WHEN LOVE WINS

FEAR IS THE LIE. LOVE IS THE TRUTH.
ALWAYS.

NICOLE D. MILLER

ND Miller
Publishing

CONTENTS

**ND Miller
Publishing**

To the youth of this generation. Let no one ever tell you that you are too young...

Jeremiah 1:6-8
"Alas, Sovereign Lord," I said, "I do not know how to speak; I am too young."
But the Lord said to me, "Do not say, 'I am too young.' You must go to everyone I send you to and say whatever I command you. Do not be afraid of them, for I am with you and will rescue you," declares the Lord.

PREFACE

When I was 19 years old, I found myself in love with God. Or rather, I found that He was in love with me. It was an interesting phenomenon because I can't pinpoint an exact moment or time when I had this revelation. It was like one day, I went to bed my regular self, and the next, I woke up in awe.

I lived in a dorm back then at Miami University in Oxford, Ohio. I had been dropped off there a year prior by my loved ones, which included the guy I was dating at the time. Apparently, engaging in a long-distance relationship and being 5 hours away from my family proved to be a bit much. I became depressed. I was recovering from an eating disorder, I had no friends, and all of that, undoubtedly, stirred up this depression.

I remember sitting in an office of one of the few Black administrators, Bill Madison, at Miami. I can't remember who referred me to him, but it proved to be a divine encounter.

Mr. Madison shared with me some pertinent information. One, that I was depressed (he did not say this in a mean way, and actually only indicated it) and then two, that Miami had a gospel choir called Miami University Gospel Singers, fondly known as "MUGS." He told me this last bit of info because once he observed my depression (I should add, I actually did not agree with his assessment), he asked what it was that I liked to do. "Well, I love music," I replied. And thus, I became a member of Miami University Gospel Singers. Then, one day, a fellow student announced that they were having a weekly Bible study through "The Impact Movement." I decided to attend, and those two decisions were life changing. I joined several other young men and women who were growing in their faiths in these two weekly programs, and a few of them are still my BFFs today!

I can't remember the exact moment or time my heart fell in love with God, but I know He wooed me on that campus in such a way that I have never been wooed before.

And I was not the only one! Several young men and women were hungry and thirsty for His presence. We banded together and were zealous for Him. We created groups and programs to spread the gospel to our peers, and though many looked at us strangely, we stood firm on the truth we had been given: that God was real, and He was with us.

We gave God our youth. And the beauty in that thing was that it didn't happen in a church building. It didn't happen by a preacher laying hands on us. It didn't happen by ministers or elders sharing the four spiritual laws. For me, it happened in the four walls of a dorm room, where the Spirit of the Living God revealed Himself.

And I haven't been the same since.

Chapter 1

Bad Blood

(Ashley)

Ashley wasn't the type to get intimidated, but this girl was getting on her last nerve.

"I mean, real talk, BJ, she think she all that," she told her best friend after they did another lap in Central Park. "She can miss me with that goody-goody attitude. And I'm fed up with her frontin' for my dad too," she sneered. "I need her gone. ASAP."

BJ shook his head with a comical laugh. "Ashley B, your cousin Natalie ain't got nothin' *on* you. Why you sweatin' her?"

Ashley blew out a stream of puffs in between strides before stretching out her short, sculpted legs to keep up with his. Huffing in irritation, she said, "Boy, why you movin' so fast? We ain't in no race." The thick forest surrounding her on each side whipped by with the speed of a mountain lion, and Ashley's chest heaved in protest.

"Yo! I'm doin' my regular. You the one slow pokin' it." But BJ slowed his pace to appease his friend.

Ignoring him, Ashley snuck a peek at her Apple watch. Her caramel face wrinkled, creating a slew of jagged lines across the perimeter of her forehead. She knew she was tired for a reason.

"My dude. I done burned 100 extra calories messin' wit' 'chu! It's time for a break." Pausing, she popped both hands on her hips, then inhaled and exhaled theatrically.

BJ sighed, watching her antics. "You just off cuz you trippin' on Natalie. You can't let that negative energy eat up yo drive." He arched his back into a long stretch, and Ashley followed his lead, extending her toned, muscular arms upward.

While keeping both hands braided together, she thought about his words. Was she being negative?

As they stretched, two young women trotted by in tank tops and short shorts, successfully magnetizing BJ's eyes to their movements. Clearing her throat with disdain, Ashley sized up the petite one with locks. *These girls ain't even that cute and he trippin'.*

BJ peeped her annoyed eye roll. "Aye. You can't blame me," he said, scrunching up both shoulders to his earlobes. "Did you see the thick one?"

He even had the nerve to smile that boyish grin that won over so many. So many, well, except for Ashley. Yeah, BJ had tried to get her back in middle school, but after she saw how he ate his peanut butter and jelly sandwich (more was smeared on his face than in his mouth), it was over for her. Without even thinking, 11-year-old Ashley checked the "no" box on the note he passed in math class, asking her to be his girlfriend.

"Just cuz Miss Thang got an *ass*, these dudes is on her." Ashley continued her vent about her cousin, working herself up so much that she quit her stretch altogether. "And I can't *stand* the way she always trying to act so freakin' innocent."

It's like it wasn't enough that Ashley had to give up her room when Natalie moved in a few months ago. Or that her father always seemed to dote on Natalie in a way he *never* seemed to do with her. Ashley was so over all the special treatment, even though it had only been a short time since her cousin had started living with them.

Exasperated, BJ's puppy dog brown eyes whipped to the sky. "Man. I'm done with talking about Natalie. You only salty cuz you think Darren is on her. If it wasn't for that, you wouldn't even care." With a knowing look, he hoisted his brows before clearing a thread of sweat gliding down the back of his neckline.

At the mention of her ex, Darren, Ashley did a small intake of breath. "Well, you know I still kick it with his boy, Tone," she admitted, "and Tone mentioned it the last time we was at the mall. And I aint' gonna lie. The shit got under my skin."

A smirk flickered across BJ's syrup-hued face. "Man, forget Tone. He still mad cuz you chose Darren over him. He'll say anything to make sure y'all stay split." When Ashley didn't respond, he added, "Yo. I'm thirsty. Let's bounce."

Ashley obliged, jogging behind BJ the rest of the way to the car, but she had to bite her tongue the whole way to keep her mouth shut. The hard granite from the park's path trembled beneath her running shoes as the warm sunny air paraded around the crevices of her face.

They soon made it to her white Mercedes-Benz GLS and headed to Devon's, the Black-owned Cafe tucked inside Central Harlem. Ashley liked to study in its classic urban decor, smooth vibes, and friendly atmosphere. Devon's was perfect for when she wanted a break from her slow-going residential neighborhood. Or, better yet, when she needed to gossip with her best friend Denise, who was a waitress there.

When the pair traipsed through the glass door, it was apparent that the cafe had once again attracted a young, vibrant weekend crowd. As a result of this growing demographic, the owner, Devon, expanded the menu to include smoothies and sandwiches, opening the kitchen in the back.

"Hey, y'all!" Denise greeted her friends, springing over, bubbly in a jean skirt and baby blue vest with a plain white T stitched underneath. Her black apron, which read "Devon's" in white cursive writing, held a tight grip on her small waist.

"Heeyyyy," Ashley called with a glowing smile. Seeing her friend had lifted her spirits. She inhaled the familiar coffee aroma, but the red Birkin handbag weighing heavy on her shoulder begged her to find a place to sit.

BJ nodded his greeting before Denise went to serve a customer, and Ashley took the lead. "Come on, B," she directed. "This way." She cocked her head to a small table in the back, and he shuffled behind. The duo flew past the charming tall stools that drifted beneath the mahogany coffee bar and aimed at a table in the corner that kissed the edge of the west wall. Martin Luther King Jr. and Malcolm X shaking hands were a picture of solidarity and peace, featured over the violet backdrop.

"Yo. I'm madd hungry!" BJ announced and thoroughly smothered his lips with his tongue. "They still got them panini tuna sandwiches?"

"Last I heard." Ashley was surveying the crowd. It seemed that almost every table busted with laughter or conversation from an assortment of beautiful brown skin tones. Lots of the regulars were there. Al from Bed-Stuy, who was always flirting with everybody. Candy and her new boo, Jeff. But then, Ashley's eyes bulged as she smacked her lips before squinting her light browns. "I can't believe she at my spot."

"Who?" BJ barely got the question out when Ashley snatched his arm, digging her long, oval nails into it, then jerked her head sideways. Alarmed, BJ twisted his head around to view the reason for her behavior. Natalie hovered over a laptop with earbuds in her ears at a table near the front where Devon's open mics were always held.

BJ laughed and looked at her like she was crazy. "Yo, dead-ass. This *is* a free country, Ash."

"Yea. But 'chu know how many coffee shops is in this city?"

BJ sighed. "Man. Just go over and say, 'Hi'. She is your dad's sister's *daughter*. That's *blood*, last I checked."

Ashley's frown reeked with venom. *Yea. Bad blood.* Instead of responding, she ripped a menu from the table to cover her face and sank deeper into her seat. BJ just shook his head in pity.

"Wuz up, y'all?" Denise was at their table, long locks piled high on the crown of her head and large silver hoops jangling with every step. "Y'all comin' from Central Park?"

"Yea. We ran a couple miles," BJ answered, and as a show of proof, wiped perspiration off his forehead with a napkin. "Shoot, I'm *still* sweating."

"A *couple* miles?" Ashley's face turned skeptical. "Girl, we ran at least five." She checked their mileage on her Apple watch. *4.8 miles.* "B always tryna kill somebody."

BJ discarded her comment with a flippant wave. "Aye. Yo, Denise. Y'all still got those tuna paninis? A brotha hungrier than a Muslim fasting during Ramadan!"

"Actually, we just stopped selling 'em cuz they wasn't doin' too well." Denise's charcoal eyes flashed an apology, and BJ sucked his teeth.

"Aww, man," he said while rubbing his white New York Nets jersey frenetically over his flat stomach. "I'm feenin'."

"But let me see if Larry will make one just for you," she added in a rush, referring to the cook.

Ashley suppressed a smile. *She been after that boy as long as I can remember.*

"Aight' cool. Good lookin'." BJ cheesed, and Denise giggled while Ashley rolled her eyes.

"What about 'chu, Ash?" Denise turned to her.

"I'm just gon' get a green smoothie. I lost my appetite seein' Miss Thing over there." A sour look pinched her face as Ashley peered in her cousin's direction, and Denise followed her gaze.

"Oh. Yo cuz' been here for a minute. Said she was workin' on a paper."

"Yea? Well, she also workin' my nerves. I can't go *nowhere*. I go to school, she there. I go home, she there. Now she kickin' it at Devon's?" Ashley's face flushed with frustration as she narrowed her eyes in contempt. "The chick is everywhere."

Denise's chuckle was accented by an awkward shrug. "I don't know, I mean, she seem pretty cool to me." But then, witnessing Ashley's crestfallen face, the waitress struck a sneaky look. Propping her tray under one arm, she added, "But umm, give me some time. I'm sure I can get some dirt on her." Denise rubbed her hands back and forth while throwing a confident smile at her bestie.

Ashley's smile back was so large, it practically blinded her. "See!" she hailed, "*That's* why you my girl. You *always* got my back." Her thick, microbladed eyebrows zoomed to the ceiling as she chucked her head at BJ. "Unlike *some* people."

"Look. I don't get in the mix of female drama." Falling back into his chair, BJ stuck his arms across his body in defense. "I *watch* cat fights. I don't join 'em."

"Yea? Then how come when Elise McWright wanted to scrap, you jumped in?" Ashley peered at him with a face full of accusation.

"That was eighth grade."

"So. It still counts."

"Aye. Elise McWright was as big as a dude. You was gon' *need* help with that one." BJ gestured to the girth of their childhood peer by stretching his arms out wide at his sides. "That girl know she ain't have *no* business bullying no-*body*. As big as she was. Shoot, she musta failed at least *twice*."

Ashley giggled, her mood chipper again. "Yea. She failed three times. That broad was big enough to catch a case."

"Y'all buggin'," Denise said, laughing too. "I'm a go put in the order. I'll be back." BJ's eyes lingered on Denise's backside as she headed to the cook.

I wish they would just hook up already, Ashley thought, then began eyeing her reflection in her phone camera. A pleased smile crept along her full, salmon-hued lips as she feasted on the mirrored image. Smooth skin, falling cozily somewhere in between caramel and honey-colored, shimmered in the glass, and the thick, long tresses adorning her head, normally cascading over her shoulders, were swept back into a ponytail. An added bonus to her face were the full, curvy legs, enhanced from running distance, and large round hips that sealed the deal. Today, a pair of Nike neon running shorts smothered those hips along with a white Champion cropped top. It was a sporty look topped off with white and gray Asics running shoes.

"Why don't 'chu just holla at her?" Ashley asked BJ, referring to Denise, but her eyes still lay stapled to her reflection.

"Cuz, man. It would be too weird. We known each other foreva. And, if it don't work, then the friendship is jacked." BJ said it as if it were obvious as to why he wouldn't pursue Denise.

"I mean, didn't *somebody* say it's better to have loved and lost?" Ashley insisted, even though she couldn't remember exactly who had said that. "And you *know* she gone' say 'yea.'." She flipped her long black ponytail over one shoulder to get it off her neck and smoothed it out so that the strays were now in-line. She was still cooling down from their run.

BJ half-smiled to himself, and she could tell he was contemplating her words. "Yea. But I don't know," he started. "You know me and

Denise both be on some trash." BJ snickered while sliding around the saltshaker on the table one-handed.

Ashley chuckled too, clicking off her phone. "You right about that. I don't know whose roster is longer. Hers, or yours." Her friend beamed, taking her comments as a compliment, but Ashley's light-hearted smile was short-lived. A deep sound reverberated from her throat, rivaling that of a growl. She couldn't believe her eyes. "No this chick did *not*!" With pursed lips, she stared daggers in her cousin's direction.

"What *now*?" BJ's smile faltered too as he twisted around so he could see what she was glaring at. Natalie was joined by a tall, brown-skin dude with a mean current of waves rippling through his fade. He was fitted in a white T, denim shorts, and a pair of Jordan's. A black Calvin Klein messenger bag shimmied across his athletic form.

"Welp," BJ announced, eyes growing wide. "She done' did it now."

Shock tumbled from Ashley's mouth with every word. "She actually kickin' it with Darren." Up until this point, Ashley had had no tangible evidence that Darren was really interested in Natalie. It was just something his friend Tone had mentioned last time they hung out.

But it looks like it's actually true. Ashley was queasy and started brushing her nails against her stomach in long, even strokes. Darren was her first. Her first kiss. Her first love. Her first everything. It had been almost two years since the breakup, and he still had a special place in her heart. She knew he always would. *Now Natalie pushing up on him! Ain't this some shit.*

BJ patted her hand on the table, knowing how she felt about Darren. "I'm sorry, Ash."

She didn't respond. *This hoe got to go.*

"Here y'all go." Denise presented their orders, and Ashley tackled her smoothie before giving it an angry slurp.

"Dang. You gone' kill that straw in a second," her friend commented with a giggle, but stopped when Ashley didn't join in.

"She trippin' cuz Darren here," BJ spit out between a mouthful of his panini and fries.

Ashley sucked her teeth. "I ain't trippin' on *him*."

"Oh. My bad. She trippin' cuz he talkin' to Natalie," he corrected, only it came out muffled and incoherent as globs of pepper jack cheese attacked his lightly stubbled chin. He threw back his smoothie to wash down the fistful still buried inside his cheeks.

"Ugh. Boy, can you *please* wipe your mouth?" Ashley eyed him in disgust. "You eat like we still in middle school." Frowning, she wagged her head in disbelief as Denise, with a silly grin on her face, handed BJ a napkin. *My girl cannot possibly* think *that is attractive.*

BJ smashed the napkin against his mouth, still chewing. "Thanks. I'm glad *somebody* know how to help a brotha out." Denise's sloppy grin only grew at BJ's statement. "Guess it's *some* sistas out here that still know how to treat a man," he added, his eyes pointing at Ashley, before he took another colossal bite of his sandwich.

"Well. You show me a man, and I'll treat him right," she tossed back with a smirk.

Chuckling, Denise said, "Y'all. I gotta get back to work," then turned to Ashley. "Text me later?"

Ashley nodded, all the while thinking, *I definitely will, cuz I'm a need my girl to help get rid of Miss Thing, most def.* With another feisty gulp of her green smoothie, Ashley cut her eyes at her ex talking to her cousin.

"Just go holla at 'em." BJ's tone was as soft as a pillow as he watched her stare. He had finished his sandwich and was once again speaking in coherent sentences. "Be the bigger person."

Ashley sighed in frustration and popped her phone back out. There was no way she was going over there. Ignoring him, she whisked through her TikTok and Snapchat accounts until a memory photo of her and BJ from seven years ago burst on the screen.

BJ smacked his teeth at the ceiling before slouching back into his seat, then eyed her. "So. You goin' over there?"

As his eyes burned into her, Ashley got that same feeling in the pit of her stomach that she did when she knew her dad expected better of her. Resigned, she huffed, "Fine" and dismissed the Snapchat memory. *Since clearly he ain't gonna let it go until I do.*

For a few moments, Ashley danced her hands around her drink, then took another long, leisurely sip. Afterwards, she peeked inside her purse for her lip gloss and dragged it across her lips under BJ's scrutiny. "Dang, B. Can I get myself together in peace?" She scowled.

BJ cocked his head in annoyance. "You're perfect. Now, *GO.*"

Sometimes I swear he think he's my damn father. Grunting, Ashley dumped her items back into her purse before easing from the table. Moments later, she greeted her cousin with an attempted small smile. "Hey, cuz'. Wuz up."

Natalie's warm cocoa eyes peered up at her as Darren's mouth slightly parted. He squirmed a little in his seat.

His ass has the nerve to look uncomfortable. Good. You know you don't need to be over here with my cousin.

"Hey," Natalie responded in an upbeat tone. "I didn't know you were here." The epitome of an ebony model for Gap, she popped up straighter in her chair. Natalie was sporting a pink glittery tank top that smartly complimented her mocha skin and khaki shorts that did nothing to hide the large round butt that Ashley always admired. All-white sandals decked her feet, each boosted by a slight tan wedge. They looked a little worn to Ashley, but still clean. Unlike herself, Natalie wore very little makeup. The only hint of it was the light shine on her lips that glistened if the sun hit just right.

What could he possibly see in her? Ashley wondered. *We couldn't be more different.* Tilting a pair of cool eyes at Natalie, she replied, "Yea. I been here for a minute." Ashley paused, doing a little two-step with her feet. "So. What y'all up to?" The question came out accusatory, and for one brief moment, she locked eyes with Darren.

He hung his head a few inches with a, "Hey, Ash," to which she gave a curt nod.

Natalie watched the odd exchange. "Uh. We're not doing much," she stated, and an open look of uncertainty settled over her almond-toned features.

Yes you are heffa. You over here blatantly flirting with my ex! Ashley couldn't stop the thoughts that bum-rushed her mind, but she held them at bay after shooting a look at BJ. He mimed for her to continue.

Out of nowhere, Darren fidgeted with a pencil and started tapping it against the keyboard section on his laptop. The beat he was making formed into a distinct sound that Ashley couldn't help but equate to Neyo's version of Zap's "Computer Love". She gripped her Birkin against her body, her knuckles beginning to balloon. *His petty ass.*

A moment of silence joined the trio, other than Darren's pencil-induced beat. Natalie watched the pair's lack of interaction in apparent discomfort, and all Ashley could think about was the damn "U 2 Luv" song.

"Can you stop that please?" she blurted at Darren, and although he ceased his tapping, he pitched her a sharp look.

"Yea. Uhh. We were just workin' on this paper our writing professor assigned," Natalie volunteered in a blatant attempt to break the tension. "I think I mentioned Darren was in my class. Right?" She pointed a finger at Darren with her hand flipped over, the whiteness of her palm facing upward.

Ashley scrunched her nose and tried to make her voice sound unsure. "Hmm...I don't remember you sayin' that."

"Yes. I did. *Remember*?" her cousin insisted. "I was sayin', this dude named Darren Ellis made a joke about the number of white people decreasing every day when they realized it was a class on Black writers."

Darren laughed, his nut-brown face breaking into a wide, charming smile. "Yo. It was real. You know it was like six people that first day, and now we got like two?" He glanced at Natalie, who also chuckled.

Ashley glared again at BJ. The truth was that Ashley did know Darren was in Natalie's class, but she had gotten so caught up in her feelings seeing them together at Devon's that it didn't dawn on her that the reason could have been for schoolwork. She nodded slowly, still frowning as she fingered the strap to her bag.

"Oh. Yea. Well, anyway... I'm on my way out, so..." Ashley soccer-kicked her chin towards the door where BJ was waiting. "Just wanted to say 'Hi'. See y'all later," she muttered and strangled her Birkin while whirling on her Asics.

"Umm. Ok. It's cool," Natalie called. "I mean... thanks."

"Yea. See you," Darren added, but it was moments after Ashley had turned, and the statement was only a whisper to her ears.

Speeding to the entrance, her legs felt like lead against the cafe's dark hardwood floor. *Ugh! I wish I hadn't let BJ talk me into that,* she fumed, but then her eyes met BJ's and he was half-smiling. Ashley could tell he was proud of her, and that caused her to feel a little better. As she reached for the handle on the door, he absorbed the tension from her body with a small squeeze to her shoulder. Before they walked out, she offered him a small smile and a quiet, "Thanks".

"So, wuz up?" BJ asked as soon as they got situated in the car. "How'd it go?"

"Awkward as hell."

"But don't you feel like Michelle Obama, knowing that you took the high road?" Laughter peeked at her through BJ's chocolate eyes, and Ashley couldn't resist laughing out loud herself. His approval was a warm blanket covering her heart.

"I guess..." She let her voice trail, but after a moment, a gleam hit her eye. She spewed in a hardened tone, "But the deal is, B, she pushin' up on him. I don't care what that heffa say."

Sighing in surrender, BJ slumped back, crunching into the peanut butter cup leather seat. "*Maybe*. But now you can at least say you did the right thing."

Ashley wasn't so sure about that. *I mean, what the hell is the right thing in this situation? My cousin going after the only man I actually ever loved? And I'm supposed to cheese all in they face like the shit is ok? I'm not feelin' it.* But she kept her thoughts to herself as she dropped BJ off at his apartment in Queens. Ashley knew he wouldn't understand; BJ had never been in love.

Studying, my ass. She on him and I'm not having it, she seethed, tightening her grip again on the wheel and strong-arming her way through freeway traffic. *Natalie is a straight 'A' student. Who the heck does she need help from for school?* Ashley's jaw was a thick line of determination as she ruminated on getting rid of her cousin the whole drive home.

Chapter 2

Close Call

(Natalie)

Natalie watched her cousin's guy friend squeeze her shoulder when Ashley met him at the front door. *Looks like he was watching our conversation the whole time. Weird.*

She was still observing BJ and Ashley when Darren asked, "Uh... where were we?"

"Sooo. We just gone' act like that wasn't super awkward?" Subtlety was never her strong suit.

Darren flashed a shrug while staring at the pencil he clutched. His dark eyes brooded over the thick, black lead corroded from overuse. "Well, I mean. I'm sure you know me and your cousin have history." He shifted another uncomfortable shoulder with a slight frown. "That's all."

"Ok. So. What history?" Natalie looked at him.

"You really don't know?"

"I wouldn't be asking if I did." Tossing both arms over her chest, Natalie sat back and waited.

"Well... I dated her for a minute. It was kinda deep. But that's been over for a while now." Darren's summary was as brief as an obituary in the Sunday newspaper.

"Wow. Y'all dated?" Natalie was shocked. "Yea. I definitely didn't know." *Now everything is making sense.*

"I can't believe she didn't mention it." Darren rolled his eyes. "Yea. We were high school sweethearts and all that." He paused, widening his gaze at her. "I guess y'all not close at all, huh?"

Natalie was caught off guard by the question. What business was it of his? "We're cool *enough*," she said in a testy tone. "We just didn't grow up together. But anyways, let's get back to this paper." A crisp nod at his open laptop was her indication for Darren to continue reading.

Truth be told, Natalie didn't know *why* she and Ashley weren't close. They had been in each other's lives, at least from a distance, since they were in diapers. They got along great as kids, even spending summers together and having sleepovers, but somewhere around junior high, Ashley became distant.

Every time I try to get near her, it seems like she has her guard up, Natalie mused in concern. *Like she doesn't trust me or something.* Natalie had assumed that moving to New Jersey after her mom's death would help her bond with her cousin. *After all, Ashley's mom died when we were just kids. If anyone understands that kind of loss, it should be her.* But instead of her cousin being a support, it felt more like Natalie was in Jersey, recovering from grief, all on her own.

I will never leave you or forsake you! The heartfelt message enshrouded Natalie's mind along with God's supernatural presence.

With a slight tilt to her head, she lowered her chestnut-hued eyes. *Thank you, Lord!*

Shifting her focus back to Darren, Natalie decided she would try harder to win her cousin's affection. *Maybe it's the Darren thing that's bothering her? He's cute and all, but not enough for me to lose my cousin over.* The thought solidified in Natalie's mind as she played with the keys on her laptop. *Whatever it is, I'm gonna make it right. Nothing could be that deep that we can't resolve it. After all, we're family.*

"So. Um," Darren's stilted voice broke into her concerns. "It's, uh, Friday." He was fiddling with his pencil again, and Natalie glanced at him, perplexed.

"Yea?" She chuckled. "Good observation."

"I know you probably got somebody you hooking up with tonight." When Darren's lips curved into an attractive smile, Natalie's stomach took a nosedive.

Before she could think up a better response, she replied, "Uhhh. No. Not really." *Please don't ask me out. Please don't ask me out. Please don't ask me out.*

Darren's eyes tinted with hope. "Oh yea? I was thinking about catching a movie. I usually kick it with my kid brother on Fridays, but can you believe his little 13-year-old self has a freakin' date?" Laughter rumbled through his muscular frame, forcing Natalie to crack a smile.

"Wow. I didn't start dating 'til I was like, 15."

"Man, these kids is growing up *too* fast. Apparently, homie snapchatted her and asked her to come over to catch a movie. My mom ain't bout to let him do nothing outside of her supervision, so that was pretty much his only option."

"Wow. I can't even think of any boys back then who would have been bold enough to ask me out." Natalie tackled her chin with her pointer finger while pondering. "I did like this kid for a while in 6th grade, and he liked me back, but neither of us was brave enough to do anything about it. We just made googly eyes all the time in class." A fond chuckle sprouted from her lips at the memory.

"Right. I think I probably got the nerve by 14, but Snapchat woulda helped a brotha out, though, foreal!" With a look of animation, Darren cocked his neck, and Natalie giggled.

"Yea. I coulda used some help myself," she admitted. "I was always too scared of boys. Probably was a good thing at that age, though." Her eyes shined with mischief.

Darren's face turned serious. "Oh yea? Well. What about now?" He inched in a little.

Shoot. Hesitating, Natalie's eyes drilled holes into her laptop screen. "I mean. I definitely want to meet the right guy," she began and slicked her tongue slowly over both lips. "But honestly, I've got a lot of stuff on my plate. I'm still getting settled, and I don't really have time to focus on that." She stole a glance at him before averting her gaze. "You know?"

Darren replied fast. "Oh. Yea. I feel you. I was just checking. Anyways. I guess we about done, huh?" He tapped the open laptop, and Natalie shook her head in agreement.

"Yea. We got through it. Hopefully, Professor Dawson sees the improvement in your writing."

"Mhmm. I'm sure he will. He loves *you*, so I'll probably tell him you helped me with the paper just so he can give me an A on GP!"

Natalie laughed and play-shoved his shoulder. "Whatever. This is *your* work. I just gave you some tips."

Darren packed his things, and Natalie toyed with the rim of her mug in thought. *Should I really not go out with him?* The question swirled around in her mind like a hula hoop as Darren stood to leave.

Natalie had just started developing an interest and finding out that Darren dated her cousin was slightly shocking. He was the first real friend she had made after her move and the only person she talked to on the regular. Her heart was dampened at the prospect of a missed opportunity.

Darren pitched another lopsided grin. "Thanks, Natalie. Appreciate you!"

To keep herself from doing something stupid, Natalie squeezed her mug and smiled her reply. *He dated your cousin. He dated your cousin. He dated your cousin.*

When Darren left, she pushed aside all thoughts of him to focus on her work. Since transferring to The City College of New York from Penn State, Natalie found it to be a smooth enough transition, but she still needed to be mindful about staying on top of things.

I know my attention span has been off since mom passed, she thought while completing her assignment for her Psych class a week later than when it was due. Thankfully, her prof was cool and had given her an extension.

Though the transfer to her new school had been a sacrifice because of the scholarships she had forfeited, when she weighed the need to be surrounded by a supportive family, the choice was clear. Natalie moved to Jersey. She had even transferred to CCNY, thinking it would be helpful for her and Ashley to be enrolled at the same school. At least then, she would know someone. Unfortunately, it hadn't worked out that way as Ashley never seemed interested in hanging out. But with her grades and hard work, Natalie figured she could still pull off landing the job of her dreams.

While finishing studying, Natalie's thoughts roamed back to Darren. *I can't believe he asked me out. Especially when he knows I'm*

Ashley's cousin. To her dismay, Natalie's social life was stagnant, and she hadn't made too many friends in her new location. Turning down Darren's offer was no easy feat.

I wonder what Jaida and them are up to? The thought straddled her mind and zoomed through her fingers to flip open her Instagram account. Trisha and Jaida had been Natalie's BFFs since middle school, and when she left Philly, saying goodbye to them had been the hardest.

A photo of Jaida, Trisha, and some guys she didn't recognize popped up as Natalie perused her timeline. Then, in Jaida's story, the same crew was at the skating rink doing tricks and line dancing on skates. *Wow. Looks like they're having the time of their lives.* A sigh of disappointment hurled from her lips. Sitting there, almost two hours away, Natalie felt every bit the effects of her move, and her heart sank worse than the Titanic.

Jaida could have at least called and told me about it. I been tryna get a hold of her forever. But she perked up a bit when she saw she was tagged in a new story from Darren.

"Who said I can't do schoolwork on a Friday?" read the caption. Darren had taken a picture of his laptop displaying his paper in a boomerang form.

A giddy smile enclosed Natalie's face as she responded in his direct messages. "You crossed over to the dark side my friend!" But thoughts of being alone tonight re-emerged when she saw how much fun everyone was having on her timeline. Another dreary sigh oozed out, and the desire to scope Darren's page became too great a temptation to resist. Natalie's fingers were swiping through his pictures when the little hairs on her arms bristled from a sudden presence by her side.

Denise had sashayed over with a tray attached and an expectant look on her face. "Hey, girl! You still workin' hard?"

A guilty expression accompanied Natalie's response. She had flipped her phone over on the table so fast, a loud clack resounded. "Yea. I've been, uh, just trying to get ready for next week's classes." She cleared her throat, attempting an innocent smile, but judging by the look on Denise's face, she had come up short.

Denise continued eying her, said "Um. Ok," and tossed her chin at Natalie's facedown phone. "Did I catch you at a bad time?"

Feeling flushed, Natalie's voice caught a little. "Naw. I'm good."

In slow motion, Denise's head pivoted up and down, her eyes glinting with humor. Still, she didn't push the subject, and for that, Natalie was grateful.

I shouldn't have been looking at Darren's profile anyway.

"Aight then. Well, I feel you on the school tip. I mean, I've only been able to take one or two classes at a time myself. I can't really take too many cuz I gotta hustle. Between working at Devon's, pushing my hair cream, and my online boutique, classes are a luxury." The young waitress's face crumpled into annoyance. "But if you can afford it, do it." She held up a palm for a high-five, but Natalie left her hanging with a polite smile.

"Yea. I definitely can't afford it," Natalie corrected, fighting concern. "I'm actually looking for work. If I don't get a job soon, I'll probably have to scale back on my classes."

Denise drew up her brows while easing closer. "You mean your rich ass uncle ain't fundin' you?" Surprised, she tossed her tray to her other side.

Natalie's eyes rounded into two large balloons. *Wow! People just be all up in your business around here.* "Well, I *guess* Uncle Malcolm *could* help if I really needed it," she murmured, thinking about it. "But I wouldn't feel right taking his money. If anything, it would be a loan."

Confusion sheltered Denise's beautiful medium-brown face. "Girl, that's blood. Why you need to pay back blood? Basically, you like a second daughter. Best believe *Ashley* ain't payin' her daddy back!" She cackled at her own humor, and Natalie agreed with an uncomfortable chuckle. She wasn't sure how she felt about the comment regarding her cousin, but she, like so many, was unable to resist the young waitress's charm.

"No. I just mean, I wouldn't feel right taking somebody's money like that," Natalie tried to explain. "No matter *who* they are. But, if I needed it, I'm sure I could go to him." She swiveled back to her computer to indicate she was done talking. *I appreciate Denise being nice and all, but I don't really know her like that.*

Unbothered by the change in Natalie's body language, Denise carried on. "Well, anyway. If you *really* need bread, you can always work here. Devon just said he was looking for a new server. One of our newbies just quit."

Natalie perked up. "Really?"

"No doubt." Denise scribbled down a number after whipping out a pen and pad from her apron. "Just call Devon. He ain't in right now, but he usually returns business calls within 24 hours. I'm sure he got something for you."

Wow. I guess Denise really is cool. Laps of gratitude swam in Natalie's almond-shaped eyes as she clasped the paper. "Thanks so much!" Easing back into her seat with her fingers still wrapped around her new gift, she offered Denise an appreciative smile.

"Bet. I gotta bust these tables. See you."

When Denise hurried off, Natalie sat in awe. She was so pleased by how swiftly God was moving. *Lord, you always supply my needs!* Once again, His nearness permeated her as soon as she set her mind on Him.

It had been that way since Natalie went on a missionary trip to Haiti in high school her sophomore year, courtesy of her mom's prompting. It was a change of pace since she usually went to summer camp, but it ended up being so worth it.

Natalie had no idea the impact that trip would have on her life. She thought she was going to help a people that had experienced greater poverty and devastation than she had. Turns out, *she* was the one in need of saving, and the faith of the Haitians to continue believing in God regardless of their tragedy deeply impacted her. The following summers, she went to two other countries on missionary trips. She had been growing in her faith ever since.

Natalie knew after so many spiritual experiences overseas that God was real. He was proving that to her again by giving her a job opportunity. Joy painted her heart like one of Van Gogh's famous works.

I've done enough studying for the day. Natalie's faith had increased when thinking about God's history of providing and she didn't want to wait another moment. Closing her laptop, she dialed Devon right then and there, but it wasn't until the third ring that a rushed, deep voice kissed her ear.

"Devon. How can I help you?"

"Hi. Uh. This is Natalie. Natalie Greene. I was referred to you by

Denise?" She paused. "I heard you had a job opening for a server?" Drumming the surface of her laptop, she sat a little straighter in her seat. *I hope I sound professional enough.*

"Oh. Hi, Natalie. Yea I do. How about you come to my office for an interview Monday evening?"

Devon sounded happy to hear from her, so her shoulders exhaled a little. "I can do that. How about after my class? Around 6pm?"

"Yep. I'll pencil you in. See you then!"

Wow! Just what I needed. As Natalie entered the appointment into her phone calendar, she beamed like the sun. *Maybe I'll splurge and see a movie tonight after all,* she thought, now that there was hope regarding her financial predicament. *Except I'll go by myself.*

She had just started a Google search for what was playing in the theater when a Snapchat notification glowed on the screen. *Maybe it's Jaida!* Hurrying to open the message, Natalie was surprised to see the notification was from Darren. *This boy.* Intrigued, she viewed his video.

"Yo. I thought I would double-check to see if you were interested in the movie tonight?" Hopeful eyes peered at her, coupled with a goofy grin, and she couldn't resist a smile.

He is too much. Natalie replayed the message while cheesing the whole time. Once again, she considered her options for the evening, and loneliness appeared. "Lord, *help,*" she whispered and bit her lip so hard, she almost punctured it. Natalie knew she shouldn't, but it would be so nice to have company. *I mean, we are just cool,* she reasoned. *It's not a date if I pay my own way...*

But instead of responding to Darren's invitation, she found the movie she wanted to see and purchased a ticket for one. With a short moan, Natalie replied, "No thanks," in text form on Snapchat, while she still had the God-given strength.

CHAPTER 3

DADDY'S GIRL

(ASHLEY)

Ashley steered up to her large, red-brick, two-story home, music bumping from one of the rappers with the name "Baby" in it. Located in South Orange, New Jersey, her house had the suburban feel but was still close enough to the city to get into a little trouble when needed.

It had only been a few years since she and her dad had moved there after his practice started booming. They lived in Manhattan, closer to her peeps, for most of her life. That was the reason she applied to and attended CCNY. Well, Darren was the other reason, but that split happened not too long after they began school. Now that she was in Jersey, the commute was just a natural part of her existence. Overall, suburban life was cool, but sometimes, her neighbors complained about her music. Too bad Ashley didn't care enough to do anything about it.

F the neighbors, she thought when Old Mr. Roberts cast a surly frown her way before entering his home next door. Delicately lifting this season's black Prada sunglasses, Ashley checked her reflection in the rearview, an act that drew an immediate smile. Tilting her head to examine her pearly whites for remnants of her green smoothie (the only reason she was thankful for those ugly braces growing up), she snapped the mirror back into its rightful place. *All good.*

Ashley wasn't even thinking about seeing Natalie and Darren at Devon's while approaching her house. It probably helped that she had checked her Instagram at the stop sign on her street corner. Her direct messages were jam-packed with requests for her presence tonight.

It's the weekend baby! she thought, still seated in her driveway and scanning her DMs. *Time to turn up!* But heavy eyelids intruded upon her excitement, a direct effect of her run with BJ. *I could definitely use a nap.*

"Aye, Ash. Come help me with your cousin's armoire!" Her dad's head hung from one of the upstairs windows as he shouted for all the world to hear.

Dag. She wasn't even in the house, and already he was putting her to work. *So much for that nap.* Ashley turned down the music to give herself more time and yelled in response out the car window. "What was that, Daddy?" Maybe he would move on if she took too long.

"Girl. Get yo butt up here and help!"

No such luck. Ashley sighed, snatched her bag, and slammed the car door before bolting inside. As was her normal, she threw her keys on the small glass table near the entrance before sifting through the mail. Bills for her dad flashed before her eyes, a notice for an upcoming event for the Black professional men's group he was in, but ooohhh! Her new issue of Vogue had come. She could read *that* when she got her hair done.

"Ash-ley!" Her dad must have heard her come inside.

"Com-ing." Dashing through the foyer in her sneakers, Ashley climbed the winding staircase to her cousin's new room, AKA Ashley's old room. There had certainly been a vengeful tug of war in her heart when she gave it up. *And even if I had volunteered, moving all my stuff was a foreal inconvenience that I wouldn't have had to deal with if she wasn't here.* Residue from Ashley's resentment still coursed through her veins.

Finally mounting the top of the stairs with a strong puff that announced her arrival, thoughts of the room change bobbed and weaved in her mind, causing anger to bubble up all over again. "It's like I'm giving up everything for this girl," Ashley muttered with each aggressive step to her cousin's bedroom.

But as soon as she neared the doorway, she posed better than a model on a Victoria's Secret runway. "Hey, Daddy!" She hit her dad with an exuberant smile.

Malcolm Bennett floated over a plethora of white wooden pieces scattered on the floor. A bright red tie lay swung over his shoulder like someone had tried to choke him and he had just scraped out of their grip.

"Baby girl." Shuffling to his feet, the older Bennett used his knee as a launching pad. When he wiped his peppered-gray brow, an exhausted expression bear-hugged his features. Even still, his light brown eyes sparkled at the sight of Ashley.

"Dag, Daddy." She giggled. "You sweatin'!" Ashley speed-kissed him on the cheek, careful to dodge all perspiration, then stood back to browse the mess he made. "You tryna put this thing together? You know you not good at this stuff." Cocking her head to the side, she asked, "Why don't you just let Natalie do it?"

"Aww. I just figured I would try to take the load off her while she's getting adjusted. You know she has classes, and she has to find a job. *And* she's trying to heal... But you right. I'm horrible at putting stuff together." Malcolm puffed a sharp breath before his words tumbled while studying his Rolex. "I also have a meeting with a client in an hour." He paused, scratching his low fade sprinkled with small curly waves. His matching light eyes did a seesaw on top of Ashley's heart. "You think you can do your old man a favor and help me out?" For extra effect, he topped off his request with a pitiful, helpless look that said, "I need a woman to aid me."

Malcolm Bennett was one of those old-school types who knew how to charm a woman proper to get what he wanted, and Ashley knew when she was getting charmed. But could she really be upset? She had learned from the best.

"Ok, Daddy," she heard herself say. "I got 'chu."

"Thanks, baby girl. I knew you would come through." Mr. Bennett whipped out his wallet and started counting cash. "I know it's the weekend, and you need some spending money. Let me know if you need more." He stuffed a few hundreds into his daughter's eager palm, just the way she knew he would.

Ashley beamed. "Thanks, Daddy! I need to get my hair done. Oh, and lashes too... so this *should* be cool..." She let the sentence hang, not wanting to be tacky and outright ask for more money.

"Oh. Ok." Mr. Bennett reached into his wallet again to peel off another bill. "I forgot about the lashes," he mumbled.

Ashley grinned wide as she choked the one hundred dollars like it was her new Birkin handbag, then eased it into her hand with the rest.

"I'm headed out, but let's try to hang out as a family for dinner tomorrow." Malcolm straightened his tie prior to maneuvering a few wooden pieces out of the way. "We haven't done that in ages."

Excitement exploded in Ashley's heart. "Yea. That'll be dope. I can order Chinese like we always did growing up."

One of Ashley's favorite memories was their daddy-daughter dates, which usually consisted of her putting on her Sunday's best and her dad ordering takeout. Her mom was either out shopping or getting her hair done, leaving them alone to bond. Her dad would lay a blanket in the living room and top it off with the spread. They would hop in the car, and she would sit on his lap so she could see over the steering wheel. She'd pretend to drive while stationed on the street. About a good 15 minutes later, Ashley would announce they had arrived at their destination, and her dad would escort her into the house for their meal. To her, it was a real outing.

A peck on Ashley's forehead from her father brought her out of her reverie. "Yep! Perfect." Before jetting to the door, he added, "Have fun tonight, honey."

Immediately, Ashley cased the room. It wasn't the fancy decor *she* had had it laid with, but she acknowledged it was nice in its own way. Natalie had a queen-size bed covered with a white down, cascading with purple and yellow pillows. Her auburn desk was catty-corner with a light gray papasan chair in front. The windows were dressed in long, flowing, translucent curtains while purple, stenciled flowers swirled along each drape. Rays of sunshine sliced into the room, permitted by dark gray shades drawn up beneath the open curtains. The decor was sweet, yet dull.

"Hmm. I wonder if cuz' has a diary?" Inspired to capitalize on this rare opportunity of being alone in her cousin's bedroom, Ashley started snooping. First, she poked around Natalie's desk drawers, only to find school papers and miscellaneous office supplies.

Hmm. What's this? In the bottom largest drawer lay a baggie with what looked to be a sturdy, sharp razor inside. She held it up while peering through the lighting. "What would she have this for?" Frowning, Ashley tossed the thing back inside the drawer, burying it beneath a stack of books and paperwork. Giving up on the desk altogether, she filtered through the tall assortment of novels and biographies, running her hands over hard and soft book covers.

"How to Be a Godly Woman," she read aloud and winced. "Ugh. Can you get *any more* lame, dear cousin?" Stumped for a moment, Ashley clicked her tongue a few times, her mind churning butter.

"Hmmm... Let's see what you hiding, Miss Thing. I know you not the saint you pretendin' to be." But after slinking over to Natalie's closet and doing a nice Inspector Gadget inspired-search, she once again came up empty. When whipping around to find another place to look, Ashley stubbed her foot on a wooden piece scattered across the floor.

Damn. I forgot I need to get this thing built. She checked her watch. *I'm gonna have to resume this little hunt another time.* "Now. Who can I get to do this project for me?" she wondered, browsing her texts. Bingo. Ashley's fingers crafted a message to Jeremy.

"Hey, bae. What you up to?"

"Nothing much, beautiful," was the response five minutes later. **"Thinking 'bout you."**

Ashley sent the heart emoji. **"Aww. You always so sweet. I've been thinking about you too, boo. I was hoping you could stop by the house for a bit. Keep me company while my dad is gone?"**

"Bet. Be there within the hour."

Ashley's lips slid into a cocky smile. Too easy. *Now I just need a shower,* she thought with a pleased saunter into her bedroom. Jeremy would expect her to be looking her best. *And even though I plan on putting him to work, I'll at least let him* think *he getting some.* The vibration from Ashley's phone in her hand stole the attention from her musings. It was Jason.

"You up for tonight? I'm thinking about going to Cleo's."

"Yep. What time?" She sent the heart emoji.

"I'll pick you up at 6."
"My hair appointment is at 5. How about 8?"
"Say less. See you then."
Ashley checked the time. Jeremy's assignment should only take an hour or two. She just might be able to fit that nap in after all.

———

Ashley had been going to Thelma's Hair & Style since she was a kid. Her mom used to take her, and her mother's mother used to take *her*. Even her *father's* mother went there. And though they had relocated to Jersey and expanded over the years, Thelma's Hair & Style was a place that represented comfort and familiarity. It also didn't hurt that there always seemed to be good gossip in circulation.

Thanks to Jeremy, Ashley made it to her appointment in record time and glided through the double-glass doors with a pep in her step. *Jeremy is definitely good for a* few *things*, she mused as her lips spread into a sensual smile. *I'mma have to make it up to him.*

The burning smell of fried hair and chemicals from the salon embraced her as she scanned the familiar facility. Thelma's now had individual rooms for clients that they had implemented a few years back. This made it nice for when Ashley wanted to get a little bit more *personal* in her dialogue with her stylist.

"Hey, Ashley. You here for Tamra?" the receptionist quizzed in a perky tone. She was petite but a little on the heavy side, and not in a cute way.

I wish they would give this girl a name tag, Ashley thought, double-checking the woman's shirt. Nothing.

"Yep. She free?" *She better be. I can't afford to be late for my date tonight.*

"Yea. Her 3 o'clock just left." The receptionist smiled, showing a dire need for some Crest whitening toothpaste.

Ugh. Does she go to the dentist? Ashley hovered over the countertop to sign in on the clipboard.

"I always love your hair, girl," the receptionist hailed. "You keep it lookin' good!"

Ashley tossed a quick smile her way. "Oh, you know. I do what I can." With untaught confidence, she patted her long, full tresses tucked beneath a black suede fedora before sticking the pen back onto the granite counter. Her roots were a mess, but she wasn't going to let the world know that.

I guess the girl has taste. Ashley figured the receptionist's skills and friendly demeanor must have made up for her appearance. *She's definitely doing better than that other sis they had with the TWA. She kept scheduling my appointment on the wrong damn Friday! I mean, how hard is it to schedule a standing appointment?*

"You can go right on back since you're signed in," the nameless receptionist informed, nodding towards the hall to her left.

"Thanks." Ashley made an effort to sound nicer than she felt toward the woman. *You always gotta be nice to the help,* she thought, then rounded the corner into the hallway. *I'm just glad Tam is free.*

Ashley just never knew with Tamra. It was hit or miss when it came to time, but she was just too good for Ashley to let her go. Tamra had been her stylist for several years now, and she didn't even want to *think* about looking for someone new.

Nearing the back, Ashley adjusted her black and white leopard printed romper that clung easily to all the best parts of her. She had it draped with several silver necklaces and complemented by a large Coach tan watch with a turquoise face. As her feet traipsed along the hall, Ashley felt right at home in the immaculate salon. Glass separated the rooms so that each stylist and their client could be seen. Most of the doors were open, so pieces of conversation nudged her ears as she passed by.

"Giiiirl, and when he ate the box. Whew! I mean, he made my toes curl!" exclaimed one woman's voice. Ashley slowed her pace and chuckled at the client's graphic description. She would have loved to hear more but had to keep it moving.

Moments later, Tamra greeted Ashley in a frustrated tone, a nasty scowl dripping from the edges of her face. "Hey, sis." She added in a hurry, "Have a seat, and I'll be right wit' 'chu," before offering her back to Ashley to resume her phone conversation.

Dag, what's up with Tam? Ashley popped her Birkin on the purse hook near the entrance, her issue of Vogue partially hanging out of it, and exhaled while sinking into the overstuffed leather chair. The room had a simple but elegant ambiance: dark wooden floors, ivory walls, and a large oval mirror that hung behind Tamra's station of hair supplies. The shampoo bowl was stashed in the corner, propped right in between the hair dryer and a large potted Monstera. Ashley had always loved Tamra's style, and the vibe of the room was right down her alley.

"Ricky. I know how much was in my account. And you tryna' tell me it's not what I know it was, and that ain't right. Don't try to play me!" Tamra spewed venom into the speaker in rushed tones, and Ashley's ears stood all the way up. She knew Tamra couldn't have been as happy as her damn Instagram account was making it look.

All those posts about her new boyfriend, and it sounds like he's stealing from her!

"Right. I got 'chu. I'm gone' be home tonight, and we gone' finish this conversation." Tamra hung up, and Ashley tried to act like she hadn't been paying too much attention by studying her phone and pulling up reels on social media. "Girl, these ninjas aint' ish," the feisty hairdresser grumbled while grabbing her scissors and starting to cut out Ashley's sew-in.

Ashley tried not to be too nervous. *I hope she don't cut my damn hair.* "Oh yea? Wuz up wit' your new boo?" Ashley was intentional to make her voice sympathetic and not a thirsty one excited for gossip.

"Girl. I'd rather not say. I just know that's the *last* time I listen to my freakin' sister. *She* the reason I'm in this mess. Real-estate my ass. The only thing that fool is sellin' is some damn lies. I mean really. He don't own a thing, and yet she tryna' tell me he a real-estate agent. Not a car, not a home, not a freakin' bicycle." She whipped up her hands with the scissors and floundered a finger as she ticked off each item with her other hand. "Bruh ain't got nothin' but the clothes on his back. And got the nerve to be drippin' in Gucci and Prada! Puh. I ain't seen no freakin' *license*. I shoulda known his ass was sus when I ain't see him pullin' that BMW no more he apparently *rented* for our first date!" Ashley let out a squeal when Tamra shoved her head to the side. "My bad," Tamra said and became gentler.

"Well, my daddy always say, 'Never let no man steal your heart who hasn't earned it. So. What he buy you?" Head bowed, Ashley admired her freshly manicured, hot pink toes in her strappy black Michael Kors sandals. She had gotten her pedicure the day before, and her toes were sparkling like lightning bugs on a summer night.

"Puh, I ain't seen a dime since that first month of us dating. It's like, when I gave it up, all of a sudden, he was broke." Tamra dragged out a sigh while working.

"Dag. I thought y'all just went on that trip to L.A? Didn't you post something about that?" Ashley tried to make it sound like she hadn't been oozing over all of Tamra's pictures when she posted on that trip. She had been green with envy because Tamra's new dude was super fine. The boy had the nerve to look just like that brother that played Emmett in "The Chi".

Tamra smacked her lips with force. "Exactly. I gave it up on that trip, and it was over. Sis, I'm tryna' tell you. Save the cookies, cuz they ain't on it once they get it." Tamra removed the rest of her client's sew-in, causing long, black locks to decorate the area around Ashley's chair.

As her stylist started unbraiding, Ashley kept silent. She already knew how to work *her* hand and thought it was pitiful that Tamra didn't. *She just as cute as me.* Ashley's eyes roamed over her hairdresser's voluptuous frame and short, 90's Halle Berry haircut. Tamra always had some new shoes that Ashley wanted and a bag to boot. *And she's older! She should know better than to let these dudes get the best of her.*

With Ashley's mane fully unbraided, Tamra said, "Come on, let me wash you."

Obeying, Ashley shimmied out of her seat and, while Tamra was getting the water ready, caught a glimpse of her reflection. Her hair was the same light brown as her eyes, medium length, and right now it was super wavy from the braids. Ashley actually felt like she had nice hair but wasn't comfortable going the natural route. *Dudes love long hair,* she reminded herself. *And my head is too large to pull off Tamra's cut.*

Ashley needed to play her hand as best she could. After all, how was she going to get what she wanted if she didn't appeal to whoever it was that she was trying to get it from? Still ogling her reflection, she felt her phone grumble with a text from Denise.

"Guess who about to work at Devon's?"

Ashley typed out, "**Who?**" when Tamra motioned her toward the washer. She was just about to sit in the chair when her phone vibrated again.

"**Natalie.**"

"That skank," Ashley mumbled.

"What 'chu talking about, girl?" Tamra's curious eyes studied Ashley as she plopped into the washer chair.

"My stupid cousin. This girl is gettin' on my damn nerves." When Tamra started massaging her scalp, the tingling sensations from the shampoo seduced her.

Masterfully working, Tamra prompted, "Hmmm...do tell." She dug in a little deeper, and pleasant sensations cascaded throughout every nook and cranny of Ashley's skull. The added aroma of herbal bliss hit its target, sailing straight into her nostrils.

"It's just, ever since she got here, she's been taking over my life. I mean, she's getting all this freaking attention, and I honestly feel like I can't compete." There. She had said it. Ashley didn't feel confident when she was around her cousin. Natalie was just so *self-assured*.

"Girl. I have never heard *you*, of all people, sound insecure." Tamra stared down with wide eyes as if she was seeing a ghost. "You sure it's not just in yo head? What females is out here competing wit' 'chu, Ash?"

"It's not just in looks, Tam. It's like, she's smart, she's driven, and has this "Saint Theresa" act down pact. Like anybody could be that freakin' square." *Damn. I feel like the shampoo is making me spill all my secrets. What does she have in this stuff? Truth serum?*

Tamra laughed. "Well, maybe you should try to get to know her. I'm sure she has her own insecurities. In fact, she could feel the same about you." As Tamra continued to massage, Ashley pondered her stylist's words.

"I don't know. But I *do* know one thing. If she knows what's good for her, she better keep away from what's mine." A flashback of Natalie with Darren from earlier that day swam across her vision. "Otherwise, I'm comin' for her ass." Ashley flicked some water off her mouth that had squirted from the sink before sinking deeper into the chair.

"Dag, Ashley! You act like she ain't even blood." Tamra's voice was a mixture of half shock and half amusement as she started on the second shampoo.

"Puh. I mean, she let that family shit go a long time ago," Ashley spewed through gritted teeth, tensing back up. "And I ain't one to forget a wrong. I don't care how young we were."

CHAPTER 4

SAVE ASHLEY

(NATALIE)

Maybe I'll be the bigger person and give Jaida a call, Natalie thought while driving home from Devon's. *Even though I know she didn't respond to my last call.* Before she could change her mind, she punched the call key on her steering wheel. "Hey Siri, Call Jaida."

A multitude of rings echoed on the other end until the all-too-familiar voicemail kicked in. "Hey, Jay. Was just checkin' in. Again. Hit me when you're free." With trembling fingers, Natalie tapped the end-call button as the road loomed ahead through her watery eyes. Her friend was MIA. She peered in sadness as words conceived from layers of emotions were birthed out from a broken heart.

"Momma, where are you?"

Grief caressed Natalie with bony fingers, and she didn't even try to eject the loneliness that passenger-ed the drive. A good half hour later, though still in her fragile state, she managed to ease into the long driveway in her 2017 Kia Optima, a much-needed inheritance item. In Philly, Natalie took the train to wherever she needed. Now, she at least had her own wheels, which was helpful in South Orange, but not so much in New York.

Natalie steadily crept into the three-car garage next to her Uncle's

Yukon Denali. Snowballs of grief tumbled around her gut, so she sat there a moment, a head full of wavy tendrils kissing the steering wheel.

Why is this so hard?

Darren's offer to hang out suddenly resurfaced. *It sure would have been nice to talk to Jaida about Darren. She was always better with guys than me.* But Natalie dismissed her disappointment at her friend's absence with a few strokes over her wet cheeks. Cradling her belongings, she trudged into a sanctuary of prestige and couldn't help but brighten some. No matter how many times Natalie came home, the Bennett's house took her breath away.

High-raised vaulted ceilings, marble floors in the kitchen, four bathrooms, and large walk-in closets in every bedroom. Ashley even had gray-slatted double-sliding doors added to the bonus room when she switched rooms. And even though there was also a jacuzzi tub on the back patio, the kitchen was Natalie's favorite part. She loved to cook but rarely had the time.

She tossed her bag and phone onto the counter and grazed her hand over the large white ivory island, inhaling with content.

Now for a snack. She rummaged through the fridge after plucking a pear from the fruit bowl and smiled. Opening one of the French doors of the large, stainless-steel unit was like opening a gate to heaven, and her eyes twinkled at a half stack of cheese. Natalie was still in awe that her new living situation was a super upgrade from the affordable two-bedroom apartment she and her mother had shared.

Momma, this house is the come-up! Gliding to the counter, she sliced up the pear to mix inside the yogurt she had confiscated from the fridge. She was taking her first bite when her phone dinged. She dove for it. *Jaida!* But disappointment stained her heart at the name glowing on the screen. Gramma Reese. Still, Natalie was tickled.

I don't know too many 70-year-old women who know how to text. Or who actually prefer it to a phone call!

"Hey, baby girl. How are things?"

"Hi, Grams. I'm good. I'm gonna call you tomorrow. Just been busy with school stuff." A stab of guilt pierced Natalie's insides, and she tap-danced a little in her wedges. *I know I need to make time to go over there and see her.*

"Ok. I look forward to hearing from you."

"Yep. Love you."

"Love you too."

Seizing her snack, Natalie headed to her room, where the armoire sat fully intact. Her eyes burst with surprise. *It looks great.* Impressed, she ran her hands along the plywood while studying the quality. *Uncle Malcolm must have done it. Wow. He really knew what he was doing.* Some scratching and shuffling drew her attention to her uncle's home office, so she took a trip down the main hallway.

"Uncle Malcolm, thank you so much for putting the armoire together!" Natalie stayed slanted against the doorway while peeking her head inside, not wanting to disturb him. "I mean, I would have gotten to it, but that helped me out *a lot.*"

"Hey, Natalie. Well, I have to be honest," Malcolm ceased manhandling his files and drifted a hand to the back of his neck, "I needed help myself. Believe it or not, your cousin did it. She's actually really good at that stuff."

Ashley did something nice for me? Natalie's brows crinkled in surprise. *She's barely spoken two words to me since I've been here.*

"Oh. Well. I'll have to thank *her* then." She backed up some out of the doorway. "I'll let you get to work."

"No. Come inside." Malcolm motioned towards her. "I want to hear what's goin' on with you."

Natalie smiled at the massive mahogany desk, plush cream carpet, and oversized brown leather office chair. Her uncle's undergrad and law degrees were tacked to the wall along with a picture of him and a grinning Ashley decked in her high school cap and gown. They both clasped the degree while posted on each side of it.

Hmmm, but no picture of Aunt Patty?

After another rapid scope of the office, searching for a picture of her aunt that she may have missed, Natalie couldn't help but think about Denise's words from earlier that day. *Uncle Malcolm* definitely *has bank,* she decided, but Natalie knew it hadn't always been that way. Malcolm and Patty had usually made ends meet, but the sudden boom of her uncle's business these last few years clearly upgraded their family's lifestyle. Natalie wasn't so sure if the effects had helped her cousin's character development at all.

"I didn't want to interrupt you, Uncle Malcolm..." She glanced behind her. She was only standing a few feet inside, just in case she had to make a quick exit.

"No interruption, Natalie. I'm never too busy for you." Malcolm's smile was her cue, and she fell into the chair across from him, guiding her yogurt container with care in between both thighs.

Removing his reading glasses, Malcolm's face became an open field of interest.

"Now. How are classes going?"

"They're ok." Easing back into her seat, she added, "I took a break after everything with mom," then lowered her eyes. "So, I'm just now getting back into the swing of things. I really like this Black writer's class I'm in, though." Natalie's countenance brightened several shades when she thought about Professor Dawson. He was hands down the best teacher she'd ever had.

"Really? What do you like about it?"

"Well, there are so many Black writers that we don't get to hear about in middle school and high school. Like Toni Morrison, James Baldwin, Langston Hughes, and Angela Davis. I mean, I read Maya Angelou growing up, but that was only during Black history month. But there are *so many* amazing writers in our history. It's a shame you have to take a special class in college to learn about them." Natalie edged forward in her seat as her voice bred passion into every word. "And really, Black culture *is* American culture. I mean, other races *should* learn about the cultures that live in this country. Not *just* white culture. It's their heritage too!" Natalie caught herself, pausing with an embarrassed expression. "I'm sorry, Unc. I just get fired up sometimes."

Her uncle's eyes exuded pride. "No, Natalie. I love hearing that excitement in your voice. It's one of the things about you that reminds me of your mom," he added in a heartfelt tone.

Natalie grew warm at the compliment but felt an ache again. She missed her mom.

"Thanks, Unc."

"Yea. She was always fighting for someone or somebody," he went on. "I mean, I became the lawyer, but your mom? *She* was the real advocate. I thought she was crazy for going into social work. I told her, 'Melissa, ain't no money in social work!' But she didn't care. She just wanted to help people." Malcolm chuckled at the memory, and Natalie soaked up every word.

He looked at her thoughtfully then. "Hey. What are you up to this evening? I know Ashley is out, but if you don't have plans, maybe we could hang together?"

Natalie appreciated the suggestion. *He must have sensed my mood.* "Well. I have a ticket for this show tonight. I was just gonna see that..."

"Ok. How about I come with you?" Malcolm's light brown eyes lightened at the prospect.

"Aww, no, Unc. I'm sure you have plans. Or work. Or *something*." Natalie was certain he had a date, even though she didn't want to say it.

Uncle Malcolm is out here just as much as Ashley.

He waved at her. "Like I said. I'm yours," he told her and held up both hands, indicating he was free. "What time does the movie start?"

Natalie glanced at her phone. "In a few hours."

"Cool. That'll give me time to finish up and get ready." A reassuring smile spread on Malcolm's face, and relief rushed through Natalie.

Now I don't have to be alone. "Ok, Unc. I'll leave you to it. Let me know when you're ready." With her yogurt stuck to her palm, Natalie trekked back to her room and flopped on the bed.

Well. It wasn't the hot date I was hoping for, but it's company. But even though she now had evening plans, she still felt glum. Hoping to lighten her mood, she turned on her worship playlist, and Mali Music piped from her iPhone. It wasn't long before the music stirred her heart, wooing her into worship where God's love ministered. His peace was upon her, lulling her into a heavy slumber and drifting her into a realm of dreams.

Natalie was in the deep sea, swimming, and the waves were fierce, but she was such a strong swimmer that they hardly fazed her. When she looked ahead, two figures on the shore jumped up and down vigorously. The closer she got, the more she recognized them.

Mom! And... Aunt Patty? *Whatever it was they were yelling was drowned out by the rushing sea surrounding her ears. Natalie swam harder to make it to shore and finally, within a few yards to her destination, heard what they were saying.*

"Save Ashley! Save Ashley!" they shouted, over and over again in unison, all the while jumping and waving while stabbing pointed fingers behind her. Treading water, Natalie ceased her strokes and pivoted to see what they were pointing at. That's when she saw Ashley in the midst of the sea, flailing her arms in panic.

Ashley's drowning! Natalie didn't think twice. She headed to her cousin, swimming as hard and as fast as she could. Even though she couldn't see her family members anymore, their voices rang inside her eardrums.

"Save Ashley!" resounded over and over.

Taking in water, Natalie spat out and pushed harder. Finally, after what seemed like forever, she reached her cousin and grabbed with all her might, but Ashley wouldn't come.

"No!" Ashley yelled in the midst of her drowning. "Not you! I don't want you!"

Natalie, fighting her, ignored her cries. "Ashley, you'll drown!" She tried again, but Ashley shoved her hand away.

"I want my mom!" she cried. "Not you! I want my mom!" She coughed out water while bobbing up and down amid the waves. At one point, she was fully submerged, then somehow popped back up, only to resist Natalie once again.

"I'll take you to her!" Natalie's scream was gripped with fear as she grasped again for her cousin. "I saw her at shore."

"You promise?" Ashley's voice was a 2-year-old child's, her eyes round with alarm.

"Yes. I promise. I saw her at shore. I'll take you to her!" Natalie was shocked her cousin was so resistant when she was on the brink of death. "Now, let me save you!"

She reached for her again, and this time, Ashley let her help. Natalie succeeded in bringing them both back to shore where Ashley lay spread eagle on the sand, coughing and crying. She curled into a fetal position as Natalie rested beside her and stroked her cheek with a shaky hand.

"Thank you," Ashley whispered. "I couldn't have made it without you."

Natalie woke from her dream, her heart beating fast and, "Save Ashley!" echoing in her mind. She understood the message loud and clear.

The movie Natalie selected wasn't the kind of film she normally would have chosen, but there weren't too many options. *No nude scenes. Minimal crazy language. Not a blockbuster, but tolerable.* Overall, she was satisfied it was one she felt comfortable watching with her uncle. Her bladder cried out for a bathroom break, though, when Idris Elba had at last figured out the woman he had been calling his best friend for half the movie was, indeed, his soul mate.

She whispered to Uncle Malcolm that she would be right back and had only taken a few steps towards the restroom on the sticky dark carpet when someone called her name.

Her eyes exploded in surprise. "Hey!"

Darren stood posted beneath a glowing sign for the ladies' restroom in a pair of dark denim skinny jeans and white polo shirt.

Natalie offered a quick smile, thinking fast. "So. You decided on the movie after all?" In one brisk gesture, she scanned his ensemble. *And changed your clothes from earlier.*

He stuttered, "Uh yea. I figured. Why not, right?" The strap to a jet-black leather Louis Vuitton handbag wilted between his fingertips. "It is the weekend."

Hmmm. Natalie fidgeted with a few strands of her twist out. *Who's purse is that?* She bit her lower lip to keep from asking the question. "Right. So anyways...I'm here with my uncle," she said in hopes that he would tell her who the heck *he* was here with.

Darren responded with more ease this time, "Oh. Yea. That's cool." But nothing more, and Natalie felt her own loss for words as he continued his swaying. She was about to excuse herself and escape to the bathroom when a tall, dark-skinned female with a voluptuous frame materialized from that direction. The girl was sporting honey-blond hair that drizzled down to the crown of her butt and a miniskirt that barely draped over it. Both of her long legs were clothed in high-heeled black suede stilettos.

"Bae. That restroom was so stank!" Honey-blond raved, snatching the Louis from Darren's grip. "I think the workers are on break or something." Darren, for some reason, appeared embarrassed as the woman begged in a sing-song tone, "*Please* tell me we going to Cleo's tonight. I just *have* to have the lobster bisque! I cannot do anything else, foreal foreal." A heavy sigh punctuated her plea, causing the two chocolate mounds on her chest to jiggle beneath her plunged neckline.

You can't be serious, Natalie thought, roaming her eyes up and down Darren's companion.

"Um. Yea," he muttered. "We can do that." He peered at Natalie, drawing the woman's immediate attention. After giving Natalie a once over, she swung her purse on top of her shoulder and indicated the door to the restroom she was standing in front of.

"Oh. Am I in your way?" Except she sounded as if she could care less if she was.

"No. Well, yea," Natalie stumbled. "I mean. I *am* about to go to the restroom." The woman just stared at her as if *she* were the one in the way. Propping one hand on her hip, Natalie met her stare. *And that is your cue to move, sis.* It took everything in her not to say the remark out loud. Darren's date sized her up, and Natalie's palms transformed into little balls at her sides.

This girl really thinks she's about something. She narrowed her eyes, and Darren interrupted, seeing that the situation was about to escalate.

"Tonya. This is Natalie. Natalie. This is Tonya."

Tonya's eyes narrowed, but that was the only indicator that she had even heard the introduction. Natalie huffed a breath.

Girl chill. Clearly, you're the one here with him. Not me. Unclenching her fists, she puffed out more air before turning to Darren. "Hey. I'll see you later, ok?"

"Bet. Have a good night," he said, and before Natalie could get in another word, Tonya snaked an arm around his waist and chased it with a quick steer toward the exit.

"Hi, Natalie. It's nice to meet you. Oh, yea. Likewise. Heard so much about you!" Natalie mumbled the pretend dialogue as she entered the stall. "Except I haven't heard a thing about you. And maybe that's for the best."

A frown masked her peanut-butter brown face as she rinsed her hands under the sink. *I can't believe that girl almost made me lose my cool,* she marveled, studying herself in the mirror. Natalie's was a quiet beauty. Like soft ripples through a vast pond, it made its entrance subtly. She was not the one to contour her face and clothe her hair with weave, yet it seemed these were the kind of girls Darren was fond of.

How could we possibly ever be anything other than friends? Again, Natalie was sure that nothing could ever happen between her and Darren for a multitude of reasons. Ashley having dated him was just one of them.

Well. One thing's for sure, she thought as her eyes glided along the overflowing trash can and spilled water over the sink. *Tonya was right. They need to clean this place and quick.*

After the movie, Uncle Malcolm whisked her to some fancy Italian spot in Times Square called Carmines. Busyness inundated her as shoppers laughed and talked with animated faces and lights exploded from crowded giant-like buildings flying from above.

Natalie's eyes inhaled the vigorous activity of streets spitting out stores from every angle in Midtown Manhattan. *It all feels so* alive!

"I know your mom probably didn't take you to many spots like this," Malcolm shared after they were seated and digging into some delightful concoction for their appetizer. It had all kinds of spices Natalie had never tasted before.

"Right. She was more of a meat and potatoes kinda girl." She laughed, and Malcolm joined in.

"Yea. That was Melissa. She wasn't one to overspend on a *thing*! I remember once going to the grocery store with her as teenagers, and she pulled out these friggin' coupons. Now, she *said* momma gave 'em to her, but I ain't never see momma cutting up those coupons. *She* was the one every Sunday, going through the paper, cutting up them damn coupons. And then would give 'em to momma and say, 'Now, make sure you use this one so you can get half off if you buy two!'" Her uncle's chuckle simmered Natalie's soul.

He sounds just like her. "Uncle Malcolm, we had a whole drawer full of coupons right by the fridge. I would tell her, Momma, you can pull them offline. You don't have to *actually* cut them. But I think she liked the old-school way of cutting up the paper." Natalie smiled, remembering her mother's process every Sunday of getting the paper and cutting up coupons. *Who knew that had started when she was just a kid?*

Malcolm's laughter trickled into a painful sigh. "Yea. She was a stickler for saving money." His eyes teared up a bit. "I miss that girl."

Natalie tugged her bottom lip with her top front tooth to keep her own self in check. Her emotions were as tumultuous as his, and they both sat there trying to get themselves together.

"But at least she left us with you." Malcolm broke their moment, and his sandy eyes crinkled while shoving a chunk of steak into his mouth. A tearful smile touched her lips. "And what about you?" Malcolm added. "Do you take after her in that way?"

Natalie munched on her lasagna with a shrug. "I do what I can. I mean, I'm not into a whole bunch of material stuff like I know some people are..." Her voice died. By 'some people,' she was thinking of Ashley and maybe that girl Tonya, but she didn't want to offend her uncle by saying so.

Uncle Malcolm eyed her. "You mean like Ashley?" He winked, and Natalie peered at him with a bashful smile. "It's ok. You can say it. I know Ashley likes her *stuff*. But really, she has a good heart. That stuff is just a way for her to enjoy life." Malcolm tackled his salad, chewing in between sentences. "I know she has some growing up to do, but I believe she'll get there."

Natalie was quiet. "Momma always said we each have our own way of getting to the finish line."

"Hey. Yea. I never thought of it that way."

Natalie sat and listened to her uncle drone on about her cousin. He clearly was so proud of her, even though she was on the slow road to finishing college, not working, nor was she treating Natalie in any way that was hospitable in the three months she had been staying there. But Natalie refrained from saying any of these things.

When dessert arrived, the vibration from her phone disturbed the peace on her lap. She hadn't had any texts all evening. Not even from Jaida. With curious eyes, she grasped the screen.

"Sorry about earlier. You didn't deserve that. Let me make it up to you."

Darren. A slow smile eased along her face as she bit into her Italian cheesecake. Natalie didn't know what Darren had in mind by "making it up to her," but she couldn't deny that she had just a smidge of a desire to find out.

CHAPTER 5

THE BARN
(ASHLEY)

Later that night, after leaving Thelma's, Ashley showered, then wrapped and concealed her 'do with a double-duty silk bonnet and shower cap. A satisfied smile slid from her lips as she posed in front of the full-length mirror. She was dressed to kill and knew it, ultimately deciding on her Gucci mini black dress number. The one that was cut low in the front and pressed up hard against her Savage X Fenty push-up bra. It was her favorite, making it look like she had more cleavage than she actually did thanks to Ms. RiRi. A pear-shaped figure filled out the rest, and the material stubbornly clung to her hips.

Beyonce has nothing on me, Ashley determined, observing her reflection with a gleam in her eye. She chose her stilettoed-heeled, cheetah print Michael Kors pumps and traded her Birkin for a black Chanel clutch, the one with the small diamond studded to the front. This was a special occasion. Ashley and Jason had been seeing each other for a couple of months now. They weren't exclusive, but she was committed to getting there.

Lucky for her, Jason happened to be in the area and picked her up in his candy-apple red Ferrari. Ashley dove inside, throwing her overnight bag in the back seat one-handed. She was that excited to see him. No one was home, but even if her dad was, he had stopped meeting her dates after Darren. "Let me know when it's serious, and I'll meet him," he told her, and she took him at his word.

Ashley looked Jason over, impressed. A Kenneth Cole black blazer draped unbuttoned over his chest, exposing a white T with Calvin Klein stark lettering. Light denim skinny jeans hugged both thick quads, ripping just so at the knees. They even had the nerve to kiss his black and white hi-top Dolce & Gabbana sneakers at the ankles. The intricate, tight curls that gripped Jason's scalp alluded to him being bi-racial, and just in case there was any doubt, his coffee-with-cream-colored skin confirmed it.

Ashley had met Jason at a block party BJ invited her to this past summer, and they hit it off in no time. Turns out his cousin lived a few streets down from BJ's apartment in Cambria Heights where the party was being held.

"You look good," Jason said, eyeing her over when she climbed into the prestigious vehicle.

Ashley dazzled him with a winning smile. "Thanks. So do you." Since Jason had the top down, Ashley let the warm air fondle her face, soaking up its rays faster than bread dipped in butter. Summer was fading fast, and she didn't know how much more good weather Jersey was going to get.

"Oh! This is my song," she squealed, and on cue, Jason cranked up the volume. They glided onto the freeway while Ashley belted Cardi B and Megan Thee Stallion's latest hit on their way to Clinton Hill.

Ashley loved Cleo's. It was upscale yet trendy. Cool yet classy, and on any given day, a celebrity or two could be spotted at one of its white-tablecloth-covered tables. One time, Ashley had even seen Alicia Keys there. Cleo's was the kind of place she pictured her and her future husband frequenting often. She didn't know too many brothers in her age group who could afford such taste, so when she did come across one, she tried to keep him around, even after she lost romantic interest.

Jason did all the right stuff. He held the door open when Ashley got out of the car, put his arm around her like she was his, and ordered for them both. Ashley just loved when a guy took charge.

"So, what chu' been up to lately?" Jason asked once the appetizers had arrived; escargot and shrimp with cocktail sauce.

"Oh, you know. Grindin'," Ashley replied. In truth, the most "grind" Ashley had done was actively keeping up on her social media accounts, but she knew a guy like Jason wanted someone ambitious. *But forreal though, isn't social media how the Kardashians got started?*

Jason responded, "Yea? Me too. My dad's been letting me work more at the office, so I'm getting a lot of experience." Dabbing a piece of shrimp in a puddle of sauce, he popped it into his mouth with a distinct air of privilege.

What is it his dad does again? Ashley couldn't remember. But really, did it matter? She had the proper response. "That's great! I know you've been wanting more experience." Leaning in, she brushed his hand with hers, a movement that shoved the table against the two melons perched happily on her chest.

Longing draped Jason's face at the view, but he continued rambling about his career goals. Ashley knew he was a full-time student at NYU and that he was majoring in something in business, but she could never remember which field. *Whatever it is, I'm sure it makes a lot of money.*

"How are your classes going at CCNY? You think you'll land a gig in fashion or do some type of artwork?" Jason's tone rang genuine. "I know you mentioned wanting to do more drawing."

Oh. Was it back to her again? *Hmm. I forgot I shared about my drawing. Must have been a weak moment.* Flirting her small fork with her Caesar salad, Ashley conjured up a vague, meaningful-sounding reply. "Yea. I've been thinking about that. I mean, I'm not full-time like you, and I only have about a year's worth of credits under my belt, but I did pick up an extra course this semester in fashion design. The ultimate plan is to transfer to the Fashion Institute of Technology. I've been drawing more during my downtime too."

Ashley took a small bite, nibbling with her lips protruding, but Jason seemed more interested in her conversation than in the sensuousness of her mouth. *This boy.* When he didn't react to her move, she continued. "Yep. I'm playing with some different techniques, and I feel like my own unique style is really developing." She took a sip of her water and added a few other crafty responses until the food arrived. The lobster with steak was divine, and she thanked BJ in her mind for making her run earlier that day, especially since she had plans to drink the rest of her calories later that night. Ashley's eyes began devouring the ensemble of Crème Brulé and chocolate-covered strawberries the waiter appeared with.

"So. I was thinking we should hit up The Barn," she volunteered, indulging in another strawberry.

At her request, a concerned expression was imprinted on Jason's scrumptious face. "I heard it was a shooting there last month. You sure about that?" His tone was wrapped in skepticism.

"Oh. They beefed up security since then," Ashley informed, shaking his fears away with one hand. "Besides, the music is always raw. *And* some of my peeps will be there. Including BJ." Ashley's light browns pierced him, radiating attraction in the dim lighting. Jason still seemed hesitant, so she slipped on an irresistible smile for extra effect. Just as she knew he would, he caved.

"Oh. Ok. But if I hear one gunshot, a brotha is out!"

Ashley couldn't tell if he was joking or serious, but figured she was getting what she wanted, so who cared? In response, a soft chuckle purred from her lips. "Cool," she said and sent a text to her crew. "**Y'all still turnin' up tonight?**"

A few seconds later came the replies. "**Yep.**"

A 1949 Clos du Bois Chardonnay tickled Ashley's lips as she drowned out the rest of Jason's conversation with her fantasies. His talking face toggled up and down like a bobblehead, and she pictured how it would look in a family photo on Instagram. Her with two kids (a boy and girl, of course), maybe even twins, and a large red-brick home located somewhere in the 'burbs.

And just as fly as my current house! she thought with glee, downing another sip. *Ohhh, and my kids will be a quarter white, so they'll have that good hair!* Realization danced in her eyes.

Yep, Jason was prime meat, and Ashley was on her way.

———

Sandwiched in the line outside of The Barn, Denise threw Ashley an enthusiastic, "Hey, girl!" along with a hearty handwave while beckoning her to come over. There were so many people, Ashley figured it would be a good 15 minutes before they even got inside.

I hope my feet can stand it. She stared down at her pumps in suspicion.

"I see you with Mr. Ferrari," Denise bubbled once she approached. Jason had just dropped Ashley off at the curb and went to park his car.

"Yea. It's nice, right?" Ashley responded. "I mean, he was kinda nervous parking it down here, but I'm like, 'Boy ain't nobody gone' jack up yo ride.'"

"Yea. That little incident last month had people shook for a bit." Denise adjusted her white leather mini, then added, "But you know that don't be happening on the regular."

Ashley agreed. "Mmhmm. Looks like it's live again." She observed the eager 20-somethings waiting to get inside, then looked her friend up and down. "Okaaaaay! I guess you tryna' pull BJ tonight, huh?" she teased.

Along with Denise's tight white skirt, she donned a white crop top with only one sleeve, the all-white illuminating her brown skin like a daytime light bulb, and a long silver necklace with a triangle-shaped medallion that circled her neck. Four-inch stilettos made her legs run longer than a water fountain as thick, stylish locks swooped to one side glistened on sight. Ashley's mouth dipped into an approving smile.

"Hahaha," Denise chimed. "Very funny. But 'chu know, if he decides to step, I *may* give him an opportunity." She wiggled her brows up and down with a mischievous grin.

"Puh! Who you foolin'? You been on that boy since middle school. You gone' give him more than that." Ashley bent slightly and pretended to twerk, her bold movements stretching her form-fitting black dress over her behind.

Denise giggled, gobbling up the attention like a Thanksgiving meal. "Well. I'm actually here with Lloyd, so..." she revealed with two sneaky eyes veering in the direction of the parking lot across the street.

"Whaaaat! You here with his *boss*?" Ashley's head fell backward hard while darting her eyes to the sky. "You on some *dumb*-ness."

Denise shrugged. "He asked me out. What was I supposed to do? Say 'No' just cuz my *friend* works for him?" Her lips drew into a naughty smile before she flicked her tongue like a lizard. "Besides, now I can get even more of a hook-up on shoes."

The girls burst into a fit of laughter, only regaining their composure when their dates appeared. Denise introduced Lloyd, who had just come from parking his black Mercedes. Ashley had actually considered buying that model before she got her own truck. She already knew who Lloyd was but participated in the introductions anyway.

"You BJ's friend, right?" Lloyd asked, looking as if he already knew. He was playing it cool himself.

"Yep. And this is my...this is Jason." Whoops! *Slow down, girl,* Ashley told herself regarding the slip of tongue. *Soon he'll be yours.*

The two men began getting acquainted, and Ashley took pride in Jason's knowledge as he engaged Lloyd in some light business talk. Lloyd was sharing how he had a deal with a nearby shoe repair shop in which he swapped referrals for customers. This agreement skyrocketed his sales since New Yorkers beat up the soles of their sneakers on a daily basis.

Ashley was especially pleased the men were hitting it off, given Jason's previous hesitancy to come to the club. She did notice, however, that he kept checking in the direction of his precious Ferrari as they edged closer to the front door. *Dag! I wish he would relax*, she thought with tempered annoyance. *It's security everywhere.*

Once inside, Ashley and Denise bum-rushed the bathroom while the guys looked for a table. "Ok, girl. What's the deets? I mean, you done brought out the 'Beyonce dress', so I *know* you goin' in for the kill." Denise quipped while viewing her reflection to touch up her makeup.

Ashley brushed against the counter beside her while doing the same. "Well," she began and ticked off her fingers. "NYU. Full-time in business. Daddy works off Wall Street." She paused, trying to think. "Selling stocks. He clearly has a nice ride, even though his daddy bought it for him. He wants to create his own wealth and leave a legacy for his kids. Yada, yada, yada. We went to Cleo's for dinner," she finished, looking pleased, and started working on her mascara.

Denise swiveled to face her, almost dropping her concealer. "Girrrrrl. Cleo's? Yassss! Did you get the steak?"

"Hell yea. *And* the lobster."

Denise hit her with a high-five, and both girls howled like hyenas, their fingers still entwined. A few ladies standing by the sinks eyed them in distaste, and Ashley smirked. *Jealous much?* She narrowed her eyes at the short, skinny one fitted in a denim Gucci jean skirt and matching Louboutin jean heels. *Ugh. Who matches anymore?*

"So. What's the problem, Ash?" Denise asked, ignoring the onlookers and invading Ashley's thoughts.

"What 'chu mean?" Ashley resumed touching up her hybrid extensions. "I didn't say nothin'."

"Girl. I *know* you. You have had a problem with every dude since Darren. So. What is it?" Denise studied her friend in the mirror. "His curls are too bouncy? His skin is too smooth? Oh wait, he has too *much* money."

Ashley giggled. "Uh, honey, there is *no* such thing!" She cackled some more, then paused to groom herself. After a moment, though, her nose pinched as she shared her thoughts. "I just think he's too interested in getting to know me." *Dag, that sounds weak, even to me.*

"See. I told you. Dumbness." Denise scoffed. "Now, how is a man *too* interested? It's usually dudes like that who are too self-absorbed."

"I don't know. I just mean, he always asking me all these damn questions about myself. Like, what are my dreams? What are my passions?" She mimicked a deep, male voice with a wrinkled forehead in the mirror. "That kind of stuff."

"Well. You *do* know that means he's tryna' get serious, right?" Denise looked at her like she was crazy.

"Yea. I guess. I just didn't expect him to want to be so..." Ashley searched the bathroom counter for the word she was looking for.

"So, what? So, *intimate?*"

Ashley thought about it. "Yea. I guess so."

"Now, *you* the one that said you was ready for the real deal, Ash. *You* the one that got this 5-year-plan to be wifey in the works. *Now* you got somebody who seems on it, but 'chu got cold feet?" Denise turned back to the mirror to paint on her pink lipstick from Mac. It had just the right amount of violet to complement her cocoa-brown skin tone.

"I mean, I also think he may be a bit too... *boogie.* I need a dude who can eat lobster *and* greens." Ashley whipped out her Rouge Roulette by Revlon.

"Girl. *You* don't even eat greens! Remember? Yo Gramma Reese made 'em at Christmas last year, and you left them things in my fridge for *weeks*. Talkin' bout, you gone' eat 'em when you come over. It took me *forever* to get that smell out." Denise shot her friend the side eye.

"D. You know what I mean. I mean, I need somebody *down* too." Ashley's eyes pleaded while dabbing her lips together in the mirror, but Denise only shook her head in disagreement.

"I think you scared to fall in love again." Denise tucked away her lip gloss, popped out her eyebrow brush, and smoothed out the crisp bristles of hair with unmatched skill.

Ashley was silent. Maybe her girl was right. Throwing a hand on her hip, she asked, "Why you gotta call me on my stuff?"

"Cuz. That's what the homie do." Denise's tone softened with affection. "Now, come on. I'm ready to dance." She tossed her eyebrow brush into her tiny, wallet-sized purse and whisked her friend back to the club scene.

The Barn wasn't the upscale environment Ashley had just come from, but she still loved the vibe. The decor was vintage, and the ambiance was always hype. A few times, she had witnessed a couple of fights, but nothing serious had happened before the shooting last month. She liked that they usually played both old- and new-school hip-hop, and she tried to make it out whenever they had old-school hip-hop night.

Denise split to find Lloyd while Ashley spotted Jason in conversation with BJ at the bar. "Hey, B. Wuz up." Jason wasted no time scooping her up, tackling her waist with his arm, and squeezing her in possession. Ashley fought the urge to pop out her phone to get a picture for Snapchat; she knew they were stunning. *We'll get one later.*

BJ had replied, "Yo, Ash. Just hollerin' at cha boy," right when Denise strutted over with Lloyd stitched to her side. BJ's face went flat, and for a split second, her friend lost his easy-going smile. "Lloyd. Wuz up."

Though he recovered fast, Ashley knew BJ well enough to know he was caught off guard. Denise snickered, and Ashley's own laugh napped just below the surface of a well-curated placid facial expression.

"Wuz up my G." Lloyd pumped his head while pulling Denise closer to his stocky build. Any closer and she would have been on top of the brother.

"Hi, B," Denise purred, offering BJ a smug smile as Lloyd's hefty hands caged her in.

"Sup." BJ buried his fists deeper into his dark blue Louis Vuitton jeans, perfecting a nonchalant stance. The rest of his ensemble included a white crew-neck T somewhat covered by a baby blue suede sports coat and a tan belt that offset all-white tennis shoes. Ashley had to admit, BJ looked good.

"You here alone?" Denise was digging for a reaction, and BJ popped a shrug.

"Yeah. You know I'm on the prowl. I think I see a cutie I'm actually 'bout to get wit', so... I'll see y'all".

When BJ made his exit, Ashley locked eyes with Denise, sure that her friend's dark browns reflected the amusement of her light ones. *I know I'm something else, but Denise is in a league of her own!*

The rest of the evening flew by with drinks, dancing, and more drinks. Someone had the great idea for their group to keep taking shots every time a song had the word "booty" in it, and that left Ashley and her crew more than intoxicated. They were strutting outside, laughing and talking about going to Wendy's, when a murderous scream erupted from Jason. Ashley had never heard a brother scream that loud. *What the hell?* She whipped her head as he stabbed an aggressive finger at his car in the parking lot.

"My car! Look at my ride! I can't believe this *shit*!" The side window of Jason's Ferrari was smashed in, and whatever it was the culprit was looking for had to be gone because they left nothing unturned. Glass was everywhere as well as his basketball shorts, shirt, and shoes that he kept in a duffel bag in the backseat. All items were strung about next to the tires. A pile of notebooks and textbooks also lay scattered nearby on the concrete.

"They got my stash in the glove compartment!" Jason's eyes bulged in growing alarm, and everybody flew into action. BJ called the cops, and Denise took pictures of the damage. At the same time, Lloyd went to talk to security to see if they had seen anything or if they could provide any video footage. Ashley was so drunk, it was all she could do to keep herself standing.

"Babe. It's cool," she slurred, "It's gone be good." Slumped against the hood of his Ferrari for support, she suddenly remembered her overnight bag. "Awww, man. Did they get my bag too?" She tried leaning into the car to peek through the broken window but stopped. Even in her drunken state, Ashley knew by the treacherous look Jason responded with that whatever she had just said had been the wrong thing.

It took almost an hour for the cops to arrive and another 45 minutes before they got the information they needed for the police report. By then, Ashley had passed out in the back of Lloyd's truck and couldn't remember even getting inside. The thieves had ruffled through her duffel bag but must not have found anything of value because all of her clothes and toiletries were safely nestled inside. The next thing Ashley knew, BJ was dropping her off at home in an Uber. He woke her up and escorted her to the garage entrance while stuffing her belongings into her hands. *So much for my overnight at Jason's.*

"You good, Ash? You need me to help you in?" BJ watched her, worry coursing through his muddy brown eyes, but she shook him off.

"Yea. I'm good," she managed, "Thanks for the lift," but stumbled after fumbling the key in the door. With a backward glance, Ashley popped a thumbs up at the Ford Focus they arrived in and took a few shaky steps inside. Whoops! She forgot the trash can was near the entrance and smacked right into it, then made a mistake and stubbed her toe on the corner of the kitchen island while squinting in the darkness.

"Ouch!" Crying out, Ashley dropped her duffel bag and purse, slipped off her Michael Kors, and stroked her foot with care. Within moments, the lights flashed on. Annoyed, her neck jerked up. She shielded her eyes from her tormentor.

"Hey. I thought I heard something." Natalie was planted by the light switch in the kitchen, appearing sleepy but concerned. Dressed in cotton pajama shorts with a complementary tank, her silk bonnet sat haphazardly on her head as if she had rushed out of bed.

"Just me." Ashley gestured with her shoes in her hands, "I'm no one," but the statement was chased by a small moan as she lost her footing near the fridge.

Natalie sped like a gazelle to catch her, but Ashley flung her hand with the one still clenching her MK shoe. "I'm *fine*," came the angry response, layered with Jack Daniels and Tito's. *I don't need you!*

In pure reluctance, Natalie conceded to her cousin and stepped back. She watched Ashley wobble across the marble floor with one shoe on and one shoe off. It was a pitiful sight.

Ashley grasped the island to steady herself, only to lose her balance again when she went to turn the corner into the hall leading to the foyer. This time though, she clutched her shoulder when Natalie jetted to her side. "I think I'm gonna be sick," Ashley announced. At that, Natalie steered her near the downstairs bathroom to the right of the foyer. The duo barely made it before all the evening's contents climbed their way up Ashley's throat. Lucky for her, Natalie whipped the toilet seat up in record time. In went Ashley's head. Goodbye steak. So long lobster.

The sound of puking echoed. The potent smell followed. Natalie cringed while Ashley heaved and coughed over and over before, finally, she was done. After running a rag under cold water in the sink, Natalie dabbed Ashley's face. When she returned from getting a cup of water from the kitchen, she found her cradled against the tub, eyelids drooping. Ashley did, however, manage to lift her head long enough to take a few sips.

"Man. I thought I could keep up with Denise," she proclaimed in a little-too-loud-voice. "But sis knows how to throw it back!" This, for some reason, struck her as hilarious, and she started cracking up. "Get it? Throw it back?" she said to Natalie and laughed all over again.

"Shhh," Natalie commanded while, once again, stroking Ashley's face with the rag. "We don't want to wake your dad. It's 3 AM."

"Oh, he don't care about me." Ashley's frown was coupled with a theatrical whisper. "As long as he pays me to stay out of his way, he gucci," she insisted, swishing around her cup of water as she talked. Some of it spilled onto her leg, but that didn't seem to be of concern as she only peered at the cold liquid crawling down her bare skin.

"That's not true, cuz'. Uncle Malcolm loves you." Natalie hunched over and began soaking up the water with the rag she was still holding. "You're all he talked about tonight at dinner."

Ashley stiffened. "Dinner? He cooked?" Her face spun a web of surprise. *He never cooks.*

Natalie clarified, "Naw. We went out."

"Oh. Y'all went out to dinner." Ashley sobered up some.

"Yea. And a movie." Now done with her leg, Natalie resumed cleaning Ashley's face, but Ashley pushed both Natalie's hand and the rag away.

"I'm *fine*," Ashley said again. This time, she set her mouth into a determined line and shimmied up while straightening her dress. Up until that point, it had been hiked up near her waistline.

"Ok, but take it easy." Natalie rushed after, watching with anxious eyes as Ashley stumbled up the stairs. She actually missed a couple, so Natalie hurried to support her, stapling her hand to her lower back. When they reached her bedroom, Ashley sprawled onto her large queen double-mattress face first.

"I'm so *tired*!" she told her comforter as a force-filled exhale caved her body deeper into the blanket.

Natalie rotated Ashley onto her side, then kicked the trash can by her bed with her foot. "Ash, if you gotta puke again, do it here," she said, indicating the bin.

Ashley's eyes fluttered open to see where Natalie was pointing. "Ugh," she grunted. *But why is the room spinning?* She slammed her eyes shut to block out the revolving window by her bed.

Natalie rifled through her cousin's drawers, settling on an oversized black t-shirt with a pair of pink glittery high heels on the front. She removed Ashley's dress before engaging in some heavy lifting. "Can you help me out here?"

It took all of her might, but Ashley heaved up her arms, and Natalie, albeit a difficult feat, managed to dress her. She pulled the blankets from under Ashley's body and wove them over, tucking her in. In response, Ashley hugged the pillow like a child as memories of a time long ago flooded onto the surface of her psyche.

"You know," she slurred, "I always wished I was *you* when we were at camp."

Natalie's face warped into a map of confusion until realization struck. "Oh yea, that's right. I forgot we used to go to summer camp together." She paused, then added, "But we were all going through our own awkward stages back then." And just as she had experienced her mother do a thousand times, Natalie smoothed down Ashley's blankets.

"Yea. But yours ended way before mine." Ashley squeezed her pillow tighter, then straddled a few fingers against her forehead. "Plus, The Hyenas liked you better." She grimaced while tightening her hold around her pillow. *Those witches!*

"Wow! I forgot about The Hyenas," Natalie commented. "I haven't thought about them in years." The Hyenas were a group of girls at camp that thought they were all that. They liked to pick on kids they felt weren't cool, and Ashley had fallen into that category back then. Natalie stroked Ashley's cheek while whispering, "But I liked *you* more than them, and that's what matters."

"You didn't like me enough to stop them." Even though Ashley had murmured the statement into the pillow, the pain in her voice was evident. "They still got away with it."

"What? Got away with what?" Natalie popped up from her spot-on Ashley's bed. "Ashley. What are you talking about?" she asked again, with more force this time. "What did they do?" But Ashley only grunted and started snoring. She was fast asleep.

CHAPTER 6

PROVISION

(NATALIE)

Professor Dawson was the old-school type and preferred to use a chalkboard in his classroom. The distinguished-looking man stood in a regal stance in front of the 'Prominent Contemporary Voices in Black Culture' class. A trusty piece of chalk in his hand served as a personal scepter. Natalie swore it was glued to him; the man was never without his chalk. A long, white, scraggly beard dipped well past his chest, and he had a habit of peering over his glasses instead of through them when he was lecturing, just as he was doing now.

Natalie adjusted herself to crank out notes on her laptop more easily. Theirs was a small group, about fifteen students, and she was glad. The advantage of a smaller class was the opportunity to receive more one-on-one attention from the instructor. This particular class was no different.

"Aye." The staged whisper played on Natalie's right ear drum. "You got a pencil I can borrow?" The blonde sitting nearby had leaned in so close that the Eclipse Peppermint gum on her breath clouded the intimate space.

I've been next to this girl for three weeks now, Natalie ruminated, *and never once has she said one word to me.* Now *she's asking for a pencil?* She was annoyed. *In the middle of lecture? Humph.* "Uh... yea. Hold on."

Shooting a hand into her bag, Natalie fumbled around a bit before wagging a blue ballpoint pen in the air. "This is all I have."

A helmet of shimmering gold bobbed up and down, and the girl grinned while jabbing at the pen. "Thanks so much! I'll take it."

"Ms. Greene. Are you ready to share on the pertinent moments that stood out to you in the assigned reading of Michelle Obama's, 'Becoming'?" Professor Dawson's stare ignited Natalie's face as 14 pairs of eyes abruptly fell on her.

Now this chick has me looking like I'm not paying attention! Natalie cleared her throat, scouring her brain for the information she had read. "Uh...yea. I would say, what stood out to me, was that even though the first lady was being raised in a working-class home *and* grew up in a predominantly Black neighborhood, she was still on an elite academic trajectory." She tightened both clasped hands along the rectangular table shared with three other students and became an expert at ducking and dodging their watchful eyes. "I mean, Mrs. Obama and her brother were able to attend an Ivy League school when her parents never even received a college education. I would think that usually, Blacks who attend higher education have *some* kind of model. But *they* didn't. That's pretty impressive."

"Good, Ms. Greene, but keep going," Professor Dawson prompted to the beat of chalk twiddling in his hand. "Are there any other ideas that stood out to you in the reading?"

Natalie took a moment to consider the text she had read but was a little hesitant to share due to the blonde next to her. *I guess she opened that door when she walked into this class.* Smoothing her tongue over her lips, she continued. "Yea. I think another important thing Mrs. Obama touched on was the need to fit into white society by adopting 'proper' language and addressing the necessity to 'code switch.'" Natalie held up her fingers in quotes while saying the words, and the professor's small smile danced with joy.

"Now, *that* is an interesting observation."

Whew!

"So often, people in minority groups must learn the language, beliefs, and values of a dominant culture," the professor added, "in addition to their own perceived subculture." His attention was directed solely at Natalie, and in some ways, it felt like they were having a private conversation while 14 other people were invited to watch the show.

"Right. Another thing I picked up on was how Mrs. Obama's uniqueness was clear, even when she was younger," Natalie continued. "And then, later in her career, it happens again. She wasn't satisfied with just practicing law and following the path of her peers. She wanted to do something more meaningful to help people. She wanted to see transformation in her community." Natalie peered at her professor like an obedient child to its parent, and he nodded in pleasure, striking his chalk in her direction.

"Excellent points! Thank you, Ms. Greene." White chalk locked in his grip, the quirky professor swaggered across the room and resumed addressing his students. "Often, it is that stirring in our belly that pushes us to manifest our true identity. When that happens, we aren't able to settle for what others tell us is socially acceptable. Had Black Americans done that, then we would have stayed slaves." With eyes fused with fire, Professor Dawson scanned the group of early 20-somethings, mostly African American, and let his last statement resonate before carrying on with his teaching.

An internal sigh pounced on Natalie's chest, vaporizing her initial nervousness. *Next time this girl asks me for a pencil, I'm throwing it at her.* She chuckled to herself.

When class ended, Ms. "I'm-in-need-of-a-pen" scooted closer. "That was really great insight you shared. I'm sorry if I got you into trouble at all. I just always use those lead pencils, and they tend to run out of lead at the wrong time. No matter how many times this happens, I never remember to pack extra lead." Still smiling that same carefree smile, she tossed her straight towhead and started packing the bookbag on top of her desk.

Stuffing her own bag with school supplies, Natalie responded, "Thanks. Don't worry about it." She was still feeling some kind of way about the whole thing.

"I'm Kate." The girl whipped out a hand.

"Natalie."

"I know I should probably use my laptop to take notes, but I like that old-school feeling of writing. You know?"

You just full of conversation today, aren't you, Kate? Kate had the preppy look. Sparkling white teeth, baby blue eyes, and a tiny frame clothed in a J Crew jacket with hat and gloves to match. She could easily have been a carbon copy of one of their models.

Probably didn't even know what code-switching was before today. Natalie grunted in irritation. *Why is it that* our *people always seem to have to teach others about our culture when we share the same domestic residence as our more privileged citizens?*

Even at just 21 years old, Natalie had been well-trained and was adept at navigating middle-class American society. But instead of sharing her internal musings, she said, "Yea. I feel you. I love writing in my journal. It's kind of therapeutic in a way that typing isn't."

"Yo, Natalie. I see you was spittin'." Darren strutted over all smiles, clenching his messenger bag, and joy fondled Natalie's heart at the cadence of his voice. "I don't remember reading about Mrs. Obama practicing law, though." His face crumpled into confusion.

"Thanks, but that's because that comes later in the book. It wasn't a part of last night's reading."

"I'll catch you later, Natalie!" Kate's tone was still upbeat but now held a familiar ring.

Natalie mumbled, "Later."

"Dag. So you already read the whole thing?" Darren looked at her, impressed, but Natalie shrugged off his admiration.

"Not quite. But I am almost done." Shoving her laptop into its case, she subsequently tossed it into her tan faux leather bookbag.

"Nice. So, what 'chu up to? I was thinking about getting something to eat," Darren proposed with a sturdy plop to her desk area. He swung his messenger bag onto his lap as she continued packing.

Being this close to him caused a flutter in Natalie's heart, and she struggled a little while feeding books to her bag. Darren's chocolate eyes were colored with interest as he watched her, so she scrambled away from his gaze. "I actually have a job interview. So, I'll have to raincheck." Natalie was grateful for the excuse, though she didn't let him know it.

"That's cool. Well, congrats!" Darren grinned, and she chuckled.

"I haven't even gotten the job yet." Adjusting her mustard-colored scarf with the blue polka dots, Natalie slipped on her gray pea coat in anticipation. The Jersey fall had set in unexpectedly early, but she loved fall, so she wasn't too upset.

"Yea, but 'chu got this. Anybody would be a *fool* not to hire you." While Darren hyped her up, he grabbed at her bag. "Let me get that for you."

Hesitating a bit, Natalie relinquished the strap. "Uhhh. Ok." She let him carry it down the steps leading to the doorway.

The duo had drifted behind a chatty group of students when Professor Dawson called to her, "Ms. Greene, can I have a minute?" A quick search of the room revealed that she and Darren were the last to leave.

"I'll be in the hall," Darren told her with a cocked neck towards the door.

With her hands still hidden in her peacoat, Natalie glided over. "Yes, Professor Dawson?"

The professor stroked fluffy cotton puffballs of hair on his face, and she giggled as little white pieces of chalk did a waltz with the threads of his beard.

"Thank you for your input in today's class," he said, his eyes laser-beaming through her.

I feel like I'm being x-rayed. "Oh. You're welcome." Natalie shifted around some.

"Do you know *why* I called on you today?" Dawson stopped messing with his beard and adjusted his glasses, successfully decorating the rims with tiny chalk particles.

"Umm, you caught me talking in class?"

"Yes. But were you the *only* one talking?"

Natalie's face was now a swamp of confusion. "No."

"So. Why then would I have only called on *you* and not your counterpart, Ms. Greene?" Dawson raised a quizzical brow, and Natalie was silent for several moments until he removed his glasses. Kindness wrinkled her professor's aging face, and it was the first time Natalie had seen him without the glasses.

"I'm not sure." She was slow to answer while swaying a little in her stance. *It's like I'm failing a test I didn't even know I was going to take, or even have the chance to study for.*

"Because, Natalie, in *this* world, *we* are not able to get away with what *they* can." Dawson laser-beamed her again before sliding his glasses back on.

Natalie nodded while processing the information. Her professor was using her classmate Kate's distraction to teach her that she couldn't afford to be distracted from her purpose, even if others could, simply because of the color of her skin. She was reminded of something her mother had told her growing up.

"Natalie, you will need to be twice as good just to get an opportunity to compete and three times as good to win." The saying was practically the Black community's secret mantra and was sandwiched inside the ten commandments as far as Melissa Greene was concerned.

"Yes, sir," Natalie responded as her mother's voice did a religious swirl in her mind. "I understand."

The professor eased behind the podium and started erasing the chalkboard. "I'll see you Thursday, Ms. Greene." His back was to her now, so she knew their talk was over.

Natalie found Darren on his phone, propped against the wall beside the classroom door. Once they were outside, he exclaimed, "Man. Dude is deep." Having clearly listened to her conversation, he repeated in a husky voice, "*We* cannot get away with what *they* can." Making his best impression of Professor Dawson, he then pretended to lower invisible glasses. He glared at Natalie over them while stroking a long, fake beard.

She doubled over with laughter before smacking his shoulder. "Yea. But that's why I like him," she said, defending her favorite teacher.

"Yea. Cuz he a nerd. Like you," Darren teased, making Natalie laugh harder. "Y'all was like two nerds going back and forth today."

"Well, I enjoy learning. But really, it's literature," she said. "You want me to talk to you about science or math, and it's crickets. I got nothing for you." Natalie rolled down her scarf, which had crept up to her mouth while they walked along the greenery leading to the pavement. "I'm barely pulling a B in my stupid Calc class."

Darren's eyes widened in sheer disbelief. "And that's a bad thing?" He tilted a perplexed brow.

"Uh...yea?" Natalie's face danced with shock, and Darren laughed again.

"Ok, Ms. B student!" He kept laughing for a minute, then added in a softer tone, "Yo. You ain't gotta dumb yo self down for me, Natalie. I know you a nerd. But it's one of the reasons why I like you." He was still smiling while taking her in, and Natalie didn't know how to respond, so she just continued in step with him. They hopped down several stairs and cut through St. Nicholas Park, their feet tracking over a few fallen leaves. The crisp air slapped Natalie's face when she snuck a glance at Darren out of the corner of her eye. He looked cut straight out of the casual section of Essence magazine, decked in a Nike hoodie and Timberlands. His hair waves did laps at every angle of his profile, and she couldn't deny the attraction.

When they got to her car, he asked, "Where's your interview?"

"At Devon's."

"Oh. Cool." Darren clapped both hands together in excitement. "*Now* you gone' be able to give me the hook-up!"

"Yea. Right. How about you give me those tips tho?"

Darren chuckled at the suggestion. "Uhh... I need a *date* if you want some tips." His eyes washed over Natalie's physique before he hit her with that cute smile she had come to enjoy. Initially, she laughed his statement off, ignoring her heartbeat picking up. But then, she looked at him.

"Well, if you want a date, you need to ask your friend Tonya."

Darren's eyes flew to the sky. "Hey. I'm sorry about that. I told you I would make it up to you. You know I wanted to go wit' chu' in the first place."

"It's cool. Cuz honestly, I'm not one to get with my cousin's ex. Or any of my people's exes, for that matter. So. We can be *friends*. But nothing more than that." Lowering her gaze, Natalie started a search for her key fob in her pocket.

Darren watched her for a moment, his expression blank, then handed her her bookbag. "Yo. I get it. But a brotha had to shoot his shot, right?" He tightened his messenger bag around his body as they were tackled by an angry gust of wind. Natalie shivered, hugging her hands together. "But I'm cool. I mean, you good people, Natalie," he added in a tender tone as he opened her car door. "So. Friends, it is."

Natalie examined him, trying to see if he was sincere. *I cannot hurt my cousin. No matter how cute he is.*

"Yo. I'll catch you later...*friend*!" Darren's playful laugh trailed behind as Natalie sank into her Kia.

Rolling her eyes, she shouted back, "Cor-neey," but she couldn't hide her grin. "Later."

After possibly escaping another close call with Darren, Natalie popped open her favorite playlist while stagnant behind back-to-back bumpers. New York traffic was its own Freddy Kruger nightmare, and if she got this job, she realized she may have to ditch her mom's Kia for a MetroCard. The fact that she could receive free rides since she was a student made this option even more appealing.

I don't know how Ashley drives like she does. But Natalie knew her cousin well enough to know Ashley wasn't one to succumb to public transportation with mere commoners.

"Cranes in the Sky" seeped out of the speakers, and Natalie pretended like she was Solange; big curly fro and all. She belted lyrics in her crystal-clear alto tone. In her mind's eye, she was singing to her love and telling him how much he meant to her. He was dark chocolate and fine, but not cocky like so many good-looking guys her age were (how she knew Darren was). Plus, her fantasy guy loved God, and that was hard to find. *It's much easier to fantasize about.* An incoming call halted Natalie's ruminating as her grandmother's name rolled onto the screen.

"Hey, Grams."

Grams's response was baked in its usual sweetness. "Baby girl! How are you? How was class?"

A guilt that was now becoming all too familiar crawled into the bed of Natalie's heart. *I still haven't been to see her.* With her eye pinned to the GPS, she responded, "It was good, Grams. I just got out of class. I'm heading to my job interview at Devon's."

"Oh. That's right. I forgot that was today," her grandmother bubbled. "Well, I ain't gone' keep ya, baby. But I *did* want to invite you for Sunday dinner. I'm gone' actually invite ya cousin and uncle too. It's been a while since I cooked and felt up to cookin', and it really *would* be nice if you went to church wit' me." When she paused, conviction and guilt took turns punching Natalie in a 1-2 combination. "I know you like those new contemporary services, but we got the Lawd too ya know."

Natalie frowned. She still hadn't found a church home, and she had visited her grandmother's before. *I appreciate Grams's church and all, but it's just not the style I'm looking for.* "Oh. Ok, Grams. Sunday, huh?" Natalie tried to think of her schedule. Of course, she had studying, but if she got this job, she may be working. "Can I get back to you on that? I need to make sure I don't miss my turn."

"Oh, honey, of course. I'll talk to you later."

When Natalie hung up, that familiar, still, small voice emerged, and she knew God wanted her to see her grandmother.

"Ok, Lord. I'll make it." Now at peace, Natalie exited the highway, crooning out the words to the rest of her playlist all the way to Devon's.

It was early in the week, so things weren't as lively as the last time Natalie had been at Devon's, but there was still a good crowd of people enjoying the cafe's famous brew of coffee. Coincidentally, Solange bellowed over the speakers of the Black-owned phenomenon stuffed inside Central Harlem, stubbornly snubbing its nose at the surrounding areas of gentrification. Natalie bounced in sync to the music, walking in and spotting the mural draped on the back wall of Dr. Martin Luther King Jr. and Malcolm X shaking hands. A soft smile of admiration met her face until Denise's profile blocked her view. She was heading right towards her. *This girl is always working.*

"Yo, sis," the waitress spit out, gripping an empty tray, her forever companion. "You here for yo interview?"

Natalie eyed her, a little put off. "Uh, yea. Devon told you?"

"Yep. I know everything around here." Denise winked, spouted "Come on!" and held up a commanding hand. "Follow me. I'll take you to his office in the back."

The back of the cafe was as clean and stylish as the front. Natalie trotted behind Denise down a long corridor colored in a cool, light gray with several closed doors on each side. Some of them had name plates that zoomed by, so she assumed they were offices. Different portraits of

Black businessmen and women accompanied their trip: Madame C.J. Walker, Oprah Winfrey, and Bernard S. Garrett, just to name a few.

Ok Black man! A smile burst from Natalie's lips in appreciation of Devon's honor for Black business trendsetters. Finally, they reached Devon's office, and even though it stood wide open, Denise tossed a rapid knock to the edge of the doorway.

"Natalie's here," she announced before backing out so that Natalie could step inside.

A brown-skinned man teetering over the threshold of 30 years old floated above a plethora of paperwork strewn across his desk. Blatant frustration wrote a novel on his almond-toned face. The office was a little chaotic for Natalie's taste, with file folders splayed open and a file cabinet gripping a few drawers that begged to be closed. Obviously, Devon had been looking for a something that she wasn't sure he had found. There were a couple of degrees pinned to the wall in addition to a bookcase, desk, and three chairs, one of which he was sitting in. Instant curiosity grabbed her when her eyes grazed over a picture of Devon clutching a little girl with a giant smile that displayed a handful of teeth.

Daughter? Natalie wondered before focusing back on the man in charge.

Devon's eyes brightened and he gestured for her to come inside. "You must be Natalie," he said with a generous shake.

Hmm, friendly and *attractive.* "Yep. It's nice to meet you."

Devon motioned to the chair opposite him and offered, "Please, take your coat off. Get comfortable." At his command, Natalie's A-line, knee-length, gray and white plaid skirt fell free. A navy-blue turtleneck and twin mocha-colored shoe-boots completed the ensemble along with a silver cross hugging her neck. Devon's eyes widened slightly as she smoothed a few loose tendrils that had fallen behind her ear. She managed to avoid the wide blue headband that secured the bulk of her curls into a sturdy bun. Natalie's look was complete with a slew of thick strands of baby hair that swam along her temples in deep, wavy strokes.

"So. Natalie," Devon uttered after a pause and a seeming need to regather himself. "Tell me about yourself." His smile was as warm as a summer's eve as he tilted back into his seat with both hands clasped over his chest, exploding with an air of quiet authority.

Ok. A relaxed interview. Natalie sat back in a posture that mimicked his.

"Well," she began, "I recently moved here a few months ago from Philadelphia. I had some, er, *unexpected* circumstances and wanted to be closer to family." She stopped to clear her throat. "I'm taking some classes now, but not full-time yet. Just trying to ease back into the whole school thing."

Interest flooded Devon's mocha latte eyes. "Oh really? What kind of classes are you taking?"

"Some standard courses and a writing class. I'm a writer. Well, at least, I'm hoping to be," she added with a slight chuckle. To her relief, he laughed too.

"I'm sure you are *exactly* what it is in your heart for you to be." The certainty in Devon's voice was piercing.

"Wow. I appreciate that." Natalie added, "Sir." She had to remind herself that this *was* potentially her future superior, even if he did look as appealing as a Macadamia Nut Sundae, her favorite dessert.

"Please. Call me Devon. We're not that formal around here." Another cozy smile sunbathed Devon's lips just when the phone rang. He lifted a finger. "Uh, hold on a sec."

As he took the call, Natalie studied his demeanor. He sounded just as amicable with whomever he spoke with as he did with her. *But he still sounds like a boss. I wonder how long he's had his own business?* Devon caressed the handle from his office phone while scribbling some notes into a planner. *He's definitely a cutie,* she decided and rubbed her toasted cheeks at the thought.

"Frank. My bad. Unfortunately, I scheduled another meeting during that time." Devon scrutinized his calendar, his brows huddling together like football players reading a play. "Can we do the following Friday instead?"

Eventually, he ended the call after settling on a good date for the meeting. Natalie browsed the room so it didn't seem like she had been staring too hard. Clearing his throat, Devon's half-smile juggled embarrassment. "Sorry about that. I had a mix-up with my scheduling." Apologetic eyes glazed his expression.

"Oh. No. It's fine," she assured him. "I understand."

"Hmmm. Where were we? Oh, yea. You're a writer!"

Natalie held back a smile. She loved the way that sounded. "Yes. I mean, I'm working to be. But right now, I'm a student. And I'm a student who needs income." Leaning languid against the armchair, she chuckled while Devon joined in, a dreamy look crossing his face.

"Ahhh. I remember those days. What kind of work experience do you have?"

"Well. I honestly don't have any serving experience. I mean, I'm a quick learner," she rushed to say. "And I did work in fast food for a year in high school, but most of my experience has been administrative."

With bright eyes, Devon bent over his desk, adding a singular hand clap. "Oh really? Do tell."

"Junior and senior year, I worked part-time for my mom's friend in construction. Organizing files. Answering the phone. Even some light bookkeeping. You know, that kind of stuff." Her eyes drifted to the open file cabinet, and Devon shadowed her gaze.

"Hmmm... interesting. I could certainly use some admin help. I've been saying for a while now that I need an assistant." He examined his desk with a sheepish grin while scouring the back of his neck with a hand. "As you can see. Believe it or not, I actually had one until she up and had a baby on me. I guess she liked the baby more than me cuz I ain't seen her since." The refreshing sound of Devon's laughter chimed into the room, beseeching Natalie to join in. "What kind of hours are you looking for?"

"Oh. I would say 20-25 hours per week would be good. Depending on the pay." She bit her lip, thinking about it. *If I work longer hours on the days I don't have class, I can swing it.*

Jotting some notes on his pad, Devon responded, "The pay is negotiable, and we are definitely accommodating at Devon's. The hours are doable." In an assertive manner, he scratched his chin. "Do you have some references? I'd like to follow up with your previous employer. If all goes well, I think we could find a spot for you here, doing what you did before."

Wow, God. That would be so awesome! "Yea. I can get you that info. I'll email it over ASAP."

"Great. I love helping out young students such as yourself. And I think you'll find that Devon's isn't just a job, Natalie. We're a community. A *family*, in some cases. That was my goal when I started this place, and I feel like I've successfully met that goal."

That's exactly what I'm looking for. Natalie's heart ballooned as her lips parted into a grateful smile. Devon's confidence invited her into further examination. His low fade, streaked with gray, gave him a polished look while large roasted-brown eyes topped off the breadth of his face. They held such kindness, a desire stirred for her to peer into them even more.

"How long have you had Devon's?" she asked, finally stating the question in her heart and fighting the longing to stare into his eyes.

A pleased look met Devon as he smoothed his hands over his stomach with a plop back into his chair. "About five years. But it's been the last two that have really taken off. I had a vision of a place where our people could connect and enjoy each other in a safe environment. But still have fun, you know? I know it just seems like coffee, but I've got more in store." His eyes sparkled at the prospect. "So far, we have our open mic night every first Friday of the month, and that's when the *real* fun begins."

Natalie edged forward a little. "That sounds dope. What all happens at the open mic?"

"Anybody can sign up. We have poets, singers, and sometimes even musicians. And they just *release*. There are moments when, Natalie, I swear, it feels like heaven on earth." Devon's mind seemed to be elsewhere as his eyes coated over while speaking.

"Wow. I would *love* to check it out." Natalie hadn't been to something like that in a while. *Plus, it will give me a chance to meet some more folks. I definitely need to up my social life.*

Her mind reeled back to times in Philly when she, Jaida, and Trisha would roller skate at Doll's Rink. It was a common occurrence and one she missed terribly.

Why hasn't Jaida returned my call? A sudden ache paraded Natalie's thoughts, but Devon's voice redirected them.

"Yea. We have a good time. And, like I said, I have some other ideas on expansion." Devon pitched her a hopeful expression. "Whether with this venue or others. So I could *definitely* use some admin help."

"And I would love the opportunity," Natalie gushed, unable to conceal the growing excitement in her voice. "Devon's sounds just like what I need right now." *In so many ways.*

"Great. I'll let you go then. Email those references, and I'll get back to you right away." As Devon stood, Natalie followed.

"Yes, sir. I mean, yes, Devon!" She smiled, receiving another friendly shake before sliding her coat back on.

"And Natalie," Devon said.

"Yea?" She looked at him on her way out the door.

"God always provides. He may not come when we want Him to, but He's always right on time." He winked, and all Natalie could do was grin. Those were her thoughts exactly.

CHAPTER 7

ON THE RUN

(ASHLEY)

"**I**'m just sayin'," Ashley taunted, "Yo face that night was *classic*. Don't front. You was *not* feelin' Denise." Swooping up a pair of Polo tennis shoes, with a militant eye, she examined them from sole to toe.

BJ hunched over to put some extra boxes of shoes on the shelf while smacking all 32 pearly whites at her. "Leave it to you to bring that shit up *here*," he growled. "And for the record, I was *good*. Ain't nobody buggin' on Denise and her games."

A humorous smile swallowed her cheeks as Ashley dismissed the Polos to capture a pair of Pumas. "Yea, right. She got 'chu, and you know it. Yo ego just too much to admit it." *Hmmm. Let me try these Pumas on real quick.*

"Yo. Dead-ass. *You* the one to talk about somebody's ego. And anyways, you got madd lit that night. I'm surprised you remember *anything*. We practically had to *carry* you to Lloyd's car." BJ guffawed, and Ashley threw him a scowl.

"Hehe," she said, a sarcastic neck roll accenting her tone. "Yea, I don't remember much. But 'chu feelin' some kinda way about Denise and Lloyd? Well. I remember *that* much." Pitching him a "you-can't-play-me" look, Ashley went back to admiring her shoe. *I guess they cute. I don't really do canvas, but it's fall, so there's still time to rock 'em.*

"Whateva. Yo, hold up." BJ trotted over to a young Asian kid that entered Lloyd's while Ashley sat studying her new prize. She had popped up unannounced to see him at work after class because she didn't want to go home to an empty house. Or, worse, to Natalie. A vague memory of Natalie clutching her hair over the toilet Friday night ate at the crevices of Ashley's mind, and she felt just a tad embarrassed that the girl witnessed her in such a vulnerable state. She had been avoiding her ever since.

BJ returned. The kid he was helping was in search of a pair of out-of-style loafers that Lloyd would never have had in stock. "Yo. You gone' have to chill on that Denise stuff while we here," he warned, slicing the air under his chin in a cutting motion. "I need this job. I ain't got daddy's bank like you."

"Ohhh. You takin' shots now? Somebody in they feelings." Ashley mumbled, "Guess I hit a nerve," then peeked at the Pumas on her feet. *They look good enough.* "Wasn't you kickin' it wit' some short chocolate chick that night anyways?" she asked in a blatant attempt to get back on BJ's good side. Crinkling her face, she tried to put together the hazy pieces from that night at The Barn. "Wuz up wit' that?"

"Oh, yea... *Janae.*" BJ's face broke into a huge grin. "That was a good night. I took a little stop by her house after I dropped you off."

"Yea, I bet."

"Damn, her ass was *fat.*"

With a sardonic expression, Ashley muttered, "Thanks for the extra info," and continued pawing the Pumas. *Ugh! I got a chip!* Her eyes bulged as she zoomed in on her index finger. Sure enough, the hot pink color laced with glitter was jagged with missing pieces. Huffing an annoyed sigh, she caressed the torn edges.

"But, wuz up wit' 'chu and 'pretty boy swag' though?" BJ eyed his friend while stocking his remaining inventory. "I know you got that on lock."

"Yea. We had a little hiccup after his car got jacked." Ashley tossed her head back and forth. "And honestly, I ain't even remember it happening until he texted me the next morning. Said he was pissed the police hadn't found nothing out yet about who did it. He had like $500 in the glove compartment that they stole."

"Damn. My man was rollin' wit' five hund' loose like that?"

"That's what I was thinking but shit if I would say it. He was already super pissed."

BJ wagged his head with an incredulous look. "Crazy. But bruh. I ain't *never* heard a brotha scream like that though, foreal."

Ashley exploded with laughter. "Right! I forgot how high-pitched he was. You woulda thought it was a chick." She and BJ cracked up, back on solid ground after her little dig at him about Denise.

"But other than that, he's comin' along nicely. I mean, he kinda salty it was my idea we went to The Barn. But damn, I ain't the one who jacked up yo ride, love." Ashley started stroking the sneaker in her hand again, playing with it like a kitten with a new toy. "I'm planning something a little more *intimate*, though, and I think that should get us back on track." Her lips spread into a calculated smile while slipping the Pumas into their respective box. Her concentration was diverted, though, when Lloyd made an appearance from the back.

"Oh, hey! Ashley, right?" Lloyd greeted her with just a little too much enthusiasm for her taste, so Ashley threw him an icy head nod foil-wrapped in aloofness.

Propping her weight on one hand, she replied, "Yep," and eyed him up and down. As Ashley lifted her chin, the black Brazilian bundles swung along her mid back in a choreographed dance. No doubt sensing her lack of warmth, Lloyd's voice wavered in uncertainty.

"So. Um. How's Denise? I reached out a few times... but, uh, I haven't heard from her." BJ smirked but was smart enough to conceal it by ducking his head over the shoe shelf.

Ashley too struggled to keep her face composed. "Oh. Is that so?" she responded. Her voice was as neutral as Switzerland. "I'm sure she's just busy."

Lloyd's thinning brows knit in confusion. "Umm. Ok. I mean, I seen her out and about on her IG stories? But um... yea, you prolly right."

Ashley cracked up internally as a half-smile rumbled to the surface. She struggled hard not to look at BJ, whose shoulders jiggled, she assumed, from his own internal laughter. *Bruh. Not stalking the IG stories!*

Lloyd's frame slumped a little, and Ashley gave him another one over. Average height. A stocky build. Nothing fancy. She knew her friend well enough to know that Lloyd was just a means to an end. *There's no way Denise is gone' go for a dude* pining *after her*, she thought. *No matter* how *much bread he got.*

Sweeping her eyes over the store, Ashley decided it was a typical shoe store, but what set it apart was Lloyd's inventory and his location. Somehow, he had a good connect on the latest shoes, and that's what kept her, and others like her, coming back. On top of that, he was in an area that sat at the crossroads of gentrification, tucked in Bed-Stuy, right off the J Train at the Marcy Avenue stop. On the east side, it was urban and gritty, but on the west side, "snow city". The benefit to Lloyd was that he had customers of all ethnicities and social classes who frequented there. Ashley knew a good businessman when she saw one. And apparently, so did Denise.

"BJ, why don't you go handle that young couple over there?" Lloyd tossed his head towards the front where a middle-class-looking Caucasian couple donned matching confused faces while ogling women's heels. BJ obliged, and Lloyd went to the register to ring up a Haitian man with fierce locks.

Ashley wasted no time whipping out her phone. **"You got 'em feenin' over here, girl! 100% thirst bucket,"** she texted Denise. A few seconds later, she received a response.

"Who?"

"Lloyd"

Three "ROFL" emojis and a "smirk" emoji flooded the screen. Ashley sent the "fire" emoji and the "queen" emoji in reply.

"Teach me your ways!" she said, and Denise sent a GIF with a white fat man dancing. Ashley burst out laughing.

BJ was back after helping the couple and smacked the air toward the Puma canvas tennis shoes abandoned on the bench. "Yo. You gone' get those or what?"

"Yea. Ring me up." As he totaled her purchase, Ashley knew BJ couldn't relax with Lloyd there. "Yo. I'm a slide. Hit me up later," she told him.

"Bet," he answered while handing her the bag.

Once outside, Ashley hopped into her truck and threw her goodies on the passenger seat but then sat there a moment, knowing there was no place for her to go. Her dad was working late, and she had no intention of having another powwow moment with Miss Thing. One night of drunken bonding was enough.

What's Darren up to? The thought popped inside Ashley's head like an unwanted pimple. *I know I'm trippin'.* But her fingers had a life of their own as they pulled up his profile on Instagram. No new posts, but when she used Denise's login to view his story, it showed that he was out with some random female from high school.

Ugh. I can't stand that broad. What was her name again? Sonya? Tonya? Wanda? Ashley didn't know, but what she *did* know was that the girl's ass was like an inflated balloon from some surgery she had gotten junior year that skyrocketed her to the top of the food chain. That was enough to piss off Ashley.

Screw Darren! This new Instagram information was all the more reason for her not to be by herself tonight. Ashley hadn't heard from Jason all day (probably due to that whole car situation), and she was being careful not to seem too available with him. She didn't want to hit *him* up since the car theft was not her fault *at all*. Besides that, she always made sure that *she* was the one being chased by her dates.

Oh, but Jeremy! Ashley dialed fast and purred, heaping mounds of sweetness into her words like an old-school pitcher of Kool-Aid. "Yo, babe. What 'chu up to?"

"Depends. You bout' to make me do slavery work again?" Jeremy's tone was smothered in suspicion, and Ashley giggled.

Yes, Jeremy was a little guarded, but she couldn't be too upset. She did kind of do him dirty by having him build the armoire this past weekend, then kicking him out so she could make her hair appointment. "Oh, boo. Don't be like that," Ashley replied in the same sugary tone. "I was hoping I could come to *you* and, you know, uh, *pay* you for your services from the other day." Eying her reflection in the rearview, she licked her plump, shimmering lips still doused in their Victoria's Secret gloss.

"Oh, yea? I like the sound of *that*." Jeremy paused. "But, I mean, my roommate here. You cool wit' that?"

"Didn't matter last time."

Jeremy switched his tone. "Say less. I'm free."

"On my way." Ashley's voice was equally promising before she ended the call, but as soon as her foot touched the gas, the dash lit with an incoming call from Gramma Reese. *I better take this*, she thought and prepared to hear a lecture on why she had been so MIA.

"Hey, Grams." Ashley tried her best to sound like the little girl she knew her grandmother still saw her as, though those days had been long gone.

Grams's vibrant voice saturated the leather interior of the car. "Baby girl! How are ya?"

"Doin' ok. Just left a visit with a friend. You remember BJ?"

"Oh, ok. Y'all still thick as thieves? Yea, of course I remember Bobby Jr., Rhonda's oldest. Followed you around like a puppy all through middle school."

Ashley chuckled at the memory while steering along Eastern Parkway. "Yea, well, that was until he started dating his first girlfriend, Gina Simpson."

"Mmhmm. It be's that way. So how *he* doin', baby?"

"Good, Grams. He's workin' full time. Tryna support his mom. You know she's been dealing with a lot, raising his brothers." Catching a glance in the rearview mirror, Ashley silently cursed at the sedan tailgating her.

"Oh yea, I understand that! A Black mother's plight if ever there was one," Grams chirped.

"Mmhmm. And I'm heading home now," Ashley replied, the lie slipping out easily while still eyeing the sedan. *This fool better lay off.*

"Oh, *good*. Now, didn't you have class tonight?"

Ashley switched to a slower lane. She didn't want to risk an accident since she was only half paying attention. She of all people knew the importance of safe driving since her own mother had died in a car crash.

"Yes, ma'am. I had my 'Design for Beginners' class. It's the first one of my major," she rushed out as the tailgater sped past in the other lane. Ashley flicked him off without a second thought, but his face was aimed forward, so she was sure he missed it.

"Asshole," she muttered.

"What?" Grams asked, shocked.

Whoops!

"Sorry, Grams. I was, uh, just clearing my throat."

"Mmhmm... well anyways, your class sounds exciting. You can tell me *all* about it at dinner on Sunday."

"Dinner, huh?" Ashley thought about her schedule while spotting her exit sign. "What time?"

"How about 4 PM? We gone' have a nice family sit-down and catch up. I done already talked to Natalie, yo Auntie Sheryl, and cousin Terrell. Now, I done called ya Daddy, but he ain't answerin'. Probably wit' some *client*." Grams's lingering on the word "client" caused Ashley to shift in her seat a little.

Is she sick of his work schedule too?

"And the man act like textin' don't exist. So, baby, do me a favor and make sure he come."

"Ok, Grams. I'll get back with you. I'm actually driving right now and need to pay attention." *I barely see daddy. When am I going to ask him about a Sunday dinner?*

"Alright now. Talk to ya lata."

"Yes, ma'am. Love you."

"Love you too, punkin'."

As soon as the line was clear, Ashley nudged up the volume to the radio to submerge her hurt. *Damn family sit-down. Some family,* she thought. *The last time I tried to have a family meal, I got played.*

Memories of the Saturday picnic let-down surfaced, and though Ashley tried to flick them away, they prevailed in shadowing her mind's eye.

"Ash. I'm sorry to do this to you, but I have some necessary paperwork I need to complete for this case coming up." Ashley's heart shriveled up when her dad backed out on their plans Saturday morning. *"I thought I would*

get it done in time for our picnic, but it's not lookin' good." An embarrassed expression crowded Mr. Bennett's face before his eyes fell to his Rolex, more out of habit than anything else.

It was almost noon, and Ashley had rolled out of bed with a horrible headache. The hangover she earned from the night before at The Barn pounded with a vengeance. She figured she could nurse it though and be at least 80% for her father's promised picnic later that day. Perched at the dining room table, she uttered a disappointed sigh. Her father shuffled around in the kitchen as she threw back the tall glass of Gatorade.

Does he have to bang the bowl on the table so loud like that? *Finally, Ashley mumbled the automatic response. "Ok, Daddy." Massaging her forehead, she squinted at the double French doors to the back patio.* It's the perfect day for a picnic, *she noticed*—Sunshine and not a cloud in sight.

"I swear I'll make it up to you, honey. I just overestimated how much time I'd have available this weekend. Well, with work and all." Malcolm poured himself some cereal, spitting out sentences in between bites.

Probably because you spent your time with Ms. Goody-Goody last night. *But Ashley's thoughts stayed buried like hidden treasures along with a treasure box of other topics left unsaid to her father. "I understand, Daddy," she replied, forcing down another swig of Gatorade.* Well, at least I can take it easy the rest of the day and knock out this hangover.

"You always do, sweetie. And again, I'm gonna make it up to you!" Mr. Bennett drifted over and kissed his daughter's forehead before rushing on to his next task. His half bowl of cereal was left forgotten on the kitchen island, so Ashley went to dump the remaining contents into the sink. She stared at the little pieces of cornflakes ravished by the garbage disposal. I feel like one of those little pieces.

Moisture decorated Ashley's eyelids at the memory, and she gripped the wheel tighter, now more determined than ever to see Jeremy. Instead of going straight to his place, though, she hit up a neighborhood liquor store, per his request, and picked up a bottle of Hennessy, Rosé, and two Backwoods. By the time she parked on the sidewalk in front of Jeremy's dilapidated apartment complex, half of the Rosé was gone, and she had a nice little buzz going.

Even though Jeremy's spot was in Brownsville, a rougher part of town, and every time Ashley came, she was a little concerned about her truck, he assured her 'his people' were looking out. Thus far, he was right, and nothing had happened to it.

Ashley and Jeremy met one night at The Barn. Jeremy was one of those dudes she knew could hold his own on the street *and* between the sheets just by the way he moved in the club. It also didn't hurt that he had a solid build from lifting all the time and the most beautiful Black skin she had ever seen.

The problem is, he can't provide for shit. Plus, he's a hustler. Not marriage material, but definitely a good time to be had. Until she was locked down herself, of course. Reapplying her lip gloss, Ashley adjusted her leather yoga pants, black knit sweater from Zara, and knee-high Chanel black boots, all accented by a long glittery scarf. Her hair was wavy and flowing, just the way she liked it. Not too much makeup. Jeremy said less was more.

Once satisfied with her look, Ashley's fingers did a deep-dive inside her Birkin, and she clasped her phone to text Denise. **"Feels like a Jeremy night."**

"Yasssss," her friend responded with the eggplant emoji.

Ashley wasn't just bragging, though. She was also letting Denise know her whereabouts for safety reasons. She rationalized, *If I ever come up missin', at least they know where to find me. Right now, I just need some company.* Thoughts of Darren with the high school random resurfaced as she finished her remaining Rosé. Annoyed, she smacked her lips, but her phone's ding stunted her annoyance. It was Jason.

"How was class?"

Damn. I know I should respond since he's probably pissed about that damn car, but this is so not a good time. If Ashley replied, Jason may keep texting or, worse, *call* to talk. Since she was about to be preoccupied, that wouldn't be wise on her part. Cementing her final decision, she dismissed the text then glided from her Benz in one fluid motion.

After hitting the buzzer to the apartment building, Ashley was let in right away. Walking up the stairs wasn't as strenuous as it would have been if she didn't run on the regular. But even if it was, she would have had to rough it out because the elevator was broken. By the time she got to the seventh floor, she was in need of a little deodorizing. *Man, it's like the workout before the workout,* she thought, cracking a smile at her own humor.

Using the camera from her phone, she paused in front of Jeremy's door to do a quick touch-up. The door swung open right before she knocked, revealing a bare-chested Jeremy, looking like a black stallion. A pleased smile dressed Ashley's lips better than Dapper Dan did NYC's finest.

Jeremy ripped the brown paper bag from her hand, then dropped it on a nearby coffee table. He drew his body to hers like a dog to a bone. One of the things Ashley loved about Jeremy was his chest, and the boy never had a shirt on. At least, not at the house. The closest he had come to one was the one time she came through and he wore a "beater." *But he didn't have that shit on for long,* she thought, snickering to herself. Ashley had made sure of that.

"'Bout time," Jeremy grumbled with passion, molding her into his arms.

Giggling at his urgency, she said, "Yea? Well, if you didn't live so high up in this damn building, I would a got here sooner. And when they gone' get that elevator fixed?" The Nautica Voyage Cologne soaking Jeremy's pores infused Ashley's nostrils. In response, she tightened her hold around his muscular frame.

"I don't know," he murmured regarding the broke-down elevator, then continued to suffocate her body with his. "It's been like that since I been here." He buried his face deeper into Ashley's neck and kneaded his fingers into her lower back, sending all kinds of sensations her way. All memories of Darren, or hell, Jason for that matter, were erased. Jeremy released her, and Ashley trailed him into the living room, eager and ready.

"And how long has that been?" she asked, ignoring the clutter mingled with the potent smell of marijuana. *At least it ain't as messy as last time.*

"Five years."

Damn, and no maintenance? Ashley rolled her eyes in disbelief. Her vision soaked up a dingy couch, flat-screen TV, and beat-up leather reclining chair. A small cloud of dust floated upward when she dropped down on the couch.

Jeremy went to grab a few items from his room before mumbling something incoherent to his roommate, Case, who was hulled up in his bedroom. When he returned, he was gripping a bag of weed and a shell. Just what Ashley was looking for: escape.

Later that night, Ashley had a hard time sleeping. She tossed and turned but couldn't get rest. After her shenanigans with Jeremy, she felt super exhausted, so she wasn't sure what the issue was. Now that she was settled in her own bed, she just couldn't find peace. "Maybe a snack will help," she grumbled with her face still smashed against a pillow.

Just in case her dad was ambling around randomly, Ashley wrapped herself inside a white terry-cloth robe and slipped into her fuzzy pink slippers. When she got to the kitchen, she was surprised Natalie was seated at the island, suspended over a mug and speaking in low tones. The closer Ashley got, the more she realized her cousin was on the phone. Listening hard, she posted by the wall in the foyer so as not to be seen.

"Yea. Yes, I know. I've been taking the medication, but I'm not sure if it's helping. I also don't like the side effects." Then a pause. "Yea. And it doesn't help that my friends have been MIA. I barely get a text, let alone a phone call from them. Which is crazy coming from Jaida, who I've always been closer to." Natalie's voice was dripping with hurt.

Medication? Ashley wondered. *And who is Jaida?* But she was even more surprised at hearing Natalie sound so upset. Ashley couldn't think of one time when she'd witnessed her cousin distressed.

Not even at her own mother's funeral, she thought before her mind whirled back to the service held earlier that year. Natalie was stoic at the funeral, and for that reason and a few others, Ashley kept her distance.

Aunt Melissa was a stellar mom, in Ashley's opinion. She often wished they had lived by each other so she could have been closer to her, especially after *her* mom had died. A memory of her aunt seeking her out to speak with her right after her own mother's funeral was one Ashley treasured to this day.

"Honey, don't let the hard parts of life make you *hard," Aunt Melissa said while rocking her and cupping her cheek.* 14-year-old Ashley hadn't understood the statement at the time, but now she could guess what her aunt was talking about.

"Who knew you would be gone too soon yourself, Aunt Melissa?"

"Huh?" Natalie craned her neck to peer near the foyer. "Who's there?"

Shoot! Ashley had gotten so caught up in her thoughts she forgot she was supposed to be eavesdropping. Embarrassment sullied her eyes as she slinked around the corner into full view.

"Hey." The word was doused in an unspoken apology, but Natalie's almond eyes rounded more from surprise than displeasure. Her own "Hey," in reply was cloudy with confusion. As Natalie went back to talking on the phone, Ashley raided the fridge.

"Yea. I appreciate that," Natalie said. "Thanks, Linda. I'm gonna let you go. I'll follow up with you tomorrow. Yea. I'm ok. Thanks again. Good night."

Hmmm. Ashley vaguely remembered Natalie mentioning a Linda she was close to back home but couldn't remember the details. Her curiosity peaked as she started the makings of a bowl of cereal.

"Munchies?" Natalie asked.

Dag, did she know I was smokin'? Ashley jerked a little, glancing at her cousin. "Naw. Why you say that?"

Puzzled, Natalie gestured at the cereal. "Uh, I don't know. Just making convo. It's late, and you're eating." She took a perplexed drink from her mug.

"I couldn't sleep," Ashley replied. Grabbing the almond milk, she did a once over of the expiration date before pouring it into the bowl.

"Me either." Natalie eyed Ashley's bowl of peanut butter Captain Crunch. Everyone knew that was the best one.

Feeling guilty for her earlier tone, Ashley offered, "You want some?" She slid the box in Natalie's direction before dropping onto one of the stools nearby.

Natalie smiled. "Sure. Why not."

It was weird because Ashley hardly ever ate cereal at night. At least, not as an adult. But sitting across from her cousin, having cereal at whatever time in the morning, made her feel... Hmmm, how did it make her feel?

After fixing a bowl, Natalie got back seated. "So, what's keepin' you up?"

Even though her tone was light, Ashley was still caught off guard by the question and tripped up on her words. "Well. I, uh, just had some stuff on my mind. That's all," she finished and shoveled her face with more Captain Crunch. *I don't know if that's the real reason, but it sounds good.*

Disappointment hid in Natalie's eyes. "Yea? Me too. I've had to take some anti-depressants the last few months, but the side effects affect my sleep sometimes." She popped a spoonful of her own into her mouth.

Ashley was surprised. She looked at her cousin while swinging her spoon in mid-air, making it float over the bowl like a helicopter. "Really? You struggle with depression?"

Natalie's gaze dropped. "Yea. My mom did too. But I didn't know she did until I started having similar symptoms," she confided. "When I opened up to her about it, she was able to share her experience."

For the first time since Natalie moved in, Ashley held a genuine interest in her cousin. "Wow. So, if you don't mind me asking, what were your symptoms?" Natalie went quiet as a lopsided frown framed her face. "Hey. It's cool if you don't wanna share," Ashley rushed to say.

"No. I'm fine with sharing. I was just thinking about that time of my life and what was going on. Well, I was sleeping a lot, and my diet was *horrible*. I gained like 20 pounds." She stroked the inside of her arm, focusing on a specific area. "I also had a lot of anxiety. Depression and anxiety can be related," she said, looking up at Ashley. "But I didn't know that then. It wasn't until I got help and was treated that I learned." Natalie stopped rubbing her arm while puffing out a breath before attempting a smile. "I got help, and now I'm better."

Ashley observed her cousin. *Even in the dead of night she seems to have it all together.* Natalie's head was in some type of updo with mounds of tiny curly tendrils piled high underneath a silk scarf, and even her pink terry-cloth robe couldn't hide the well-endowed behind she had.

You know people are paying thousands *for that ass?* Ashley wanted to yell at her cousin. *And you always coverin' it up!* Ashley was thinking about Sonya from high school. *Or is it Tonya?* Continuing her assessment, she noticed Natalie's skin glowed without any makeup. Ashley didn't think *she* looked so hot unless she put on *at least* some foundation, and she had to go through great pains to make sure *her* hair was wrapped super tight each night to keep her tracks in place. Shaking away her thoughts, she asked, "So, what did your treatment consist of?" and took another bite.

"I did a holistic approach initially," Natalie explained, her face now tainted with worry. "I really didn't want to take medicine. My mom had been on something that was helping, but I was leery. So, I met with a holistic doctor, and they showed me foods I should be eating and exercises I could do. They also directed me to some herbal remedies."

Hmm, I wonder if weed counts? It sure enough calms the hell out of me. Ashley took a few more bites and sat with her cousin in silence as a weird sensation sprung in the pit of her stomach. She didn't like the feeling. "Well, I'm glad you figured it out," she said. "So, you going to this Sunday dinner Grams is having?"

"Oh. Ok. Yea." Natalie looked put off by the abrupt topic change. "I figured I'd go to church with her too. What about 'chu?"

Church, huh? Grams didn't invite me *to church.* But Ashley abandoned the left-out feeling as soon as it appeared. "Yea. I figured I would. It's been a while," she replied. She steered a particle of cereal around with a spoon, making it do laps, and Natalie peered at her with a cocked head.

"Yea? So, y'all don't get together like that?"

Does Thanksgiving and Christmas count? Ashley's face scrunched up. "Not really. I mean, we used to. But now everybody kinda does their own thing." She tossed an indifferent shrug, her stomach now full enough to lead her into a coma. Hopping off the stool, Ashley poured the remaining milk from her bowl into the sink. "I'm gonna head to bed now."

"Umm. Ash. There was something I wanted to ask you." A concerned expression shadowed Natalie's features.

Does she know I was snooping through her room? I thought I put everything back in place. Ashley's mind sizzled as she nodded, cooking up a good excuse.

"Do you remember talking to me about 'The Hyenas' the other night?" Curiosity flooded Natalie's eyes as Ashley's skin went cold. She stumbled backward against the sink.

"What? When was this?" *Damn. I have no memory of this conversation* and *had it with somebody I can't stand.*

Natalie eyed her with intent. "Friday night. When you came in drunk. You mentioned something happened with them back at camp."

Sudden tears clung to Ashley's eyelids, and she turned around to hide them. *I can't believe I said that.* With her back still to her cousin, she swiped a trembling hand over her cheek and rinsed it along with the bowl. *That's the last time I mix Tito's with Hookah,* she thought, sliding the bowl into the dishwasher. "Yea. I definitely had too much to drink if I was talking about some stuff from years ago. I have no idea what I was on." Twisting on her heels, she grabbed for a sponge while adding in a rush, "I'm exhausted. 'Night."

"Oh. Alright then... 'night."

Natalie's eyes brimmed with resignation, and Ashley ducked her head while brushing off the part of the counter where she had been sitting. Even still, her cousin's stare burned her neck, and the desire to open up wrestled against the hedge of fear encircling her heart. *There's no way I'm confiding in this heffa about some shit from back in the day.*

"Hey, Ash?" Natalie called.

Ashley had just about reached the opening to the foyer. Irritated, she stopped in her tracks. *What now?*

"Thanks for building the armoire." Natalie's warm smile melted Ashley's hedge into confusion.

Ashley pitched her cousin a puzzled look until it dawned on her. *Dad must have told her I built it.* "Uh. Yea," Ashley replied. "No problem. Trust me. It didn't take much from me at all."

Ashley snuffed a giggle before hurrying through the foyer and up the steps. When she made it to her bedroom, she discarded her robe and buried herself deep beneath the blankets. She was still annoyed that she had brought up The Hyenas to Natalie, but there was also something else. It wasn't until she was settled and almost asleep that Ashley recognized what that odd sensation she had felt downstairs while eating and talking with Natalie was. It was a feeling of nostalgia.

CHAPTER 8

A FATHER'S LOVE

(NATALIE)

Ugh. I can't get used to this dosage, Natalie thought. *I'm definitely gonna have to ask Celia to adjust it.* Natalie's new counselor had put her on a higher dosage of antidepressants after her last counseling appointment, but her body seemed out of whack as a result. Every time she thought she was good, another side effect would pop up. First, she kept getting dizzy all the time; then, her appetite had taken a nosedive; and now, her sleep was sketchy. She half-rolled, half-limped out of bed in a haze. Dragging both feet to her desk, she flicked away the crumbs of sleep before propping open her computer to check emails.

Professor Morris wants my Calculus assignment in today. An odd sound of frustration resounded from Natalie's lips. *I guess I* did *tell him I would have it done by now.* Her brows wrinkled in concentration as she tried to remember the date it was due. *I think it was last Friday...* The bulky textbook on the corner of her desk titled "Calculus 1 for Beginners" stared up at her with dread.

Beginners, my butt. It's just like what I told Darren: if I escape with a B- in this class, I'll be good. With skeptical eyes, Natalie leafed through her notebook of calculus problems. Then, there was Psych. "Somebody, please tell these people I will *never* be a mathematician or a psychiatrist," she murmured before speed-reading for Wednesday's class. The vibration from Natalie's phone disturbed her focus. She answered with her eyes still glued to her Psych paragraph.

"Hello?"

Jaida's perky voice burst through the line. "Hey, girl. Wuz up?"

"Hi, stranger." Surprised, Natalie jerked up. "I see *you* alive." She tried to keep her voice light and not heavy with the annoyance she had accumulated from her friend's absence. "I called you like three times." Flopping back into her papasan chair, Natalie folded her limbs to get more comfortable.

"Yea. Yea. I know. But you know how it is. I been super busy with the youth ministry, and me and Trisha started that new line dance class at Doll's. Oh. And I met this cutie pie, David, in class! Giiiiiiiirl, he is *so* fine!" A playful giggle tickled Natalie's ear, inducing a fond smile from her lips.

Jaida and her men. "Yea? I did see you take a pic on Insta with some dude. But why you couldn't have at least *texted* is beyond me..." She let her voice fade.

"Well, I did DM you, though. I was asking about how things were going."

Natalie rolled her eyes in disbelief. "A DM? Since when is a DM enough for best friends since middle school?" Jaida went quiet. *I can't believe she thinks that's ok with everything I'm going through right now.* Natalie's heart sank while she fought the urge to fill the space in their conversation. Peering down at her nude-colored fingernails, she opted to play with the hem of her pajama pants.

The reply from her friend came through guilt-ridden. "You right, Nat. My bad. I guess I got caught up. But, actually... I umm... I only have a second to talk... I gotta get ready for class," Jaida admitted. "So. I'll hit you up later, ok? And we can *really* talk."

Disappointment riddled Natalie's sigh. "Fine. I'll talk to you later." She stared hard at the end call screen on her iPhone with hurtful eyes. *What is that about? Why did she even call if she was just gonna get off that fast?* Natalie was still stewing over her friend's flakiness when another buzzing from her phone resounded. It was a text from her bank.

"OhmyGod." Her stomach did a double somersault as she slid the text open in fear and skimmed the notification that she had overdrafted her account. "Not again! I *swear* I deposited a check last week." Seizing her laptop, Natalie swiped open a few tabs to make a transfer from a stash her mom had left. It was now dwindling all too fast.

I really hope this gig with Devon pays off. Thinking about her money troubles birthed another aggravated sigh, and Natalie's mind cycled back to a time when she wouldn't have been able to handle the pressure mounting internally. Her heartbeat accelerated.

"Take deep breaths, Nat. Take deep breaths." Fidgeting with the laptop still on her lap, Natalie tried to get a hold of herself. Still, a familiar temptation scraped at her psyche. Stealthily, ripping at its edges, unwinding it like the thread from her favorite pair of distressed denim jeans.

"Nat. Keep it together," she whispered while trying desperately to remember the techniques Linda had taught her, but a creeping, growing anxiety multiplied until she couldn't take it anymore. She caved, and her eyes began searching the room.

Where is it? she wondered, having popped out of the chair to rifle through her top desk drawer. Then the middle. Then the bottom. Until finally, under a stack of file folders, notebooks, and a copy of "The Love Songs of W.E.B Du Bois," she saw it: a bright, shiny razor, almost sparkling, crammed inside a small sandwich baggie.

Butterflies soared in Natalie's abdomen. Biting her lip in anticipation, her fingers tapped against the top of the drawer. *Nat, don't do it.* The tapping began sporadically at first, then sped up. Excitement brewed with fear clouded her typically-sound judgment. She was a dog in heat as she eyed the razor. Its smooth surface. Its sharp edges. The way it glistened in the sun rays that filtered through the window...

I just want to hold it, Natalie reasoned. Even though she knew better. Sometimes, though, she did just hold it. Somehow, it empowered her to hold it and not use it. But this time, she knew something was different. And just as Natalie was reaching for the glossy metal object, just as she was about to commit to doing the unthinkable, there was a loud knock at the door. Startled, she slammed the drawer, peering up with wide, dilated pupils. Taking a deep breath, she called out, "Come in!" in what she hoped was a perfectly normal sound and not the screechy, high-pitched one she had heard with her own ears.

"Good morning, Natalie." Uncle Malcolm poked in his head, resembling an arc angel. "I was just seeing if you were up. I know you've got a big day ahead."

"Good morning. Yep. I'm up." Natalie tried for a smile. "I appreciate the wake-up call."

Malcolm's expression collapsed into concern as he eyed her. "Everything ok, kiddo?" He opened the door wider while inching onto the threshold, revealing a three-piece, navy-blue Boss suit.

Natalie squeezed both hands together, trying her best to be strong, but her resolve crumbled. "I don't know, Uncle Malcolm." Her voice broke. "I guess... I just. I just, uh... I miss my friends." She settled on the thing that seemed the easiest to say.

"Oh, honey!" Malcolm was near her in seconds, melting her beneath a warm bear hug. "I know it's hard. You just let it out." He held her, and the smell of his aftershave mingled with love swarmed all around.

The tears Natalie had been holding in ran a marathon down her cheeks. "I'm sorry. I'm sorry," she murmured over and over between hiccups. She was on the floor now. At some point, she sank down there without realizing it. *When was the last time I cried in a man's arms?*

"Nothing to be sorry about, Natalie. I'm here." Malcolm was rocking her on his knees in his three-piece suit, hunched over the soft cream carpet. "I'm here."

And Natalie believed him. He *was* there. It was the thing she knew she needed. It wasn't the razor she kept hidden in her room, and yet still somehow couldn't get rid of after all this time. It was the love of a father.

Malcolm convinced Natalie that he could move his 9 AM appointment to 11 and took her to Denny's. She threw on a jean skirt and a white tank with a yellow cardigan and was ready in 15 minutes.

I don't want to make him late, she thought while swiping her favorite crossbody handbag from Marshalls. Not long after, they were seated at a small booth and browsing their menus when the waitress came by.

"Y'all know what you want?" she asked as a wad of gum straddled her two front teeth.

Natalie wasn't that hungry but didn't want to disappoint her uncle. "I'll have a couple of eggs and a cup of coffee."

Malcolm peeked over his menu. "You sure? You've got a big day ahead, remember? You should get some more protein." He turned to the waitress and added, "She'll have a side of bacon, and I'll get the big breakfast," before closing his menu.

Natalie's half-smile at her uncle was full of endearment. "Thanks. I guess I wasn't thinking about that."

"Yep. Now, I know you start Devon's today. You nervous?" His bright eyes crinkled in pride, his obvious care warming her insides.

"A little. I mean, it's like, a 'big girl job,' you know?"

"Ahh. Yea. I remember my very first job. I helped print newspapers and was a clerk in the mailroom. Back then, we actually *read* the paper and didn't just pull up the news online." His lips tilted into a teasing smile. "Or social media. I know you kids don't read nothing that's not on a screen."

Natalie poked her chest out a little while clearing her throat. "Uncle Malcolm, I'll have you know I'm reading *two* books right now that are *paper* versions." She held up two fingers coupled with a sassy look.

Malcolm chuckled. "Yea. You're a rare breed. You're probably the only one in your whole generation, though." The waitress stopped to pour their coffee, and both sipped the warm liquid in gracious silence. Natalie added several creams and sugars to hers while Malcolm preferred his straight black.

"So, Nat. How are you adjusting to being here? I know you mentioned your friends earlier." He watched her with intention, and Natalie fought embarrassment as flashbacks of this morning's episode resurfaced.

It's definitely been a while since I've struggled on that *level.* "Yea. About that." She spoke after taking a moment to choose her words. "I think I'm just a little off right now because I'm on some new medication. It's made me more emotional than I normally am." Brushing a tendril of hair from her neckline, she added, "I mean, my friends haven't been as available... but I'm sure it's nothing." She waved a carefree hand. "They're just busy right now. That's all."

"Mhmm." Malcolm was silent as he drew in another sip. "I know it was hard for me after Patty died." His voice grew quiet. "I definitely needed more support during that time. Especially raising Ashley."

Intrigue waded in Natalie's eyes. "Really? In what ways?"

"Ashley was 14. Well, you both were. And I'm sure you know from your own experience that a 14-year-old girl needs a mother in ways that a father is never going to be able to provide." He paused and stroked the smooth mug between his fingertips. His caramel face settled into a blend of sadness and deep thought, and a pang pinched Natalie's heart.

I can't even imagine how hard that was for Uncle Malcolm, being a sudden widower and single dad. "How did you get through it?"

Malcolm studied the table for a bit before meeting her eyes. "Do we ever really get through it, Natalie? I mean, you fill up your life with things that bring you joy and hope, but that person's absence is always felt. It's like you're navigating around it all the time."

She nodded, soaking up his words. *But I definitely don't want to feel this way forever.*

"Well, isn't there a time when it doesn't hurt *this* bad?" Natalie's voice cracked without her meaning for it to, and Malcolm shot out his hand to shelter hers on the table.

"Oh, hon, yes. I would certainly say there isn't the sharp, agonizing pain that accompanies loss initially. I only meant to say that..." He searched for the right words. "Life is never the same. It can be good at times and even fun. But never the same." Malcolm stopped rubbing her hand when the waitress delivered their meal.

After finishing a mouthful of eggs, Natalie said, "I don't know. I think one of the hurtful things is that my mom isn't here. And she was this constant in my life. You know? And then, on top of that, my best friends, who have *always* been there, aren't there either. And Jaida calls me this morning with no real apology as to why she hasn't returned my calls. And I admit it. I wasn't happy to hear she and Trisha have been so tight lately." Taking a swig of her water, she swallowed her distress. "I was always the closest to both of them. Now I feel like the one being left out."

Natalie couldn't stop herself, even though she knew she was rambling. "And she thinks a DM is enough. Like a DM means you really care!" Her eyes were two brown slits aimed at the piece of bacon in her hand, though she wasn't really seeing it. Instead, she was seeing her two best friends skating at Doll's Rink and having the time of their lives.

"Have your friends ever acted this way, sweetie?" Malcolm asked in a gentle tone. "I mean, have you witnessed them being unreliable when you needed them?"

Natalie paused while licking her lips. *Have I seen this type of behavior with them?* She was silent and munched on her bacon. "Honestly. Jaida has always been flaky. And Trisha. Well, Trisha has always been guarded. Even though they're both my best friends, there's just stuff that Trisha doesn't talk to us about, and we find out after the fact."

Like when she slept with Rashon, and nobody knew until she got pregnant, and then gave up the baby for adoption. Natalie shook her head at the thought. She still had a hard time with that one, but she never told Trisha how she felt because her feelings weren't the focus. Trisha needed a friend, so Natalie focused on being there for her. *And now she isn't there for* me. She tossed her head with a sad frown.

"It sounds to me like they're probably just being their normal selves. The difference is, you're in a time of need, and your needs aren't getting met."

"Hmmm. Wow. I didn't look at it like that."

"Did you go to them before to get your needs met? In the past, I mean?"

Scrunching up her face, Natalie answered, "I don't know?" Her eyes fluttered to the window and she glimpsed a man outside who, to her surprise, resembled Devon. "No. I probably didn't," she said, more solid this time, as her view drifted back to the Devon look-alike. "*I* was probably the one that was always there for *them*." She tilted her cup inward to take a drink but cried out instead. "Ohh!" She had missed her mouth entirely and splashed hot coffee onto her shirt. An ugly brown stain exploded on Natalie's vibrant yellow top, just missing the base of her neck. "Ugh! Just great."

"Here." Malcolm was on his feet, snatching napkins from the dispenser.

"Thank you," she muttered, accepting the paper towels. "Just what I needed." Shaking her shirt away from her skin, Natalie speed-wiped. *Can this day get any worse?*

"I think I have some clothes in the trunk that belong to Ashley," Malcolm announced. "Let me take a look." Before she could respond, he was up and moving. Natalie kept working at the stain and was so busy trying to clean it that she didn't even notice someone standing nearby.

"Hey there. Looks like I get to see you twice today."

Natalie inched up her eyelids, almost too afraid to look. "Devon. I um... I thought that was you." She tried for a smile while slicing a self-conscious hand through her kinky ringlets. *Of course, it's you, because I'm a mess right now, and this is the day from hell.*

"Yea. I was on this side of town for a meeting and had to use the bathroom *so* bad." He chuckled. "I figured this was the most sanitary option. What are the odds?"

That smile! Sheer attraction stirred Natalie's gut as she peered up at her new boss. "Oh, yea? I'm just having breakfast here with my uncle." Although she made herself sound nonchalant, she was still gripping her soaked shirt. Her eyes then skirted to the crumbled, damp napkins on the table.

Following her gaze, Devon finally saw the mess she had made. "Oh! Do you need some help?"

"Uh, no. I'm good." Natalie's hand hovered over her chest so he couldn't see the stain. "I got it covered." *Literally.*

"Nat. I got a shirt for you." Uncle Malcolm appeared at the table, a Black superhero with a blouse flying around in his hand like a white cape. Devon stepped back to make room. "I see you got company." Malcolm looked at Devon before sticking out a hand. "Malcolm. Natalie's uncle."

"Devon Woods."

"Yea, I know. I've been to your cafe several times. You're doing a great job over there, young man."

Devon's eyes brightened. "Aww, thanks. I appreciate that. It hasn't been easy, but I'm thankful for the growth we've had the last few years."

He jammed both hands into his pockets then while rocking a little in a boyish manner.

Malcolm glanced at Natalie. "Well, you should definitely be proud. I know my niece is in good hands over there."

Natalie chimed in. "Yep. I'm really looking forward to my first day." This time, her smile was genuine.

"Me too." Devon agreed. "But I don't want to interrupt y'all. I'll see you later, Natalie. It was nice meeting you, Malcolm." He stared at her some with those coffee browns, and once again, warmth flooded Natalie's cheekbones. If she were a shade lighter, she would have actually blushed.

"Yep. Later," Natalie replied. *Ugh. But why did you have to see me with this massive stain on my shirt?*

When Devon exited for the men's stall, Natalie found her uncle eyeing her with a mysterious expression. In hopes of distracting him, she asked, "That's Ashley's shirt?"

Sitting in his seat, he handed it over. "Yep," he answered, but he was still watching her with that strange gaze and a knowing smile. "So. Devon, huh?"

A tingling sensation pulsed through Natalie's heart that she tried to ignore, but a smile eked its way to the surface. "Mmhmm." Still not meeting his gaze, she captured the shirt and assessed it. "You sure Ashley's gonna be ok with me wearing this?"

"Oh yea," Malcolm assured with a dismissive hand. "She gave it to me to donate. I just haven't gotten around to it. Ashley hasn't worn that thing in forever."

Relieved, Natalie went to change in the stall. On her way there, she bumped into Devon coming out of the men's room, and they both laughed.

"I just keep running into you," he teased, smoothing over a crisp plaid blue and gray tie while backing up from their encounter.

Natalie bounced her coily tendrils to the side. "Yea. I promise to be more *inconspicuous* when I'm at work."

"Well. You don't have to do that, Natalie. I like seeing you too much."

Did he just say what I think he said? Natalie was glad her face wasn't made of glass, or it would surely break from smiling so hard. But before she could think up a reply just as witty, Devon had turned to leave.

Once in the women's restroom, Natalie slipped on Ashley's shirt and checked out her reflection. *I guess this day is getting better after all,* she thought, turning to view her profile and continuing to admire her figure. The blouse fit like a glove.

Chapter 9

Class Act

(Ashley)

Professor Simone wasn't your typical professor, and that's exactly why Ashley liked her. With glistening skin that looked like it was dipped in a pool of Hershey's chocolate and a thick, layered charcoal bob, she could dress her butt off. This, of course, made sense because she was leading a design class at the academic level. In her late 20s, Professor Simone was graced with the unique experience of being liked and respected by peers and students.

"Ok, class. What have we learned so far regarding Chanel's onset in the fashion world in the early 1900s?" While asking the question, she kicked her head at an angle. The gesture caused the long part of her bob to somersault into the air. Each midnight-black strand shimmied amid the silence that settled over the classroom. When no one replied, she crossed one ankle over the other, teased her butt against the edge of the desk, rested a palm on each side, and surveyed the room with untaught class. The woman was fierce.

Ashley studied her professor's long cream shawl wrapped elegantly around each slender shoulder and draped over a black cashmere turtleneck. Her top, tucked into black jeans with subtle slits at the knees, was drowned into a pair of black Louboutin boots. *I know those things are red bottoms,* Ashley thought with envy. *I don't even have to look.*

"Ashley?"

"Huh?" Yanking her head up from her assessment of her teacher's shoes, Ashley struggled to regain her composure and combed a hand through her long store-bought tresses.

"Would you please explain what you've learned regarding the Coco Chanel era?"

Aww, man. A ball of nerves swelled in her belly as Ashley slipped a tongue over her top lip. *Why she gotta pick on me?*

The class was pretty diverse, and Ashley liked the idea that she could blend in and not be the only brown face. Her attempt at blending in was one of the reasons she sat with intentionality near the left, in the middle, a few rows behind the geeks and a few in front of the potheads. Her seat choice, however, didn't seem to be helping much today.

"Sure," she responded after a beat. "Why not?" A student snickered behind her, and Ashley's eyes darted, piercing him with her best, "You're going to be working for me one day" facial expression.

"Chanel arrived on the scene just when the hourglass figure was in, and so corsets, bodices, and such were in style." Waving a dramatic hand in the air, Ashley's mind conjured up images of the clothing items of the day. "Her style changed the game, and she introduced a new concept along with it to her consumers." Pausing for effect, she waded in the attention.

Professor Simone hoisted up an arched brow while crossing both arms. "Oh, yea? What was that?"

"That a woman didn't have to be uncomfortable to be stylish." Ashley sampled her cafe latte floating in its Starbucks to-go cup, then added in a humorous tone, "That she could be cute and still breathe."

The class laughed, and even Professor Simone cracked a smile. "Yes. That's a great way to put it, Ashley." Ashley beamed. She tossed back her drink again to mask her smug expression.

As Professor Simone continued her lecture, Ashley ear hustled without appearing to do so. She had mastered this ability and chose to use it, whether listening in on gossip or when she didn't want to appear too smart. Like she did with men. And sometimes in school.

"Never let 'em see your hand," her father always said. Of course, when *he* said it, he was referring to his work in the courtroom, but

Ashley had learned fast how to apply the method to her personal life. Especially after Darren.

"Now I want you all to listen up." Professor Simone's smooth, eloquent speech serenaded the room near the end of her lecture. "I'm going to give each of you a chance to attend Fashion Week. This spring. With me. In Paris." Dabbling in a stroll with her hands clasped behind her back, she perused each student. A collective intake of breath exuded from Ashley's peers. Ashley hadn't even realized she had inhaled right along with them. Leaning over the desk, she strangled its edges.

"Although all of you will have this opportunity, only one of you will get to attend." The chic professor continued treading the classroom, taking in the students' responses and capitalizing on the moment. "I'm going to assign an extra credit project. If you choose to do it, you'll be eligible for the fashion event and be accredited with additional points for your grade. If you choose not to do it, it doesn't affect your grade." She shrugged. "But, you lose out on this opportunity. If you're the winner, you'll spend five days in Paris with me. All expenses paid." She punctuated her speech by pivoting in the middle of the room, both hands still braided together.

Straight up powerhouse, Ashley thought, being sure to conceal the approval in her eyes.

"I'll assign the project next week, and it will be due at the end of the semester. You'll receive details via email, so check Blackboard."

"*Maaannnn,*" one of the students whined, a redhead with thick glasses who sat in the front. "We can't know *now?*"

Ashley jabbed her head in annoyance. *Thirsty.* Her peers knew nothing about the element of surprise. *Professor Simone has everybody in the palm of her hand right now.* She scoped the room, impressed. *She knows how to play* her *hand.*

Professor Simone tossed a patient smile to the student. "Check your Blackboard. That's all. Class dismissed." She turned her back to the class and rummaged on her desk but moments later swiveled around and made eye contact with Ashley. "Ms. Bennett. Can you come here for a sec?"

Ashley strolled over, trying not to appear too intrigued. "Yes?"

"Ashley. Clearly, you're a smart young woman, and I know you have a lot of potential, but your talent could really be enhanced if you showed up to class more." She whipped out a small black binder and viewed it before speaking again. "I show you've missed several classes thus far, and we're still in the beginning of the semester."

Ugh. Why is she trippin' on me? Ashley's mind spun its web. "Well, you know... I've just had some stuff goin' on..." she started.

The older woman whipped up a handful of long, shiny, pointy fingernails. "Save it, Ashley. I want to see you go far. I know you may not believe this, but I think you can be great."

Wow. Ashley was taken aback. *I can't remember anyone ever shutting me down like that. And damn if a teacher ever had my back all like that either.*

In uncharacteristic fashion, she found herself stuttering. "I. I. Ummm...thank you. I'll do better."

"I know you will." Professor Simone politely smiled before waving her away.

When Ashley went to pack her things, she found her friend Gary waiting. Only a few students remained. Although she could hear them still talking with excitement about the opportunity in Paris, she kept her expression nonchalant.

"Yo. What did Professor Simone want?" Gary asked right away.

Ashley shrugged a shoulder. She kept her head low so that her eyes didn't reveal anything different than what her mouth was saying. "She just wanted to thank me for my participation in class. That's all."

"Oh. Cool. But wow. This is crazy, Ash! Paris?" Gary was gushing. He was tall and slender with tanned-skin and short, stubby locks high-lighted by a smooth goatee. The artsy type, and Ashley kept him around because he was hilarious. Plus, she had known him since high school, so if she needed a study buddy, he was it.

And, I don't have to give him any. Ashley watched Gary pack his things in his dark Hermès jeans and red Polo T-shirt buried beneath a tan vest. *Because he's gay, which is even better.*

"Yea. It's nice," she answered with a flip of her hair over one shoul-der. She braced her bag, and once Gary was ready, they exited the room in synchronized swag.

"I mean, the closest *I've* come to France is eating French fries," Gary said, and Ashley chuckled as they stepped into the hallway.

"I ain't even got no French kiss lately!" he added, pitching his Burberry backpack over the roof of his arm.

Ashley swung her head in amusement as they turned down the hall. She was just about to respond when she spotted Natalie with Darren near a classroom, talking. *Ugh. I keep forgetting she's in this building at this time,* she thought with an instant glare toward Natalie. Ashley and Gary had to pass them to get to their next class. As they drew closer to the duo, she began fake-laughing loudly and looking at Gary like he was God Himself.

Gary threw Ashley a look that said, "Dang, girl. I'm not that funny!" But he still seemed pleased she was laughing so hard.

"Hey, Ash," Natalie bubbled while tearing her face away from Darren's.

Darren pitched his extra crisp waves in her direction. "Sup".

"Hey," Ashley called but kept walking. *I know she don't think I'm 'bout to act like we friends now just cuz we had one bowl of cereal together.*

Natalie's voice sailed towards her, "You just leaving class?" Her back was against the wall next to the classroom, and Darren was a foot or two in front of her. He eased back a little, seeing Ashley and Gary approach.

Natalie's attempt to engage Ashley in conversation only made her more annoyed. *The last thing I want to do is talk to this heffa, then watch her flirt with my ex. Like I ain't date the man for three years.*

"Yep," Ashley huffed. But then, she zeroed in on Natalie. Without warning, she swirled on her heels and halted in front of the pair. Her eyes narrowed at the shirt Natalie was wearing. *What the hell?*

Unfortunately, when Ashley stopped, Gary ran smack into her backside. "Dag!" he mumbled. "My bad."

"Yo. Wuz up, Gary." At the same time, Darren greeted Gary with a pump of his head. Gary, straightening up, returned the favor while Ashley glowered at Natalie. Her eyes inflated to the size of a magnifying glass.

"Is that my shirt you wearing?" A murderous expression took form as Ashley dipped her head sideways, engaging in an intense study of the creme cashmere sweater. Yep. It was a Louis Vuitton throwback. She hadn't worn it since high school, but that was beside the point. *No. This ho. Did not!* Before Ashley could even think about her movements, she lunged and yanked at the material in stark disbelief.

Natalie's face crumpled in surprise as she clutched her chest in protection. "Ash. Uncle Malcolm gave this to me after we had breakfast this morning and I spilled coffee all over my shirt," she hurried to explain, both shoulders frozen upward in apology. "My bad! I didn't think it was a big deal."

"*Your* bad? Nobody asked *me* what the hell *I* thought about giving up my damn top! Nobody asked me what I thought about giving up my room, for that matter! You mean to tell me you couldn't traipse your ass upstairs to your own closet?" Her finger was aimed at Miss Thing's face now. "Oh, excuse me. *My* old closet, and pick out something that belongs to you?" *This is some straight bull!*

Natalie's voice was a blend of nervous frustration. "First of all, the way I heard it was that you *volunteered* to give up your room because you wanted the bigger space. And second of all, I was out with Uncle Malcolm. We were at Denny's, and he had it in the trunk of his car. He said you gave it to him a while back to donate to the Goodwill, and he never did. So. It was just *there*. I was running around all day and needed to get to class. I didn't have time to change." Visibly upset, Natalie gritted her teeth, both hands clenched into little golf balls.

Darren stepped up and shoved Ashley's finger downward. "Ash. You don't want to do this." Wrapping her hand in his, he steered her a few feet away for some privacy.

"Darren. She's wearing my damn top." Ashley's voice squeaked out, whiny as a three-year-old toddler's. She peered at him with eyes cloudy from hurt. "I know it sounds petty. But it's my shit!" While taking short, intense breaths, she threw another furious glance at her cousin.

Darren watched her in silence before speaking up. "Man. You need to figure out what's really important. Before it's too late."

"What the hell do you mean by that? You of all people know that I know what it's like to lose what's important!" Ashley's voice quivered as she drew her arms around herself.

"Do you?" Darren looked at her for a second before walking back to the group, leaving her there. Alone.

Ashley's face cooked with anger and embarrassment as several puffs of air smoked out. *How the hell he gone tell me what I need to do? He lost those privileges a long time ago,* she convinced herself. Speeding past Darren and Natalie without so much as a "goodbye", Ashley called to Gary. "Come on. We gone be late."

Poor Gary shuffled behind, trying to keep up. "Yo. You out!" he said, juggling his backpack on one arm. "Man, slow down. We got like ten more minutes before we need to be there." They were rounding another corner in the building when he ran into her again after Ashley all of a sudden slowed her pace.

"My bad," she sputtered this time. Gary stumbled, catching himself. "Sorry. I'm just not tryna be late," she added.

Ashley's Guess leather boots were still clacking on the tile floor as she tried to stifle the fury bubbling like lava in her heart. *Why he got be all up on her? We are in public.* Ashley knew her ex well enough to know he was crushing hard on her cousin. *And how he gone check me in front of her?* Suffocating her black Coach leather backpack even more, she blew out another herd of oxygen. Darren still did that to her: made her mad as hell.

"I don't be liking nobody wearing my drip either. I mean, I get it," Gary said, but Ashley was hardly listening. She was too caught up in her own thoughts. "Man. I remember when y'all was *that* couple, though," he went on raving, ignorant of her inner angst. "Ya'll was glued at the hip in high school."

Animation masked Gary's expression as Ashley kept walking, a little slower this time. She figured he was referring to her and Darren and she didn't appreciate the topic, so she pretended she didn't know what he was talking about.

"Who? I was never that close with Natalie." That was the best she could come up with.

"Naw. Not yo cuz'. Darren." Gary nodded in the direction where they had seen her ex, his small, neat locks tinted by the hallway lighting.

Man. Gary is funny as hell, Ashley thought with a frown, *but he can be slow.* "Yea, well. That was then. This is now."

They reached the classroom, and Ashley waited for a student in front of her to enter before jetting through the doors. Gary plopped down next to her, and for the first time in their friendship, Ashley wished he would shut up.

"But why tho? What happened 'wit y'all?" Gary set down his Burberry bag and pulled out his iPad, propping it on the desk as he pried. "I mean. You can tell me. We cool like that."

Dang. Is he that clueless of social cues? Shoving aside a few clothing items she had stored, Ashley fished her laptop mini out of her bag. "Let's just say I outgrew him." *A half-truth is always better than a lie.*

"Yea? I had a situation like that. We weren't as serious as you and Darren, but I still had feelings after it was over." Gary gave her a knowing look, but instead of responding, Ashley repositioned herself in her seat and started previewing her notes section.

Gary's ass is getting on my damn nerves, she thought. *If I wanted to talk about relationships, then I would have initiated the conversation.* Students were still getting settled, and the instructor hadn't appeared yet, so she sifted through her texts. *Jason wants to hook up tonight. Good. It's time I reel that brotha in.*

"You know what, Gary?" Ashley offered while looking back at her friend. Gary peered up from his iPad, his fingers paused on the screen. "Darren was the minor leagues, but I'm playing in the big leagues now." Ashley threw her phone back into her bag just as Professor Johnson walked in. "And I'm 'bout to hit a freakin' home run."

Class went the way it always did: with little relevance to Ashley's life. She knew what she wanted and how she was going to get it. *Jason* was all she was thinking while leaving. She all but skipped into the restroom in her new Jessica Simpson thigh-high boots. After a quick dip into a stall to change, she whipped out a low-cut black tank from her bookbag. Ashley always kept extra clothes around, just in case. When she reached her car in the parking garage, she overlaid it with a black leather jacket confiscated from the backseat and ditched her boots for some old-school red and white Adidas. As a last-minute thought, she stuffed a couple of Prada pumps hidden underneath her seat into her bag. She intended to change when she reached Jason. *I gotta keep it hot for him,* she decided as she headed to Jason's dorm from CCNY. *And ain't nothin' hot about no Adidas.*

It was a 15-minute walk plagued by nasty smells floating from nearby sewers and noisy whistles from the trains running at all times. Ashley thrived off each step. The hustle of New Yorkers on their grind invigorated her like no cup of coffee ever could. That feeling of never being alone. That opportunity to witness a talented artist expressing themselves or a panhandler on every corner begging for attention could never be rivaled in any city.

In no time, she slid into Jason's studio apartment on the cusp of NYU's campus. "Hey, baby," she breathed while dodging a pile of clothes loitering on the floor near the entrance. A small coat hook sat near the door that she smothered with her Birkin.

Jason glanced from his post on top of his covers, muttered a quick "Sup," and stuffed his nose back deep into whatever subject he was studying.

Ok. So you still trippin'. Ashley rolled her eyes and perused the room. *There's crap everywhere. How the hell does he find anything?* After almost tripping over a sizable black textbook, she removed her heels, determining it was safer to navigate the floor barefoot. *So much for keeping it hot.*

"Baby. How was your day?" Ashley eased onto the corner of Jason's bed, slinging her bookbag on the floor near her newly polished toenails. She had to kick aside a few t-shirts and jerseys in the course of doing so. *Ugh. That one smells like it was rolled in sweat!* She eyed the crumpled Steph Curry jersey with a slight grimace and flung *it* the furthest distance.

"Fine," Jason grunted, only inching over to make room. He was decked in a pair of shiny black Armani reading glasses, the classic depiction of an NYU scholar.

Hmmm. So you invite me over to study, and now the silent treatment? Trying to read him, Ashley sloped her head sideways, her black bundles brushing up against her elbow.

"Okkkaayy. Well. Mine was good up until Ms. Thing freaking stole my damn shirt!" She started ranting while thinking again about seeing Natalie in school earlier that day with her precious Louis V. "I mean, who the hell does she think she is? I can't believe she feels like she can just have access to anything that I have. Like we that damn tight. Shoot. I can't remember the last time Denise even borrowed something."

When Ashley saw the expression on Jason's face, she rushed to add, "And of course, I would let her if she needed it. I mean. You know, Denise is my girl, foreal foreal. So I'm definitely not gone play *her*. But me and Natalie ain't that. So I don't know what the hell she was thinking." Ashley was fuming again, and her hands wound as tight as the braids under her sew-in. She unwrapped and re-wrapped each finger around the edges of the bed to calm herself.

Jason exhaled, pitching aside the highlighter he was using. "Ashley. Isn't she your cousin?" He looked at her, confusion shimmering in his beautiful chestnut eyes. "You would think that would mean something."

Of course your *ass don't understand. Why the hell am I talking to you about this anyway?* Ashley clasped her lips to keep from responding. After all, she was here to try to get back on Jason's good side, not push him further away.

"So, anyways," she said with an abrupt change to the subject, "What's up with yo ride?" Ashley dug into her backpack for her English Lit book, searching for "Queens of Egypt: When Women Ruled the World". Unfortunately, she was so far behind in the reading that she had resorted to using Cliff Notes to study for the weekly quizzes. But since she was trying to spend time with Jason, and wanted to seem studious, she figured it would be wise to actually do some work. *Ahhh! There it is.* With a victorious smile, Ashley maneuvered the book from her bag, tackling the brown and black cover.

"The police are a joke." Jason sneered. "They ain't said nothing since I filed the report. And my dad's insurance isn't covering the theft part."

Dropping her book onto her lap with a thud, Ashley peered at him with sympathetic eyes. "What? That's crazy!"

"Yea. They said they don't cover personal property that's stolen."

"Well. I guess that makes sense." She paused. "I mean. Most people know not to keep valuable stuff in their car..." Letting her voice trail, she opened up the syllabus for her class. *Dang. We on chapter eight already?* Again, she poked through her bookbag. "You got a highlighter? I can't find mine."

Jason peered at her with a hardened countenance, his attractive features dripping with offense. "So, what? You saying the shit is my fault?"

Whoops. "Uh. Naw, bae. I was just sayin'..." Nervous laughter expelled from Ashley as she swooped her hair to the other side of her neck. Leaning forward, she made sure that her low-cut top fell just right. "I mean, I'm sure you had a good reason..." she offered, trying to clean up her earlier statement. She then zeroed in on the green highlighter perched on Jason's open book. "Can I use your highlighter?"

"I told you I was supposed to pick up some shoes off my boy that night, but he flaked on me." Jason gawked at the ceiling in exasperation. "That's why I had the cash. But you obviously weren't listening."

"Babe. I was too." Ashley danced her tongue over her lips before adding, "I must have just forgot," then shrugged while reaching for his highlighter.

"Honestly, Ashley. I don't think I'm up to studying with you." Jason let out a laugh of disbelief while popping into a sitting position, then ran a frustrated hand through his loose, soft curls. His nose pinched in irritation as he added, "I feel more distracted with you here. And I got a test in the morning that I can't afford to half-ass." He looked at her in expectation.

"So? What you trying to say? *You* ask *me* to come over, and now you want me to leave?" *He done' lost his mind!*

"*I* asked *you*? I just texted to check up on you, and you said you wanted to hang out." Jason served her an incredulous look. "Puh. You a class act. Foreal." He was shaking his head in shock.

Scoffing in response, Ashley said, "Whatever," and started thrusting her things back into her bag. "Have fun *studying*." She hooked her Birkin over her arm and slammed the door behind her, all the while thinking, *What the hell is a class act?*

CHAPTER 10

MAD AS HELL

(NATALIE)

As Natalie sat in Devon's office, the little cocoons in her stomach morphed into full-blown butterflies. *Wow. I didn't know that working for Devon would be* so *much* work, she thought while trotting her hands over her lap for the umpteenth time. It was her first day, and even though she was thankful for the opportunity to make some extra cash, she hoped she'd be able to deliver. As Devon outlined her job responsibilities, Natalie fiddled with the threads dangling off her distressed denim skirt.

Her nervousness must have become apparent because Devon said, "Look. I don't want you to be overwhelmed. I'll let you know what's priority. And trust me. *Any* help you offer is appreciated!" He stood and smiled his signature calming smile, and his words smothered her with enough peace to slow her heart rate by several milliseconds.

"Oh. Ok." Natalie's smile back was relieved. "Thanks."

Her new boss led her through one of those closed doors she had seen when she had done her interview, located right across from his. *Wow. My name plate is on the door!* The office was medium-sized with a desk, chair, and guest chair. The floor, hugged by a classic blue carpet with small gray specks, looked just like Devon's, and a hue of light gray painted the walls, mirroring the corridor. Natalie was already thinking of how she wanted to decorate.

"This is so nice. Thank you!" Now that her nerves had settled, she could finally be excited. *My first real job with a real office and a real name tag and everything.*

Devon swept his eyes around, doing a quick inspection with a sturdy hand stuck to his waistline. "No sweat. I had Denise in here earlier cleaning, so it should be up to par."

"Man. She cleans *and* serves?" Natalie joked.

Devon chuckled with gleaming eyes. "Yea. When you're a small business owner, your people wear a lot of hats like you do. I'll take you around today to meet some other servers." He indicated for her to have a seat in her new office chair, and Natalie did, swiveling one good time. Appreciating her vibrancy, Devon folded his muscular arms over his powder-blue collared shirt and grinned. The top two buttons had come undone, and he had removed his tie from when she had seen him that morning at Denny's. "We're gonna love having you added to the family, Natalie."

She was touched. "I'm going to love being added." Joy was her friend as she sighed in content. Rays from the sun cast a spotlight on a red robin outside the window, and it became the lead in a Broadway musical.

After reviewing some items in her new office, Devon introduced Natalie to a few other staff members: Monique, the Office Coordinator, and Alvin, his Marketing Consultant. In addition to Denise and Alice, the other server, Chuck, was a longtime worker there.

Chuck turned to Natalie with a soft smile after they were introduced, saying, "Natalie. Welcome!" His eyes were sweet as he took her hand.

"Thank you." She peered back, warm inside. *Devon was right. These people already feel like family.* For the first time in several months since she had moved to South Orange, New Jersey, Natalie felt genuinely welcomed.

After leaving Devon's, Natalie took the A-train. Now that she had a moment to breathe, thoughts of Ashley's blow-up from earlier that day haunted her mind. *I can't believe she had the nerve to put her hands on me.* She worked on her bottom lip in agitation. Because of her cousin's excessive response, Natalie ended up stopping back home and switching her shirt, even though doing so almost made her late to work.

"I swear I don't know what that girl's problem is," she murmured, gazing at the time. It was 7:45 PM, and she only had 15 minutes to make it to her therapy session. She had told her new counselor that her first day of work was today and she wasn't sure if things would run over, but declined Celia's offer to move the appointment. It was only their second meeting, and she hated to delay her progress. *The sooner I can heal,* Natalie thought, *the better.*

Celia Johnson was supposed to be really good, and Natalie got a lot out of the one meeting they had last month. Her counselor back home, Linda, had referred her.

"I actually went to Howard with her," Linda revealed. *"I love her work and I think you'll like her too."*

"Come *on...*" Anxiety built with each rattle from the train and every minute that ticked by, but lyrics from the worship playlist blaring through Natalie's earbuds caught her attention, and she had to laugh:

"I'm not in a hurry

When it comes to Your spirit..."

Ok, God. I know. I need to be patient. Sucking in a wad of air, she kicked it out slowly while counting to five. It was one of the breathing techniques she had learned from Linda. She had learned so much from Linda.

When the conductor announced her stop at 7:48 PM, Natalie lunged to her feet. *See, Father. If I wait on You, I get there right on time.* Gathering her things, she booked it down 37th street until she was captured by the tall brick building housing a variety of suites and offices.

"Natalie, it's so good to see you," Celia greeted her new client in an upbeat tone when she entered the office. With cinnamon skin and a slender frame, Celia's eccentric beauty was cemented by pouty lips and large, oval, onyx eyes.

"Thanks, Celia." Natalie shook off her jean jacket and masked the coat hook near the door with her belongings. "Same to you."

The room was warm and peaceful, just as it had been last month when she came. Lavender clouded the airwaves of the office, drowning its visitors' noses in a field of purple aroma. Two overstuffed plush chairs sat opposite each other in conversation against the east wall with a small table stitched between them. A desk posed near the middle of the room against a large window with a standard office chair as a small potted Peace Lily perched on the windowsill. It was displaying quite a few lilies modeling on their individual stems. If Celia had designed her office to create the sense that she and her client were just two old friends chatting, then she was successful in her endeavor.

Celia motioned towards the Keurig in the corner. "Would you like a cup of tea?" But when Natalie declined, the psychiatrist folded herself into one of the overstuffed chairs. Sliding her files and notes onto the quaint table, she said, "Ok. How was your first day? I know you started Devon's."

"Yea. It was really good! I'm so blessed by this opportunity God provided." Natalie was all smiles while telling Celia that Devon had given her her very own office and how welcoming the staff had been. "I never would have guessed I would be doing admin work. I mean, I thought I was going to have to be a server." Her eyes shined with relief.

"Well, it sounds like Devon saw something in you that made him offer you that position." Celia's smile was as kind as her tone was inviting. She made a few notes on the pad on her lap as her soothing demeanor infiltrated the atmosphere of Natalie's heart.

"Yea. I guess so." Natalie shook her head in agreement, her expression remaining thoughtful. "Devon is super affirming. I don't think I've ever met a man as affirming as him." She sighed. "And his vision and what he's been able to do with his cafe is so impressive," she finished as excitement sparkled in her eyes.

Celia lifted a brow. "Oh, really? How so?"

"Yep. Devon created job opportunities for others. He's made a safe place for our people to have fun. *And* he has even more plans for expansion! I think a Black man making moves like that is so inspiring." Natalie cheesed again, thinking back on her first day of work.

"Mmhmm. Well. It sounds like you're in good hands then."

Wow. That's exactly what Uncle Malcolm told Devon this morning.
"Yep! God is faithful." Natalie shifted to one side, sinking deeper into the soft fabric.

"I'm so glad you're getting settled. Now. How have the anti-depressants been working for you?" Celia studied her with pen in hand, ready to take notes.

A pensive look engraved itself on Natalie's smooth brown skin, and she swallowed while stroking her arm. "Yea." She hesitated. "About those. I really haven't done too well with them," she admitted. "I feel like my sleep has been broken, and I'm losing my appetite again. I mean, I never had a huge one before, but now it's really being affected." Confusion straddled her shoulders as she shrugged.

Celia responded with concern and a healthy click of her tongue. "Mmhmm. Ok. Let me look into a lower dose, and if that doesn't work, we can research other options. Now. Are you trying to eat the right foods when you *do* have an appetite? And are you getting regular exercise?"

"I can say I've been walking a whole lot more while commuting. But no. No other workouts."

"Why don't you try to look for more physical activities then? Also, what about your writing? Are you still journaling?" The psychiatrist was flipping through some papers in front of her. She had gotten a lot of information from Linda and, thankfully, had copies of Natalie's file.

"Yea. I've been blogging and writing down my dreams."

"Good. So, how would you say the depression and anxiety have been at this point?" Celia took a break in her note-taking to examine her client's response.

The struggle Natalie had just this morning resurfaced. *I wasn't* really *going to use the razor*, she reasoned. *I* just *wanted to hold it*. She knew she had been feeling sad, of course, from missing her mom. She was lonely because her friends back home were MIA and she hadn't made a ton here. *Not to mention all of the drama with Ashley.*

"I think I'm ok. I would say I'm at an eight if ten is the best you can be." Natalie etched invisible sketches along the threads hanging off her skirt with her forefinger.

Celia peered at her with the expertise of someone who had been in her profession a long time. "Mmhmm. Now. How are things with your family?"

"Well. I've gotten to hang out with my uncle a few times, which has been great. Growing up, I always wanted to spend more time with him, but because of the distance, it never really happened. He's such a good dad." *Ashley just doesn't know how good she has it.* "He took me to breakfast this morning, and that was nice. I'm also finally going to see my grandma this weekend. She's having a family dinner."

Celia made a tisk sound while looking at her file. "Ok. So, what about your cousin... Ashley, right?"

For the first time since Natalie had entered the office, her countenance dimmed, and a subtle frown stole her lips. "Right. Ashley." What could she say about Ashley? *No matter how hard I try, her walls stay up.* The girl was Fort Knox. Natalie took a moment before meeting the psychiatrist's eyes. "I think I'll have some tea now. If that's ok."

"Of course." Celia covered the table with her files and hopped to the Keurig to prepare some herbal tea.

Natalie accepted the mug with a small smile when it was ready, letting the warmth feed her hands and her heart. "Thank you."

The psychiatrist reiterated her question with a bit more force this time. "You're welcome, dear. Now. How are things going with your cousin?"

"Well... Ashley is... *Ashley,*" Natalie responded with a wild eye roll packed with frustration. "She flipped out on me today about a freaking shirt. I mean, come *on.* She has a *million* shirts. And she was even *giving* it away and not wearing it anymore."

Celia pitched a shocked look. "Really? What happened?"

"I literally spilled coffee on my top this morning and borrowed her shirt *after* Uncle Malcolm said it would be cool. She saw me with it on at school today and *blew all the way up.* I thought she was gone' rip it off me!" Natalie bit her lip in distress. *Sometimes, I just don't understand what her deal is.* But then she was reminded of the dream God had given her with the message "Save Ashley," and guilt sabotaged her. "But I know she's dealing with pain," she added. "And she must not be aware. But that's what makes it hard. She's like a missile that can go off at any time." Natalie's eyes swirled with pity for her cousin.

Taking notes, Celia commented, "Hmmm. That's an interesting assessment."

"Yea. And I feel like it's directed at *me* most of the time. No matter how much love I show her. How much I reach out, she pushes me away. You know what's so crazy?" Hurt swam Olympic-sized laps around the circumference of Natalie's irises as she peered at her counselor. "Ashley came in drunk off her butt one night, and I literally *held* her hair away from her face while she puked in the toilet." Natalie cringed, and Celia's mouth parted in surprise. "If that ain't love, I don't know *what* is. And do you know, she never even *thanked* me? She avoided me for days like I wasn't there for her, cleaning vomit off her face." Natale's voice hardened on her last statement, so she took a couple of breaths to calm herself and gulped her tea.

With coal-hued eyes drilling holes into her client, Celia asked, "So. How does that make you feel?"

"I mean. I get it. Hurt people hurt people and all that." Natalie slapped the air with an annoyed hand while repeating the mantra. "She said something about The Hyenas from back in the day." She stopped at Celia's confused expression. "These girls we went to summer camp with. I guess something happened with them, but she won't talk about it." Natalie sighed. "It's just hard because I'm hurting too." She set the tea on the table and tasted her bottom lip soaked in the salty wetness. Not sure what to do with her hands, she settled on folding them in her lap, then fondled the ring her mom gave her. *Momma, I wish you were here.*

"True. Hurt people do hurt others." Celia laid down her pen and looked at Natalie with eyes of compassion. "But that doesn't mean the people they hurt deserve to be hurt."

"Right. I'm not trying to hurt anybody. But, I mean, I have other resources and support. So I know I can't act out like Ashley does."

"What other resources and support?" The psychiatrist angled her head to the side, her large, wavy hair swaying in the same direction.

Natalie swooped her hand around in a wobbly circle. "Well. I have my family. I have you. I have... *God.*" She looked at Celia as if it were obvious that *she* was more equipped than Ashley to face her pain.

"Yes. But Ashley has all those things too. *And* she has friends here in the city. *And* she didn't *just* lose her mother this year." Natalie was quiet. "Natalie. You haven't found a church home yet. And didn't you also have to forfeit some scholarships to transfer here?" The psychiatrist paused to review her file as Natalie twisted a little in her chair. "So. I presume you have added financial stressors in addition to a lack of community."

Natalie grappled with Celia's words. *I guess she has a point.* She picked up her tea again. "I didn't look at it that way."

"I would say, at *minimum*, Ashley has the resources you have. The difference is, *she's* not choosing to use them." Dr. Celia rested back in her seat while massaging the files on her lap. "I'm not saying you have to act out, Natalie," she clarified. "But you *should experience* your feelings. *And* process them. I mean, since you've been here, has Ashley supported you *at all* in dealing with the grief of your mother?" Celia's statement hung in the air like a kid on monkey bars, and in the stillness of the office, Natalie had to be honest with herself.

Ashley never even said she was sorry for my loss. After placing the tea back onto the table, Natalie mumbled, "No. She hasn't."

"Instead, *you* said she's taking her pain out on *you.*" Celia looked at Natalie and asked again, "So. How does that make you feel?" Relaxing her hand with the pen still in it, the doctor awaited a response as another pregnant pause clung to the room.

In the vulnerability of the moment, Natalie let herself be totally honest. With a weighty exhale, she squeezed the sides of the soft, cushiony chair arms, mildly consoled by the sturdy microfiber fabric. "Celia," she started, her jawline hardening and her lips tightly pursed. "It makes me mad as hell."

***

It had been several days since Natalie's counseling appointment, and there was a lot to process. Sunday morning, she reached for her journal for the first time in a long time and wrote down more of her thoughts from the revelations she received from Celia. After getting dressed, she headed to the kitchen for a quick meal before meeting Grams for church.

I know her service will be going for hours and I can't afford to be starving by the end of it, she thought, hopping down each step. *Celia was already getting on me about eating better.* When she turned into the foyer, Natalie peeped Ashley spread out on the living room sofa, flipping through a magazine with the phone cupped to her shoulder.

"Yea, girl. I put it on him!" Ashley cackled, then whipped her head behind as Natalie approached.

"Uhhh. I'll fill you in on the details later." Then a pause. "Actually, let me just call you back."

Irritated, Natalie pointed her eyes to the ceiling. *Nobody wants to hear that mess anyways,* she thought, then grabbed a box of cereal out on the counter. She perused the inside of the fridge, her eyes roaming.

"Is there any more milk?" Natalie didn't really want to engage with Ashley (she was still processing her anger about the flip-out over the forbidden shirt) but, her hunger motivated her to ask the question anyway.

"Daddy was supposed to get some, but he probably forgot," came the lackadaisical reply.

Great. Natalie wanted something to eat that was quick. *Maybe they have some granola bars?*

"There's some granola bars in the cupboard," Ashley tossed from the couch, and a surge of surprise stroked Natalie.

I guess there's a heart in there somewhere. "Uhh. Thanks," she uttered, discovering the box of bars hidden behind a can of oatmeal. She took two.

"You going to meet Grams?" Suddenly, Ashley seemed very interested in her happenings, and Natalie didn't know how to take it.

"Uh. Yea. For church." Her red blouse caressed the ceramic tabletop as she bent over the counter and studied her cousin. "You wouldn't want to come, would you?" Natalie almost didn't ask but couldn't help herself. *Even after all of her craziness, I still want her to know Him.*

Ashley smirked. "Naw. I'm gonna meet a friend for brunch. But you have fun with that."

Natalie shrugged. "Will do." She was about to head out but doubled back. "And Ashley?"

Ashley threw her head up from her spot on the couch. "I love you. But don't ever put your hands on me again." Natalie didn't wait for a response, and instead, walked to her car. But even as she turned the ignition, her heart raced with thoughts of Ashley. The drive to Grams's was a film strip of Ashley's drama, and one incident after another bombarded her mind's eye. *Why is she always so difficult? The girl has everything, but she's always trippin'.*

Extend grace, child. The message saturated Natalie's mind as she veered onto the freeway.

I know, God. I know. The Father's love for Ashley coursed through the arteries of her heart, and Natalie knew her desire for her cousin's inner healing was supernatural. Her worship playlist became her companion as her little Kia blared Lauren Daigle during the short drive to Bloomfield, NJ. Lauren's jazzy tone, belting lyrics full of hope, love, and joy successfully diminished her anxiety. The pesky thoughts of Ashley had morphed into worship by the time she turned into her grandmother's driveway.

"Hey, Grams," Natalie said through her car's BlueTooth. "I'm outside,"

"Ok, baby. Here I come!"

A few minutes later, the small bungalow expelled an almond-skinned, plump elderly woman. Though a large purple church hat shadowed the bulk of her pie-shaped face, the brightness of her countenance radiated. Every item on her body was chosen in a crafty purple, from scarf to shoes. Even a purple alligator-skinned purse dangled on her arm.

"Baby, it's so good to see you!" Grams greeted, but as soon as Natalie stepped out of the car to help her grandmother down the sidewalk, her heart plummeted like a speeding bullet.

The resemblance between Mama and Grams is so strong. I forgot how much they look alike. Natalie froze, and unexpected, unruly emotion heaved her into her grandmother's arms where she began to weep.

"Baby. It's ok." Grams held onto Natalie's body, now wracked with a cohort of ugly sobs. "You just let it out."

"Grams. I'm sorry. I'm so *sorry!*" But Natalie couldn't stop crying.

Grief erupted like a volcano, and the soothing beat Grams was drumming on her back only made the tears gush even more.

"Ain't nothin' to be sorry about, chil'. You just let it out." Grams rocked Natalie back and forth, rubbing her back up and down until her cries were less frequent. They stood by the car in the drive, embracing for what seemed like forever. Finally, Natalie was able to pull herself together, and her grandmother handed her a purple handkerchief.

Natalie dabbed her face a few times, knowing her makeup was running like Forrest Gump. "Let me help you in the car," she offered, walking to the passenger's side to open the door. Once Grams slid into the vehicle, Natalie did the same. *Wow. I didn't expect that.* Natalie was embarrassed and couldn't think of one time she had lost it like that. Not even as a kid. *Now I'm two for two. First, I break down with Uncle Malcolm, now Grams.* She tilted the rearview mirror downward, searching for evidence of tear streaks as Grams tossed her a worried expression.

"You ok, baby?"

Natalie tried for a smile, but it only came out as a grimace. "Yes, ma'am. I just miss her. That's all." She blew into the handkerchief, then dropped her eyes to the purple cotton cloth. It smelled like Grams.

"Me too, baby. Me too." Her grandmother heaved a painful sigh, nearly choking the bulky purple bag buried in her lap. Stress and pain raced each other down her fingertips until they wrapped around the thick, plum strap. It was the first time Natalie remembered that, yes, she had lost a mother, but her grandmother had lost a daughter.

That has to be worse.

"I'm sorry for taking so long to come see you." Natalie turned to her grandmother, still clinging to the handkerchief. "I just think... it was probably too hard for me. You know?" When she peeked at Grams, there were a few more wrinkles and worry lines, but the soft brown eyes, wide nose, and rosy cheeks all belonged to her mother.

"Honey. I get it. There ain't a day when I don't pray for God's strength to get through it!" The older woman's mouth trembled when she paused. "But He ain't *never* failed to give me that strength. And I *know* it's cuz He's with us." She gave her granddaughter an affectionate gaze, and Natalie exerted a much-needed exhale. "And, honey, you have that same strength in *you*. I know this has been a rough season, but trouble don't last always. Joy is sure to come in the morning!"

This time, Natalie's smile met her eyes as she gripped Grams's hand in one hand and the handkerchief in the other, letting her elder's words wash over her. *Thank you, Lord, for this woman,* she thought, squeezing her grandmother's hand with love. *Thank you for her strong faith!*

Grams licked her thumb and wiped Natalie's cheeks with it. "Now come on. We gone' be *late*. And I ain't tryna miss the announcements. I'm selling my peach cobbler in this month's bake sale, and they gone' be tellin' the congregation *all* about 'em." The older woman sat back in her chair, her mood changing like the seasons, and waited in expectation.

Natalie's chuckle filtered through a watery smile. *Grams is something else!* "Yes, ma'am," she replied and, handing Grams back her handkerchief, she obediently switched the gear in her Kia to drive.

C H A P T E R 11

———————

S U N D A Y   S U R P R I S E

(A S H L E Y)

After Natalie left for church, Ashley meandered to the dinner table with a cup of coffee and a quick perusal of her Instagram account. A tinge of regret stained her heart as she remembered how she spazzed about her shirt last week. *And then Natalie lightweight checked me about it.* A soft, embarrassed chuckle crept through her, beginning in her torso. *I can't even be mad at that though cuz I know I would have went ham had she come at me like that if the roles were reversed.*

Last night, Ashley talked the shirt situation over with Jason, who started making a little more sense that she should be nicer to her cousin. This morning, she put his advice into practice. Telling Natalie about the granola bars had been her good deed for the day.

I just hope she don't think we super tight or anything. Drawing little slurps from her cup, Ashley's eyes punctured her news feed. *Whaaaaat! Tamra got a new dude? Ok, Tam!* Double-tapping the picture of her hairdresser boo'ed up with a tall Hershey's-chocolate bald brother, Ashley oooo'd and ahhh'd over the photo.

I guess we both on our way, she thought with a crocodile smile stretching her lips. Ashley was referring to the fact that she had decided to forgive Jason for his foolery in kicking her out of his room after their little spat the other day. She popped up last night at his dorm room in a trench coat and lingerie; a classic move. What could she say? She just wasn't one to give up on a challenge. By the time her dad made an appearance, Ashley was caught up on her newsfeed and her cup of coffee had run dry.

"Good morning, sweetie." Mr. Bennett addressed her with a bright smile before pecking her forehead and shooting over to the coffee maker. "I thought you had plans this morning?"

"Hey, Daddy." Ashley uttered an exuberant yawn. *Whew! That boy wore me out last night.*

"Yea. I was supposed to hang with Denise, but she got caught up and had to reschedule. So I'm a just chill.'"

"Ahh, Ok. You want more coffee?"

"Sure." *Maybe* that *will help me wake up a little faster.* She was still weighed down by a ton of bricks from her escapades with Jason.

Mr. Bennett cruised through the kitchen before approaching with a refill of the steaming hazel-hued liquid, and the smell of freshly crafted caffeine whiffed with joy through her nostrils. "How about we sit out on the patio?" he suggested. "It's a nice fall day."

Pure bliss captured Ashley's heart like a kid on Christmas morning. It was so rare that she had one-on-one time with her father. He was usually rushing to get to some meeting or some date or some *something*. *But why is he in such a good mood?* Her suspicious nature cut through her momentary happiness.

"Ok, Daddy," Ashley agreed. *Might as well take full advantage.* She tied her robe, cradled her mug, then popped up from the table to lead the way. Her father was right; it was a beautiful fall morning. The sun was shining, and the temperature was just cool enough for her plush terry-cloth robe. Any cooler and she'd need to grab a blanket.

Mr. Bennett relaxed his paper on the patio table with an element of respect, and the duo fell into their matching wide patio chairs in silence. Both held onto their warm mugs in a way they rarely held onto each other. Unfortunately, the small table separating them hardly compared to the mound of things that Ashley never said, which separated them even more. As the birds serenaded their morning song, she eyed the steam emanating from her cup.

Mr. Bennett asked, "How are classes?" while taking a generous drink of his brew, and Ashley shrugged the typical way a young person does with their parents.

"Classes are cool. I mean, now that I'm getting more into my major, it's definitely gotten more interesting."

Malcolm offered his full attention, shifting to face her. "Really? How so?"

"Now I get to learn more about fashion, the history of fashion, and actually designing it," Ashley elaborated before drinking from her mug that read "Learn to Dance in the Rain" in bold, wispy letters. It was her mother's mug, and she loved it just because of that.

"Yea?" Her father's eyes were hungry for information.

Inspired by his interest, Ashley proceeded. "Yep. And my one professor is madd dope. She's super cute like Ryan Destiny, as fly as a Kardashian, and fierce like Beyonce." Ashley's eyes were aflame over the mug while thinking about Professor Simone.

Malcolm chuckled, amusement hidden like two sea shells in his sandy brown eyes. "Oh, really?"

"Yep. *And* she's giving us an opportunity to go to Paris with her next year!" Ashley had almost forgotten and sat straight up at the prospect, spilling a little coffee on her robe.

"What? That's great, Ash." Malcolm grinned, looking like the proud father that he was.

"I know. I can't believe I get this opportunity. I'm still waiting on her to send the assignment. It's extra credit, and there's only one winner. Whoever wins gets to go."

"Well, I know you got this. You can do anything you set your mind to."

Ashley was touched. It was something he had told her her whole life, but it always warmed her heart whenever he said it. "Thanks, Daddy. I don't know, though." She pursed her lips. "Designing at the collegiate level is a whole other thing, but it's definitely a way for me to step my game up since the plan is to transfer to FIT."

"Oh. So you still wanna transfer? I didn't realize..."

Ashley tried not to be offended by her father's tone of surprise. She knew she had been dragging her feet with taking classes and that she wasn't the most ambitious student in the world. *But a degree from a prestigious school will look so good next to Jason's in our future shared home office.*

"Yea. That's still the plan," she said and quenched the hurt feelings that squeezed her heart. "I just gotta get a few more classes in to finish my pre-reqs and keep up my grades." *I mean, damn, if you don't believe in me, Daddy, who will?* Ashley thought, having already forgotten his earlier affirmation of her.

"Oh. Ok." Mr. Bennett nodded in agreement before sipping his drink, but he didn't sound as convinced as she would have liked.

With false confidence, she added, "And Professor Simone would make a great recommendation for sure." Ashley wasn't so sure if she actually had the talent to swing a recommendation from any professor, let alone Simone, who was killing it, but she didn't want her father to know that. *Especially since he already seems to doubt that I could get into FIT.*

A few leaves waved in the breeze, and she paused to admire them as they sashayed on their chosen branches. Beauty was never missed by Ashley. She could appreciate it in all its forms, including nature, even though she was more of a mall and boutique kind of girl.

"Definitely, honey! Now, what about your drawing?" Her dad watched her with unabashed curiosity. "How has that been?"

Ashley was silent. She hadn't drawn in a long time. She threw a lopsided shrug his way. "I don't know. It's not something I'm into as much anymore."

"Well, you can't ignore your gifts. You're so talented."

Comforted by her father's words, a weak moment overcame her. "I haven't drawn since mom died," she blurted. *Shit. I didn't mean to say it like that.* Ashley and her dad never talked about her mom, and nervousness sabotaged her. She stroked her mug as her eyes drilled into her large Chanel pink slippers, a present from Darren. Even though it had ended a while ago, she held onto them for reasons she wasn't yet ready to admit.

"Oh. Ok," was all her father offered in response.

Ashley waited for more, but it never came. Instead, he went on to talk about his new case and some board meeting he was a part of. She sighed. *Of course you would change the subject.* Following his lead, she asked, "You going to Grams's later. Right?"

"Oh shoot." Mr. Bennett slapped his forehead, his lips forming an "O." "I forgot that was tonight." Ashley figured as much. He cleared his throat and shared, "I actually had other plans, uh, but I'll figure something out." He paused. "This *is* probably a good time to tell you about 'em."

Her tone curious, Ashley replied, "O-K."

"Remember that conversation we had when I asked that you introduce me to your date if it was serious?"

Aww man. Did he catch me with Jason? The boy had only been over a couple of times. Or maybe he saw me with Jeremy? Now that would be worse cuz that ain't serious at all. Shoot, he could have even seen me with Brian. But Brian hasn't been over in a while...

"Ashley?"

"Huh?" Ashley shook her head to escape her crazy train of thoughts. "Yea. Yea. I remember," then braced herself.

"Well. I think that should go both ways. So, sweetie, I'm seeing someone." Uncertainty flashed in her father's eyes as her heartbeat sped up something serious.

"You're seeing someone?" Ashley repeated, stunned.

"Yea, and I think you'll *love* her. She's smart and driven and loves all the stuff you love. Like fashion and art. I think y'all gone' really hit it off." Her father was so excited, hopping up in his chair and leaning over with his mug, that it broke her heart.

Hit it off? What the hell is he doing getting serious with somebody? Ashley went frantic as a ten-pound weight soared over her mind, but she kept her face a crisp, white blank sheet of canvas paper. She had never known her father to love another woman other than her mother. He dated as much as she did, but never once had he introduced anyone to her. Ashley had found security in knowing that her mother was the only one who had his heart all these years.

"Well, Dad. That's, uhh... that's great," she managed in a, "I'm a little girl, but I need to grow up" sort of way. "I-I'm happy for you." She slurped the lukewarm mug to conceal the anger eating her heart.

"Really? Because, Ash, I want you to feel ok with this move." Her dad set his own mug near the newspaper on the table before holding out his hands. "I know it's a change, and we've been doing our regular all these years," he started, "but I finally feel *connected* with somebody. You know?" His eyes begged her to understand like a homeless person begging for change, and Ashley sighed.

He's practically groveling. In a feeble tone, she repeated, "That's great. I'm happy for you." She plopped a short kiss onto his forehead. "I'm going for a run. See you later."

"Ok, baby girl." But Ashley's back was already turned, and the comment sank onto deaf ears.

Back in her bedroom, Ashley started stripping and throwing her workout gear on, then scoffed at herself in the mirror. Her mind was so distracted she had put her shirt on backward!

How in the hell is he gone' add another woman into his life for me to compete with? She reversed her shirt and double-laced her Asics running shoes with the intensity of an Olympian. *I already have Natalie to deal with. Now I got this broad too?*

Fuming, Ashley stomped down the stairs and out the door. The pavement trembled beneath her soles as she took her usual route, heaving heavy gulps of air fighting into her lungs. She shoved each one out with vengeance every step of the way.

"Ha! Take that!" Ashley yelled at her bestie while sprawled out on BJ's living room floor. They were playing Street Fighter on his PS4. Ashley chose Cammy, like she always did, who could do a mean backward kick and had the best jumps that knocked down any male opponent. *The girl can slay.*

"Yeah, right. You betta come wit' it!" BJ shouted as he created an insane combination, punching the controller and knocking her flat on her butt.

"Aww, man. Cheater," Ashley mumbled, and BJ cried out a victorious laugh. "Why I gotta be a cheater just cuz you lost? *Dag*, you *hate* to lose."

Ashley knew he was right and couldn't deny it, so she chose another player to see if she could win. Ashley liked days like this, even though she could count the number of times she was able to beat BJ at one of his games. It was one of the few times she could let her hair down and just be, even if her hair was corn-rowed under a sew-in.

"Give me back my shoe!" BJ's little brother Tony came hurling down the hall, chased by Lionel, until they both invaded the small living room. Lionel sported one shoe and one sock, his other foot bare. Tony waved his brother's missing shoe high like a trophy in his left hand, a smile of glee plastered to his young walnut-colored face. Because he was a few inches shorter, every time Lionel jumped to reach the shoe, his attempts went unsuccessful. Tony threw back his head in menacing laughter whenever Lionel swiped and missed. The boys were 18 months apart but looked exactly like BJ.

They gone' kill it with the girls when they hit puberty, Ashley thought, not for the first time, with an affectionate smile.

"Yo! Y'all need to cut all that out." BJ wore his grown-man voice, and Ashley smirked. It tickled her whenever she witnessed him as an authority figure. "You know Ma 'bout to be home soon."

"He won't give me my shoe!" Lionel whined, trying but failing again to capture it from his brother's hand.

"That's cuz he took my hat!" Tony was quick to inform. He pitched his hand up again, dangling the shoe above Lionel's head.

"Give him his shoe!" BJ aimed a threatening stare at Tony until he complied.

"He started it," Tony muttered and pointed at Lionel, but Lionel took the defensive. Whipping exaggerated scrawny arms over his bird-sized chest, he poked out his lower lip and swung his head back and forth.

"Nuh unh!"

"Unh huh!"

They went on long enough for BJ to yell, "Quiet!" Leaping to his feet, he shot them an angry scowl. "Matter of fact, y'all need to clean yo room," he charged, motioning to the back hallway from which they had run.

Ashley chucked him a side-eye. "Boy. Wasn't 'chu just fightin' wit' me about this game?"

BJ rubbed the edges of his temples as if he were an old man. "Yo. It ain't' about that. They need to dead that noise."

"Well, it wasn't too long ago *you* was takin' *my* stuff and chasing *me* around," she reminded him as memories from their childhood sprouted in her mind.

"Yea. And I'm sure it bugged the hell out of whoever was around." BJ chuckled, and his brothers, who looked up to him like Lebron James, fidgeted on the couch. A chorus of them begging to play the game soon resounded in the intimate living room. "No. What did I just say?" BJ reprimanded, but Ashley felt bad.

"Come here, Lionel," she called to the younger one and sat up so he could sit with her. Wrapping her legs around him, she clasped his little hands over the controller and sheltered his with her own. "Now. I'm gone' tell you what to do, and you can kick your brother's butt. Ok?"

Lionel's eyes swelled with excitement, and a giddy smile decorated his sweet, round face. "Ok!"

Tony's lips scrunched into a pout as he stuffed his hands under his armpits while jumping to his feet. "Hey! That's not fair!" Huffing, he extended his small frame, attempting to look larger than life.

After a moment of watching his pitiful antics, BJ caved. "Come here, little man," he said and sat Tony in his lap. "We not gone' let them whoop us, are we?"

Tony beamed. "No way!"

"That's right. They know they trash. Team Harris, let's go!" BJ raised his hand, and Tony slapped it.

Another half hour flew by with Ashley laughing and playing with the boys. This time, she picked Laura. She and Lionel were actually winning when Ms. Harris walked in with a handful of groceries overtaking her slender arms. As soon as she entered, BJ paused the game, inducing a series of groans and complaints from his younger brothers.

"Hey, Ma." Since BJ was on his feet to help, his brothers did the same.

"Hey! Man, it's *crazy* at the store. It's the first of the month, so people is *ruthless* out there." Ms. Harris chuckled good-humoredly. "I swear, I had to fight an old woman for this can a beans I need for my baked beans today." The hard-working single mother of three waved around a can from a grocery bag before shrugging off her jacket. "It was the last one," she explained. Ashley smiled at Ms. Harris's anecdote while standing to help. "Oh, hey, Ash." With warm eyes, she greeted her in a familiar tone. "I didn't even see you. I was so busy tryna' get in the door." When Ms. Harris embraced Ashley, the usual fragrance of Rose from Bath & Body Works entangled with cleaning solutions clogged her nostrils. Since she worked as a maid for one of her jobs, the smell lingered, even on her days off.

"It's cool, Ms. Harris. I'm gonna head out soon anyways." Ashley trailed BJ into the kitchen to help him unpack. "My grandmother's having a family dinner."

"That's nice. I ain't talked to Ms. Mabel in a *minute*. I used to see her *all* the time at Thelma's Hair & Style. But shoot, I ain't had *no* time, or money for that matter, to be up in there." With an embarrassed smile, Ms. Harris patted her long, thick ponytail self-consciously. "You tell her I said 'hi' when you see her," she chortled, bringing up the rear into the kitchen.

"Yes, ma'am," Ashley replied. She folded up a grocery bag that BJ had emptied. Since he was stocking the pantry, she started to tackle some items for the fridge.

"Now, I see y'all was playin' that game." Ms. Harris directed her attention at her two youngest with solid hands on her hips and narrowed her stern eyes. "But did y'all clean yo room the way I told you to?" Dual heads hung low as gangly arms twiddled behind their backs.

"Umm, yea. Umm, kinda. Umm," the boys mumbled in incoherent unison.

"Go back there or you ain't gettin' no dessert!" Ms. Harris's face indicated she meant business, and her rigid finger aiming toward the bedroom solidified the threat. She snuck a look at Ashley and winked. "I'm making my sweet potato pie today."

Hearing this, the boys flew down the hall to do as they were told. Ashley grinned while watching them fight for who could get to the bedroom first.

"Looks like you know just what to say, Ms. Harris." Ashley's tone of admiration escorted the two cartons of almond milk she shoved into the fridge. Moments later, she crowded the same shelf with several containers of Greek yogurt.

"You will too when it comes time." The mom of three's smile shined with encouragement, revealing a faint dimple, but Ashley was a deer caught in headlights. She kept her hand tacked to the open refrigerator door, holding onto it like it was a life raft.

"Oh, yea. Well..." Ashley stuttered. "I got time for all that." BJ's laugh was loud and boisterous at the look on her face.

"Yea. Ash ain't in no rush for kids," he agreed, sliding a few boxes of off-brand cereal into a cupboard. "She likes getting *all* her attention."

Ashley smacked her teeth and yelled, "Shut up!" then elbowed him in the side when he handed her a block of cheese. BJ pretended to double over in pain.

"Ain't nobody listening to him," Ms. Harris quipped. "You gone' make a *good* momma, Ash. I see it in ya." Smiling wide, she balanced her petite frame on a stool, then tossed the flour and peanut butter into the cupboard.

An uncertain smile caressed Ashley's lips. Could someone make a good mom if they didn't have a mom? She wasn't so sure and really didn't want to think about it too hard. *Except for when I'm lost in fantasyland, pretending to play house with Jason.*

"I think that's the last of it," Ashley announced with satisfaction. Packing up all the plastic bags, she buried them beneath the sink like everyone in every household she had ever been to.

"Alright. Thanks, dear." Ms. Harris dressed in an apron before pulling out what she needed to cook while Ashley headed to the living room to retrieve her purse.

"I'll catch 'chu later," she said to BJ as he walked her to the door.

"Aight'. Let me know how the dinner goes. I'll prolly be at Lloyd's, but you can text." BJ held the door open, but Ashley was hesitant to walk through it. In some ways, it felt like BJ's was more of a home than the one she was about to go to. In most ways, in fact.

"Bet," she responded, then left before she lost her nerve and asked Ms. Harris if she could stay for dinner.

Grams's house was large enough for just her, a two-bedroom with a full basement. Ashley felt cramped just thinking about being that close to her relatives. *How we gone' act like we ain't seen each other since Christmas?* she huffed, veering her Benz into the narrow driveway. Her aunt and cousin's cars were parked, but her dad hadn't arrived yet. *Great. Even more uncomfortable.* Letting out a sigh, Ashley jumped out. Her yoga pants, Ralph Polo flannel, and new Puma tennis shoes were a nice change of pace. Of course, she still rocked her Prada shades and Birkin.

"Hey, baby girl!" Gramma Reese answered the door before swaddling Ashley into her large, cozy arms.

Returning the favor, Ashley replied, "Hi, Grams."

As usual, Grams's tone was a hearty basket of love. "You just in time to make the dressin'!" When she stood back to let Ashley in, the smell of soul food seduced her nostrils, and her stomach rumbled in eagerness.

Whoops! She hadn't really eaten today.

"I see you brought ya' appetite, honey." Grams took Ashley's purse, flinging it on the nearby coat hook. "You won't be needin' this big ol' thing."

Leave it to her grandmother to downplay a $10,000 bag! "But, Grams. My phone is in there." Ashley swiped for her purse, but to her surprise, her grandmother moved with lightning speed and captured her arm. *She sure is a quick old woman.*

"You ain't gone' be needin' *that* either, honey. Come on." Grams held tight before leading Ashley directly to the kitchen. When they arrived, Aunt Sheryl was rolling some kind of dough on the counter and Natalie was cleaning what looked to be Collard greens.

"I thought the food was already done, Grams?" Ashley sucked on her lower lip with her two front teeth. This little situation was way too close for comfort.

"Yea. Most of it. But I thought it'd be nice if the women of the family had a little bonding time." Without awaiting a response, Grams glided to the side of the pantry to choose Ashley an apron.

"Hey there, niece," Aunt Sheryl called. "Come and give me a hug."

Ashley assessed her. Her aunt had what looked to be flour all over her apron, and some on her nose, and a lot on her hands. Ashley's caramel brown features scrunched in distaste. "Uhhh. How about we air hug?" she suggested. She couldn't help herself. *I don't want food all over my shirt. Even if it is flannel.*

"Girl, come over here!" Sheryl stopped kneading and swung open her arms, leaving Ashley no choice.

Sheryl can be so damn demanding. After disentangling herself from Aunt Sheryl's messy welcome, Ashley started a dusting session with her shirt. Sheryl was a shade lighter and a few inches taller with the same light eyes as Malcolm. She was the only one of her siblings who fully took after grandpa Jesse who died over 10 years ago. Malcolm had Grams's features and his dad's eyes while Melissa had Grams's features, almond eyes, and even-brown skin coloring.

Natalie lifted her head from the greens she was picking. "Hey, Ash."

Guess she knows enough not to force me into a hug. Ashley chuckled to herself, replying with an indifferent, "Wuz up."

"Your plate of cornbread is right over here, baby." Grams steered Ashley to a spot on the counter next to Natalie.

Ugh! She whined, "But, Graaamms. I ain't never made dressing before," and started fidgeting with the tie on the apron Grams handed her. The stupid sharp points of her nails kept getting in the way every time she tried to knot it. Repeatedly, Ashley twisted and turned to get the strings into the right place. *This thing is so aggravating.* "Maybe I should be in the basement with Terrell," she suggested, now one hundred percent frustrated with the apron. Ashley assumed her cousin Terrell, Aunt Sheryl's adult son, was in the basement with his baby and the baby's mother, Gina. *They probably down there watching TV since that's all Terrell do anyway,* she mulled, fiddling with the long apron strings.

"Well, you 'bout to learn, honey," Grams said, referring to the dressing, and came over to help her. "I ain't gone' be here foreva, and y'all need to know my family secrets." She drew Ashley closer while tugging on her apron. "I'm sorry I didn't teach you sooner," she added in a low tone closer to her ear. After knotting the fabric, Grams rubbed an affectionate hand on Ashley's shoulder, then landed a light kiss on her cheek.

Ashley sighed. *Come on, Daddy. Hurry up and get here.*

But it would be another hour before her father walked through the door, and Ashley would be settled in by then. Aunt Sheryl filled up the time telling tales of her and her siblings' escapades growing up, some of which her own mother hadn't been privy to.

"I remember when Melissa and I decided to sneak into a college party. Oooh, we bout' *died* when we saw the good lookin' brotha's in *there*." She smiled with mischief, her brown eyes flames of joy as she flashed back to memory lane.

My aunts were kickin' it like that? Ashley perked up, intrigued. *Who knew?*

"I mean, they was *gettin'* it on the floor." Sheryl spouted, "We had never seen brothas movin' like *that* before." Ashley's ears hung on every word. "My homegirl Dorothy invited us. She was a couple years older, and her sister went to school there. We was only 15 and 16. Melissa had just got her license but still didn't have a car, so we rode with Dorothy." As she talked, Aunt Sheryl rolled out dough and crafted small circular balls from her medium-sized palms.

Perplexed, Grams asked, "Now, baby, where in the world was me and yo daddy while y'all was out frolickin' the streets at 15?" Grams started buttering the ham, making it drizzle with gold and moisture in its pan.

Tiny drops of saliva congregated on the skin of Ashley's tongue as she eyed the delicious entrée. *Damn. My mouth is actually watering.*

"Yea, Mama. About that." Sheryl tried to suppress another smile. "See. *Melissa* had this idea to spike you and Daddy's drink," she started.

Grams gasped. "What? Chil' you can-not be serious."

"Yea, and how we know it was *my* mama?" Natalie cut in. "How we don't know it wasn't *you* that had the idea?"

"*Cuz*, chil', I ain't gone' lie!" Sheryl exclaimed with mock offense and a doughy hand plastered to her round hip. "So anyways, we did. And it worked. Y'all was out like a light." She looked at her mother, eyes sizzling with humor.

Grams whipped her head from side to side, gray curls bouncing in sync. "I can't *believe* y'all." Amused, she threw her hands at her daughter before shoving them atop her swollen hips. "*Horrible!*"

Aunt Sheryl's laugh was warm with delight. "Yea. But it didn't matter, cuz *Malcolm* found us out and totally put us on blast. I mean, when that brotha showed up at that party, he almost *knocked* the door down!" Ashley smiled, thinking of her father crashing a college party to confiscate his teenage sisters.

"I don't know *how* he fount us out cuz he *still* won't tell me to this day. But I'll never forget how embarrassed we were. He was basically yellin' through the whole house, 'Y'all seen my sisters?'" She lowered her voice to sound like a man's and twisted up her face, impersonating her brother.

She looks just like him, Ashley thought fondly. She continued pouring the ingredients for the dressing into the pan.

"And back then, we ain't have cell phones, so this brotha is goin' around with his wallet, showing everybody and they mama our school pictures from like eighth grade." The kitchen burst with laughter and love, and something stirred deep inside Ashley that she hadn't experienced in a long time.

"And then what happened?" she heard herself ask while mixing in the diced celery and onions with the cornbread, hoping to God she had put in the right amounts.

"So. All I know is, I'm on the floor dancing wit' this tall *chocolate* brotha. Learning moves I'm *still* usin' to this day." Her aunt wiggled her brows in good humor. "Until suddenly, I feel a hand squeeze me so hard on my shoulder and turn me around so fast, I got whiplash!"

"And it's Uncle Malcolm," Natalie finished, hovering over the counter and looking like she had all but forgotten about the greens.

"Yep. And he grabs me and makes me go get Melissa, who was out back makin' out wit' some dude. Then he drags us away in his beat-up old Dodge Neon and threatens to tell on us the whole way home." Sheryl grabbed her stomach while releasing a jovial sound and spattering dough all over her apron.

"But he never did," Ashley guessed, knowing her father; all talk.

"Nah. He never did. And we learned our lesson. We was so embarrassed. I don't think we tried anything *that* spectacular again. Of course, Melissa could have, and just didn't tell nobody." A sad smile formed on Natalie's face, and an unexpected wave of sympathy hit Ashley.

I guess I haven't really thought about her missing her mom, she realized.

"Sheryl. I'm gone' have to get on yo brotha when he get here," Grams declared, shaking her head and cutting up yams. "I can't *believe* he ain't tell me!"

"Didn't tell you what, Mama?" Malcolm stood in the kitchen entryway, confusion grabbing his honey-brown features. "I told you I was bringing Samantha."

At the sound of her father's voice, Ashley shifted her eyes upward. He had his usual Sunday wear on, which consisted of a pair of slacks and some kind of high-end cardigan. Today, it was a black one from Ted Baker. She recognized it as a Christmas gift she had gotten him last year. What she didn't recognize, however, was the tall, curvy silhouette embedded in his shadow. When Malcolm stepped forward, the woman bloomed into full view. Brown like molasses, with large almond eyes and killer lips, she was in all black, matching Malcolm. It was apparent she had chosen her pieces well. A long black shawl with a V-neck T draped over her torso while leggings and boots shot up just below her kneecaps. One high ponytail dropped from the top of her head before racing down her back. Her look was made complete by a plush pink lip and edges so fierce a surge of jealousy ignited in Ashley.

"Well now!" Sheryl said, her voice weighty with fascination. "Who is this?"

Competition, Ashley thought, instantly annoyed, as she proceeded to busy herself with finishing the dressing.

CHAPTER 12

FAMILY FEUD

(NATALIE)

"Everybody, this is Samantha!" Uncle Malcolm smiled wide as he held his hand toward the young woman nearby. Natalie's smile back was slow yet polite. His companion looked to be about 30, which put her age somewhere in the middle of both Malcolm and his own daughter. Everyone said hello when Malcolm gave the rounds, but Ashley barely said a thing once her father arrived. Instead, she kept her head low while working.

She's guarded again. Natalie assumed it had something to do with Uncle Malcolm's female friend, and her heart sank. *So much for our good ol' family bonding moment.* Turning back to the stove, she stirred her pot of greens, which were now almost done.

"Honey, why don't 'chu tell Terrell and dem to come on up here," Grams whispered while nudging Natalie's arm. "Dinner be ready soon."

"Yes, ma'am." Tossing her apron to the side, Natalie switched her view from her cousin to her uncle, then back to her cousin again. Ashley was scrubbing her area with a sponge, but Natalie didn't see one crumb in sight; the dressing was now in the oven.

"*Now*, honey," Grams whispered again with a little more umph, and Natalie rushed off. She flew to the dining room towards the back door and down the basement stairs, doubling them so she could return faster.

"Y'all, dinner almost ready!" she yelled, only halfway down the stairs. "Grams said come on!" There was some stirring, so she waited a few more agonizing moments until Terrell, his girlfriend, Gina, and their baby, Stacy, made an appearance at the bottom step. That was her cue. Natalie dashed back to the kitchen, wanting to see what she had missed. Everyone but Ashley and Gramma Reese had trickled into the living and dining room areas. Uncle Malcolm and Aunt Sheryl were setting the table while Samantha had "The Real Housewives of Atlanta" blaring on the TV. Sitting alone, she twirled her phone in her hand repeatedly as her eyes mirrored the screen.

"You want something to drink?" Natalie offered. She felt bad that the woman seemed so out of place.

Samantha looked up with appreciative eyes. "Yes please." When Natalie returned to the kitchen, she caught a few sentences from her cousin talking to Grams.

"She's half his age!" Ashley whined.

Grams responded in a hushed tone. "She *ain't* half his age. She just younger! And anyways, love don't got an age. Yo grandad was 10 years older than me."

"Whateva."

"Girl, you betta watch yo tone wit' me."

Not surprisingly, the conversation died when Natalie walked in. "Just getting some water for our guest," she explained.

Gramma Reese spun into action, popping open the fridge. "Yes. Of course. Honey, why don't 'chu put out this lemonade and the appetizers too." She was already handing Natalie the pitcher of homemade lemonade before turning back to a sulking Ashley. "And you. Help ya' cousin." Ashley stood like a little girl who had lost her way, and Natalie's heart squeezed as a scripture flooded her mind. She knew, without a doubt, it was God's desire for Ashley.

"O Jerusalem, Jerusalem, who kills the prophets and stones to death those messengers who are sent to her by God! How often I have wanted to gather your children together around Me, just as a hen gathers her young under her wings, but you were not willing!" (Mathew 23:37)

If only she would let You in! Natalie cried in her spirit, conflicted. Even though she was both frustrated and hurt by her cousin's hostility, she was still touched by her pain. So often, flashbacks of their time together as kids would surface, and she wondered if they would ever reconnect in that same way again. Natalie could also sense *God's* longing to be reconciled with Ashley. The way that God desired to embrace the Israelites, she was sure He wanted to embrace her cousin.

It's sad, Lord, but she just isn't ready. But Natalie didn't have long to meditate on the word on her heart.

"Go on, y'all," Grams said. "Move!"

At Grams's command, Natalie gathered the items Grams had given her and propped them on the mantle in the dining room so as not to disrupt the table setting.

"Nat. How are you?" Uncle Malcolm enclosed her with a tight squeeze when he finished with the table, oblivious to the drama he had caused in the kitchen.

"Doin' good. I brought your, uh, *friend*, a glass for water." She pointed at the pitcher. "Or lemonade."

"Thanks. Hey Samantha, you want water or lemonade?" Malcolm held up the glass until Samantha tore her face away from the TV.

"You ain't ask me what I want, Unc," Terrell called. He was slouching next to Gina on the couch across from Samantha while Gina gripped the baby in her lap, fighting to keep her content with a toy bear.

Natalie hadn't seen Terrell in years and didn't think he looked to be doing too good. *He's at least 15 pounds heavier, and he was already husky before.* His girlfriend didn't look so hot either. *She must be exhausted.* Gina rocked the baby on her lap while trying to watch TV. Photos on Instagram from when the couple first got together manifested in Natalie's mind. *Gina used to be super put together.*

"That's cuz you a grown man, boy," Malcolm responded to his nephew. "You betta get it yo self." He was joking, but Natalie knew enough of the dynamics of her family to know that Terrell needed to grow up. Her mother always said that a baby and a girlfriend does not a grown man make. Natalie frowned at the thought.

"Aye, babe. Why don't 'chu get me some lemonade?" Terrell asked his girl, and she scowled in frustration.

Gina held up Baby Stacy, who was less than a year old. "You see I got this baby. Why don't 'chu get it?" Stacy giggled, thinking Mommy was playing a game, before swiping at her toy bear.

The back of Terrell's neck sank onto the top of the couch before he muttered, "Never mind," and Natalie rolled two disgusted eyeballs.

Since when do men not serve women in this family? She grunted, along with another incomprehensible sound under her breath.

"What was that, cuz'?" Terrell must have heard her.

Natalie just looked at him while unwrapping the cheese and crackers. She returned to the kitchen to get the other plates where Ashley emerged with a few of her own. Grams always did the most when it came to food.

As the evening flowed, the crew fell into chit-chat about weather and work and who was getting paid more, Nene or Phaedra this season? Natalie voted Nene hands down, and it was almost 7 o'clock by the time everything was done.

"Now, look at that!" Gramma Reese said, gathering everyone around the table.

Natalie's breath was taken away. *It looks amazing!* And to think, she actually had a hand in making it. Greens, yams, cornbread, dressing, ham, mac & cheese, homemade rolls, and baked beans all donned the table in style. Natalie peered around at her family, her heart bursting with gratitude.

"Malcolm, bless the food," Grams ordered, and everybody joined hands while Malcolm led them in prayer.

"Lord. Thank You so much for Your provision. For time with loved ones. For putting it on Momma's heart to get us all here. And for always leading us back together, no matter how long we've been apart. Amen." Malcolm lifted his head and glanced around with a loving smile.

"Amen!" came a cheerful chorus from the table.

As everyone sat, a spirit of unity touched Natalie's heart. *Wow, God, I've missed this.* She couldn't think of the last time she had gathered with her family. So often, it was her, her mother, and their friends for the holidays. *Lord, thank You for new beginnings.*

"Baby. Can you hand me those greens?" Aunt Sheryl asked. She sat on Natalie's right with a palm already extended to receive them.

"Yes, ma'am." Natalie passed the bowl, and pretty soon, everyone was passing plates of food to serve themselves.

Sheryl cut up pieces of ham into thinner slices while asking, "How are your classes coming along, Nat?"

Natalie nodded while digging into her mac and cheese. "Great! I love the writing class I'm taking. And the fact that I'm still able to work around my class schedule is truly a blessing."

"Oh, yea. Malcolm did mention you got a job." Sheryl smiled broadly. "That's awesome, baby."

"Yea. She's over there at Devon's. I love that place. I mean, I haven't been there in forever, but I sure do remember how good the coffee is," Malcolm chimed in. "Nat and I ran into him the other day at Denny's. He is definitely a fine young man doing big things."

"Yea. Devon is amazing. He's a great business owner, and I'm learning a lot from him." Natalie tried to keep her face from grinning too much by ramming more food into it.

"I'm proud of you, honey. You doing so well," Sheryl said with a short pat on her back. Natalie was thankful for the praise but also somewhat embarrassed. She stole a glance at Ashley, who had been unusually quiet.

For some reason, Samantha chose that moment to lean over Malcolm towards Ashley. "Ashley, your dad tells me you're studying to be a fashion designer?"

Uh oh. Natalie was reminded of the conversation she had walked in on earlier in the kitchen between Ashley and Grams. *Ashley is not trying to hear from this woman.*

Ashley's eyes darted to Samantha. She gulped down some of her lemonade before answering flatly, "Yea."

"Well. I'm a little versed in the industry," Samantha replied in a bubbly tone. "I'm actually a Fashion Marketing Manager." Ashley chucked her chin up and down, her face remaining blasé.

Malcolm piped up, "Yep. Samantha has been a great asset to her company. You could learn a lot, Ash." He peered from one woman to the other on either side with a lopsided, mushy grin. Ashley rolled her eyes before shoveling a spoonful of baked beans into her mouth.

A moment of silence hit the room, and Aunt Sheryl gestured to the new couple, switching the subject. "Now, how did y'all meet exactly?"

Malcolm told the story, saying they were at some networking event he went to for his firm. "I was thinking I was going just to get clients, but I walked away thinking of nothing else but this young woman." The fondness in his eyes was evident as he chomped on a piece of ham.

"*Young* is the right word," Ashley muttered, only she said it loud enough for everyone to hear. Natalie's mouth dropped, and Malcolm pitched his daughter a look. Everyone else busied themselves eating, including Samantha.

Ashley commented with a shrug, "What? She is," as her eyes sank to her plate.

Malcolm's voice was stern. "That's enough, Ashley."

"What's up with your job search, Terrell?" Better than any race car driver, Ashley switched lanes, veering her attention to her cousin. Popping both elbows on the table, she held her fork in mid-air as Terrell's face screwed up.

"Still lookin'," he said, munching on his food.

"Oh?" Ashley's voice slithered into an eager edge of taunting. "You been lookin' for a while now, huh?"

Aunt Sheryl jumped to her son's defense. "Leave him alone, Ash," her tone warned.

"What?" Ashley batted two long-lashed eyelids. "I'm only asking a simple question. I just never known nobody to take *that* long findin' a job." She heaved up her shoulder, then inhaled more cornbread. "That's all," she finished with a smug smack to her lips.

Terrell stated in an irritated voice, "Yo. It takes *time* to find the right position. I mean, I don't just want to take *anything*." Gina rubbed his hand to comfort him, but he flicked her fingers away.

"Really?" With a jut of her chin, Ashley swallowed her food. "Don't 'chu think you *should*? You got a *whole* family to take care of." Right on time, Baby Stacy cooed in Gina's lap. The young mother pulled out a bottle, but Stacy pushed it away, reaching her chubby hands for the yams on her mama's plate. She wanted the good stuff.

Oh Lawd. Natalie fought a sinking feeling in her stomach regarding the interaction between her cousins. *This can't be good.*

"Yo. Why you worried about me anyway?" Terrell said. He puckered his lips into a sneer. "You ain't doing much yo self. I bet chu' don't even know how to spell the word *job*." His round mocha face contorted into spite as he fired out each word. Ashley had hit a nerve.

Natalie wrung her napkin under the table while shooting a telepathic look at Grams. *Grams, do something!*

"Y'all just gon' *love* my pecan pie!" Grams declared, gazing at everyone from her prominent seat at the head of the table. She clasped her plump hands while giving a hopeful smile. "It's a new recipe!" But it was as if Grams hadn't said a word. Ashley would not be distracted.

"Yea?" Ashley answered her cousin. "I'm doing more than *you*." She held her gaze steady on Terrell. She was a vetted soldier who would not miss aim. "I'm going to school. Doing *something* with my life," she spat. With another jut of her chin, Ashley crossed her arms, foregoing the meal on her plate.

"Puh! A few classes every now and then ain't *nothin'*." Terrell glared. "All you do is pamper yo self with yo daddy's money and post on social media."

His tone was callous, and was it just Natalie or was the temperature rising in the room? *The walls gotta be sweating, it's so hot.*

Ashley fired back with the accuracy of an M80. "Oh. *You* the one to talk about livin' off yo parents, dear *cousin*." Snarling, her voice rose as she flicked an accusatory hand at Gina. "You got a whole damn family living up in yo momma's house."

"I'm using a cinnamon recipe this time," Grams practically sang out, not that anyone was listening.

Natalie's eyes swapped back and forth between her cousins in alarmed intrigue. *Who needs Housewives of Atlanta when the freaking show is at the dinner table.* Ashley sat with arrogance as if she were the Queen of England. Terrell's hands were tightly balled like Mike Tyson in his prime, positioned and ready on the table. Natalie thought in unnerved humor, *Hmm. I wonder who would win in a fight? The Queen or Mike?* Her eyes flew from one relative to the other.

"Y'all need to calm down," Malcolm finally cut in, piercing a threatening stare at his daughter. "Ashley. Chill out."

"Yea," Aunt Sheryl agreed and leaned over to soothe the baby since

Gina was still struggling. She snuck a pinch of mashed sweet potatoes into Stacy's mouth, and the child stopped fussing. "Y'all ain't gone' raise my blood pressure today!" her aunt declared. "Nunt unh, not *today.*"

"Boy, you ain't took a class since 8th grade." Ashley ignored her elders and went in on her cousin. "You cut *all* through high school. I'm surprised you know how to read." She paused and examined her nails with a pleased expression. "Wait. You *do* know how to read," she snickered, slicing vicious eyes at Terrell, "right?"

"You an arrogant, selfish, b-"

"Terrell!" Sheryl cut off her son while jumping to her feet, but the intended expletive still stained the atmosphere. "That's enough." Startled by her abruptness, the baby started crying, and Gina rushed to quiet her by bouncing her on one knee.

"Shhh. Shhh," Gina whispered to Baby Stacy in quick, soft tones.

"Daddy. You just gone' let him talk to me like that?" Ashley's tone was incredulous while hopping up from the table.

"Ashley. You need to stop antagonizing people. Now sit down and eat yo food." Malcolm wore an exhausted expression as he glared at his daughter. Time seemed to stand still as each Bennett sized the other up.

Feverishly rubbing her leg under the table, Natalie puffed out a breath, her heart rate escalating. *Lord, what should I do?*

"Save Ashley", came the instant reply.

"Oh, ok. Because I'm not *Natalie,* I don't get defended." Ashley's voice was loud and tearful. "I bet 'chu if somebody called *her* out of *her* name, you would be tryna *fight* dude!" She backed away from the table, her eyes aiming daggers at Natalie with both arms folded.

Natalie gasped. "What? How did *I* get brought into this?"

"Ashley, if you want to eat your food *alone,* then you can do that and go in the basement. But I'm not doing this wit' 'chu. You're embarrassing yourself." Malcolm had had enough. He slammed down his utensils and wiped his mouth with more force than was needed.

"Oh. So *that's* your solution, Daddy? Just get rid of me, huh?" Ashley's shrill voice bounced off the walls of the small living room like a boomerang. She was practically yelling now.

Natalie was torn. *Should I say something? Or will that only make it worse?*

"Save Ashley", beat along with the rhythm of her heart.

But Lord. How?

"Honey. You are *loved*. Nobody is gettin' rid a you." Grams's soft tone carved through the tension in the air, heartbreak written all over her gentle, round features.

"Maybe *you* love me, Grams, but I don't know about anybody else here." Ashley scoped the room. "Love ain't bringing a woman around I never even met in *person* and then introducing her to the whole family at *once*. As if— as if—" she stuttered, and raw emotion transformed into tears. They spilled out lavishly, but she was quick to wipe her face while avoiding everyone's gaze.

"As if what, honey?" Grams asked with compassion. She moved to stand but was having a hard time.

Natalie winced. *Poor Grams. This can't be good for her.*

"Grams, don't entertain this. She just wants attention," Terrell said before stuffing another forkful of mac and cheese into his mouth.

"Honey, I'm sorry. I didn't think bringing Samantha tonight would upset you." Malcolm grabbed for his daughter's hand, but Ashley jerked away, offering her back instead. She seized her purse, which she had snuck on the back of her chair when Grams wasn't looking and started for the exit.

"You know what? Terrell is right," Ashley announced, turning around with fiery, bright eyes. "I just want attention. So I'm out. I'll get my attention elsewhere." Before anyone could say anything, she stomped her Puma canvas sneakers out of the dining room.

Natalie ran after without even thinking; she just felt her legs carrying her forward while having no idea what she was going to say. With every step, *Save Ashley* echoed in her mind. "Ashley, wait!" She called to her cousin, speeding to the front door, a desperate prayer sailing from her heart. *Lord, give me the words to say!*

"What do *you* want, little Ms. Perfect?" Ashley spewed, and Natalie shrank in shock.

"Is that how you see me? You think, *I* think, I'm *perfect*?"

Her cousin just stared at her. "Look. I just need to get outta here. I can't be here right now." Ashley shifted towards the door, all personal items jammed inside her tensed red knuckles.

"Then I'm going with you," Natalie announced, her voice firm, while taking a step forward.

"What? What are you talking about?" Surprise wrestled Ashley's anger, but after a few moments, it seemed to have won the match.

Natalie took another determined step towards her. "If you go, I go." She looked at Ashley with her jaw set as her cousin's conflicting emotions combated in her light brown eyes.

"Fine," was all she finally said, so Natalie followed her out the door.

Somehow, Natalie convinced Ashley not to leave, and instead, they went for a long walk. "You're always running away. You have people here for you. *I'm* here for you." Natalie's sincerity pushed through the clouds of pain like sunshine on a rainy day, and Ashley's eyes bloomed with surprise. She softened enough to let her guard down.

"I can't believe he brought that skank here," Ashley fumed with each step during their walk.

Natalie struggled to keep up with her pace but dared not express it. She was just happy Ashley was confiding in her. "So, you didn't know about Samantha?" she ventured. *I hope that's a safe question.*

Ashley huffed a breath while squeezing her arms tighter against her body. She had tossed her Birkin in her car when Natalie convinced her to walk. "Nope. He literally just told me about her this morning."

"Wow. I didn't know," Natalie offered. They were now several blocks from Grams's house. It was a decent neighborhood; only a few older people sat on their porches. A kid also played outside in his yard at the house across the street that they walked past.

"Pure bullshit. Who brings a whole stranger to a family dinner? I mean, you don't see me bringing my dude to dinner." Ashley was speaking out loud, but Natalie felt her statement was directed more at herself than anything.

"Wow. I didn't even know you were dating." Natalie's eyes widened in surprise as she tried to keep up with her cousin's pace. *Man, everybody is boo'ed up.*

"Exactly. Cuz I ain't tryna bring somebody around unless it's serious. And foreal foreal, I wouldn't have played *him* like that and just dumped him on the family all at once." Ashley kicked a pebble to the side, and Natalie fought the urge to touch her shoulder. Physical contact was *not* something her cousin was easily receptive to.

Lord, help me help her. "I don't know if he was thinking about it that way. He was probably just excited to find somebody he felt was good enough to share with the family." Natalie gazed with caring eyes and held her breath, but Ashley's mouth was tight enough for a gymnast to balance on, her pretty face set in stone.

"I guess that's the problem," she finally said, her balance beam crumbling into a sad frown. They walked a little further until the cul-de-sac forced them to turn around.

"What is?"

"He's really moved on." Ashley's voice cracked with emotion, and Natalie's heart felt like it was being squashed like one of Devon's stress balls.

Without thinking, she drew closer and rubbed Ashley's back. Though she stiffened, Ashley didn't move away, and Natalie took that as a good sign. "Has your dad ever dated somebody seriously?"

"Nope," Ashley replied, her eyes now focused on the sidewalk. "Not ever." Her words fired out while shaking.

Wow! It had been seven years since Aunt Patty unexpectedly died in a car crash. Hit by a drunk driver, the coroner said she died upon impact. Natalie remembered when they were kids and it happened. Everything was so sudden. One day, her aunt was there, and the next, gone.

Now Uncle Malcolm is so serious about somebody that he would introduce them to the whole family. Natalie marveled but kept her thoughts to herself as they continued their walk. When they got near the house, the little kid across the street was gone and the streetlights were on.

Natalie released a cautious sigh. "I think you should talk to him. I know it's hard to picture our parents as humans. And I know we think they're just parents and kind of here just for us," she paused, "but I'm sure Uncle Malcolm's been lonely these seven years. As much as he loves your mom, I'm sure he wants to have someone like the rest of us." Natalie was thinking of her own desire to have someone when she made that last statement. She was thinking of Devon.

Natalie waited in anticipation, hoping her words didn't set off the invisible bomb that lurked in Ashley's heart. But she must have made some kind of sense because her cousin's expression became a little less defiant. A little less angry. And she nodded slowly with an enigmatic expression.

When they reached their grandmother's house, the two young women stood side by side on the porch steps in total silence. Finally, Grams came out, embraced them both, then brought them in for pecan pie.

C H A P T E R 13

B R E A K T H R O U G H

(A S H L E Y)

"Come *on*. Let's go!" A sharp stinging trekked through Ashley's palm from jamming her hand on the horn so hard. Jason had been waiting for at least a half hour. "Freakin' New York traffic," she mumbled while confiscating her phone from her black leather Dolce & Gabbana purse.

"Baby. I'm coming." She typed out the text as the van in front inched forward. Rushing, she dropped her phone and clasped the wheel. *Shoot!* The phone now sat on the floor, stubbornly nudging her right foot. But Ashley couldn't worry about that now. She was finally moving. *I got to find a new route to La Repas de Michelle,* she mused. *This is ridiculous.*

Minutes later, she saw the real reason for the holdup. It wasn't traffic, but a horrific accident. An audible gasp flung from her lips as she crept by a blue 4-door sedan flipped onto its side. Not too far away, the entire front end was smashed in on a white SUV very similar to her own. An ambulance and police crawled like roaches on the scene. The air was pierced by heart-wrenching cries from a woman standing by the truck as a young child gripped a strong chokehold around her leg. Both looked unharmed, but the other person hadn't been so lucky.

Ashley gaped in horror. *This is bad.* Chills swarmed her arm like a colony of bees, and she couldn't escape the heaviness in the pit of her stomach. A body lay on its back on top of a stretcher, and although an EMS team huddled over it, she could still see that it was covered in blood. *I can't see this!* But she couldn't look away.

Traffic dragged forward as each car took turns merging into one lane. Ashley turned up the volume of her radio, but it didn't work. Her breathing grew labored, and as dread suffocated her heart, air became a precious commodity. *Oh God!* Alarmed and fighting to get oxygen to her lungs, she did a frantic search with her right hand for her phone. *I can't breathe!* Once her fingers laced around the glittery case, she punched buttons, trying her dad. No answer. *BJ!* He picked up on the first ring.

"Hey, Ash. Wuz up?"

"B-J. I can't b-reathe!" Ashley exhaled panic into the phone, her eyes still stapled to the accident. Why wouldn't these damn cars move faster?

"Ash. Calm down. Calm down!" BJ's voice escalated to concern, and comfort stroked her heart just hearing it. Still, she struggled with getting air. "What's wrong?"

"B— I can't..." was all she could say.

BJ's alarm dove through the speaker as his tone rang with worry. "I'm comin' to you. Send me your location. I'm comin'!" Ashley dropped a pin for her location just as a bead of sweat popped onto her forehead. It slid down to her eyelid, blurring her vision, but she was too frozen with fear to wipe it away. "Ash. I'm staying on the phone wit' you. I'm comin'!"

The car in front was moving again, so she used all her energy to steer and press the gas. "B," she whispered.

"I need you to stay calm. I'm en route, but 'chu gotta get somewhere safe."

"I'm get-ting-off," Ashley stammered. Once the cars in front passed the accident, the highway was clearer and she could gain speed. There were only a few miles until she reached the nearest exit, but each mile felt like an eternity.

"Just take your time," BJ soothed while she drove. "Drive slow. Stay calm."

With all her might, Ashley focused on his voice, and it did give her the strength she needed. Hopping off the exit, she swerved into the parking garage near a random bodega and sent the new location. *What is wrong with me?* Ashley thought, sitting there heaving and sweating in distress.

"I'm gonna sing to you." And within moments, her ears reverberated with BJ's rendition of "My Girl."

Ashley had always loved BJ's voice. When they were younger, he tried to pursue a career in music, but his need to work and help his mom prevailed. She sat in the car with her head against the wheel and the door propped open as he sang. With the phone nestling her ear, she listened hard, but when BJ appeared in Lloyd's Mercedes, she was on the verge of tears. He rushed out of the vehicle, moving so fast that he left the door wide open while speeding to the driver's side of her truck. Ashley's eyes met his, and the moisture gripping her eyelids ambushed her cheeks.

With care, BJ gazed into her water-stained face. "You ok?"

She was still heaving, but her heart rate had slowed. With her shoulders now trembling, she whispered, "I don't know what's wrong," and bowed her head in confusion.

"Come on." Helping her out of the truck, BJ cupped his hand around her waist and guided her. Once he got her situated, he grabbed her bag and locked her car. "We'll get it in the morning," he said, referring to the Benz.

Ashley nodded, her head still low, while accepting her bag and keys. "I need to text Jason," she mumbled. "I was meeting him."

"Let me do it." Without waiting for a response, BJ typed a message on her phone that she was ill and would call later. When he started driving, Ashley's anxiety dissipated. Her breathing gradually returned to normal, and at some point, she stopped perspiring. Worry lines decorating his normally smooth forehead, BJ looked at her. "What happened?"

"I'm not sure. I saw this car... and this *woman*." She shuddered, the goosebumps once again turning into ants crawling along her forearms. "At least, I think it was a woman. Her face..." Ashley held her hands in front of her own face, then dropped them and peered out the window. She couldn't even finish.

"What? You saw an accident?"

"Yea." She went quiet and studied her lap. *Why am I trippin' about an accident?* Ashley was perplexed. It wasn't like *she* was in it. "And I just couldn't breathe," she finished with trembling lips.

A crisp frown creased BJ's mouth. "Ash, I think you had a panic attack."

"What? *Why*? I mean, why was I struggling to breathe over an accident? It didn't even involve me." But Ashley had said the question more to herself than to her friend. Growing quiet again, she fiddled with her phone in her hands. Her ink-colored leather skirt had hiked up, so she dragged it down toward her knees. *So much for a lovely dinner at a fancy French restaurant,* she sulked.

Ashley had dressed to the max for her date in high-heeled Gucci black pumps, a coal-black bodysuit, and a Ralph Lauren blazer that topped it off fantastically. Before the rainstorm on her face, it was adorned with a soft pink lip and glittery eyeshadow. *I must look a hot mess,* she thought with a frown but was too upset to double-check in the mirror.

"Well, you look nice," BJ commented, glancing over.

She chuckled. "You must be joking."

"I mean, outside of the boogers and runny mascara." He appeased her with a teasing smile, making her chuckle balloon into a full-out laugh.

After a moment, she said, "I'm sorry. I feel like a fool for having you come all the way out here." She stared at the road through glassy eyes.

"Yo. I'm just glad I got the message right away and that Lloyd let me use his ride."

"Yea, my bad——" the ring from her cell stopped Ashley mid-sentence. *Dad.* His picture lit up the screen, flashing like the sirens from earlier.

BJ caught a glimpse. "Yo. You gone' get that?"

"Naw. I'm cool," she replied, flipping the phone over. "Ain't no point in worrying him."

"Well, you *definitely* need to tell him what happened. What if you need to go to a hospital?" BJ's eyes were heavy with affection as he switched on the windshield wipers to fight the new raindrops coming down.

A sharp exhale protruded from Ashley's lips. What was the point of telling her father about a panic attack when he wasn't there to help her through it? "I'm good now. I'll be ok," she insisted. "Can you drop me off at Denise's? I don't feel like going home."

BJ's big brother training was in full effect. "You sure? I can stay wit' 'chu..."

"I'm sure. You gotta get to work." Ashley smoothed a hand over her head, making sure her hair was intact. "I'm sorry this took you away from it."

"You ain't got nothing to be sorry about. I told Lloyd it was a family emergency."

That warmed her heart, and a small smile met her lips. "Thanks, B." Ashley texted Denise, wanting to make sure she was home, even though it was her night off work. Denise responded that she was home, and yea, she was up for company. To tidy up her face, Ashley slid open the camera on her phone.

The pair rode silently until BJ's gentle tone interrupted it. "You think it was your mom's accident that triggered you?"

Ashley was surprised. She hadn't even considered it. "Oh. I don't know," she answered with a smooth shrug, then dabbed on some lipstick.

"I think you should talk to somebody, Ash. I mean, that was pretty intense. You was on the road and *everything*. What if you had an accident yourself just from seeing one?" BJ's voice was thick with emotion, and Ashley didn't know what to say.

"I don't know. I mean. I know I've seen accidents before." A shiver ran through her while tucking the lipstick back into her bag. "But it was just something about that one..." *Maybe it's cuz that one car looked like mine. Or maybe it was the mother-daughter duo...*

BJ stopped at a red light and peered at her with a grave expression. "*Promise* me you'll talk to somebody."

Ashley swished around uncomfortably in her seat. If it was anybody else, she would have brushed them off, using her charm, or maybe her attitude, to deflect. But this was BJ. This was her brother. And he knew her too well. She hesitated while gnawing at a fingernail. "Ok," she finally relented, slowly meeting his eyes. "I'll talk to someone."

"Girrrrl, I cannot *believe* yo cousin Terrell was buggin' like that!" Denise jiggled her lock-filled head, prancing around the tiny apartment she shared with a roommate who worked three jobs and was barely home. She stole another bottle of wine from the fridge. She and Ashley had already killed half of the Pinot Grigio, but it was only half-full when they started drinking it.

Not missing a beat, Ashley offered a smooth neck roll in response. "Yea, sis. I'm like, bruh, you tryna come fa me? Yo broke, baby mama havin' ass?" Getting more comfortable, she crossed her legs while seated on the floor.

After arriving nearly an hour ago, Ashley changed out of her dress attire and slipped into a pair of joggers and a crop top from Denise's closet. She was a size larger than Denise and a few inches shorter, so it wasn't the best fit, but it would do.

"Puh! He had the nerve to call *you* spoiled. Like he be up here grindin'." Denise plopped onto the sofa facing Ashley with eyes of disbelief. "*And* he got a whole damn family."

Even though they didn't have a lot of furniture, Denise's space was still nice. In Ashley's opinion, it gave chill, cute vibes in a vintage sort of way. The sofa was a pull-out belonging to the MIA roommate, Cat, and served as her bed at night while Denise copped the intimate space in the back. It was more of a cubbyhole than a room with a large maroon blanket nailed to the opening instead of an actual door. Denise did her best to make it inviting, crowding the walls with shelves of varying items like candles and pictures of loved ones. Jars of the homemade hair products she hustled were sprinkled throughout as well. There was also a sizable hand-painted portrait of a marijuana plant overlooking the pallet she slept on.

Denise and Cat had had a third roommate, Jeff. But Jeff had just moved out, and they were looking for a replacement. Ashley had no idea where Jeff had been sleeping. Denise swore up and down he wasn't sharing *her* room, but Ashley didn't believe her. The only other space would have been the kitchen. Even the bathroom was barely a full bath and resembled more of a closet. But since Cat spent ample time with her boyfriend in Brooklyn, there was a slight possibility Jeff had alternated between the sofa and the floor when he was home between jobs.

Ashley's eyes shifted out of habit in a low-key search for mice. Though she had never spotted any, she couldn't seem to untrain herself from looking anyway. She grazed over the treasure-chest-designed wooden table with drawers that sat smack dab in the middle of the floor and then to the large painting of a brown-skinned woman, half-naked with long locks, sprawled on the wall over the sofa. The woman's locks swirled in the air while a black bodysuit swallowed whole her bulging butt cheeks. Ashley secretly thought Denise had the portrait painted of herself, but never took the time to ask.

Feeling confident no rodents were running rampant, she resumed her conversation. "Yea. It's a shame Auntie Sheryl spoils Terell like that. I wish my daddy *would* let me move in a dude *and* have his baby, and I be sittin' on my butt all day while *he* pay our way." Sipping her Moscato, Ashley sucked the juicy taste lingering on her lips in pleasure.

"Girl, you know yo daddy got *bank*," Denise was quick to say. "He gone' be funding you *and* yo grandkids." With a ruckus laugh, she lit another incense. Once the sweet fragrance cascaded into the air, she pulled up her playlist from her phone and selected Jhené Aiko's *Sativa*. The hit ballad flowed through the BlueTooth speaker, and both girls vibed to the tune.

"Yea. You may be right," Ashley admitted, then offered a light chuckle before slanting her head to the side. "But I could *never* be with a dude who wasn't a 'go-getter' like that. I mean, that shit is just unattractive." She frowned in disgust.

"Ain't it tho'? Why a man is comfortable with letting *his woman* pay his bills is craaazy to me." Having whipped out the contents from one of the coffee table's drawers, Denise started rolling a joint. Ashley sat up in anticipation, forgetting the drink next to her.

"And you *know* I only got hittas on *my* roster," Denise bragged, then swiped the small paper with her tongue. She was referring to the fact that Ashley wouldn't date a man unless he was working and agreed that she, too, could only be with a man who had means.

"Yea, yea." Ashley rolled her eyes. "I know. So. Speaking of hittas... wuz up wit' 'chu and Lloyd?"

Denise's full lips eased into a half-smile. "Oh, you know. I hit him up when I need him." She swooped up the lighter she used for the incense, put flame to paper, and drew in long and hard. Smoke caressed the space around her, doing a tango with the scent from the incense.

Ashley giggled. "I knew he was a goner when I saw him *thirstin'* after you at the store. I wanted to be like, 'Brotha, you need a Sprite'?" Snagging the joint from her friend, she sucked. *Ahhh.* Now *that* was the relaxation she was looking for. *This shit is better than a massage*, Ashley thought with pleasure, then passed the rolled substance back to Denise.

Denise switched the subject. Her skin clad in fitted jeans and a skimpy tank, she lay flat on her back with a foot propped on the sofa arm. Both articles of clothing clung to her slim frame, only opening at the rear.

Ashley admired her friend's figure. *Yep. Just like the painting.*

"Did you talk to yo dad about 'Miss Fashion Marketer'?" Denise asked.

"Naw. I mean, what is there to say? If you can bring a chick to meet the *whole* family at once and not me *first,* then you don't give a damn *what* I think." Ashley's half-full glass of Moscato peered up at her before she swooshed it back, swirling the sweetness around and letting it ease down her throat.

"Yea. Dead ass. *That* was some trash." Denise gave her two cents before passing the herbal treat back to Ashley. "I can't believe Mr. B is seriously datin' tho'! He ain't seen *nobody* since yo mom."

Inhaling, Ashley bobbed her head in agreement. "I know," she said before a fit of coughing grabbed her. Smoke had gotten tangled in her lungs, and Denise giggled as she struggled. "The shit is crazy," she finally got out.

"Ohhhh! So, guess who got a crush on Devon?" Flying up from the couch, Denise looked at her friend with two shining eyeballs.

Ashley knew Denise well enough to know that when she looked like that, it meant good gossip. "Who?"

"Natalie," she said, awaiting her reaction.

Ashley almost dropped the remaining joint while passing it. "Whaaat?"

Denise lunged to seize it before ashes hit the cheap carpet and she had to pay a cleaning bill she hadn't budgeted for. "Yea, girl."

Ashley's voice was as skeptical as a diehard Atheist's. "How you know?"

"Cuz, she gets all wide-eyed when she's around him. Nodding up and down like, 'Yes, Devon. Whateva you say, Devon.'" Doing her best version of Natalie, Denise's pupils enlarged as she batted her lashes and tossed her hair.

Ashley howled. "Girl. She *is* his assistant." *Denise is ridiculous.*

"Yea, well, she wanna do more than assist him at *work*," Denise insisted, finishing the joint and smothering the bud deep into a nearby saucer. She knew most of her peeps went the vapor route, but there was nothing like that old-school feeling of a fresh joint rolled in between her fingertips. It must have been the hippie in her. "Just listen to how she talk about him."

"I don't know. I don't really be talking to her," Ashley admitted. "*You* would know better than me." She threw her head back and downed her glass in one clean gulp. "But 'chu know what? I ain't even mad." Ashley's voice turned an octave louder than normal. "Ms. Perfect deserves a little boo thang. I mean, she *did* help me out at the family dinner." *Shoot, and all this time, I thought she was gonna marry Jesus.* This thought tickled her, and she started to laugh.

Denise's eyes shifted sideways. "Whaaat? Since when are *you* 'team Natalie'?"

"I'm not. I'm just sayin'. " Ashley shrugged a lopsided shoulder. "She was there for me after my daddy wasn't when Terrell was a straight-up ass. And Devon is a good dude. I mean, he definitely *older*. And would she even know how to *handle* an older dude?" Ashley snickered, thinking about her goody-goody cousin dating a more experienced man.

"Right! Can you picture Natalie with a Zaddy?" Denise smiled.

Spreading onto her back, Ashley stared at the ceiling. The sound of laughter filled the air, and her mood from seeing the car accident had totally dissipated. It took her a minute though to realize it was *her* laughing that loud. *Dag. I* must *be high.* She flipped onto her side and gripped her stomach; it hurt from laughing. Amused, Denise watched while sprawled on the sofa. After a minute, Ashley started fumbling around in her bag for her phone.

"Yo. Let's look at Darren's page," she suggested. Her speech had started to slur, and she was already opening her Instagram account.

"Aww, here we *go*." Denise proclaimed, but out of boredom, she dropped to the floor near her friend. "Every time you high, you wanna IG stalk him."

"Whateva." Ashley logged out and handed the phone to Denise so she could log in. Denise and Darren were still friends on Instagram, so it wasn't weird if she was on his page.

"Yo. I'm a stop doin' this fa you one day, homie," Denise announced, shaking her head in pity while taking the phone. "It can't be good for a sista."

Ashley sucked the air between her teeth in annoyance. "Girl, if you don't give me that phone!" Snatching the phone, her eyes devoured Darren's page while Denise hovered over her arm so she could see too.

"See. He ain't wit' nobody. He broke up with that thot Sharon a minute ago," Denise informed as Ashley zipped through different pictures. "And I think he be kickin' it with that ho Tonya, but she only good for that much," Denise went on.

Ohhh, that's that girl's name. "Yea. I saw them out a while back," Ashley admitted. "I mean, I saw them out on his story." Ashley kept perusing, but she only saw Darren and his little brother, Eric. Darren with his new sneakers. Darren with his boys and some other miscellaneous portraits. "Let's look at his story," she said, still unsatisfied. Ashley just couldn't shake the desire to see what was up with her ex. She knew she was being "extra," but she had this need to know that *she* had been Darren's first and only love.

"Yooo. I told you he ain't on nobody," Denise insisted once they finished investigating his stories and Snapchat.

Ashley muttered with a sigh, "Well, nobody *serious* anyway." Leaning against the table, she yawned as the corners of her eyes sagged. "Shoot! What time is it?" As he usually did, Mr. Cannabis was making her sleepy.

"After 10 o'clock," Denise murmured, stretching out on the carpet. She was getting tired herself.

Ashley's voice had turned sloppy, and her tone was now fully slurred. "*Dag.* I ain't know it was *that* late. I forgot to call Jason. Shit. I'm messin' this all up." She stumbled to her feet and arched her back hard to try and sober up some.

"Girl, you don't want that dude," Denise said while flopping over. "You just *think* you do." She was facedown now with her head heaved onto both arms.

"What 'chu meeeean? Jason has *everything*," Ashley started showering her phone with a text message to Jason. "*Of course,* I want him."

"Babe. Sorry about today. I've still been trying to recover. I'll call you tomorrow!" She added three sad face emojis to hammer home her point.

"Yea, ok," Denise mumbled, half asleep. "If you wanted him, you wouldn't be cyber stalking Darren."

Ashley hoisted herself onto the couch and curled up since, per Denise, Cat was with her boo tonight. *I'm way too tired to pull out the sofa bed.*

"Whateva," Ashley responded to her friend and yawned again before shutting her eyelids. Denise didn't know *what* she was talking about. *I'm so over Darren.*

Perched on the couch in her living room with both legs folded, Ashley checked her email on her laptop. *Professor Simone sent the extra credit assignment.* Delight and excitement simmered in her eyes as they swept over the email.

"Students, if you choose the assignment, it is to create your very own original design of a man and woman's complementary ensemble. The style can be vintage or modern and should stem from a time period we will have discussed in class by the end of the semester. It should be submitted two weeks prior, and the winner will be announced once final grades are released."

Still reading, Ashley lifted her favorite mug with the words "Diva" in large, bold, cursive letters. "Ok. This is cool," she murmured, swallowing a mouthful of the brown, steamy liquid.

The phone's ringer interrupted her mind racing with possibilities. "Yo. You good?" BJ's anxious tone ignited Ashley's memories from yesterday.

Damn. I forgot about the accident. "Yea. My bad. I'm good. Wuz up wit' 'chu?" It was weird for him to call so early, and now she realized why; he was worried.

"Nothin'. 'Bout to head to work but wanted to check on you."

Ashley appreciated BJ's concern, but it also made her nervous. She didn't like thinking about the panic attack.

"Yea. I'm cool. Me and Denise was fried last night, so that helped a *lot.*" Closing her laptop, she clasped the phone close to her ear and kissed the rim of her mug.

"Oh, fa real? That's wuz up. But you gone' still talk to somebody. Right?"

Dag. Here he go. Ashley peered into her mug, watching the steam rise, then tossed an irritated eye roll to the ceiling. "I mean B. It was *one* time."

BJ pushed back, his tone swamped with worry. "But you could barely *drive* you was so upset. I *never* seen you like that."

Ashley knew BJ sounded just like her father would if he knew about the incident, so she stayed quiet. Instead, she tap-danced her fingers around the mug. Who the heck would she talk to? Her dad didn't even know. Still, she needed to appease BJ. *I don't want him tweakin' on this foreal.* "Yea, I'll look into it," she finally said. *Maybe I can talk to Grams.*

"Alright. I'm a hold you to it. Yo. Did you get yo car, though? I meant to try to get up early enough to check about that, but I overslept."

"Yeah, I got it. Thanks." Ashley didn't mention that she had Jeremy swoop her from Denise's that morning in his brother's Prius. She didn't like BJ knowing *too* much about her escapades, even though he probably could have guessed. They dropped Denise off at work and then took her to get her car.

"Oh yea? Who took you?" BJ asked, "Cuz I know yo boujee self ain't about to hop on no train."

Man, he all up in my stuff. "Jason," she lied, ignoring the dig at her wealth, but BJ sounded like he didn't believe her.

"Yea. Ok. Just make sure you get somebody to talk to." His voice softened. "I'll check on you later."

Ashley smacked her teeth and hung up before drifting over to the kitchen to pour another cup. She was just thinking about moving to the patio when Natalie entered the room decked in a floral-printed peplum top, fitted navy blue jeans, and pink high heels to boot. *She actually looks nice in her little outfit. But I wouldn't have worn the peplum top over those jeans. It's hiding her butt too much.* Ashley snickered to herself. *With an ass like that, you* have *to flaunt it!*

Of course, Ashley knew there was no use in encouraging her cousin to be a little more revealing, so instead, she chirped, "Ok, cuz'. I see you!" then trotted her eyes over Natalie's physique for good measure. Clusters of hair twisted in the front and fell in thick, buoyant curls down Natalie's neck. A nice nude lip and light blush enhanced her even-toned brown skin, and long, thick lashes dressed her eyelids.

Natalie responded, "Oh yea? Thanks." But she touched her hair with uncertainty while resting against the kitchen island. "You don't think it's too much? I don't usually wear heels like this." She peered down at her shoes and stretched a foot in front of her.

"Naw, girl. I think you look *good*." Ashley threw a dismissive wave. "Besides, they only a few inches. You work in the back, right?"

Natalie nodded. "Yea."

"Well, then, tis' the perks of having an office job." Ashley drank long and hard from her "Diva" mug. "You want a cup?" Without waiting for an answer, she whisked away a mug from the drying rack for Natalie, who took it, before pouring her own.

"I gotta work soon, but wanted to chill for a minute," Natalie explained, squirming onto one of the stools.

"That's wuz up. I was just about to head out to the patio, so..." Ashley wasn't usually interested in spending time with Natalie, but she was too amused by Denise's revelation that her cousin had a little crush. *Now seems like a good time to get the tea.*

"Oh, ok." Natalie responded, "I'll leave you to it," and made a little hand motion as if she were seeing Ashley off.

"I mean. You can come too..." Ashley tilted her head to the patio. That was the closest the girl would get to an invite.

Natalie must have known because she started stammering. "Oh. Yea. That's cool."

Both girls skated through the French glass double doors into a bright, sunny morning. It was much cooler than when Ashley had come out with her dad. "Let me go get a couple of blankets," she offered before resting her mug on the table and traipsing back inside. In no time, she reappeared with two cozy fleeces, one burnt orange and the other navy blue.

She handed Natalie the blue one and got situated in a chair then grew quiet while observing a couple of birds fighting over a piece of bread. *Crazy how even animals fight.* One bird decked the other bird, then flew away with the bread in his beak, leaving the hurt bird to waddle a little before he flew after him. *Only the strong survive.* Ashley clucked her tongue in sympathy and thought about her own childhood events where she had to learn that lesson fast. *Damn Hyenas.*

Natalie cut into Ashley's bird-watching and trip down memory lane. "What you got going on today?"

"Uh, I have an afternoon class and some studying before then." Ashley also had some making up to do with Jason for their missed date at the French spot, but Natalie didn't need to know all that.

"Yea? What class?" Natalie looked over, and Ashley had to fight the desire to switch the subject.

See, that's the trouble when making intimate conversation, she thought. *People want to know about* you. "Design for Beginners," she answered, then turned to face Natalie head-on. *Ok, sweetie, let's get to it.* "So. How *is* working for Devon?"

Natalie's face spread into a grin as she dove into her long tale about how great Devon was to his workers, how great a businessman he was, and how everything he did was just so great!

Ashley bobbed her head up and down with a serious expression, but inwardly, she was cracking up. *I am too weak!* she thought. *Denise is right. Ms. Perfect is* sprung.

"And there's an open mic night coming up I'm helping to plan. I can't wait," Natalie was saying.

"Yea. I've been to those. They're pretty dope." Natalie's eyes brightened even more, and a hint of envy from her evident joy pricked

Ashley's heart. Ashley hadn't liked somebody like that in a long time, and thoughts of Jason surfaced while her cousin kept talking. *I mean, Jason is the freakin' come-up!* Ashley convinced herself. *Who cares about feelings when I would be set for life?*

"My counselor encouraged me to work out more, so I'm going to try this Zumba class," Natalie said.

Wait. Back up. Ms. Perfect has a counselor? "I didn't know you had a counselor," Ashley said while drawing her mug to her face.

"Oh." Natalie appeared surprised and licked her lips. "Yea. She's actually a psychiatrist," she added in a much softer tone, and Ashley focused on keeping her face a vacant mask. "I've been in counseling for a while now..." Natalie looked away as she threaded a few tendrils of hair between her fingertips.

Interesting. Depression. A psychiatrist. Who knew? Ashley chuckled, thinking that her cousin had more issues than she did. But then BJ's voice popped into her head. *You need to talk to somebody, Ash.*

Shoot! Damn boy. Now how is it that he's able to get on my nerves, and he ain't even here? She wrestled in her seat while crossing her legs to stifle her stomach's queasiness.

"Having a counselor can be helpful," Natalie explained. "Even if you're not going through trauma, but especially if you are. My counselor has helped me in a few areas."

Her voice ping-ponged in and out of Ashley's mind, taking turns serving with BJ's and a growing angst in her stomach. *You need to talk to somebody.* BJ's voice repeated like a scratched-up old CD that skipped.

What is *this*? Ashley thought, regarding the growing pit and the disturbing feeling that she was going to have to do something she really didn't want to do. She tried to focus on the conversation and pretend it wasn't messing her up in all kinds of ways. "Oh, yea?" she replied to Natalie. "That's cool."

"Have you ever talked to a counselor?" Natalie's voice was cautious as she sat with her mug to her lips, awaiting a response.

Ashley answered fast, "No," then looked away. *I don't need counseling,* she told herself, but BJ's voice kept skipping. *You need to talk to somebody.* He was pleading with her, and his large, worried brown eyes loomed in her mind. *You need to talk to someone.*

And now *his* voice tag-teamed with Natalie's. *Have you ever seen a counselor?*

Her shoulders deflating from their smugness, Ashley repeated, "No. I've never seen a counselor." She then huffed a sigh with impending defeat as the gentle tug of relent traveled to the forefront of her heart. "But I'm looking for one."

CHAPTER 14

BEING THE ROCK
(NATALIE)

After working a few weeks for Devon, Natalie saw he desperately needed time-management improvement. She knew an air-tight agenda would help with that, but this week, she was struggling to get that for him.

I'm supposed to be typing up his agenda, but I'm so distracted by all the drama from Sunday's dinner. Natalie played with a file folder nearby. *How could Ashley possibly feel unloved?* Mindlessly, she pecked at random keys on the keyboard. *She has her dad,* and *she has Grams right here. That's more than what I've had.* She smacked her teeth in frustration and was staring at the screen of her laptop with blank eyes when Monique stopped by.

"Hey, baby, you almost done with Devon's list?"

Natalie threw an anxious expression to her colleague while pushing out a breath. "Almost. I'm just a little slow today. That's all."

Her round face showered with concern, Monique hustled into the room before easing the door closed. "Oh? You wanna talk about it?" She scooted the chair across from Natalie, promptly invading it with a robust figure and friendly eyes.

Natalie tried to find the right words. Monique's tone was kind, and it would be so nice to confide in someone, but she didn't want to betray her family like that. While trying to get her thoughts together, she drummed her nails on the desk a few times, stalling.

"I guess. It's just some family stuff. I mean, my family is pretty great, but we just aren't that close. You know?"

"Mmhmm." The woman's eyes morphed into two deep pools of understanding.

"I just wonder if me moving here was such a good idea." Natalie's shoulders slumped, bogged down by the weight of her worries. "I mean. I came to get support. But I feel like *I'm* the one supporting."

"Well, sweetheart, I can tell you that there is always *somebody* in the family who is usually the "rock". I'll say that I've been *that* in *my* family. Before me, it was my grandmother."

Hmmm. Grams is definitely the rock. But was Natalie also the rock? At 21 years old?

"But. What happens when the rock needs a rock?" Natalie asked. She plopped back in her chair and patted a hand over her knee-length, black pencil skirt.

"Honey. Jesus is the ultimate Rock, and I can attest to *that*. If you feel weak, then, baby, lean on *Him*."

Her coworker's presence and words oozing compassion reminded Natalie of the faithfulness of God in her life. *I wouldn't even be here at Devon's if not for God providing.* "You're right, Monique. I do know *that*. Thank you for the reminder, though."

"Yep. He is ordering your steps, chil'." Monique stood to give the younger woman a cheery squeeze. "I know this for a fact."

"Really?" Natalie looked doubtful. "How do you know?"

"Because. He brought you to *us*. And Devon for sure needed you."

The warmth emanating from her elder hugged Natalie's heart. "Thank you for your kind words, Monique, but Devon was doing fine without me."

"Oh, child, nonsense. I been workin' for this man for *years*. I know he a good businessman and all, but he *definitely* needed your assistance. I can't tell you how many meetings he had been late to or completely forgotten about or double-booked before you got him together with this here *weekly agenda*." She motioned to Natalie's computer with a short chuckle. "You know how bad it is to leave a potential investor *hanging* because you thought the meeting was at 7 *PM* and it was at 7 *AM*? Girl. It's done happened. And it was *not* a pretty site."

The tip of Natalie's chin grazed her chest from her mouth dropping. "Wow. I didn't know it was that bad."

Monique nodded her thick fro and was about to elaborate when a rapid knock rattled the door. Both ladies' heads turned to see Devon.

"Natalie," he called, "you ready?"

Monique, covering for her, said, "Oh. Can you give her a few minutes? I done took up her time talkin'." Natalie slid her a grateful look.

"Sure. I'm in my office." Devon disappeared as fast as he had entered, and Monique winked.

"I'll let 'chu get to it."

"Thanks, Monique." Natalie felt ten times better since their talk. "For everything."

Monique smiled before grabbing the doorknob, her full, brown face aglow like a chocolate-covered angel's. "Anytime, honey."

After her conversation with Monique, the ability to work flowed, and Natalie's concentration was restored. She found Devon in his office working on his PC.

He rewarded her with a friendly, professional smile but was clearly in his zone, as evidenced by the small creases lingering on his forehead. "We're preparing for our monthly open mic night that I told you about," Devon started. "As a result, we have a lot of arrangements we need to go over, which you'll only need to be concerned with once a month." His eyes burned with intensity, and Natalie sat poised while balancing her laptop on her lap as he spoke.

"Also, I've been asked to do an interview with a friend of mine, Lisa Doris. She's a journalist for *Jazz* Magazine and wants to do a piece on Devon's. This has been a while in the making and seems to *finally be* happening." Devon's smile was broad. "The open mics have been popular, but I'm hoping this move with the article in *Jazz* will increase revenue to back up some other ideas I have." His face was saturated with animation, and with the energy of a stick of dynamite, he started juggling a stress ball.

"Oh yea?" Natalie was curious. "Like what?"

"I would love to create a line dance night. I got a friend who's a DJ, and I think people would enjoy the idea of a safe place to move around in. Without all the drama. You know?" He looked at her as if for approval, and Natalie nodded in adamant agreement.

Doll's Rink has a line dance night now. This could be a great replacement for what I know *I'm missing back home.* She continued stroking keys on her laptop while her brain buzzed.

Devon's excitement was contagious as he talked, and his words were a magnet, drawing her into his vision for the future. "The problem is, my schedule has been so chaotic. I haven't had time to sit down and figure something out with Lisa. The one time we did have something scheduled, I accidentally forgot about the meeting." He hung his head in embarrassment. "And it's been on the back burner ever since." Stopping in his tracks, Devon gripped the ball with four fingers and pointed to her with the other. It was as if Natalie were his most important employee. "And that's where you come in."

Wow! This is so dope. While hitting computer keys as fast as Devon talked, she stole a second to admire him. He was clad in a stark blue blazer stitched smartly over a white T nestled inside stone-washed jeans. The cloth dressed his legs to perfection while classic, clean, all-white Nike sneakers wrapped each foot.

Business casual with a touch of swag. Natalie held back an appreciative smile but couldn't keep her eyes from loitering on Devon's nut-brown skin.

"Since you've been able to get my schedule for the whole month, which is something *I've* never been able to do, by the way, I want you to call Lisa and schedule the interview." Devon's instructions directed Natalie back to attention as he engaged in an urgent pacing back and forth behind his desk. "Then I want you to work with Monique to contact the suppliers and ensure we have enough inventory. Normally this is *her* job, but I'll need your help with this every month for the open mics. Ok?" Devon turned to her while in mid-pace, making sure she understood what he needed.

Natalie piped back, "Yep, I got it." And she did. Everything was in her notes, strategically organized from most important to least.

"Great. I appreciate your hard work, Natalie." Devon smiled and was handling the stress ball again when his cell phone rang. Without hesitating, he took the call. "Hello. You want me to help out with that?" His voice softened to an almost tender tone. He sounded affectionate, so Natalie sharpened her ear to the conversation. "Ok. I can do that." Devon looked at his calendar and pecked on his phone keys before adding in a consoling tone, "It's going to be ok. Trust me. I got it." He was practically choking the cell with every word, and it seemed like whoever was on the other end was upset by his attempt to calm them. Another pause. "Debra. Don't worry about it. I got it. I can be there."

When he ended the call, he threw Natalie an apologetic glance, but all she was thinking was, *Who is Debra?*

"Sorry about that." Devon drilled a few more notes into his phone, then laid it on his desk, only to pick it up seconds later. Mumbling, he held up a finger as he typed. "I also need to call Deacon Carlton about Sunday." His brows furrowed in concentration with the chiseling of more notes.

"Oh. Do you go to church often?" Natalie didn't want it to sound like she was prying, but interest pricked her heart at the possibility that Devon was a churchgoer. *Maybe he's a Believer too.*

"Yep. *New Life* is a great place to worship! Very diverse and non-denominational." Her boss's eyes shined with pride before he fell into his seat and slipped his phone back onto his desk.

"Nice. I had a really good church back home. It's been hard to find something similar here, though," she confided.

Devon's eyes illuminated in interest. "Really? Well, you can visit *us.* The word is good and sound, and the people are genuine."

"That would be great. I mean, I'd love to." Natalie resumed writing Devon's directives and included his church's name and address in her notes. *I'll check out their website later.*

"So. Outside of church, how you been adjusting since your move from, uh, Philly, right?" Devon eyed her with thought, and Natalie was touched by his regard.

"I mean, I definitely could go for a cheesesteak," she chuckled, only half kidding. "But honestly? It's been a little difficult in the social department." *Wow. I can't believe I said that. But Devon is so easygoing. I always feel relaxed with him.*

Devon appeared surprised. "Aww. Come *on*. An attractive, intelligent, *talented* woman like you?" He tilted his head to the side, pointing at her and saying, "I highly doubt it," then offered the most charming grin Natalie had ever seen.

I have to be blushing right now. "Well. When you put it *that* way…" Natalie made her face completely serious when speaking but broke into a smile. "What is *wrong* with the rest of the world? I mean, clearly, it's not *me*." She was joking to lighten things but mainly to calm her own attraction.

Devon laughed. "*Exactly.* I *know* there will be brothas waiting around the corner tryna take you out."

"Shoot, when I get home, I'm probably gone' see the line outside," she shot back, and his eyes sparkled.

"You are somethin' else." The look Devon gave her made her insides move. "Well what do you like to do for fun?"

Devon's voice had deepened and was thicker than usual, and Natalie could have sworn he had never looked at her quite this way before. If he had, she hadn't noticed.

"The usual," she answered. "I went to dinner and a movie recently——"

Devon sat up in his seat. "Now, *see*. I told you you had dudes."

"With my *uncle*," she finished, laughing and closing her laptop. *I guess this meeting is over.*

"Ok. Ok." Holding up his hands in concession, Devon said, "but I'm surprised to hear it." His brown eyes pierced hers, and after a moment, Natalie had to look away.

"And what about 'chu, Devon?" she finally asked. "I'm sure your social life is poppin'."

He smiled. "I would say it hasn't been *poppin'* for a while now." He checked behind her, making sure the office door was closed. "I took a break from dating to focus on my business goals."

Interesting. Natalie nodded, studying him even more, and Devon seemed to be doing the same. Silence reached with long, wide arms, filling every inch of the room, and all Natalie could hear was her own heartbeat.

"Well. I think I have it all," she managed, breaking their shared moment. "I'm gonna head out and start working on these items tomorrow." *If I don't leave now, I know I'll embarrass myself.*

"Oh? Uh, yea," Devon stammered. He seemed to be trying to clear his head while sinking back into his office chair. "Sounds good," he added, but the smile he gave wasn't quite as large as before.

Did he want me to stay? Natalie was uncertain but packed her things to be safe. She was almost at the door when Devon's voice beckoned to her.

"I meant to tell you, Nat. You look really nice today." The look in his eyes exuded an appreciation Natalie knew wasn't appropriate for him to express in the office, and she couldn't hold back her grin.

Postured in the doorway in her heels and peplum top, she replied, "I was hoping you would say that," then left fast, afraid of his response. But the question of the hour lingered in her psyche. *Who is Debra?*

With a mix of giddy intrigue, Natalie headed to her office, tucked away her files, then glanced around the newly decorated space. The windows were styled with crisp white curtains, and a small pot of lavender adorned the sill, an influence from her time with Celia. Natalie knew the importance of her mental health, and lavender had a great calming effect. An abstract gray and white 5'x8" rug gave the space a more "homey" feel, reminding her of her old living room with her mom. Additionally, she had brought in a few books from her collection and buried them inside three white 8"x 8" floating shelves nailed to the wall.

"Let me not forget my journal," Natalie murmured and hurried to retrieve it from the sanctity of her desk drawer. "I definitely don't want to leave that." She had brought it today, thinking she'd have time during lunch to work on some poetry for her blog. After cradling all of her belongings, she made a beeline to the restroom and was surprised to see Denise hanging out in the mirror.

"Hey, girl. Thought you'd be gone by now." The waitress gazed over while twisting a chunky lock in the air. She slathered on some white gook from a miscellaneous container on the sink, then rubbed it in profusely, proceeding to pin the yarn of hair like a tiara to the crown of her head.

"Yea, me too. But Devon had some last-minute items for me to review." Natalie pitched her coat and bag on the chair in the restroom before sliding into one of the two stalls.

"Oh yea? He's probably gearing you up for the open mic this month, huh?"

"Yep. He is," Natalie called through the stall door. "I'm super excited too. It sounds like a good time!" She checked her texts and saw that Jaida had reached out asking when she was free. *Hmmm. Maybe I'll give her a call,* she was thinking when some rumblings emerged from outside of the stall.

"You know, girl, you should let me hook you up with some of my hair moisturizing product. I got this dope new line that adds extra moisture and holds in all the water so your hair follicles don't run dry. You can go *weeks* without washing using this stuff."

Natalie thought about it. Even though Denise's hair was all the way goals, she wasn't at ease at the thought of trying other people's homemade remedies. She had just read "The Other Black Girl" and knew you couldn't just be putting *anything* in your hair.

"Oh. Uh. My hair is super sensitive to different products. I have to watch what I'm putting in it," Natalie explained. "But thanks, though." While swiping through her Instagram, her eyes lit up. *Devon's following me!* With a joker's grin, she followed him back, then skimmed his page in excitement, searching for *anyone* who looked like they could be a Debra. *I wonder if Jaida would do a search for me?* But then she thought, I *don't need him figuring out I'm cyber stalking him.*

By the time Natalie exited, Denise was leaning near the chair stuffed with Natalie's things at an awkward angle. Her tub of hair cream was neatly tucked inside the pocket of one arm. Seeing Natalie, her head jerked upward.

"I meant to tell you, sis," Denise raved with a weird smile. "You look super cute today!"

The vibe was off, but Natalie didn't know why. "Thanks. I figured I would do a little something different." She turned on the faucet to wash her hands, but still felt "off."

"Yea. It's working, sis, for sure. I mean, I probably wouldn't have covered up those jeans like that. But you know. Next time." Denise winked, and Natalie laughed.

"Well. I wouldn't feel comfortable in a shorter top…" Letting her sentence hang, Natalie moved to retrieve her things.

"One day, we gone' get you to cross over to the wild side." Denise cradled Natalie's lower back while holding the door open, and Natalie chuckled again.

"You never know…" She threw on her coat and hooked her back-pack over her shoulder but couldn't shake the odd feeling that something was wrong. *Denise is always friendly, but not this friendly.*

Still, Natalie had to meet Darren and didn't have time to focus on the strange experience. She and Darren had reserved a room at the main branch of the New York Public Library to study for an upcoming quiz in their writing class. Natalie pushed through the swinging door after passing by the kitchen, and the smell of coffee brewed with the sound of chatter permeated her senses. Servers bustled around while people were scattered on stools at the bar and tables. "Comfortable" by H.E.R painted the airwaves.

I love Devon's! The thought sprung out of Natalie's being, and she couldn't help but cheese the whole time to the subway. She was so thankful for finding this place, and her bank account was grateful too. *Now I can pay back that loan I took from Linda last month.*

Swarmed by the after-work crowd, she snagged a seat on the D train and inhaled the recycled air. There were so many people, it always felt as if her breath was being swapped with someone else's. Once seated, she dialed Jaida.

"Hey! Was thinking about you," Natalie said when her friend picked up.

"Yea. I wasn't sure what your schedule was. I think you worked today, right?"

"Yep. Just came from work. I'm on my way to meet up with a, uh, friend to study." Natalie wrinkled her nose at the onslaught of various bodily odors that mashed the inside of the subway, then glanced to her left at an older man with a toupee.

"Cool. So. How *is* work?"

"Great. My boss is nice. He's an entrepreneur. He's super kind and caring. And I'm learning a lot." Natalie paused, smiling to herself. *Should I tell her I'm interested in Devon?*

"Mhmm," Jaida responded. "Sounds like there's more to this story with this boss."

Natalie could just see Jaida's teasing eyes on the other end. "Dag. I barely said two words about him." She marveled. "How can you say that?"

"Girl. We been friends since we were kids. I know you, Nat. Now, give me the deets. I want to hear all about this super cute boss Devon, the entrepreneur!"

Natalie chuckled. "I said nothing about what he looked like. I just said he was nice."

"Mhmm. But he is cute, though. Right?"

Smiling from ear to ear, Natalie whipped her head from side to side, accidentally bumping Mr. Toupee with her movements. He pitched her a heated glance that she brushed off as a New Yorker's standard facial expression.

"Yea. He is," she answered and proceeded to tell Jaida about the things stirring in her heart toward Devon. Talking to her friend was like wearing her favorite sweater. The conversation was just what Natalie needed, and they were able to catch up a lot by the time she reached her stop.

"Ok. So this next phone call, I got to hear about this friend you meeting to study with, cuz it sounds like it's something there too!" Jaida analyzed.

Man, how does she do it? Natalie laughed, impressed. "Girl. That's a whole *other* story. But I'll call you later for sure."

Natalie found Darren already seated in the room they had reserved and dove into her reading after greeting him. They had been studying for a good two hours when she realized she was no longer comprehending the material. Darren begged her to call it quits, so reluctantly, she walked with him out the door into the chilly evening air. When a mean breeze hit, she clutched her scarf around her neck.

"Come on. Let's walk a little," Darren suggested.

Natalie was tired. It had been a long day, and she was tempted to just go home, but she remembered her counselor's encouragement about exercise. *I could probably use the extra walk.* "Ok." She started to swing her bag on her back, but Darren held out his hand to remove the weight and Natalie felt grateful that she had a friend to help her.

As they strolled side-by-side, he said, "Yo. I was thinking about going to this spot this weekend if you interested."

"Yea? What spot?"

"It's a kid-friendly spot. They do performances and stuff. This weekend, they doin' a play." He led them around the corner from the library, his profile shimmering in the dim lighting of the streetlamps.

"Hmmm. That sounds cool." Natalie kept her hands hidden in her pockets. It was getting colder by the second. "What's the play about?"

"Look. Do you have to know everything?" Darren looked at her in exasperation. "Can't I just surprise you?"

Natalie felt bad. *I am a super planner.*

"So, if you down, I have an extra ticket," he continued.

She was silent. *Is going to a kid-friendly spot a date?* "Well... I don't think that's a good idea." They passed a few storefronts, and Natalie was glad she had Darren with her. There were some sketchy-looking guys in front of one of the stores. She knew they would try to say something to her if she was alone, but Darren had this air of manhood about him. Even though he *was* kind of a pretty boy in her opinion, he still gave off the impression that he could hold his own.

"Yea. I know you think it's sus. But honestly, I invited a *few* people." Darren added, "So. It's not just gone' be me and you."

Hmmm. Well... maybe if it's not just us. "Ok. I mean, as long as it's a *group* thing," she emphasized and could see Darren's face beaming, even in the moonlight.

"Bet! Come on. Let's turn down here." He motioned to a nearby alley between a closed beverage store and a women's boutique.

Natalie halted, folding both arms in front of her. "What? Boy, I'm not goin' down no alley with you." She looked at him like he was crazy.

"What? You don't trust me?" Darren whipped his hand over his heart, a hurt expression clouding his mocha-brown face.

He even has the nerve to sound *hurt,* she thought, tickled. "It isn't that. But it's pretty dark. I think we should be gettin' back." Natalie glanced around, and though she didn't see anyone in sight, her mind started racing. *What if those guys come by and jump us, and I was wrong about Darren's ability to hold his own?* She toggled her weight from one foot to the other, entertaining all kinds of scary scenarios.

"Come *on*. I wanna show you something." Darren sounded excited as he snatched her arm and dragged her into the alley.

Natalie mumbled, speeding up her pace. "Hmph. Ok. But I'm running if we get jumped."

Darren only laughed. "Girl, I got 'chu. *Chill*." When he held onto her a little longer than necessary, Natalie didn't mind. She felt safer that way. Even when he let go, she stayed near him as they walked.

In the alley, there were a few trash cans and a homeless guy parked on top of a bed of crates. Darren drew out his cell phone, using the flashlight app to aim it at one of the walls, and the homeless guy grumbled, "Hey!" while shielding his eyes at the onslaught of brightness. He flipped over on the crates like a rotisserie chicken on a skewer, wagging his back to his visitors.

"Sorry, sir," Natalie breathed an apology, but her eyes bulged as she focused on what Darren was pointing at. "Ohhhh!" All kinds of pictures were painted on the wall depicting the creativity of several street artists. "*Wow*!" she said in wonder as they kept walking. "This is fire."

Darren steadied his phone on the wall so she could see better. "Yea. I know, right." Pleased, he watched her face convert from worry to amazement. Before them was a woman with an afro nursing her child in one hand and throwing the other into a balled-up fist.

"This one makes me think of feminine energy and strength," Natalie shared. She stared in awe.

"Yea. My boy Kingston did that one," Darren said with a proud nod. "He was inspired by his baby mama."

"Wow. You know the artist?" Natalie was impressed, and he winked at her in the dim lighting.

"Yep. Some of 'em."

The next one portrayed an older man building a store. A long line of pre-existing customers was waiting. "This one makes me think of the importance of Black-owned businesses," she said, and they both gaped in admiration. "It makes me think of Devon's."

"Yea? How is that goin', by the way?" Darren turned to her, and a faint smile graced her lips.

"Really good. I mean, it's a lot of work, but I really like the people there." Natalie choked her coat more tightly around her as a breeze met them, and her long, thick twists fluttered upon its arrival. "And the money is right on time," she added.

Darren laughed. "That's wuz up." He started maneuvering the blown strands of hair from her face. She caught his hand, but he brushed hers away until he completed his mission to put her hair back into place. Natalie's heart skipped a beat. Without a word, Darren showed her to the next painting.

Natalie was enjoying walking down the alley and seeing so many demonstrations of Black art in an unexpected area, but it wasn't until they neared the end that she was totally speechless. Facing her was a mural displaying a woman with caramel skin; long, thick, wavy hair; beautiful brown eyes; and a smile that induced any passerby to want to live in it. She stood by the ocean, hair blowing wildly in the wind and arms outstretched in unparalleled beauty. A peaceful smile rested upon her full rose-colored lips.

Wow. She looks just like she did in my dream. Murmuring and inching to the wall, Natalie smoothed her fingers over the bricks as if she could somehow touch the woman herself. "I can't believe this." Aiming the flashlight from her own phone illuminated more of the design. Darren was beside her, still shining his light, but his presence barely registered, and a deep devour of every detail of the woman kicked Natalie's heart into overdrive. Her smile. Her eyes. Her skin. It was all so *accurate*!

"Yea," Darren whispered. He had been watching her reaction. "Ashley did it." His voice took on a touch of tenderness when he spoke, and Natalie caught it, along with the emotion in his eyes.

Still, she stayed silent. She would never have guessed her cousin was *that* talented.

Swallowing over the lump in her throat, Natalie tore her arm away from the mural and turned to Darren

"I know," she said with tears staining her pretty brown face. "It's my Aunt Patty."

CHAPTER 15

FUN ON A STICK

(ASHLEY)

At last, it was the weekend, and Ashley was looking forward to her date tonight with Jason, especially because they hadn't had as much quality time as she would have wanted since, in her opinion, he studied too much. She knew he was going to ask her if they could be official tonight because he kept alluding to it in their recent conversations on the phone. Saying things like, "Yea, we been on this thing for a minute now," and, "I'm at a point in my life where I want more stability with a woman."

I'm so ready to be yours, Jason Marcellas! With a swift roll to her backside, Ashley peeked at her phone and flicked through her texts. Her jaw slammed to the floor in surprise.

"What?!" A series of messages from Denise flooded through detailing scandalous pictures of Natalie's diary. Apparently, her friend sent them last night, but Ashley had been working on the extra credit assignment from Professor Simone. She hadn't checked her phone for fear of losing ammunition. Now she kind of wished she had at least taken a break.

Oh shit! Eyes the size of bowling balls, she inhaled the information with the speed of a corvette before dialing. "Girl. How the hell did you get her freakin' diary?" Ashley went stiff against the blush-colored velvet headboard, her mouth propping all the way open.

Denise's chuckle was more like a shriek of glee. "I told you I got yo back, homie. I copped it while she was in the bathroom yesterday. I called you like three times last night, but yo ass was MIA. Let me guess. You was with Jeremy?"

"Actually, I was doing schoolwork, believe it or not." Amazement seized Ashley again as she made a "pshh" sound. "Damn. I can't believe you got her diary. I tried looking for it a minute ago and couldn't find it."

"That's cuz you not as smooth as me."

"Whatev." Ashley slapped the ceiling with her eyes at her friend's cockiness. "But girl, the pages you sent me is cray-zee. I mean, I *definitely* didn't know all that."

"Right. Natalie got a lot going on. So. I guess Ms. Perfect ain't so perfect after all, huh?"

"Facts. You got me tweakin' fa real." Ashley flickered her fingers back to the images detailing Natalie's diary entries. *Hmmm. They're dated about a year ago.*

"Anyways, homie, I gotta get back to work," Denise's voice broke Ashley's examination. "I had to run to the bathroom to pick up cuz I figured you was gone' trip on the texts I sent at some point. I'll call you later though."

"Later." An unsettling sensation tumbled around the core of Ashley's abdomen as she sat slightly dazed. *It's crazy. Cuz all this time, I been after getting rid of Natalie, and now that I got some dirt, I ain't even trippin' on her like that.* A flashback of Ashley and Natalie's walk after her outburst at Grams's dinner sailed past her mind's eye.

It was like she was actually there for me that day. Like a real friend. Kind of like the way we were before that summer. Ashley's stomach continued doing gymnastics, but a knock at the partially-open door tore through her thoughts.

"Hey, Ash." Her father pitched his head inside, already dressed and peering at her with a smile. "You up?"

She flipped her phone face-down on her lap as if he would somehow be able to read its contents. "Good morning, Daddy. Yep."

"Good. Natalie made breakfast. You want to join us on the patio?"

An unexpected warmth swaddled Ashley's heart. "Yea. That's cool. I'll be right down." But as she slipped on her robe and slippers, she mulled over the information she had received from Denise, and an uneasy feeling escorted her all the way downstairs. By the time Ashley hit the kitchen, Natalie had just finished cooking.

"Good morning!" Her cousin's smile was genuine as she hovered over bacon sizzling in a skillet, decked in a pair of flannel PJs. She plopped a couple of pieces down on a plate with a joyous two-step.

Ashley couldn't remember the last time somebody had cooked a real meal in their house. "You made breakfast?" she asked, for lack of anything else to say. Not knowing how to respond to the act of kindness, she glided towards the island in her Chanels and made a job of rubbing sleep out of her eyes.

"Yep," Natalie replied in a sweet tone. "Your dad's already out on the patio. I was gonna bring him a plate." She resumed sliding the omelets on all three glass plates before pouring a cup of coffee, then swiped some napkins from the table.

Ashley offered, "I'll get dad's plate," and shuffled a few steps forward. "And don't worry about cleaning up. I got it."

"Oh. Ok." Natalie looked surprised but ceased wiping down the counter. She then handed over Malcolm's plate before confiscating her own.

Straddling one dish in each hand, Ashley shadowed her cousin through the sparkling-clean double French doors to the patio, courtesy of the cleaning lady who came in once a month. The cobblestone flooring caressed Ashley's slippers, and a soothing calm saturated her when the morning's cool air kissed her face. *Wow. It feels like... I'm being...* She searched for the word. *Hugged.* The encounter was almost holy, and she waded for a few seconds in the moment.

"This looks great!" Malcolm boasted. His happy smile added to Ashley's experience, and she smiled back, handing him his plate.

It's been a while since I've seen him this happy. I wonder if it's the Samantha chick?

Natalie sat, but Ashley went inside to retrieve blankets for the three of them. Ashley couldn't ignore the sensation bubbling in her heart as the trio grew quiet while eating. It had been a while since she had felt it, and it took her a moment to pinpoint the feeling. Gnawing on her strip of hickory smoked bacon and studying the clouds floating in the sky, she inhaled, then exhaled. It finally dawned on her what it was exactly that she was experiencing.

It's peace! And along with that realization, Ashley knew deep in her heart that she couldn't use the information she'd gained from Natalie's diary. Because she also realized that the very peace she was now experiencing in her home had come through her.

After a grueling run with BJ (this time, he had them do six whole miles), Ashley checked her Apple watch. "Hey. Why don't we go to a movie instead?" she spoke into the watch, then told it to send the message to Jason. She really wasn't in the mood to do anything high-maintenance. Ashley actually enjoyed being low-key sometimes, and having breakfast with her father and cousin reminded her of that.

BJ hopped on the train to run some errands for his mom, so she fished inside her leather Coach fanny pack for her key fob and slid into the warm climate of her vehicle. It was freezing out, but Ashley was cool as long as she was moving. When her car let her know she had an incoming text, her finger collided with the button on the dash.

The mechanical, reticent voice resounded through the BlueTooth speaker. "I'm actually looking forward to the art museum."

Dag. Jason wants to do the art museum. An annoyed sigh burst from her lips. *I guess I'll have to take one for the team. Especially if I'm going to lock this in tonight.* Ashley was still trying to make it up to Jason for standing him up at the French restaurant. He didn't seem too upset about it, but she knew her timeline of him committing to something permanent was dwindling. Nervousness pounced on her abs.

I need to get this boy and fast. I'm not really in the mood to get my hair done, but there's no way I'm 'bout to be half-stepping at this art museum. Ashley had moved her appointment to Saturday because of her date tonight. She wanted her locks fresh for when she and Jason became official. *Besides, I don't think Jason has ever* not *seen me bringin' it.* And really, none of her guys had. Just Darren.

But I was younger and naive then. Jerking her head out of her reverie, Ashley floored the gas, tackling the George Washington bridge and bulldozing through aggressive drivers in every lane. The radio was set on Neo Soul to mirror the mood she was in today.

"Maybe it's the fall weather," she murmured with a somewhat somber expression. When she took her exit, brightly colored leaves whisked by, triggering memories of picking similar leaves with her mother. They had loved creating projects with them, whether it was a poster Ashley could hang on the fridge or a picture frame they stashed in her dad's home office. That's where Ashley got her creative gift; her mother was an artist.

"But she never got to shine the way she should have," Ashley spat with a bitter frown while weaving through the residential streets. *She never got to go where I know she would have gone with her art, especially in NYC.* With eyes piercing the windshield, Ashley's honey-hued skin heated up, and anger tagged along for the rest of the ride, eventually punctuating at an empty house. After breakfast, everyone had disappeared into their own thing.

As loneliness fermented with fury danced through Ashley's mind, it became more and more difficult to catch her breath. *Mom. I just don't understand why you had to leave so soon,* she thought, her chest heaving while working to get air into her lungs. *I needed you!* Ashley shook herself upright, practicing the breathing techniques she had looked up online. *Deep inhale, Ash. Come on.* Sputtering waves of oxygen crept in, but it wasn't enough.

Maybe I should call BJ. But she dismissed that idea as fast as it occurred. *I can't keep calling him. And I don't want him worrying.* The leather from the steering wheel scraped into the grooves of each palm from her tightened grip as she concentrated hard on the garage door in the driveway. Willful, intentional breaths wrestled to escape Ashley's lips, but she caught a glimpse of Old Mr. Roberts bent at an angle over his garden, and that served as a good distraction. He no doubt was diligently massaging his precious snapdragons.

I guess if I needed to, I could honk and get his attention, Ashley thought between tiny gasps of air. *But how ironic if Old Mr. Roberts ends up saving me if I pass out? And this dude looks like he could keel over at any moment!* Even in her difficult time, Ashley found laughter.

When her breathing was finally under control, she remembered the counselor information Natalie had given her. *I guess now is as good a time as ever.* Before she could change her mind, Ashley tapped a sparkling, pointy fingernail onto her phone's keypad and scrolled to "Regina Caldwell-Healing Hearts Counseling." When the voicemail picked up, she left a brief message asking for a callback to schedule an appointment.

Well, at least she sounds Black. And with a name like Regina, she may even be a little hip. A light-hearted chuckle tickled Ashley as she hustled from the car, now able to fully inhale. She felt better that she had taken some sort of action in that regard and was even more relieved that Old Mr. Roberts wasn't going to have to be her savior.

Now short on time, she dashed to the bathroom and stripped, promptly bathing beneath the rainfall massage shower for a 20-minute run. Emerging from the steam with baby-smooth skin, Ashley dusted the fog off the oval mirror above her double sink and assessed her reflection.

I mean, I wish my boobs were just a size or two bigger. And maybe my ass could use a little bit of something extra. She swiveled around so that her butt was seen in the mirror and craned her neck behind. *But other than that, I'm gucci.*

Smoothing a towel over her curves, she floated to her walk-in closet with newfound confidence. *Jason is all mine.* "Alexa, play BIA," she commanded, and the music throbbed. Ashley was Vanna White, running her hands through a series of sweaters, blouses, and shirts in a walk-in closet that was exceptionally divided by styles. Nightlife clothes hung in one section, academic gear in another, and chill apparel in another. And then, within each of these sections, items were segregated into seasons. But then came the absolute best part: her shoes. Boots, stilettos, sneakers, flats, pumps, and more all dressed the walls, each inhabiting their own quarters. Another nook gripped her accessories, such as scarves and hats, while an assortment of jewelry congregated within a handmade wooden jewelry armoire. Her father had bid on the armoire at an auction his colleague was hosting. It was an antique.

Ashley settled on a pair of black leggings, an oversized pink Nike hoodie, and a light blue Ralph Lauren jean jacket. She decided, *I'll change after I get my hair done*, and shimmied on her quilted Guess leather black boots. While tossing on the final touches, a text dinged, and with a swift glance, she ripped her phone off the dresser. *Grams.*

"Hey, honey. You going to the salon today? I was thinking I might catch you there."

Grams is the biggest texter I know and the woman is 70 years old! A soft smile invaded Ashley's cheeks. **"Yes, ma'am,"** she responded. **"My appointment is at 2."**

"Great. How about we get lunch after? I'll be done around 4."

Pleasure bungee jumped its way down Ashley's spine. *Man, what is up with the fam? All of a sudden, people want to be around each other.* She started calculating her meet up time with Jason while figuring if she could get ready for him that fast. **"Can we do 3:30? I have evening plans."**

"Baby," Grams replied, **"I don't think I'll be ready by then, but I'll try."**

Ashley said 'ok' and continued getting dressed. It was 1:30 when she left, and she just made it to the salon on time. Tamra had her wait a little, and she ended up finishing around 3:45 PM herself. She was supposed to meet Jason at 7 PM. Rooted in the salon's waiting area, Ashley flipped the page in the Ebony magazine she had swiped. Drake was rumored to be dating Megan Thee Stallion.

Puh. Yeah right! She scoffed in disbelief while circling her eyes, but then thought about it again. *I mean, even though he a little corny, he's still fine... Shoot, get it, Megan!*

"Hi, honey," Grams greeted her in her typical jubilant tone, and Ashley hoisted the magazine back onto the coffee table. **"So glad you were available."**

"Hey, Grams. Ok! I see you, Grams! Who you tryna impress out here in these streetz?" Folding her grandmother into a hug, Ashley drew back to take her in. The older woman blushed and pushed her away with a slight turn of her head.

"Oh, stop, honey. I mean, I *am* meeting Mr. Wilson later. But, you know..." Twirling her body at an angle, Grams posed in her peach pants suit and low tan heels, all aglow with thick bouncy curls masking her round face.

Grams is fly! Ashley smiled with affection and steered her grandmother toward the exit. "Oh. Mr. Wilson, huh? Well, you'll have to tell me all about *him* at lunch."

"Y'all have a good day now!" the secretary called, and the two Bennetts turned back to reply, "You too!" in perfect unison.

When they neared the door, Ashley whispered to her grandmother. "Grams, what is that woman's *name?*"

"Oh, sweetie. It's Shelly." Grams's Manolo Blahnik heels led the way while trotting on the sidewalk, and Ashley laughed in relief.

Shelly, she repeated over and over. *That's crazy I never paid attention before. I need to remember that.*

They walked side-by-side to her truck as Ashley's smile blanketed her whole face from being in her grandmother's presence. As they drove, Grams wouldn't allow her "new school music," as she called it, so Ashley had a playlist ready and waiting labeled "Grams." Marvin Gaye crooned in Ashley's truck, and Grams crooned too. By the time they were at the restaurant, Ashley was singing her favorite songs right along with her.

I forgot how fun Grams is.

As Ashley hopped to the passenger side to help her out of the vehicle, Grams announced, "Now *that's* when music was *real* music!"

Ashley grabbed the overstuffed white and peach-colored purse, spouting, "Yea. Ok, Grams," and the two ambled inside the large Chicken & Waffles establishment. The restaurant was packed with noisy conversation and frenzied activity, but not as crazy as it would be the next day during the after-church crowd. Ashley hardly ever went there, but it was Grams's favorite, so she indulged her.

"Now, Grams. I know you love soul food," Ashley started after they were seated. "But really, you gotta watch your cholesterol."

"Hmmm? Oh, honey, I'm *fine*." Grams circled a hand in the air before swooping up a menu and licking her lips. She added with a toothy grin, "Chil', they ain't *made* the pork chop that could take *me* out." Ashley shook her head in surrender while popping open her menu.

"What can I get 'chu ladies?" A young, Godiva-chocolate-looking brother addressed them with a pad and pen. His teeth, white as winter's snow, were set in perfect succession beneath skin that sparkled like fireworks on the Fourth of July.

Damn, he is fine! Perking up, Ashley quickened in her seat, coiling a finger of intrigue around a loose thread of hair. *I'm glad I just got my hair done.* She was rocking a wavier style for the fall season and had Tamra layer it, sprinkling in highlights. *But I wish I wasn't in these damn sweats,* she thought, staring up at Mr. Fine.

"Um. I'll have water to start and a regular coffee," Grams answered. "But my granddaughter will have you, sir, on a stick." Grams said the last statement with a completely straight face, and Ashley's own all but burned like a forest fire.

Her eyes incredulous, she chastised her grandmother. "Grams!" Ashley was horrified, but the waiter only released a hearty laugh.

"You *do* come on the menu. Don't you?" Grams's expression was still dead serious, and if Ashley wasn't so embarrassed, she would have been highly entertained. Instead, she glared at the table, wishing it would swallow her whole.

"No, ma'am. I don't," the waiter replied with a small, flattered chuckle, taking it in stride, "but I can suggest a few things that do."

He probably hears this shit all the time. Ashley was still too afraid to make eye contact and buried her face in her menu, her nose brushing against it.

"Oh, he know I'm playin', Ash. Don't be such a stick in the mud!" Grams sprinkled a thick hand over Ashley's menu to get her attention and guffawed. "Don't 'chu know I'm playin', er, uh...?" She squinted at his name tag. "Steve."

Steve laughed and replied, "Yes, ma'am. Hehe. It's fine." Steve folded both palms over his apron, flexing the immaculate muscular definition of his arms.

My God. Ashley couldn't help but think. *Excellent workmanship.* She laughed internally and, mustering up the nerve to make eye contact, told Steve she would have water to start. She then added that she and her loose-tongued grandmother would need a minute with their order.

"Sounds good. I'll be right back." Steve's tone was professional, but his eyes were teasing when they met hers. They even seemed to linger before he turned away.

"Now, Grams. You can't just go around tellin' people stuff like that," Ashley reprimanded as soon as Steve was out of earshot. Leaning over the table, she spoke in rapid, low tones, as worry stenciled her face. "These days, you could get sued for sexual harassment. Ever heard of the 'Me Too Movement'? It may be for women, but I'm sure there's one for guys too."

"Oh, honey, hush. I have discernment! That boy was checkin' you out *way* before we even sat down. Trust me. I was helpin' *you* out." Grams danced her hand in the air in dismissal and proceeded to study the menu. "I saw him eyein' you when we was waitin' to be seated," she added with a huff, and Ashley marveled.

Whaaaat? Grams got game? Ashley sat back in her seat to study her grandmother. Grams was older but vibrated with so much youth. *I'm glad to have this time with her.* Browsing her menu, Ashley decided on the chicken and waffles. Why not? She had her run this morning. And as Steve returned to take their order, another tantalizing thought popped into her mind. She envisioned Steve with his chocolate self, slathered down in baby oil, skin sweet as apple cider, chest bare, on a stick.

CHAPTER 16

BURGERS, DUDES & PLAYS

(NATALIE)

Natalie was already in a good mood this morning, which had inspired her to make breakfast for the family, but Ashley's receptiveness was the buttercream icing on the cake.

On her way to Devon's, she thought in amazement, *Lord. You're really moving with her. Wonders never cease!* She shimmied in between two women on the New Jersey Transit. One had silver curls that rivaled the bounciness of Grams's locks. The other was decades younger, straddling a toddler in her overladen arms.

And now, she's even open to therapy. I'm sure that will help her process whatever her issue is. While thinking about the promises of God manifesting in her life, Natalie's heart swelled. Moving to Jersey had been such a leap of faith, but now everything was coming together. Cranking up the volume to her morning worship playlist on her iPhone, she piped along internally with Elevation Church all the way to Penn Station.

By the time Natalie reached her second stop, she was immersed in absolute peace and joy. It was in this state that she entered the soothing ambiance she was easily falling in love with.

"Hey, sis!" Denise was her typical upbeat self, and Natalie found it a comforting familiarity, but then, that same strange feeling touched her soul.

With a confused frown, she disregarded it. "Hey, Denise."

Denise had sauntered over in her work apron and balanced a tray like a pro, her goddess-like locks conducted into a half updo. "You look *nice*!" Denise piped.

"Yea? Thanks." *Hmm. I feel like she's being extra again.* Natalie peered down at her burnt-orange sunset utility skirt and oversized cream sweater beneath her open peacoat. *I'm not even dressed up all like that.* But before she could figure out what was going on with Denise, Alice appeared.

"Hey, Natalie."

Natalie turned her attention to the quiet server while Denise went to assist a customer.

She had connected with Alice a few times at work and found they had a lot in common. The waitress was a few years older, an aspiring writer, and lived with a cousin who was a struggling model. Her literary agent had just submitted a few query letters for her first completed manuscript to several well-known publishing companies.

Maybe she can help me with some of my writing goals, Natalie had pondered after one of their conversations, inclusive of their shared passion. Ending their short chat with a warm wave, Natalie headed to the door to the staff offices where Devon was putting away dishes.

When he saw her, he broke into an easy smile. "Natalie, good morning!"

Natalie's lips seemed to have a mind of their own as she beamed back, then she straddled a giddy arm on the glistening mahogany counter, just to be closer. "Morning, Devon. How are things?"

"Busy as always. But that's how I like it." Devon gave a light chuckle while wiping some plates set out by the cook. "I didn't know you were coming in this early."

"Yep. I decided to get some work done since I was free. That's ok, right?" Concern wrinkled Natalie's syrupy brown face.

"Of course. I told you. You can work the hours *you* need as long as the tasks *I* need get done," he assured her.

"Great. Just wanted to make sure. Talk to you later." Smiling, Natalie thrust the door open to the back, counting her lucky stars again that she had found this position.

After a quick check-in with Monique, she traipsed into her office and sidled into her chair, swiveling, before turning on her PC. *Now. What's first?* she thought, eyeing her planner. *Ahhh.* Devon's interview with Lisa Doris, the journalist for *Jazz.* Since it was Saturday, she sent an email in addition to a voicemail, marking off the item on her planner with a flick of her wrist. The rest of the morning consisted of reviewing emails, organizing files, and entering Devon's financial transactions into his accounting system.

This brother is so behind. Natalie frowned while keying in his expenses for the month into QuickBooks. When she finally got a handle on Devon's bookkeeping, she made much-needed calls to vendors and placed the orders Monique had given her for the upcoming open mic.

At noon, Natalie called it quits. While releasing a sharp, well-earned sigh, her eyes settled on the portrait on her desk. She and her mom were featured together at Christmas two years prior, wearing matching white sweaters and large bright smiles. Cancer lurked in the shadows, only revealed by the tender drooping of her mother's eyes and the dark circles from restless nights that no amount of makeup could hide. Mrs. Greene hovered behind with both hands-on Natalie's shoulders, simultaneously protective and nurturing.

Natalie's mom loved Christmas. Every year, she would go all out to decorate the house. Even their pet rabbit, JoJo, would get a stocking full of toys and treats. Some of Natalie's favorite memories were picking out the tree and the smell of maple pine that saturated their home. But nothing compared to helping her mom bake Grams's Christmas cookies from scratch every Christmas Eve. Natalie would cuddle up next to her mom with JoJo on her lap while Mrs. Greene read the story of Christ's birth directly from the Bible. They were a small and intimate family, but they always had each other.

Natalie caressed the frame with a sad smile and a tender finger, thinking there would be no more Christmases. *I miss you, Mama.* As sorrow dug deep roots into her heart, she wondered if the tentacles would ever be removed. Even JoJo passed away shortly after her mom died.

Plunging her head into both palms at her desk, Natalie prayed.

Lord. Help me through this. One lone tear seeped out, but she didn't bother with it. She was too weighed down by a hurt that trembled through her lips with each word. The soft vibration from her phone halted her prayer. Darren had texted. He was checking in to make sure she would be available for the surprise play tonight.

"Yep. I'll be there," Natalie responded then flung her hand over her cheek to wipe it.

There was also a missed message from Jaida, who had sent a picture of her and Trisha. They wanted to know when she was free for a group video call.

Natalie texted back, **"Maybe tomorrow evening"**. *I guess there's hope for my friends after all,* she thought with a watery smile, then peered at the picture through fond eyes. A few minutes later, she was packing her things when Devon snuck his head inside the partially open doorway.

"Hey there." His cheery tone perked Natalie's heart even more, along with his attractive smile. "How are things?"

Ok, God, I see You! Natalie chuckled, recognizing that God was operating through the people in her life as she struggled with grief. She tossed her phone on her desk before responding, not wanting Devon to think she hadn't been working. "Great. Just finishing up for the day."

"Oh, yea? Cool. A few of us are going to lunch if you wanna join," he offered.

Lunch with Devon? Yes, please! In an attempt to look more casual, Natalie half-shrugged. "Ok. That would be great."

"Awesome. Meet us out front when you're ready."

When Devon left, Natalie exited her computer systems faster than a sprinter running a 100-meter dash. She was so excited she almost left her phone, but doubled back to snatch it off the desk. *God, You sure move fast,* she thought, thankful for the community he had given her in the midst of her grief and pain.

The burger joint in SoHo that Devon took his staff to was in full force. There was a half-hour wait for a table, so Natalie and her coworkers chilled at the counter with shakes. She was perched on Devon's left while Monique and Alvin sat on his other side, knee-deep in conversation. Due to their seating arrangement, Natalie could only catch bits and pieces of it over the crowd. Something about who was the better blind artist, Stevie Wonder or Ray Charles?

Looking over her menu, she angled her body towards Devon's. "What do you suggest?" she asked. He was sitting so close that their legs grazed. She tried not to notice but knew nothing in the world could make her budge.

Devon's eyes goaded her. "Are you a big appetite kinda girl?"

"Depends. If I'm hungry, I can eat. But otherwise, I can get by," she admitted.

"Ah. Then you probably can't hang with what *I* normally get." Devon smiled with faux arrogance before taking a copious gulp of his chocolate shake.

Natalie toyed with the spoon in her vanilla one, encased in a 1960s tall glass that she had only seen on reruns her mom watched, like "Happy Days." "Oh, yea? What's that?" She bobbed her head to "The Twist," currently playing in the throwback restaurant.

"I love the Chubby Checker Double Decker burger." Devon chucked his chin at the name on the menu, and her eyes followed his lead.

"Are all the burgers named after music artists?" Further down the menu, there were other artists' names Natalie recognized. *But who are The Four Tops?*

"Some. But, girl, I bet 'chu don't even know who Chubby Checker is." Devon was wagging his head with amused eyes. "Shoot. *I* barely know," he said with an adorable half-smile.

Natalie's look was coy as she cocked her neck to the side. "Don't ever underestimate what I know, Devon." She pointed at the speaker in the ceiling. "Isn't he playing right now?" They both glanced upward and listened to the lyrics from the classic hit.

Devon sat back with an impressed stare. "Ok. I see you, Ms. Natalie Greene." He grinned a grin that could melt her in a New York winter snowstorm.

Natalie smiled, thanking Grams in her mind for playing her oldies when she and her mom were visiting. "Do you really see me, Devon?" Natalie asked. Her tone came out light and airy, but Devon licked his lips in response. Silence ensued. Feeling unsure, Natalie tugged on her shirt sleeve and started wrestling out of her peacoat. Had she overstepped her bounds?

When Devon stood to help, she thanked him, but her almond eyes played hide and seek from his gaze. Devon was still standing when she draped the coat over the red-top stool and sat. "Yea, Natalie," he uttered in a low tone. "I see you." His eyes indicated he wanted to say more, but instead, he sat and drank from his shake.

Natalie's heart flew to her chest. *Lord. Help me with my feelings for this man.*

When Devon turned back to watch her, his forehead was creased the same way it always was when he was working on something important.

I wonder what he's thinking?

"Hey, y'all." Monique's voice was a knife slicing into their intimate gaze. "The table's ready," she chirped, showing off the buzzer flashing little red lights in her hand. The group confiscated their belongings before a young, ebony-toned woman with the name tag "Latisha" glided over on roller skates. Devon took up the rear, pressing his palm against the small of Natalie's lower back and they formed a train after Latisha.

"I meant to tell you earlier," he whispered as their group kept moving, "you look really nice today."

A rush of delight slid down Natalie's spine, and the tiny hairs on her neck tingled in pleasure. Shifting, she indulged him with a smile, then followed Monique to their seat. *I guess Denise was right about this outfit,* Natalie thought, her cheeks warm the whole way there. *I do look good.*

That evening, Natalie sifted through her tumultuous feelings surrounding Darren. His surprise play started at 8:30 PM, but her indecision on whether or not she should even be going motivated her to study just a little longer than she had intended. It was 8:15 PM now.

If Ashley knew where I was going, would she be pissed? Natalie slammed closed the psychology book on her bed before sliding it into the bookshelf. *Is it really a date if Darren is inviting other people?* She swiped her wallet and keys from her desk and shoved them into her purse with the strength of a football player. But the real question, the one Natalie wasn't even sure she had an answer to, plagued the fringes of her mind. *Do I like Darren?*

These thoughts stirred around like a marshmallow in a cup of hot chocolate. Thoughts that eventually intertwined with thoughts about Devon. Darren, Devon. Devon, Darren. During their work lunch outing, Natalie had a little more time to hang out with Devon, and he invited her to church in the morning. She was looking forward to getting to know him better outside of work, but she was still unsure if he was interested.

"Yea, there's been some flirting here and there," she murmured, "but that's about it." Natalie glanced at the mirror and patted a springy lock of hair into place. Her do' was cute and curly, but she had to sit under the dryer for two whole hours to get the look she wanted.

I wonder what Jaida would tell me to do about Darren? But then she chuckled. Natalie could hear Jaida's voice now.

"Date 'em both!"

"You comin'?" Darren's text provoked Natalie to move faster as she snatched her jacket, scarf, and handbag.

Locking the outside door to the house with the swiftness of a panther, she replied, **"On my way"**.

During the commute, Natalie entered into a boxing match with her fears. *This is platonic,* she recited. *Darren is a friend.* And, more importantly, *I* need *a social life.* Speed-walking to the building, Natalie decided that Darren *was* just a friend *and* that she had successfully won the fear match. At least—this round.

Drawing closer to the entrance, she tightened her coat, peering up at the 'Martin Luther King Jr. School of the Performing Arts' sign overhead. *A performing arts school?* A thin line slid across her forehead as she crept inside the propped-open door with caution. Her eyes darted around the unfamiliar building.

"Hello!" a pimply-faced teenage girl with braces manning the table by the auditorium called out. "You gotta ticket?"

Natalie stumbled. "Oh. Uh. No. I…" *Darren didn't mention a ticket.* She started to text him but froze at the sound of his voice.

Darren appeared at the table sporting a Cheshire cat's grin. "It's cool. She's with me."

Surprised, Natalie gazed at him. Donning a black Polo sweatshirt, dark denims, and the latest Yeezy's, he had a platinum chain dangling around his neck with a sparkling crucifix. "Hey." Her lips curved into a small smile as she opted for a half hug, thinking that was safe. Even still, the scent of male intimacy lingered. One inhale and Natalie went right back into the boxing ring. *We're just friends!* she told herself adamantly.

Darren slid a ticket to the young girl and turned to Natalie with excitement mounting in his dirty brown eyes. "Glad you made it. Follow me. Our seats are near the middle." He grabbed her hand to guide her, and darkness met them both until the spotlight revealed kids over-flowing the stage in costumes and reciting lines.

His surprise was a middle school play? Natalie was humored but also just a little warm inside. As she tailed Darren along their row, she tried not to step on anyone's toes. The two weaved in and out of strangers' legs in the dark lighting before being swallowed whole by empty seats.

Darren whispered, "That's my brother." He pointed to a kid whose face was slathered in muddy brown paint and a stark black nose. A tall, pointy hat flopped happily on his head as strands of straw stuck out. More straw emerged from his arms and legs from a bulky costume that made him look rounder than he probably was.

Natalie whispered back, "Is he the Scarecrow?" Her eyes drizzled with intrigue. On cue, Darren's brother Eric staggered to the front of the stage near a leggy, slender girl who must have been Dorothy before he broke into song and dance.

Eric belted lyrics from "Ease on Down the Road" in a beautiful, soulful voice, giving Michael Jackson a run for his money.

Natalie flashed a broad smile and hopped around in her seat to shrug off her coat. *This kid is amazing!* She caught Darren's eye as he helped, and his own face was a map of pure, unadulterated joy. *Every-one's so talented,* she thought and marveled the rest of the show.

"Yay! Get it, baby!" When Eric took the stage to bow, a woman on the other side of Darren jumped to her feet and yelled like nobody's business.

Darren's mom is here? Natalie tried not to stare when the lights popped on.

Darren looked over with a pleased expression. "What'd you think?" he asked, sliding from his chair.

Natalie also stood. She raved, "It was great! I grew up off The Wiz. I wish I had seen the beginning." A smidge of regret surfaced as she followed her row into the aisle with Darren just seconds behind. The crowd ballooned into the hallway, smooshing the duo even closer, until a stream of folks surrounded them on each side like a parting of the Red Sea. Natalie tried to back up a little to create some distance, but it was a tough feat, given the size of the crowd.

"Ma. Aunt Sue. Uncle Leonard. I want you to meet Natalie." Darren pointed to an older man and two women shadowing him, one of which she recognized as the woman feverishly applauding Darren's brother.

Mrs. Ellis greeted Natalie with a cordial shake and easy smile while his aunt and uncle chucked their chins in unison. Trying not to freak out, Natalie responded with a polite, "Hello." Darren's mom was tall and slender, and her eyes crinkled in the corners the same way her Uncle Malcolm's did. Natalie decided that Darren must look like his father and peered at him with large eyes. *I can't believe he has me meeting his family!*

Darren must have noticed her concern because he stroked her lower back, then tackled it with a soft nudge. "Let's go to the back and wait for Eric," he directed. His hand was still in position as the group headed down another hallway where a slew of middle schoolers were exiting. Kids of all shapes and sizes, mostly in costumes, chatted in enthusiasm with their loved ones. Smoothly untangling herself from Darren's grip, Natalie hung back while the others circled Eric.

"Hey, big man." Darren stooped to give his little brother a high-five. "You did great!"

Eric jumped and smacked his hand with the aggression of a linebacker. "Thanks, bro!"

Natalie could tell his little face was grinning even under all the face paint. She smiled.

Mrs. Ellis removed Eric's hat, then smoothed a hand over his intricate cornrows. She promptly imprinted a sloppy kiss on his cheek, tattooing her ruby-red lipstick all over it. Eric's eyes flashed around to see if anyone had witnessed the horrible transgression. He scrubbed with intensity, saying "Aww, Ma!" and made a puking face. Everyone laughed.

Squeezing his brother on the victimized cheek, Darren chided, "Boy, you ain't too big for all that yet," and play-shoved him.

Eric puffed out his chest. "Yea I am!"

A sweet chuckle escaped Natalie's lips. *They seem like such a nice family,* she thought, and longing stole her heart.

Eric looked at his mom with wide, pleading eyes. "Ma. Can we cop a pie?"

"Yeah. I guess. Since you did so good tonight, baby." Mrs. Ellis draped one arm around him, and the group started towards the exit.

"Wait y'all. Let's get a pic," Darren announced. He found Natalie with his eyes and pumped his hand back and forth for her to join them.

"Ok. I can take it for you," she suggested, already extending an open palm.

Darren stared at her like she was being silly. "Naw. I want you in it." Everyone was watching, and Natalie felt bad saying 'No,' so she let him scoop her up into the family photo. For ten long seconds, she was squeezed like a lemon between Darren and Uncle Leonard.

"Now let's do one with just us," Darren demanded, but Natalie whipped her curls back and forth with extra force.

"I don't know, Darren." But again, she didn't want to make a scene. His whole family was there, and how awkward would that be for her to keep saying "No"?

Darren cocked his neck. "Don't be such a lame. We out having a good time. Come *on.*"

He's right. We are having a good time. Natalie's resolve sank fast, and it seemed like all eyes were on them as Darren took the selfie.

"Okaayyyy. *Now* can we get some food?" Eric begged.

"Yea, yea." Darren patted him on the neck, and the group ambled outside. Darren's aunt and uncle sped up a few feet, accompanied by his mom and brother, while he and Natalie strolled side by side. A feisty breeze traveled with them.

"Where are the other people you invited?" Natalie gazed at Darren over the rim of her plaid scarf and rubbed her hands together. *It's freezing!*

Darren grinned and pointed at his family. "You met 'em."

She clucked her tongue in disbelief. "Oh my God. You are the worst. I'm the only friend you invited?" She shot him a suspicious side-eye.

Darren led her to his car, then opened the door on the passenger side, his voice growing husky. For a moment, Natalie was frozen more by his tone than the weather. "Natalie, you're the only one I wanted to be here."

"Darren. I meant it when I said we are *just* friends." But her own voice was soft and unsure.

Instantly, his tone lightened. "Girl, chill. We just goin' for a pie with the fam." He proceeded to help her into his Tangier Orange Chevy Silverado adorned with jet-black tinted windows. "*Friends* do that, you know," he added before shutting the door with her inside.

Natalie sighed. *I guess...* When Darren drove and turned on jazz, she smiled in surprise. "You listen to jazz?"

"What? You didn't think I was cultured?" An insulted expression outlined his profile in the evening light. "You think I only got Travis Scott and Pop Smoke on my playlist?"

Uhhh... Yea, she thought, having no idea who either of those artists were. But instead of starting an argument, or at least a very passionate discussion, Natalie sat back to enjoy the ride.

The seats were heated, and it was so relaxing she felt like she could fall asleep as the gentle vibration of the car rocked her. One minute, her eyes were droopy, and the next, Darren was tickling her.

"Oh! My! God!" she cried out between laughs. "Please! Stop!" Darren howled in glee before letting up and huffing a few times. Natalie straightened her clothes, her face now a wet blanket of tears. "You're ridiculous," she grumbled, but her lips betrayed her with a silly smile, and she couldn't be too mad.

"Hey. That's the rules, Ms. Greene. You sleep in my car, you pay the consequences." Humor stained Darren's chocolate eyes. "But come on. We here." He extended a hand to help her, but when their fingers kissed, the reality of being out with him jolted her, and Natalie re-entered the boxing ring.

Am I really ok to be doing this? Her stomach expelled a loud, embarrassing sound and became the referee to her fears.

"I see *somebody's* hungry!" In true Darren fashion, he wasn't about to let her get away with the uncomfortable moment.

Instead of responding, Natalie took his hand. They were within walking distance of John's Pizzeria, and the potent pizza fragrance whooshed down the street, tempting her nose. *Well, I gotta eat.*

Darren's family was already seated in a booth in the corner, and Natalie gave everyone a polite smile while sliding in next to him. Their butts had barely warmed the black plastic booth when Eric asked, "This yo new girl, D?" Though he had taken off his costume, he still had his face paint on.

Extreme embarrassment rushed Natalie. With a startled tone, she declared, "No," a little too loudly.

"No, E," Darren echoed within seconds while pitching his brother a stern look. "We *just* friends."

Eric responded, "Yea. Fa now," and whipped his head back in rambunctious laughter.

Mrs. Ellis rebuked her son, first with her eyes, then with her tone. "Boy, stay outta grown folks' business." She peered at Natalie with an apologetic shrug. "I'm sorry, honey. He's 13..."

"Oh. No problem, Mrs. Ellis. I get it." Natalie ducked behind her menu, studying it with unrivaled intensity. *Hmmm, meat lovers sounds good...*

"Natalie. How did you get your hair so pretty and curly like that?" Darren's aunt's voice invaded her focus on the assorted pizza options. "I tried goin' natural two years ago, and sis, I couldn't do it! I gave up after I broke the *second* comb." She stared in wonder at Natalie's mane, then laughed good and hard, her large chest heaving up and down with each giggle.

Natalie's palm slid from her menu to her hair. "Oh. Uh. I used this product by Shea Moisture when I blow-dried it and did a perm rod set."

She offered while making a face, "I had to sit under the dryer for a while, though."

"Ooh, girl. You gone' have to show me *that*." Darren's aunt fingered her hair, which resembled a long, thick wig with a cute brimmed hat covering the top. Donning a frown of disgust, the older woman added, "I just can't seem to get this mess under control."

"Definitely. I'll send you a few YouTubes," Natalie volunteered while shedding her coat to get more comfortable. When Darren leaned over to help, their legs touched, so she scooted away a few inches.

The rest of the evening flew by as Natalie enjoyed getting to know Darren's loved ones. They were a beautiful family, just as she figured, but she wondered if his father was in the picture.

While driving back and vibing to the sounds of Daniel Caesar, Darren said, "I hope you had fun tonight."

If Natalie was tired before, she was exhausted now as a few slices of meat lovers pizza swam into the deep end of her belly. Rubbing her full stomach, she smiled with contentment in the warm vehicle. "I did," she said, surprised. "Thanks. I needed this."

He looked her over. "Yea. I know."

"What do you mean?" She glanced at him. "How did you know?"

Darren shrugged a nonchalant shoulder. "I know you haven't had it easy, Natalie. And yea, I like you, but believe it or not, I care about 'chu and respect you too. That means I want what's best for you." His brows raised in sincerity. "I want to be here for you. In whatever way you'll let me."

Natalie was quiet. *If I'm honest with myself, I am fond of Darren. And I know I could probably date him. But I also think God has other plans.* "I appreciate you saying that." She hesitated, hoping she wasn't being too nosy. "There *is* something I've been wanting to ask you though..."

Darren's eyes shifted to her, then back to the road. "Ok."

"What happened with you and Ashley?"

Before answering, he drummed his fingers a few times on the steering wheel. "Yea. I kinda figured that's where this was headed." They rode in silence until he parked near the train station on 7th avenue.

Turning in his seat to face her, he plopped an arm on the steering wheel for support.

"Ashley was my first love. And honestly, I'll probably always have a deep affection for her." He puffed out a short sigh. "But we were young. When we got involved, we were still growing into the people we're kinda still becoming. You know?" Darren seemed thoughtful and a little vulnerable when he made the last statement, and Natalie was surprised at his depth.

"Go on," she said, studying his expression.

"To be honest, I outgrew her." While brushing a few fingertips over his chin, he thought back. "I mean, when we first hooked up, Ashley was everything I wanted. She was gorgeous, fun, funny, and exciting. And then, when I got to know her, there were these amazing gifts she had, like her art and her loyalty to the people she's close to. But then I saw this hardness there. This bitterness at life. And I guess our focuses changed. She was all about this material crap." He lifted his chain before plopping it back onto his chest. "And honestly, I'm over it. I grew up with it. And it's not all it's cracked up to be."

Natalie stayed quiet, listening. For a moment, Darren stared out the window before his words tumbled into the vehicle. When he spoke again, his voice held a slight edge to it. "You wanna know where my dad was tonight, Nat?" She nodded, knowing that he wasn't even watching her, but feeling a need to respond anyway. "He was at *work*." The word must have left a bad taste in his mouth because he spit it out fast. "He's *always* at work." Darren hung his head, his shoulders deflating from their usual cockiness as he fiddled with his leather jacket zipper. Up and down. Up and down. He zipped and unzipped until he spoke again.

"Can you imagine living yo whole life and you grind, and you get all this crap, but you miss out on the most important part? Which is your family? Your loved ones? Your *blood*?" Looking at her, he swallowed with a tightened jaw. "I don't want to do that." Darren's eyes cried out with his voice, both playing a vengeful tug of war with her emotions.

Natalie wet her lips before speaking and chose her words with care. Even though her voice was soft, her words were weighty. "Yea. I get it. There's a scripture that says you can gain the whole world but lose your own soul."* Running her eyes along his profile in the moonlight, she studied Darren's face. Natalie knew that face all too well. *He's broken with grief.*

"That's exactly it, Natalie," Darren said, finally meeting her eyes. "And that's what Ashley *wants*. She wants a man who is willing to lose his own soul."

*Mathew 16:26

CHAPTER 17

DATE NIGHT

(ASHLEY)

"Graaams. I'm just sayin'. I wish he hadn't brought that heffa to our dinner. It makes no freakin' sense." After a fun-filled afternoon, Ashley ranted by the salon near her grandmother's car. Following lunch (and after she got Steve-the-waiter's number), they took a rideshare to Madison Avenue and browsed a few boutiques. Shopping bags from Tiffany's, Prada, Gucci, and the like exploded in her hands from their little excursion.

"Honey. I understand how you feel, but you have to realize your father is a person too. He needs love and affection too. And not just the platonic kind." Ashley's grandmother threw her a knowing look, and a vivid memory of Ashley climbing into her lap as a child resurfaced.

When did that stop? she wondered with longing. *And can we go back?* "Grams. I get it. I'm just sayin'. I feel like he should have slowed it down. He really was doing the most, bringing Samantha to meet the whole family. I mean, who the heck is this woman really to be up around our family like that? As if we don't have enough of our own issues. " A few women entering the salon with scarves, bonnets, and everything in between to masquerade their new growth and rough edges caught her attention.

Grams's hand crawled on top of Ashley's shoulder in concern.

"Baby," Grams said, "we not always gone' do the right things. But know that those who love you never intend to hurt you." Leaning over, she caressed Ashley's cheek with a soft kiss, and Ashley bit the inside of her mouth in thought.

Maybe Grams was right. Maybe her dad didn't intend to hurt her. *Him bringing Samantha to that dinner was still thoughtless as hell, though.* Without a response, Ashley began feeding packages into Grams's red Buick Envision.

The older woman tucked herself into the driver's seat, cheery and bright-eyed. "Honey, we need to do this again!"

"Yes, ma'am." *I definitely need to make more time for her going forward.* Ashley hit Grams with one last peck on the cheek through the car window and watched her take off before navigating to her truck. With a launched foot off the running board, she sat inside and, almost as an afterthought, glanced at the dash. She almost screamed. *It's 6:15 PM! When did it get to be after 6 o'clock? Shit. I'm gonna be late.* Ashley all but yelled into her car speaker, "Siri, text Jason!" while racing from the salon.

"Jason. I'm going to be late. Let's do 7:30," she spit into the Blue-Tooth. She was supposed to meet Jason at his friend's in Hoboken, and if she could get there by then, then *maybe* they could get to the art museum around 8 PM. *I hope he's cool with that.* She caught herself and snatched the nail from her mouth just as her cell rang. Worry stormed her eyes as her voice became a jumble of nerves.

"I'm so sorry, I got caught up with my grandmother shopping after the hair salon, but I *promise* I'm on my way home and should be there in the next 20 minutes." She spoke so fast that it all came out as one statement.

"Ashley. I got tickets for the Belle da Costa Greene exhibit at the Morgan Library & Museum." Jason's voice was tense. "It *starts* at 7:30 PM."

Uh oh. "Can we just see the other exhibits then? Maybe they can give you your money back?" Lowering her foot on the gas, Ashley increased her speed.

"I bought these as a surprise for *you*," Jason continued, this time with an element of hurt in his voice. "I was gonna surprise you."

For a split second, she felt like a jerk. *But it's a valid reason I'm giving him. It's not like I just blew him off.* "Jason. I didn't do it on purpose," she said, her words now defensive. "I didn't know you had a surprise planned. My grandmother wanted to spend time with me." How was it *her* fault he had a surprise planned? And who was Belle da Costa Greene anyway?

"Yea. OK. Well. I'm taking somebody else. I ain't got time for this."

"What? You takin' somebody else? Fine. Do what 'chu gotta do." Ashley hung up without another word. *I can't believe this fool. I can't believe I was doin' all this shit for him. Trying to make this work.* Switching gears, she headed to Devon's since Denise was getting off soon.

"Maybe she'll want to go out tonight," she murmured while perusing her Instagram between stops. There were several notifications as she swiped through her DMs at a traffic light. "Any one of these brothas would be tryna kick it tonight."

Oh! Ashley suddenly remembered Steve, the young waiter from earlier that day. A half-hour later, she was parked near Devon's, shooting Steve a text before climbing out of her vehicle. She strutted into the cafe with newfound confidence. *On to plan B.*

"Hey, sis," Ashley greeted Alice, the quiet one, while trying to hide the frown on her face. *The chick could use some freakin' makeup.* "Is Denise here?" Alice peered at her while adjusting her thick lenses. *Or at least get some frames that fit.* This time Ashley wasn't able to conceal her frown.

"Yea. I think she's in the back. You want me to get her?" Alice's tone was strained as she balanced a tray crowned with dirty mugs. But even though the waitress appeared overwhelmed, she was willing to do it. That was good enough for Ashley.

Ashley smiled at Alice in a way she hoped was friendly enough. "Could you? That would be great." Alice serviced a customer before going to the back while Ashley occupied one of the free stools at the bar. She got comfortable and threw her crossbody Michael Kors leather bag over one side of her body as Devon poured a cup of coffee for the old guy next to her.

"Hey, Devon," she greeted.

"Hey. How are you?" Devon's response was polite, although Ashley knew he probably didn't even know her name. Only that she was "Denise's friend." And now, maybe, "Natalie's cousin." His smile was pleasant enough, and his kindness seemed sincere, but Ashley had never really talked to Devon all like that. Mostly because she didn't have a need for him.

I could see why cuz' likes him, though, she thought, trotting two keen eyes down his physique. Low black fade with a gray streak. Nice build. Nice little butt. *Not that Natalie had probably noticed.* Ashley chuckled hard at the thought and swept her eyes over his ring finger. It was bare.

"Doin' OK. Mind if I get a regular?" She tilted her head to the side and tossed a flirty smile his way. *Might as well see where he is in the dating world.* But if Devon found Ashley attractive, he kept it to himself.

"Oh, of course." He hustled to pour her some coffee with heaps of cream and sugar before setting it on the counter. Devon was all business.

Ashley rolled her eyes while taking the mug. *Straight up square.*

Shortly after, Denise popped out of the back of the cafe with Alice in tow. "Girl. I didn't know you was comin' by." She propped a hand on her hip, her face a mask of confusion. "Uhhhh... actually, don't 'chu have a date?"

Ashley's face turned impish as she swiveled around. "Yea. That... I had a change in plans." With a half-smile, she lifted the mug upward, letting the steam tickle her top lip.

Denise grinned. "Oh? Change in plans?" Her eyes grew questioning. "I guess that means you dropped Jason after you realized you still in love with—"

Ashley cut her off. "Ain't nobody in love with nobody." Her voice was stern as her eyes said, "You bet not say his name". At that moment, the vibration from her phone stole her attention, and she grabbed it with eager fingers, followed by an even more eager grin. *Steve is in!* "But I do have a new boo I'm tryna check out. Wanna turn up tonight?"

Denise peeked at Devon and spoke in a low volume, even though her boss had moved to the other side of the counter. "What time? I get off at eight."

"Cool. We'll make it after nine. I gotta get home and change anyway." Ashley indicated her sweats and took another sip.

"Yea? That's wuz up. I'll invite BJ."

Ashley raised an arched brow in surprise. "Oh? So you makin' a move, huh?"

Denise shrugged. "More like *he* made a move. We hung out a few nights ago," she revealed with a teasing smile.

Ashley was shocked. "Since when? And how come nobody told *me*?"

"We ain't gotta tell you *everything*. Anyways. Let me know what 'chu got planned, and I'll let *him* know."

A weird sensation buzzed in Ashley's belly. Her two best friends dating? It was fine in theory, but where did that leave her with getting all their attention in real life? *Hmmm. I don't know how I feel about this.* But she didn't have time for all that. The more immediate problem was having a date tonight herself. *Nobody is about to drop me and I be sittin' at home alone on a freakin' Saturday night,* she thought as she finished her coffee and Denise returned to work. Not Ashley Janae Bennett!

Ashley and her friends settled on a show that started at 10:00 PM. Some action/comedy mix, and she was glad because she still didn't feel like getting all glammed up.

Still, Steve needs to know I got something more than what he could see earlier in those sweats. She slipped on an emerald green cashmere turtleneck bodysuit and squeezed into her best-fitted high-waisted Valentino jeans. Her knee-high Burberry rain boots were stunning with the emerald. It wasn't raining, but they were so cute Ashley couldn't resist. Searching her armoire, she recruited a long gold necklace with a single pearl on the end, then viewed her reflection while starting on her makeup. *Almost perfect.*

"Going somewhere?" Natalie hovered against the door frame, a long turquoise cardigan falling nicely over a white V-neck T and skinny jeans. Her hair was a voluminous field of wild curls, and Ashley was shocked by how great it looked. She tried not to stare.

I guess going natural isn't so bad. With a pivot back to her reflection, Ashley replied, "Yep. Meeting some friends for a movie. What about 'chu?"

Natalie murmured, "Um. Yea. Meeting a friend for a play." Fidgeting some in the doorway, she looked uncomfortable as hell.

What's her *deal?* But whatever it was, Ashley figured it couldn't be too serious. It was Saturday night, and from what she knew, her cousin wasn't dating. *She's probably just pining over Devon, wishing her friend Alice wasn't her date tonight. Speaking of Devon...*

"I saw your boss earlier today," Ashley announced, slanting her eyes in the mirror to catch Natalie's response. "He was definitely filling out those Levi's." Her cousin's eyes ballooned into golf balls, and Ashley chuckled so hard she almost messed up her eyeliner.

"Ashley, you're ridiculous."

"Oh, come *on*. You can't tell me you ain't had the chance to check out his package all that time working in the back office with him." She busted out laughing at the blatant shock on Natalie's face. "I know *I* couldn't be trusted to be working back there with him."

"Definitely *not!*" If Natalie had been lighter-skinned, her face would have been as red as a tomato, and Ashley was weak. "I can't believe you."

"Oh, now, I'm just messin' with you. I know you don't get down like that." Ashley resumed her primping by brushing the highlighter on her cheeks in long, even strokes. It eventually blended in with her foundation and gave that nice glow she was looking for. "So. What play you going to see?"

"Actually, I'm not sure." Natalie nibbled a little on her bottom lip, then shoved her hands deep into her back pockets while flipping up the cardigan. "It's a surprise."

"A surprise, huh? Well, if it's a dude, he likes you," Ashley remarked offhandedly. She was thinking of Jason and the surprise he had for *her*. The one she blew, and now he was mad.

"Yea? Why you say that?" Natalie didn't look too happy to hear this. She slid to the middle of the entryway with her brown knee-high boots set a few feet apart and rocked her hips from side to side.

Ashley shrugged, self-interested eyes glued to her reflection. "Cuz. A guy is only going to put effort into a girl if he really likes her. Or, he could just be playin' games and makin' her *think* he likes her." She wrinkled her nose, thinking about it. "Either way, he put in effort." Applying her rose-colored lip gloss to pursed lips, she rubbed them back and forth.

"Hmmm. Well. I'm gonna let 'chu go." A worried expression now accompanied Natalie's cute hair. "Have fun," she mumbled before making her escape.

Why she look like that? Ashley wondered. *Strange.* But her cousin *was* strange. After she got all into Jesus, she changed. While cleaning up the mess she'd made at her vanity, Ashley started reminiscing. Growing up, she had always looked up to Natalie, even though her cousin was only older by a few months. In kid-time, that felt like at least a good year.

She used to be a good time. I mean, before she played me. But Ashley swatted away the memories from summer camp and The Hyenas like an annoying fly on a hot summer day. Reaching for her leather jacket, she poured some contents into her bag and grabbed her Birkin before heading outside.

Maybe this is a new start between us, though. Maybe we really can *start over.* The cool air hit her like a Mack truck, so she tightened her thick gray wool scarf, careful not to smudge her makeup, then texted her friends that she was on her way. Steve was cool with meeting at the theater since they had just met that day, which was great. This little foursome would be a good situation for Ashley to get to know him without the pressure of a one-on-one.

Also, BJ can check him out, she decided while backing out of the driveway. *He may just be the new Jason.* Jason. Ashley was still pissed that he played her but was determined he would not have her brooding all night in her feelings. She then noticed Natalie leaving the house and locking up the door behind her. *Guess her little play is starting soon.* Ashley veered off the street in one fell swoop and by the time she reached the theater, she felt totally optimistic about the evening. But when Denise strutted towards her, linked hand in hand with BJ, she had to regroup.

"Hey, girl!"

Ashley gave herself a mini pep talk, *OK. Your best friends are dating.*

Get it together, then rocked her best Colgate smile. Waving, she replied, "Wuz up?" Still, she had to fight to unglue her eyes from their entwined limbs.

"Wuz good?" BJ pumped his chin towards her one good time.

"Not much with *me,*" she said, "but I see *you* boo'd up." But Ashley's teasing smile didn't quite meet her eyes.

"Yea, yea. Whatev. So where yo boy at?"

"He already inside. *And* he got the tickets. Looks like he's a keeper." Ashley's laugh was a bit too loud while she tried to compensate for her inner weirdness. Joining the pair, they trotted to the entrance where Steve waited like a faithful puppy dog.

He cleans up nice. Smoothing her tongue over an appreciative smile, Ashley was now eager for some companionship of her own. "Hey there," she crooned. And just as she knew he would, Steve swallowed her into his arms. After disentangling herself from 'Fine on a Stick,' as Ashley and Denise were now calling Steve, she made the proper introductions.

On their way to the screening room, his hand found hers. "You look good," Steve said.

"Thanks!" Smiling wide, Ashley flipped her tresses over one shoulder. *I'm so glad I kept that appointment with Tam,* she thought for the second time that day, but seconds later, her smile scurried. Standing in the line for popcorn was Jeremy's roommate, Case. He was posted next to some skinny, tacky-looking girl hanging on his arm. Not that he was much to look at himself. *What's he doin' in Yonkers?*

Unsure if Case had seen her, Ashley jerked her head in the other direction, the process causing her to tug onto Steve more tightly. He smiled, thinking she was flirting. Ignoring him, she sped up to get by the concession stand unseen. Steve trailed along, oblivious to her change in behavior, while BJ and Denise were several feet behind, lost in their own rendition of "Love Jones."

After they were seated, Ashley peeked at Steve in the dim lighting. His black sweater clung to the muscles she'd caught a glimpse of earlier that day and complemented a pair of cold-blue pants and black Timberlands. She sniffed the sweet fragrance of his aftershave.

"You want popcorn?" Steve asked, looking at her like she was dessert.

"Naw, I'm good." Falling back into her chair, Ashley thought again about Case. *I hope he didn't see me. That's all I need is him telling Jeremy I was out with another dude.* She and Jeremy weren't exclusive, but the boy acted a little jealous sometimes, and Ashley liked for her men to think they were her one and only. It gave her more control over the relationship.

The movie started when Tiffany Haddish appeared on the screen, and it wasn't long until Steve's hand found hers. All the eager sensations she usually had when meeting someone new occurred, but her mind trailed to the person that always seemed to lurk in its shadows. Especially when it came to love.

I wonder what Darren is up to tonight? It wasn't too abnormal, though, for Ashley to think about Darren after a breakup. *But am I really broken up with Jason? Or did we just have a fight?* Ashley really didn't know. One thing she *did* know was that she didn't want to be alone tonight. Stealing another glance at Steve in the darkness, she decided he would do. *At least for tonight.*

In utter exhaustion, Ashley climbed atop her one-thousand-thread-count sheets and drew up the covers. It had been a decent night. There wasn't anything spectacular about Steve, so she wasn't head over heels, but she did find out he was a student at Kingsborough and working his way through college.

So, he's not a bum, she thought. *And not just a waiter, which is even better.* As she stretched out, now completely relaxed, her phone beeped with an incoming text. *It's probably Jason apologizing for overreacting today.* Cracking open one lazy eye, she slid the phone off her nightstand to peek at the screen. *Denise.* Fully expecting Denise to be gushing about BJ, Ashley viewed the text. *They were super boo'd up tonight.* Instead, her heart flip-flopped as her eyes inhaled the messages.

"What the hell?" Swiping the screen to open the message, Ashley sat up so fast that the fluffy feathered duvet flew from her body. Her eyes ran back and forth, sending important signals to her brain, but it took her a minute to truly process what she was seeing. Finally, she dialed her best friend, and Denise answered on the first ring.

"Did you see what I sent 'chu?" Denise sounded as shocked as Ashley felt, and Ashley had to fight to stay calm.

"If you mean, did I see the picture you sent me of Natalie out with Darren tonight? Yea, I saw that shit." Her mouth tightened into a hard line, and when her breathing started increasing, she forced herself not to hyperventilate.

"Ash. What chu' gone' do?" Denise's tone was colored with surprise and brewing with sympathy for her friend.

A momentary pause straddled the line before Ashley answered in a cold, no-nonsense tone. "I'm comin' for her ass."

CHAPTER 18

THE FAMILY BUSINESS

(NATALIE)

Sunday morning, Natalie woke up bundled in refreshment. Last night, hanging out with Darren had been so much fun and was so needed. *I can't believe he opened up to me like that about his dad,* she thought and studied her reflection in the mirror with bright eyes. She wore her silk bonnet to bed last night and was happy to see her perm rod set was still intact. Throwing on a pair of leggings and a navy skirt, Natalie started the job of sorting through her closet for a shirt.

*I think I'll go with my light gray sweate*r. It was one of her favorites, and today, she wanted to look her best. *I get to see Devon!* The thought made her smile a smile she rarely had since her mom died. *And, of course, worship Jesus.* She chuckled to herself. Natalie told Devon she would meet him at his church around 11 AM, and he agreed to wait for her in the foyer to get her seated.

"Hey, cuz'." Ashley swung the door, which was slightly ajar, all the way open. "Going somewhere?"

Dang. I just put my shirt on. Whipping around in irritation, Natalie replied, "Uh. Yea. Why? You need something?" She finished dressing and started on her jewelry. It was almost 10 AM, and she needed to catch the New Jersey Transit at 10:15.

Ashley's eerie tone floated back. "Not really. Just wanted to see how your play went last night."

Natalie peered up, still fiddling with a heart-shaped earring near her earlobe. "Oh. Yea. It was fine." What was up with her cousin? Ashley leaned against the doorway in her PJs, gripping a cup of coffee and a strange expression. "What you got goin' on today?" Natalie asked. She wanted to get off the topic of the play ASAP.

Ashley half shrugged. "Not much. I'm working on this extra credit assignment for this class."

Natalie's brow lifted. "Really?" She didn't want to judge her cousin, but it didn't *seem* like Ashley had ever been about going the extra mile with her schoolwork.

"Yea. This one is a little different. The reward is a trip to Paris, so I'm on it."

Now *that* made sense. "Gotcha." Natalie copped her watch from her desk. "Well, good luck!"

"And the surprise?" Ashley asked, doing a smooth U-turn back to their earlier topic. "What was it?" She looked genuinely interested as her gaze drank Natalie in.

Natalie fidgeted a little like a bug beneath a microscope. "Uh. Yea. It wasn't anything special," she rushed to say. She kept her tone light while sliding on her chocolate brown shoe boots but struggled with getting her foot inside as thoughts of Darren distracted her. "Stupid things are being difficult," she murmured with an awkward chuckle. When her foot finally eased inside, she grew excited again. "But I'm running late. I'm meeting Devon at church today." Natalie was so giddy, her voice came out almost in a sing-song tone.

An aura of mystery surrounded Ashley's stance as she posed in the doorway. "Devon, huh?" Pencil-thin lines drew onto her forehead, and she cocked her head to the side. "Well. I don't want to keep you then. I know how much you like Devon."

Ashley left as fast as she had appeared, and Natalie frowned. She grabbed her coat and purse before dashing out of the bedroom. *She knows how much I like Devon? Is it that obvious? Well, as long as he doesn't know, I'm good.* All she needed was for her boss to think she was some little girl with a crush.

Somehow, Natalie arrived at the church only ten minutes late. When she reached the front of the large, cream building, a giant Jesus statue towered over it and rivers of people were streaming inside. *Good. I'm not the only one late.*

Devon hit her with a friendly smile when she entered the foyer. And *at least I know one person. There's so many people here.* Following the flow of the crowd, Natalie was blanketed by a nice ethnic collage of folks. Black, white, Puerto Rican, and everything in between. There was even a woman with Native American features handing out programs as an usher. The music began to play, and announcements were being shared at the podium. As soon as she was in earshot, Natalie called to Devon, "So sorry I'm late!"

"No worries," he responded in his usually supportive way. "Let me show you where we're sitting."

He offered her a good old church hug, which triggered a low gasp from her lips. It was probably the first time they had ever touched, and Natalie hadn't anticipated it. Her face was a picture of pure delight while following him to her seat. *God. I know I've been trying to be content being single, but if you give me this man, I won't ask you for another thing!*

When Devon craned his neck over his shoulder, making sure she was still behind him, his smile sent her heart into overdrive. He was his customary smooth self, fitted in a gray cardigan over a light-blue button-down and navy slacks. Natalie's eyes grew wide in realization. *We're matching!*

They reached their destination, and he pointed to a row with a few empty seats. Then, like the perfect gentleman, Devon eased beside her and helped her remove her coat. The first song started, and the whole church seemed to move at once. Mostly everyone stood, and Natalie was on her feet, too, closing her eyes while tilting her face to the sky in absolute awe. God was here, and she was elated to be in His presence.

Her hands stayed raised while singing the familiar lyrics of "I Could Sing of Your Love Forever" in her alto tone. The song was a classic, but instead of the acoustic melody she was used to, there was a Caribbean beat, and a young Black man at the front led everyone in worship.

Wow. I love this version! she thought while swaying with joy to the melody. It had so much more rhythm to it. There were a few more songs that the worship team sang, and most of them were ones she knew, but for the ones she didn't, she could follow along by reading the massive screen in the front. When they finished, Devon sat with his head hovering over both knees. Paper-thin slits creased the visible side of his forehead as his lips reverberated in low tones. *He must be praying.* Natalie smiled, but a whisper from her right stole her gaze.

"Natalie!" Kate, the blonde from her Prominent Voices writing class, was in the same row

a few seats over.

"Hey," Natalie whispered back. *Wow, I didn't know she went here.* Her hand formed into a short, surprised wave.

"Please turn to Psalm 37:4," the minister directed, a Puerto Rican man with wavy hair and a thick accent.

It's like the nations at this church. Natalie could barely contain her excitement while sliding open her Bible app.

Devon glanced over, asking "You need any help?" but she already had the scripture pulled up.

"Nope. I got it, thanks," she said and noticed his leather-bound paper copy of the New International Version was spread open and waiting on his lap.

"Now, many take this scripture out of context," the minister explained. "However, let's observe it *in* context." He paused with a serious gaze landing on the audience. "Some believe that if you follow God, you can get whatever you want. Kind of like a genie. Some believe that you're actually *entitled* to. However, when we study the life of Christ and look at the *entirety* of the Bible, we find that He actually taught and demonstrated the opposite. Instead of living *for* this world and the things of it, He *gave up* his life and desires. He laid it all down." The minister cleared his throat as Natalie's heart resonated with the message.

"I'll say, my understanding is that God wants us to have nice things, and He loves giving good gifts to His children. But there are times and seasons for all things, and knowing that, we can view this scripture as a promise. However, the promise may not manifest how or *when* we want." Pausing again, he placed his hands on the podium and watched the congregation with heartfelt eyes. "And it may even be that God *replaces* our desires with His so that *we want* what *He* wants. If we don't already," he added. The minister spoke with the passion and the conviction of someone who had walked through and overcome many things.

He reminds me of Pastor Jackson. Natalie nodded in response to the message as she sensed the Spirit of God speaking. Peeking at Devon from her peripheral, she wondered, was God saying this desire for Devon was His, or hers? She didn't know, and it wasn't until that moment that Natalie realized she hadn't even bothered to ask!

Father, please show me your heart concerning Devon and me. And if it's not of You, help me to lay it down. Bowing her head, that familiar sense of surrender engraved her heart. Just like it did when she came to Jersey on the whim she would be provided for. Even though she had to give up her scholarships and friends to do so. After a moment, Natalie exhaled, now at peace. When she raised her head, Devon was looking at her, and embarrassment crowded her face, simmering both cheeks. He pitched her a small smile before turning his attention back to the front. The service lasted another hour, and when it ended, she sucked in a breath, long and deep, soaking in every moment. *It's been so long since I've enjoyed church this much.*

"Natalie, I need to help with some things," Devon said, "but let's get some food after if you're free?"

"Oh yea? That would be great."

Abandoning his belongings, Devon zipped to the front of the stage where he spoke to a young woman with cocoa-brown skin and a Lupita Nyong'o hairstyle. They stood so close that Natalie swore they could kiss if they wanted to. Her brown eyes narrowed as she studied the exotic stranger. *Debra?* The girl seemed about Devon's age and was definitely cute. *I sure hope not.*

Kate slid closer with a sunny smile staining her lips. "Natalie, is this your first visit?"

Natalie wondered how she could have missed that her peer was a Believer in Christ. She kicked herself for being judgmental. *I guess what I thought was white privilege was really the joy of the Lord.* "Yea. It is. Is this your church?"

"Yep. For the last three years. Did you enjoy the service?"

"I did. I'll be coming back for sure." The two started packing their things as people began to leave.

"Awesome! I'm meeting my boyfriend Lamont for lunch, but maybe we can do lunch after next time?" Kate had her coat and purse in hand as hopeful sapphire eyes decorated her round peach face.

Boyfriend Lamont? Natalie tried to hide her shock with a casual shrug. "Oh. Um. Sure." She turned to search the front of the church, but Devon was no longer there. "Lupita" too had vanished.

"Great," Kate said. "Here he comes now. He's on the worship team," she explained while pointing to the man who had led worship. Tall and large with a full beard and a bald head, Lamont took long, brisk strides toward them.

"Oh. Ok. Guess I'll see you later." Natalie stepped back for Kate to pass and eyed the two as Lamont met Kate at the end of the aisle. Kate flashed a wave before exiting with Lamont in hand. *Everybody got a boo.* Sighing, Natalie checked her cell and saw that Devon had texted her. He was handling some church business and would be free in 20 minutes. *Well, it may not be a boo, but it's still nice.* She tried not to smile too hard while sitting back in her seat, and though he took a little longer, Natalie wasn't about to complain. Time with Devon was always worth the wait.

They caught the train to Fort Greene and entered the front door of a quaint gray building. It had *Jack & Jill* stamped on the window in cursive and a white awning protruding over the entrance.

"Breakfast is madd good here," Devon told her. "I think you'll like it."

The aroma of eggs, sausage, bacon, grits, and coffee welcomed Natalie, and she whiffed in eagerness. *I did forget to eat this morning since I was running late,* she realized as her stomach rumbled at all the smells. But then she became nervous that she would have a repeat of last night when she was with Darren and she willed her stomach to stay silent. Although the small restaurant was at total capacity and people waited in line to be seated, Devon headed straight to the greeter. He huddled the small woman into a bear hug before turning around and indicating for Natalie to come closer.

"Excuse me," she mumbled, sliding by the strangers who had probably been waiting for some time. Customers took turns staring at her in curiosity and blatant annoyance. "Umm, sorry." She kept moving, dodging all the angry eyes. *I hope he doesn't have us cutting the line!*

Devon's smile was stuffed with joy when Natalie reached him as he held one possessive arm around the young greeter's shoulders. "Natalie, this is Debra. My baby sister." He nodded to Natalie, and happiness hugged her heart. Debra was a dead-on resemblance to her older brother.

She shot out a hand, nearly shouting, "Nice to meet you!"

Startled, Debra half-smiled, studying her, then responded, "Same," but with not nearly as much vigor. Debra turned to her brother with a questioning gaze that no doubt held more than one question. "You want yo usual table?"

"If it's free." Devon drifted closer to Natalie so a couple could exit behind them while Debra peered at a table in the corner where an elderly man was drinking coffee.

"Mr. Kent will be gone soon, and I'll make sure Cynthia clears it for you," Debra said, eyeing the older gentleman.

"Thanks. Daddy in?"

"He in the back." Returning to her work duties, Debra called out the name of a group of people waiting to be seated: "Walters, party of four!"

As the Walters crowded the podium, Natalie drew closer to Devon, and now she could see the little bristles of hair sprinkled on the top of his upper lip. The way they laid so gracefully. The soft crinkles beneath his eyes. *Nat, be cool.* But her heartbeat sped at his nearness.

"Come on, Natalie. You can meet my pops." Devon swept her hand into his as if it were an everyday occurrence, then steered her to the back of the restaurant.

Natalie's excitement went into overdrive. *I'm meeting Devon's family?* She was a little disappointed when he let go of her hand, but her adrenaline heightened when he pushed open the door with the nameplate "Owner" on it. Trailing Devon, Natalie was a collage of curiosity and nerves. She tried to calm herself by focusing on the interior. It was a medium-sized space with dark wooden floors and a desk near the back stapled in front of a large window that donned sturdy blue curtains.

The decor was similar to Devon's style, and that detail offered Natalie some comfort.

When they entered, a burly-looking man sat at his desk pounding on the keypad to his Mac computer. His eyes sped back and forth across the screen, then lept in the duo's direction. "Son!" he called in a gruff but loving tone, then stood to give Devon a squeeze.

Natalie clasped her coat while resting against the entrance and sifted through which emotion she should be feeling right now. *I'm going to go with nervous as heck,* she decided and strangled her coat against her stomach.

"And who do we have here?" The burly man adjusted his glasses and smiled while squinting at her.

"This is Natalie. Currently my most valuable asset." Devon looked at her with shining eyes, and Natalie did a slow cat-like creep into the room.

Whipping out a hand, she offered, "Hi, Mr. Woods," and he swallowed it whole in his.

"Ahh. The new admin, huh?" Mr. Woods's voice was a booming echo in the intimate space, bouncing off all four walls until it pounced upon its intended target.

"Yes, sir." Natalie couldn't help but grin. *I can't believe I'm meeting Devon's dad.*

"You keepin' my boy straight?" His lips ventured into a teasing smile, and she nodded her head in enthusiasm.

"I'm tryin'."

"Yea, Pops. Natalie is a great admin," Devon said, vouching for her. "She's really helped me get more organized." Devon wore a proud grin near his father as both Woods men observed her. "I haven't missed a meeting in a whole month!"

"Is that so? We may need your service over here then one of these days." Mr. Woods eyed Natalie as he flew a hand toward the documents covering his desk. "I mean, if Devon will lend you out sometime," he added. Smoothing his meaty palm over his swollen belly, he patted it like a woman expecting.

Natalie wasn't so sure she could fit in another job. *My schedule is already full as it is.* Her eyes pleaded with Devon, and he chuckled.

"Maybe one day, Pops. But for now, Natalie's all mine." Devon winked, and Natalie was relieved. She also really liked the way Devon put things.

Interrupting the trio, Debra peeked her head inside. "Devon, your table's ready."

"Pops, I'll talk to you later," Devon said quickly.

"Ok, son." Mr. Woods shoved his hefty frame back into his office chair. "Nice to meet 'chu, Natalie!" he blared before ducking back over his keyboard.

"Same to you, sir." Natalie smiled, now at ease, thinking, *Whew. That wasn't so bad,* and with Devon on her heels, she shadowed Debra to their table. The restaurant held the usual busyness of any after-church crowd on a Sunday, and Natalie couldn't help but stare in wonder at the place. There were cute little curtains decorating the windows and crisp white stools at the counter. The atmosphere was lively as families laughed and chatted with loved ones, couples ogled each other over their meals, and children stuffed their mouths with content. *It's like Devon's,* she thought, impressed. *Except for families.* Unable to remove the awestruck note in her voice, she asked, "So. This is your *parents'* restaurant?"

"Yep." Devon passed her a menu. "They've had it for at least a decade," he explained. "They had another one before it for several years too." He pointed to a dish on Natalie's propped open menu. "You gotta try the grits. They're *phenomenal.* My cousin Reggie is the cook." He gave a chef's kiss and said, "Magnificent!" in his best Italian accent.

Natalie laughed, refreshed to see Devon outside of his work environment. "Will do then." She looked over the other items on the menu.

"Hey, Devon. You want your usual?" A curvy server with stunning almond eyes, long lashes, and a tiny waist manifested at their table. She didn't even look in Natalie's direction, though, seeming only to have eyes for Devon.

"Sup, Cynthia. Yep." Devon bent towards Natalie. "You know what 'chu want?"

She smiled. "Oh, yea. Of course, the grits." The waitress finally looked her way, sans her pleasant smile. "And some scrambled eggs with cheese and... a side of fruit, please," Natalie added.

"Sure." Cynthia scribbled on her pad and tossed a tight smile her way. "I'll get your coffee, Devon," she cooed before sauntering off. The woman's hips beat harder than an African drum.

Natalie puffed out a stream of air in response to the waitress's rudeness. Stretching her legs underneath the table, she straightened her skirt to shake off the girl's attitude. "So, being an entrepreneur is kinda in your blood, huh?" she asked, catching Devon, once again, staring at her.

He jerked his head and sat up straighter at her question. "Yea. I guess you could say that." His unopened menu lay on the table as he drew his fingers over the cover. "I grew up seeing my mom and dad try one thing after another. My mom would work full-time and carry the load while my dad would struggle to get some vision he had in his head off the ground."

"Gotcha. And where *is* your mom?" Natalie was curious while fondling a thread of hair and wrapping it around her finger a few times. Devon's eyes followed her gesture, so she stopped, concerned she was being childish.

"Your hair looks great," he said, with just a tad of tenderness.

Pleasure exploded in her smile. "Thank you."

"But. You always look good..." he added, then chuckled before looking away after the words left his mouth.

Is he blushing? Natalie couldn't be 100 percent sure, but there was a definitive reddish color to Devon's mocha-brown skin. Her tone a soft caress, she replied, "I feel the same about you." They looked at each other in easy silence until Devon spoke again.

"Yea... so my mom." He cleared his throat while continuing to toy with his menu, then kicked his head toward the front in Debra's direction. "My mom isn't in the restaurant today. She usually has my niece, Bella, while Debra's working."

"Ahhh. Niece, huh?" Natalie asked. She *must be the one in the picture in his office.* "How old is she?"

"18 months. You wanna see?" And without waiting, Devon ripped his phone from his pocket to toggle through a few photos. In seconds, the screen flooded with a chubby round face, grinning, while the next image showed Bella and Devon cheesing together.

It was definitely the child from the picture in his office. Observing

Bella in her glory, Natalie ooh'd, ahh'd, and shrieked, "She's a cutie!" at all the right moments. Dressed in a pair of overalls, Bella sat perched on her uncle's lap as he gazed down, completely smitten. She was very obviously the center of his entire world, and Natalie's affection towards Devon couldn't help but skyrocket after glimpsing this.

Devon's eyes were a well of love as he tucked his phone back into his pocket. "I was gonna stop by after this to go see them," he explained. "I try to make it over there on Sundays since it's the only day Devon's is closed."

Cynthia returned with their drinks just then, propping a mug of coffee on the table along with two waters. Turning to Devon with purring lips, she said, "Two creams and one sugar."

"Thanks." Devon squeezed the mug and sniffed its aroma as Natalie tried her best to bite her tongue by squeezing her water glass. It didn't work.

"Cynthia," she said, her tone syrupy sweet, "I don't get offered coffee?" Natalie narrowed her eyes at the woman.

Cynthia tilted her face in Natalie's direction while shifting all her weight to one side so that one of her bulging hips protruded outward. "Would you like coffee?" Her voice was as dry as the Sahara Desert when she replied.

Natalie lifted a saucy chin. "No. Thank you."

Devon's eyes switched from Natalie to Cynthia and back to Natalie again. The server smacked her teeth before leaving, and Devon uttered an uncomfortable laugh. "Sorry about that. She be buggin' sometimes."

"Yea, well, she needs to get some manners." Natalie slid her water closer and took a drink, her mood somewhat dampened.

Devon chuckled again while edging towards her. "What did you think about the service?"

Natalie's countenance lightened like the sky when the sun first blooms in the morning. "It was great! I really needed it today. The worship and the message were both right on time." She peered at him with eyes of joy over the rim of her glass, and Devon seemed pleased to hear it.

"Yea. I've appreciated the heart of that church since I found it."

"I've been looking for a church where I feel like I fit since I moved here," she chatted in growing excitement. "I *loved* that version of 'I Could Sing of Your Love Forever.' I've never heard it sung like that before."

"Oh. It was the version by CalledOut Music."

"Hmmm. CalledOut Music. I'll have to check them out." She was already pulling out her phone to type in the artist in her music library.

"Yea. And it's a *him*," Devon clarified. "He's from England but was raised in Nigeria."

"Cool. I'll check *him* out then." Natalie ran her hands up and down her water glass with a thoughtful expression. "I would definitely want to come back to visit." As Devon continued talking, Natalie couldn't help but think of how nice it was to meet someone she could share her faith with. *As much as I care for Darren, I know I need this. I need someone stronger spiritually who I can grow with.* When she was with Darren, Natalie felt like *she* was usually teaching *him*. It was actually like that in a lot of her relationships. *But with Devon, I feel like he teaches me too.*

"I love how diverse my church is," Devon continued. "Sometimes we forget that heaven isn't just one group of people. It's *all* nations. *All* ethnicities." He gestured with his hands while speaking passionately, and Natalie nodded in agreement. She was thinking about her previous travels to other countries. Oh, how her heart longed to travel again.

"I agree. It's not easy to find that diversity. Inside the church, or outside." Without even realizing it, Natalie had plucked a curly tendril from her head and was wrapping it once again around her newly manicured fingertips. The corners of Devon's lips curled upward, his eyes pinned to each movement.

"Here you go." Cynthia set their plates down, practically salivating over Devon, while Natalie had to reach a little to get hers.

She inspected it closely to make sure nothing was funny with her meal. *You never know how somebody can take getting checked.*

"Thanks. But um, next time, you'll want to be more gracious to *all* your customers, Cynthia." Devon replied over a plate mounted with pancakes smothered in butter and three plump sausage links. He looked at Natalie, and Natalie was pricked with pleasure.

Cynthia teased her lip with her tooth while glancing at Natalie in hesitation. "Yea. I got 'chu. Sorry," she mumbled. She punctuated her apology by wiping both hands on her apron with a lowered gaze.

Natalie's reply was sincere. "It's cool." It was enough for her to be avenged. She didn't want the girl to lose her job over it. If anything, she was even more impressed by Devon coming to her aid. It felt like they were on the same team.

When Cynthia skirted away, Devon held out his hands on the table and asked, "You wanna pray?"

Without question, Natalie agreed, but when she locked her hands in his, a current zipped from the top of her head to the soles of her feet. *Whoa! What was that?* Natalie's head whipped upward, and Devon's eyes met hers. Surprise crossed his features as they sat in stunned silence. In small, circular motions, he began fondling her fingers which were now in the palms of his hands. Natalie flashed back to the statement from both her uncle and her counselor on two different occasions.

Sounds like you're in good hands. Her heartbeat stampeded, and she could sense God's presence the way she was used to experiencing Him.

"I'll pray." When Devon bowed his head, Natalie followed suit but couldn't get over the feeling she had when they first touched. She had never felt anything like it.

And it seems like Devon felt it too, she thought while dispensing her silverware from the napkin to eat her eggs. She unwrapped her fork and caught his gaze before he bent his head back over his plate and inhaled another sausage link.

Yea. He definitely felt it too.

Natalie reflected on her time with Devon as she was getting ready for bed that evening. "I can't believe Debra is his sister," she murmured in relief while twisting her 4B tendrils into round, thick Bantu knots. She needed to keep her curls going for a few more days before she was due for her bi-weekly wash.

She was finishing the last knot with a black bobby pin welded between her teeth when the phone vibrated. Dropping the bobby pin in her hand and glancing at the screen in confusion, she wondered, *Who could be calling this late?* It was close to bedtime, and typically her people would just send a text, knowing Natalie was an early bird. To her surprise, "Devon Woods" lit up the screen in bold, white letters. Puzzled, she answered, "Hey. Devon. Wuz up?" *Maybe he wants to run over some things for work tomorrow?*

"Natalie," he paused and cleared his throat, sounding unsure for the first time ever. "Um... I just wanted to thank you for spending time with me today."

A sweet smile burst from Natalie's lips as she lay back on her bed. She slid the hand with the bobby pin behind her neck, creeping around the small, round bulges. "Yea. I had a good time. I enjoyed every part."

"Yep. Me too. A lot, actually." Devon's nervous chuckle gave way to another sudden pause, and Natalie eyed the ceiling, wondering if he was going to say something more. He finally broke the silence. "Um, the real reason I'm calling... is that... I uh... I can't shake this desire to get to know you better. I mean, I know I'm your boss." Devon exhaled another skittish sound. "But I want to be something more." His voice came out rich and sure on that last statement.

Natalie's stomach flopped as she popped up in her bed, bobby pins flying all over the fluffy gray comforter. She gripped the phone so tight she feared it might break.

"Natalie?"

"Huh? Oh! Yes!" She was smiling from ear to ear. *I can't believe this is happening.* "I'm here," she added, trying to make her voice a standard octave but clutching the phone with two hands. Her body was tense and hunched in fear that if she moved, she would wake up from this dream.

Devon's laugh was wrapped in pleasure. "So. What chu' think? You want to give us a shot?"

Natalie was floored. *Do I want to give Devon a shot?* She stared at the ceiling, a huge grin masking her full pink lips as a bobby pin sat nestled in her fist gripping the phone.

"Devon. I would love to."

CHAPTER 19

FALLING HARD

(ASHLEY)

I t was closing time at Devon's, and Ashley huddled in a corner, waiting. Nursing her chai tea latte, she gazed with unseeing eyes at Denise cleaning tables.

"Almost ready," her friend informed after half an hour of sweeping and straightening the cafe.

"No worries, homie. I'm good." Ashley's eyes wandered for a bit, and within minutes, the real reason she was there made her debut. Natalie trotted inside, bundled in a hoodie and exercise gear underneath. By the looks of the frizzy bun on her head, it appeared she had been working out. Her face shimmered with a smile as she swung a blue Nike gym bag from side to side without a care in the world.

Anger strangled Ashley's heart at the sight. The kind of anger that came from years of repressed, unexpressed hurt. The kind that she was now finally ready to unleash. *She must have come from Zumba class*, she deducted with slitted eyes. In preparation, Ashley shut down her laptop and started packing her things in her school bag. A sense of acidic determination ate at the intestines lining her gut.

Spotting Ashley in the corner, Natalie struck a hearty wave. "Hey!" While doing an about-face in her direction, she swung her bag along with her.

It's definitely time for us to chat, dear cuz'. Ashley fake-smiled back but kept packing, creating ample room at the table. The last customer had left shortly after Ashley had entered, and they had turned off the music at Devon's 30 minutes ago when Alice, the other server that night, headed out.

"How are you?" Natalie sauntered over, happy as a clam, and slipped into the chair across from her.

Ashley smirked to herself. *The girl is oblivious.*

Natalie was glowing as she gushed about how she was here for Devon. She didn't need or wait for any kind of response from Ashley. "We're going for a late snack. It's hard to find time together since he works so much," she bubbled. Her eyes were as bright as the sun in mid-afternoon on a summer day in Florida. Natalie wasn't telling Ashley anything she didn't already know. She had talked to her cousin that morning and knew she was coming here tonight. Coming up for air, Natalie finally asked, "You waitin' on Denise?"

"Yep," Ashley said. *And you.*

Devon called over the bar, "Nat, I'm almost done," while darting and dashing a rag on top of the counter.

"Ok. No problem." Natalie turned back to face Ashley with a cheesy grin stamped across her peanut butter brown face.

"Whew! I am *whooped*," Denise said, dragging a chair to their table and falling into it. "Natalie, you don't want nothin', do you? Cuz, sis, I'm *done*."

Natalie threw up a hand. "Naw. I'm good. Just waitin' for Devon." A dreamy expression stuck to her as she watched him work behind the counter.

Ugh. I can't take it anymore. Ashley tried to hide the deep frown embedded on her lips with her mug of chai.

"Oooo. Ok. So, how is *that* goin?" Denise's voice became conspiratorial while asking about Natalie's budding relationship with Devon. She threw a glance at her boss, who was well out of earshot, then bent forward.

Ashley was tickled to pieces when Natalie started cheesing again. *She is so sprung*, she thought, trying but not succeeding to smother another spark of jealousy.

"Pretty good," Natalie answered. She brushed her lips with her tongue and eyed Devon again, her eyes portraying a glint of nervousness this time.

"Now. You can tell *us*, Nat. How *close* are y'all gettin' exactly?" Denise angled her head to the side and tilted in just a bit closer, her thick, neat locks pinned over one shoulder, serving as a stylish accent.

Ashley wanted to burst out laughing at Natalie's shocked expression. *Leave it to Denise!*

A giggle of discomfort escaped Natalie as she heaved a shoulder in mid-air. "I mean. We're gettin' close. I love that Devon respects me, and you know he *values* me, so he's willing to wait for me." In a skittish rhythm, she tapped a nude fingernail on the table, then stole another look at Devon.

Ugh. Give me a break! "We hear you, cuz'," Ashley said, "But *come on*. Devon needs *sex*— I mean, *intimacy*, like every other brotha out here." She hit her cousin with a sly smile.

"Mmhmm. I *hearrrrd* that!" Denise chimed in, dragging out the word to accentuate her point. She raised a hand for Ashley to slap.

"What did you hear?" Devon, finished with his cleaning, straddled the chair next to Natalie with a questioning look.

"Oh! Nothin'," Natalie said a little too quickly.

Ms. Perfect is for sure embarrassed. Unable to help herself, Ashley snickered. "Well, you know. We were just talking about the importance of *intimacy* in a relationship," she explained in a matter-of-fact tone. An enigmatic expression branded Ashley's face while she eyed the couple in front of her. Devon chuckled with amusement, but Natalie's chin slanted downward, her hands now two buried rocks beneath the table.

Devon took the lead in a smooth tone. "Gotcha. Well, there are various levels to intimacy." He placed a palm on Natalie's chair, leaned back into his own, and crossed one leg over his knee in one fluid gesture.

Natalie echoed, "Right," catching courage from her boyfriend. "There are more important components of intimacy than just *physical* intimacy."

"Of course," Ashley agreed. "There are emotional and mental components. I mean, y'all are probably working on that stuff, too, right?" She gazed, eyes shining in anticipation, before cocking her mug to her mouth to hide her grin.

Natalie scratched Devon's Levi's and caught his eye before bobbing her head up and down. "Yea, of course." But her tone was hesitant.

"And doesn't that mean sharing intimate details about yourselves?" With knitted brows, Ashley whisked her mug back onto the table.

Denise glanced from Ashley to Natalie and Devon. It seemed like she, too, should get more comfortable to watch the show, so she sat back in her chair and prepared for the action.

"Yea. Part of intimacy is building a safe place for your partner," Devon explained. "Conversing. Getting to know each other. All of that plays a part." He looked at Natalie with an easy smile, and her body visibly relaxed.

"Exactly. And I'm sure you guys have talked about all *sorts* of things in getting to know each other. Right?" Ashley pressed. "I mean, Natalie's probably told you stuff she hasn't shared with *most* people." Natalie danced around in her chair, and Ashley reveled in the feeling that she was causing Ms. Perfect some discomfort.

No fool to Ashley's antics, Natalie cut her eyes. "Chill out, Ash." Her tone was cool, and Ashley feigned a look of surprise.

"Did I say something wrong?" In a theatrical manner, she threw her hand to her chest. "I haven't even said anything foreal... yet."

Natalie turned to Devon, "I think we need to go," and regressed back to her earlier nervousness. She drew her cell from her jacket pocket in a showy way of checking the time. "It's getting late, and... we have plans."

Ashley's voice dripped with disappointment. "Oh, cuz'. You always sayin' we don't hang out enough. Now you tryna bounce." She managed a full-on pout, and Natalie's voice flirted with uncertainty.

"I mean, I still need to change..." Natalie peeked at Devon again, who gave her a look that said, "It's up to you."

"Well, I was just asking. Cuz I know you can be, er, *private*," Ashley replied. "But if Devon is to you who you *say* he is, then I'm sure you told him about your situation you had. Right?" She batted her lashes in fake sympathy, and confusion dressed Natalie's features. Her eyes blinked with questions, and Ashley etched the image deep into her mind. She had the girl's full attention.

"What situation?" Natalie's tone had morphed from confusion to testy. "I don't even know *what* you trippin' on right now, Ashley, but I'm not on it."

Ashley's face contorted into a Cheshire cat's grin. *Gotcha.* "Oh. You *know.* Your situation that you were dealing with a while back." Ashley dug into the side pocket of her bookbag to reveal the baggy she had hidden there earlier that day. "The problem you had... with... *cutting.*" Letting the statement loose like a cannon firing, she hurled the baggie onto the table. A shiny metal razor beamed, glistening beneath the crinkled plastic.

Natalie popped up in her seat at the word "cutting." "What? What are you talkin' about?" Her eyes shot to the razor. She was dumbfounded as she stared in disbelief at the evidence. "Wh-where did you get that?"

"You know you were cutting yourself for a while there, cuz'. I mean, the wounds are probably healed by now, cuz *I* haven't seen them anyways." Ashley looked over the table, studying Natalie's arm covered by her workout jacket as if she had x-ray vision. *"But why would you have this razor if it wasn't still an issue?* is what I kept asking myself. And really, how would *we* know unless you showed us?" She reached for Natalie's hand and ripped back her jacket sleeve. Natalie snatched her hand back in horror, stumbling to her feet.

"Ashley! What in the hell?" Devon was up also and jerked Natalie to him, wrapping a protective arm around her.

"How long has it been since you last cut, Natalie?" Ashley's tone was as sweet as one of Grams's pecan pies.

"Hey. Ash," Denise interrupted in a soft tone. "That's enough."

Natalie gritted her teeth as the tears started to form. "Why are you doing this to me?" She cradled her arm, and Devon jetted a hand to her lower back in support, looking both confused and upset.

"Why am *I* doing this to *you*? What about all the shit you've done to *me*!" Ashley lost her cool and was on her feet as well. *Damn if I'm going to let her play the victim!*

Natalie cried out, her eyes overshadowed by pain. "What the hell have I ever done to *you* but try to *love* you?"

Ashley's glare was menacing. "How about the fact that you've been all boo'd up with Darren since you got here!"

"Darren?" Devon asked. He looked at Natalie in surprise.

"Darren and I are *just* friends!" Natalie sliced the air with a shaky finger at her cousin. "You *know* I'm with Devon. Why would you try to ruin my relationship?"

"You just pick 'em up and put 'em down when it's convenient for you, huh, Nat? You was kickin' it tough with Darren just a couple weeks ago." Ashley popped her neck and folded her arms over her chest. "Had to be if he introduced you to his whole damn *family*. And you ain't think I would know. Backstabbing traitor!" She snickered with eyes of rage.

With fiery eyes of her own, Natalie spewed, "That was *one* night. We are *just* friends. You know how many times I coulda been with that boy? I didn't even go out with him because I was respecting your *selfish* ass!"

Ashley gasped, her mouth dropping to the floor before she whipped her hand over it with dramatic eyes. "Oooo! Did Ms. Perfect just *curse* at me?" She looked at Denise, and Denise shook her locks, eyes pleading for Ashley to stop.

"You think you run every-*body* and every-*thing*." Natalie spat in frustration. "Like we ain't got free will apart from you. Like you can just bully everybody to do things *your* way!" Her voice was sky-high as both fists were gripped at her sides. She started shaking, and Devon moved to calm her.

"Babe. Take it easy." He stroked her arm, but she ignored him.

"Why you always comin' for somebody, huh, Ashley?" At last, Natalie's true feelings were being laid out in the open. "You have *every-thing*. A father who loves you. A family who tolerates how crazy you are. Friends who are there for you. Why the hell are you even miserable? And why you gotta make everybody as miserable as *you*?"

Although she was shocked, Ashley charged back, not missing a beat. If manipulation was an art, *she* was the master artist. "Oh. Poor little Natalie. Always the victim, huh? Well, who was the victim when I nearly *drowned* from The Hyenas *dragging* me into the freakin' lake *after* stripping me and shoving my head underwater?" She jabbed an acrylic finger at herself with each word.

Denise got up to stand next to Ashley and looked at her friend in concern. "The Hyenas? Ash, what are you talkin' about?"

The group gaped at her, but her mind's eye was years in the past. Ashley was a 14-year-old kid with braces that decorated large teeth, excess baby fat rolled over wide hips, and no style. It was only a few months after her mom died. She wanted to be accepted so badly and was willing to do almost anything, but these girls were mean. They were bullies, and the only time Ashley didn't seem to get bullied was when Natalie was around. Well, ironically, Natalie *was* around that night. She had told Ashley that The Hyenas liked to play pranks, and if she went along with them, she could join their clique.

"*You* said they liked to play pranks. That it would be like hazing. That I would be a member after. But shoving my head underwater, slamming it against the rocks! It was cold," Ashley's voice reverted into one of a younger version of herself, "and I was in my underwear." She enfolded each hand over her arms, her eyes clouding with pain.

"But. I-I didn't know," Natalie stuttered, reaching for her cousin. "I... th-they didn't do that to *me*."

Ashley stepped back, her tone laced with bitterness. "Yea? Well, they did it to *me*. I cracked a tooth on a rock. They took turns punching me in the gut, seeing who could hit the hardest. They had me in the middle of the woods. I didn't know where I was. I blacked out." Ashley's words were a river now, as if a broken dam had unleashed her hidden trauma.

"I'm sorry!" Natalie cried. "I was *14*. I thought I was giving *advice*." Devon massaged her shoulder as she defended herself, but Natalie only had eyes for Ashley.

Ashley proceeded in her strange, youthful-like tone coupled with a dazed expression. She hadn't heard a thing. "And you know what was the worst part?" As she looked off into the distance and recalled the scenes of her past, her breathing grew labored. She was still gripping herself, and even though Denise was standing nearby, she felt so alone.

And so cold. Why am I so cold? "I woke up, and they were all standing over me," Ashley spouted, still holding herself. "*Laughing*. I'm in my underwear, and these girls are pointing and laughing." Between each word, her breathing grew more rapid. "I'm *bleeding*, and *they* laughin'." She glared at Natalie through tears and brushed the spot on her forehead, right underneath her hairline. The scar was there from a rock that had punctured her skin that night. It was barely visible now, but she knew it was there.

"And you were right there, Natalie," she huffed, her breath catching. "You were right there!" Redirecting her gaze, Ashley squeezed both eyelids close. When she reopened them, her vision was double. Natalie was double. And she kept hearing this sound. It was like rushing water. *What is that sound? Why am I so cold?* Now she was dizzy. *I can't breathe!*

"Ashley, honey. You need to sit down," Denise said in a faraway voice.

I'm fine, Ashley tried to get out, but she couldn't. She couldn't make a sound. And she couldn't catch her breath. She was huffing and heaving. Her vision grew blurry as muffled voices spun around until everything went black.

CHAPTER 20

THE HYENAS

(NATALIE)

Natalie sat in the waiting room, twiddling her fingers like she was playing an old-school game of Super Nintendo. Her right leg had a mind of its own and kept shaking in her white and black Adidas sneakers on the linoleum tile flooring. She was still wearing her workout clothes from Zumba class, never having had a moment to change into the dress she had brought for her date with Devon. They were supposed to go to his place before heading back out so she could get cleaned up. Being the good boyfriend that he was, Devon sat next to her, and she vaguely felt his fingers running along her back in a soothing fashion. *What would I do without him?*

Denise and BJ huddled together across from them with twin grim expressions dressing their faces. Grams and Uncle Malcolm were in the hospital room with Ashley. Everything happened so fast once Ashley fainted. She hit the ground with a sickening thud. Although Denise was the closest, she still couldn't seem to catch her. Devon called 9-1-1 while Natalie and Denise lingered over Ashley, calling her name repeatedly. Devon said not to move her, so they didn't. Thankfully, the ambulance made it in time and helped her come to, but from what Natalie knew, she had been in and out of consciousness all evening.

Natalie frowned, expelling an anxious breath, and Devon peered at her with a worried expression. He thumbed her lower back. "You ok?"

She nodded in response, but her thoughts were elsewhere. Natalie was having flashbacks of a time she had forgotten. *Or maybe I blocked it out?* She rubbed her hands together over and over as if the act itself would rid her of her pain and fear.

Like Ashley had said, Natalie *was* there the night of the assault. She and Ashley shared a bunk with a couple of other girls, and The Hyenas had told them they were going to hang out. Said they would have beer and asked if the girls wanted to join them. So Natalie and Ashley waited until their bunk mates fell asleep to sneak out after curfew. The fuzzy details of that night cracked through the lens of Natalie's psyche as she wrestled with her inner turmoil.

"Now. They be doin' some crazy shit sometimes," 14-year-old Natalie had told Ashley. "But if you just go along with it, I'm sure they'll accept 'chu." They were waiting outside their cabin for The Hyenas in matching jean shorts and yellow "Camp Chippewa" tank tops. Natalie had hung out with The Hyenas a few times on her own after curfew, and it was always a good time. They were exciting, and she would have called them her friends if they weren't so mean.

"Ok." Ashley gave an obedient head nod as a gust of wind blew and the trees around them began to dance. There was rustling from the corner of the cabin, and Natalie looked over, catching a view of a shadow.

"Hey!" The shadow cried in a staged whisper, and both girls turned as one of The Hyenas, Renee, approached. Renee was chunky with a habit of laughing when nothing was funny. She was also the reason Ashley and Natalie dubbed them "The Hyenas." Her laugh sounded just like one.

"Yo. Wuz up!" another girl said, crossing over from the other side of the cabin. It was Felicia, the leader of the threesome. She was taller than everybody, and her long, thick hair ran down her back like a horse's mane. Natalie suspected Felicia was mixed with Indian, but everybody at camp was too afraid to ask.

"Hey, y'all," Shaniqua tossed out, peeking from behind Felicia. Shaniqua was Felicia's cousin and always agreed with whatever Felicia said.

Felicia whipped around and snapped at her, "Shh! Girl, you too loud." She swung one of her thick, long braids over her shoulder. It melted down to her waistline, hanging just above her well-endowed bottom.

"My bad," Shaniqua said in the same loud whisper.

The girls formed a tight circle while Felicia looked Natalie and Ashley up and down.

"Where's the beer?" Natalie's tone was bold. She stood toe-to-toe with Felicia and stared up at her with a fearless expression.

Felicia's tough exterior caved into an approving smile. "Ok. This one got heart!" she announced, sounding impressed. "But um, we ain't out here walkin' around with no alcohol, girl. We hid it earlier in the woods." She nodded in the direction of the woods, and Natalie squinted at the dark trees in the moonlight.

"Ok. Cool," Natalie responded in approval. "Let's go then!"

"Yea. We gone' have a lot of fun tonight!" Renee giggled her signature high-pitched giggle.

"Shh!" Felicia shot up a finger, said "Follow me," then led the girls into the middle of nowhere. The group extended their cell phones and shined their lights to see where they were walking, and Natalie craned her neck back at her cousin. She had never been that deep into the woods and didn't really know where they were.

"You good?" she asked, making Ashley out in the dim lighting.

Ashley's eyes peered back, drizzled with worry. "Yea. I'm cool." But her voice wavered.

Natalie assumed she was pretending to be brave, so she smiled to make her feel better. "We're almost there," she whispered, but she was basically lying because she had no idea where 'there' was.

The girls walked for a good 15 more minutes until they met a crowd of large rocks surrounding a campfire. A lake couldn't have been too far away because water sloshed when the wind blew, even though it was too dark to see it.

"Yo. It's still here!" Giddy with excitement, Shaniqua lifted a couple of six-packs from behind a nearby tree.

Natalie's eyes brightened, but she tried to stifle the admiration in her tone. "How did y'all get beer?"

"Oh. Felicia has her ways," Shaniqua answered with a sneaky smile.

"Yea. If by making out with Chris is "her ways," then yea. She got 'em!" Renee added, and a fit of hysterical laughter tackled her.

"Chill out, y'all. Tellin' my business like that." Felicia sank in front of one of the rocks and tried to look embarrassed, but a proud smile shadowed her light brown face.

Dang, she kickin' it with a camp counselor? *Natalie thought. Now she was all the way impressed. Chris was at least 17 years old and was one of the junior counselors at camp.* He must have a fake I.D., *she assumed.*

The other girls sat on rocks and placed their cell phones on the ground facing upward so the flashlights beamed like strobe lights at a concert. Shaniqua took charge of handing out beers, but when it was Ashley's turn, she said, "Yo. You ain't gettin' none."

"Yea. We'll tell you when you can get some," Renee echoed. She swiped a Miller Lite can from Shaniqua and popped the top to take a swig.

"That ain't cool, y'all," Natalie said. "Give her a beer." Her heart sank as she looked at Ashley. Maybe I shouldn't have brought her here.

Felicia eyed Ashley from head to toe. "Naw. She gone' have to earn it. She ain't did nothin' to earn it yet." Felicia stayed seated on the ground with her arm propped on the rock behind her. As she gripped her can in one hand, her pretty features were aglow in the dim lighting.

Natalie thought, Felicia has the nerve to look cute, *while taking a beer from Shaniqua,* even when she's mean as hell.

A timid Ashley asked, "What 'chu mean, earn it?" Swooping her legs to her chest, she cradled her arms around them while drawing herself inward.

"We'll let 'chu know when the time comes," Felicia informed. "But you can't just kick it with us for free, *girl. Ask yo cuz'. She* had *to earn it."*

Felicia nodded in Natalie's direction, and Natalie tossed her chin in response. She did have to earn it. It was some stupid prank they had her do a couple of summers ago that she didn't even remember now. Then they were cool with her. I'm sure it will be the same for Ashley.

With a level of uncertainty, Ashley said, "Oh... ok." She looked back at Natalie, and Natalie offered a reassuring smile.

The girls hung out for a good hour, drinking and joking around. Felicia bragged that she let Chris, the camp counselor, get to second base with her, but little did he know, she let his twin brother get to third. The boys lived in her neighborhood, so she had access to them outside of camp. The girls peered at her with wide, shining eyes as she gave them tips on how to attract older men.

Natalie knew she was intoxicated when her eyelids started drooping. She ended up sprawled on the bare ground using her arm as a pillow. There was some movement circling her and muffled voices, but Natalie couldn't remember anything that happened between falling asleep and going back to the cabin. Felicia woke her up sometime later, saying that Ashley went to the 24-hour care center because she had started her period and needed a tampon. Natalie had no reason not *to believe her. She was disoriented and tired, and the other girls were gone. Only Felicia was there. Natalie tailed her back to her cabin, assuming Ashley was already inside. After seeing a lump of a shadow lying in Ashley's bed, she hopped into her bunk and went to sleep, thinking everything was good.*

But I was so wrong! Natalie reflected while chewing on her lower lip like a piece of fried chicken. *I'm so sorry I let you down, Ash.* A fat tear crawled down her cheek, but she didn't even notice it.

"Hey. Hey. Shhh." Devon caressed her wet cheek and held her close while Natalie nuzzled her face into his neck. "Everything's gone' be ok."

She nodded in silence, but was it really going to be ok? Natalie had no idea her cousin had been assaulted by those girls. No idea at all. *And Ashley's right. It's all my fault.*

<hr>

After visiting Ashley at the hospital, Natalie found herself at Devon's apartment, an emotional, mental, and even spiritual bucket of exhaustion. The events that transpired that night propelled her into a mental frenzy. *How did Ashley get my razor? How did she know about the cutting? Am I to blame for the crazy Hyenas?* But regardless of the rat race of questions in her mind, she knew she at least owed Devon some answers.

"When I was little", Natalie started, "my dad walked out." She gripped the large mug with "Africa" engraved in cursive as her fingers ran over the black and white illustration. Devon told her it was his favorite, so she chose it to mess with him and left him with a mug he didn't care too much for.

"My mom was great. The epitome of motherhood." She dragged out a sigh. "But a girl needs a father. Just like a boy does. But for different reasons." Natalie paused to glance at Devon anchored on the other end of the sofa until he nodded for her to continue.

Devon's apartment was the typical bachelor's. A studio with one bath, clean but sparse. His parents had assisted with the rent, he admitted, until the cafe got off the ground. A dark blue futon with some throw pillows served as his bed, and a round polyester gray ottoman lay stationed in the middle. He didn't have a TV, he explained, because he preferred reading in his spare time. There were, however, various books on shelves, stacked on his walls, even dressing the wall by the bathroom.

"I was a pretty happy kid," Natalie said. "But I struggled with some things. Perfectionism was one of 'em. I strived to do well at school. I strived to be a good member at church. I strived to fill the hole in my heart that felt so empty from my dad walking out." She took a sip of her tea, soaking up Devon fondling her legs beneath the plaid quilt he'd draped over her. His facial expression was an open sky.

"I think, I thought, if I worked hard enough, no one would ever leave me again." Natalie fell silent before inhaling more of her ginger lemon tea. "At some point, the cutting started. It-it was a way to control what I couldn't control. When hard things happened, I cut. It took me *years* of counseling to understand it. To understand *why* I did it. And to stop." She licked her lips before her eyes settled on the view outside. It was gray and cold, and she was glad to be with Devon, who had somehow become her warmth in such a short time.

"Nat, thank you so much for sharing this with me." Devon changed his pattern from rubbing to stroking the top of her leg, his eyes glistening with endearment. "I'm sorry with the way things went down and that we were forced to discuss it *now*... but I'm grateful you trust me enough to share such a sensitive topic."

Natalie attempted a smile, but her brown eyes moistened. "Yea. Mental health is a big deal to me. I've come a long way, but it's not easy. I-I see a counselor. A psychiatrist, actually. I was so afraid it would start up again after my mom." She shuddered. "Along with the depression.

I've definitely had some close calls." A flashback of her struggle just last month surfaced. "But thankfully, it hasn't gone there. Thankfully, I've been ok. Not perfect. But ok." The chocolate hardwood flooring stared up at Natalie as she bared her soul. "I mean, don't get me wrong, I *have* had some hard days. But not like before."

Devon set his mug on the floor and leaned forward, placing a gentle hand on her chin. He lifted it with the utmost care, and a pleasant sensation coursed through Natalie at his touch. It was like his hand belonged there. "Natalie." He breathed her name, and she had never heard it sound so good. "I'm here for you." He paused. "I know what it's like to lose someone. My-my younger brother died a few years ago. Cancer," he spat, saying it like a four-letter word. "My family is still dealing with that." Dropping his head, he whispered, "*I'm* still dealing with that."

"Oh. I didn't know." Natalie placed her mug on the floor also before capturing Devon's hand in hers. "I'm so sorry."

"How could you know? I only share for you to know that I can be a support." Devon's jaw was steady as his care for her swam laps in his eyes.

Natalie nodded with a heavy head. "Cancer is a horrible death. It took my mom out in two years. We didn't have much time by the time we found out. Two years may seem like a lot, but it's fast when you want forever with them."

Devon agreed. "Exactly. There's never enough time." His eyes clouded over as he looked off into the distance. "I used to go to Darion's bedroom at night and check on him, just to make sure he was breathing, you know? I didn't even live there no more, but I would drive to my parent's house after closing Devon's each night and go to his room. They were taking care of him." A spooky look glazed his eyes. "They saw the worst of it."

Pulled to him like a magnet, Natalie brushed her hand over his, creating a comforting rhythm. *Lord, please help this man.*

"I would check his breathing," Devon continued, "and, satisfied, I'd sit in a chair in the room and watch him sleep for at least an hour. It was like... I felt like if I just *stayed* there long enough, and he sensed me, he wouldn't die. He would stay." His voice caved. "Because I was there."

"But eventually, you had to leave," Natalie whispered, knowing that road all too well.

Devon replied, "Yea," but the tears covering his eyes spoke even more.

"And eventually, he had to leave too," she finished.

Quiet seeped into the room until Natalie shifted her body closer to his. She sheltered his legs with hers, drew his face to her chest, then enveloped him in her arms. Devon's even-brown skin weaved into hers as she lifted up their intertwined palms. Now she was his warmth.

"I know this life is temporary, and because of that, I want to enjoy *every* moment." Natalie smothered her lips over the salty tears streaming down Devon's cheeks. She took her time kissing each one.

"Me too," he croaked in a hoarse tone as she pecked his lips. "I want to enjoy it with *you*." Devon's voice was husky before squeezing her against him.

Natalie let him hold her and kiss her, and she thanked God for his finding her. She thanked God for giving her the desire of her heart.

CHAPTER 21

SURPRISE VISIT

(ASHLEY)

Ashley's eyes fluttered open, and her father and grandmother's blurry frames trickled into view. The two were seated side-by-side in the only two hardback chairs in the room. Her dad kept rocking back and forth in his seat, arms crossed, while Grams knitted what looked to be the beginnings of a yellow scarf. *She only knits when she's super worried,* Ashley thought with a perplexed frown. "Oh!" She whimpered while trying to sit up. *My head is killing me.*

"Sweetie! You're awake!" Her father scrambled to her side as her grandmother leapt to her feet and waddled over to the bed.

"Where am I?" Ashley squeezed her eyes back shut. *And why is the light so damn bright?*

"Get the doctor, Malcolm," Grams commanded. Moments later, a tall Black woman in a white coat bent over her, poking and prodding at the bandage that sealed Ashley's head. Her tone was kind but thorough.

"Ashley, I'm Doctor Michaels. Do you mind if I check you out real quick?"

Ashley eased her head up and down with one eye open but wondered, *Why do I need to be checked out? And why am I in the hospital?*

Dr. Michaels used a small instrument to test her pupil dilation. She then monitored her heartbeat, having Ashley at one point sit all the way up so that she could rest the stethoscope on her back. Afterward, she examined her reflexes, knocking her knee with a small hammer. Ashley groaned with each movement and stole a peek at her father.

I hope he can't see nothing. She felt exposed. The thin hospital robe was way too loose and had the nerve to open wide at the back.

"Ashley, what's the last thing you remember?" Dr. Michaels studied her with intense dark oval eyes.

"Hmmm..." Ashley thought about it. With knitted brows, she concentrated on the black and white checkered floor. "I was at the cafe —with some friends..." she finally said, then drifted off again. She couldn't remember *who* she was with exactly, just that she was there with people she knew.

Dr. Michaels tilted her head in encouragement. "Ok. Anything else? Do you know *why* you were there? Do you know these friends' names?"

Ashley went quiet while wetting her lips.

"It's ok, sweetie," her dad chimed, standing behind the doctor. "Take your time."

Why was I at Devon's? "Denise. Denise was there," Ashley managed.

"Who is Denise?" Dr. Michaels turned to her father.

"Her best friend."

"Ok. That's good." The doctor threw a stern head nod. "Well, I'm not going to push. Sometimes the brain can't handle too much at once, but the fact that you're accurate in where you were and who you were with is a good sign." Dr. Michaels's lips spun a soft smile. "You fainted, Ashley. You were in and out of consciousness, and it does look like you have a mild concussion." Her face took on a look of deep concern. "You hit your head pretty hard there. How are you feeling?"

I can't believe I fainted. That's crazy. "Not the best," Ashley mumbled through tight lips. Her mouth was dry. "Can I get some water?"

Malcolm went for the pitcher sitting on the tray by the bed and poured it with speed into a plastic cup before raising it to Ashley's lips.

Guilt reclined in her heart, laying its head back and getting comfortable. *He looks tired. I hope it's not because I fainted.* When she finished her drink, she muttered, "Thanks, Daddy."

The doctor looked at both Malcolm and Grams. "I've reviewed her X-rays and CAT scan, and there's no sign of brain damage or internal bleeding. I think she'll be ok, but she's probably going to be in some pain in the coming weeks. She'll need physical therapy for sure, and I'll prescribe some pain meds. I also want her to come back for a follow-up in a week."

Relief washed over Malcolm's face as he rubbed his hand over the back of his neck. "Doctor, thank you so much. How long will she need to stay?" His expression turning hopeful, he asked, "Can she come home tonight?"

"We're still waiting on the MRI and want to keep her for 48 hours or until those tests come back. I would say, after that, she should be free and clear. As long as there aren't any other issues that surface. I do, however, want to refer her to a neurologist to take a look as well." Doctor Michaels's comforting smile re-emerged as she grabbed her clipboard off the bed and turned to Ashley. "If that's alright with you? You are a legal adult, so we need your permission."

Ashley grimaced in response. *My back is on fire.* "Yea. That's fine. But can I get those meds now?" Curling onto her side, she tried to ignore the pain.

"Of course. I'll have the nurse bring it."

"Honey. I'm going to stay here with you *all* night," Grams volunteered while tossing the yellow yarn and needles into her seat and moving to Ashley's side.

Ashley mumbled into the stiff pillow, "Oh no, Grams. That's fine. I'll be ok."

"Nonsense. I'm stayin'!" She patted her granddaughter's hand with insistence. "They just gone' have to bring me a blanket, that's all."

Malcolm shook his head in disagreement. "Momma, don't worry about it. I got it. I'm stayin'."

Ashley was in way too much pain to pay attention to their arguing. She figured her father must have won because when the nurse brought in the blankets and pillow, he was the one who took them. It wasn't soon enough before the nurse injected something into her IV.

"Ash, you have some other visitors if you're up for seeing them," her father informed her with a gentle pat on her hair.

Her hair! *What the hell do I look like right now?* But at least she was feeling a little better; the meds had kicked in. "Uh, yea. That's fine." Who was here? Had Darren come? But Ashley felt entirely silly thinking it. *Darren is no longer relevant.*

"Ok, sweetie," her father answered. Throwing his neck over his shoulder at Grams, he asked, "Can you tell them it's ok for them to come back, Ma?"

While Grams rooted around, Ashley tried to sit up, at least to fix her hair, but when she glanced around, she didn't see her purse. "Daddy, can you hand me your phone?" He passed it from his pants pocket, and, using the camera, she tried her best to make herself presentable. *Where is my phone?* But Ashley was too tired to even ask.

"You up here tryna look fly at the damn hospital?" Denise's cheeky tone was the first to float into the room from the doorway, and Ashley craned her head in her direction with a lopsided grin.

"Well, you never know what fine doctors is walking around in here." When Denise leaned over to give her a hug, Ashley's Birkin jiggled on her shoulder. *Good. She has my phone.*

"Aye. Ain't nobody tryna hear all that." BJ skated in right behind and swiped her forehead with a peck. It wasn't until he moved out of the way, though, that Ashley saw Natalie propped against the doorway behind Grams.

"Oh!" Ashley jerked out a small cry of surprise, and everyone looked at her. She hadn't even realized she had spoken out loud. All *she* knew was that her reason for being in the hospital slammed into her mind at the appearance of her cousin.

Everyone shuffled around to make room for Natalie, who loitered in the doorway like a lost puppy. Ashley was polite but curt. Natalie kept her distance, and the whole ordeal only made Ashley more upset. Her face must have shown it because shortly after, her father made everyone leave so she could get some rest. And rest she did. She was out like a light as soon as the coast was clear.

The next evening, Ashley tossed and turned in the rock-hard bed, still wearing the dingy hospital gown. No matter how many times she asked the nurse, they wouldn't let her change. She had even tried to get

BJ to bring her some clothes when he came to check on her earlier, but he just laughed.

I don't understand how me wearing this ugly thing is gone' help me get better. Ashley glared down at the drab gown with spite. Her dad was passed out in one of the hospital chairs nearby when the nurse returned to give her something for the pain. Ashley thought it would help her sleep, but her mind was wide awake. Thoughts about her childhood, about how Natalie wasn't there for her as a kid when she needed her most, spun around like a ballet dancer doing a series of pirouettes.

"Hey, you." A familiar male voice sailed into the room, slicing through her musings. But it couldn't be. There was just no way.

Ashley's eyes darted to the partially open door. She jetted her hands over her eyes, rubbing and thinking that somehow, she had fallen asleep after all. *I have to be dreaming.*

Darren slid inside, easing the door closed while hugging a bouquet of flowers. *Wow.* If Ashley *was* dreaming, she decided she would go to blows with anybody who would try to wake her.

"Hey," she replied back, then ran her tongue over her lips a few times to ease her own tension. "I-I'm surprised you're here." When she shifted upward to sit, Darren rushed over to help, but when he dropped the bouquet at the end of the bed, Ashley's heart raced. He was even closer now.

"Yea. Natalie told me what happened after class today, and I wanted to come see you." He hesitated. "To make sure you were ok."

Ashley frowned. *Natalie told him what happened?* She started fidgeting in the stupid hospital gown. "H-how much did she tell you?"

Surprised by her tone, Darren stammered, "Uhh, that you fell and hit your head?"

"Oh. That's all?"

"Yea. I mean, I don't know why you so damn clumsy that you fell in a freakin' cafe, but uhh, yea. That's what she said." The teasing smile on his lips squeezed her heart, and Ashley chuckled. Her dad jerked in his chair at the noise but resumed snoring.

"How you doin'?" Darren's voice was as tender as his brown eyes that perused her.

"Ok. I was hoping I could get out of here tomorrow, but they want to keep me for a few days." She sighed.

"Yea. That's what Natalie said."

Wow. I can't believe she told him, and he came to check on me. "Yea. And they won't let me wear my freaking clothes. They got me in this God-awful hospital gown." Ashley's face contorted into a frustrated grimace, and Darren tilted his head back in easy laughter.

"Well. It's not a Louis Vuitton sweater dress, but I brought you these." He held out the bundle of yellow tulips from the bed.

Ashley strangled them in excitement, sucking in their fragrance with her nostrils. "These are better than any dress." She couldn't have hidden the emotion in her voice if she had tried. "You know they're my favorite."

"I know." Darren's eyes took on a look of sincerity as he watched her inhale the scent. "Look, I-I didn't want to intrude. I just wanted you to know..." His voice broke, and his tone was thick when he resumed. "I don't care *what's* goin' on with us. I'm always gone' be here for you."

Ashley was too nervous to make eye contact, so she only weaved and bobbed her head over the flowers. Darren was always there for her? "I-I appreciate that." She paused, relinquishing another sigh. There was so much to say. *But where the hell would I start?*

"I'm gone' let you rest." Darren pocketed his hands back into his jeans and shuffled a few steps toward the door. "You just reach out if you need anything."

"Oh. Ok." Ashley was disappointed he was leaving, but too overcome with emotions to ask him to stay. He was making his way out of the room when desperation surged through her. "Wait!" Darren's head pivoted upward in surprise. "I-I just want you to know. I-I *do* know what it's like to lose what's important."

Darren stopped in the doorway with confusion swirling in his eyes. "What? What are you talking about?"

"You said I didn't. When we were at school a few weeks ago. You said I needed to decide what was really important. Before I lost it."

Understanding blanketed his face. "Ahh. Don't worry about that. Just focus on getting better."

"But I want you to know. I *do* know what it's like." Ashley took a deep breath, searching for courage. "I know what it's like. Because... because I lost *you*." After a moment, Darren heaved a breath and started towards her. Ashley prepared herself for the worst.

I know it's too late. She was still grasping his flowers as he drifted nearer, his face encased in shadows. The whole time, her dad's light snoring resounded in the background like the soundtrack from a bad movie, and it seemed like everything was happening in slow motion.

Finally, Darren's hand was on her face, his palm cupping her cheek. It was the perfect fit. "I'm always here, Ash," he said, his voice now a croaked whisper. "You haven't lost me." And before she could reply, his lips on her cheek sent a tingle down her spine. "Get some sleep," he reinforced, then left before she could ask him to stay.

Smothering the flowers against her chest, poignant vulnerability swaddled Ashley, and she lay back thinking about Darren's kiss. She couldn't deny that she was in awe. Not just because of the care he obviously still had for her, but the care demonstrated by Natalie.

Natalie could have told him how I flipped out and put her on blast. But she didn't. Ashley knew that, without a doubt, if the roles were reversed, *she* would have. She also realized her cousin had more loyalty than *she* did. Somehow, she would try to make it up to her. She had to. Because that kiss from Darren meant everything in the world. It was worth more than a million Louis Vuittons.

CHAPTER 22

———————

RIGHT ON TIME

(NATALIE)

The days turned into weeks and before Natalie knew it, she was falling for Devon. Since her first experience at his church, she had been spending more and more time with him, but after she shared about her mom and he opened up about his brother, they were pretty much inseparable. At work, she was his assistant, and everything was business, but after church, they hung out by going for walks or spending time with his family at their diner.

This particular day, they were meeting Kate and Lamont for lunch after church service. The air was mild, at least for New York in the fall, and she tasted a sweet breeze with her nostrils.

"Over here, guys!" Kate was mounted near a table with a frantic wave attached to her wrist, ushering the couple inside the little cafe. Lamont stayed seated with a menu propped upward but popped his eyes over it in greeting.

"Hey!" Devon smothered Natalie's hand with his, pulling her forward into a stream of chatter and various food smells as they headed towards their friends. Natalie crinkled her nose in pleasure, partly because of the food, but mostly because of Devon's hand in hers.

"Wasn't that the best service ever?" Kate piped when everyone got seated. Natalie scanned the crowd. Many of the tables bulged with people, and they had just managed to capture one of the few free ones.

"Yea. Pastor Luis has such a knack for expanding on the most common scriptures," Devon answered in awe. "I mean, not that scripture is common," he hurried up and added, and Natalie patted his knee with understanding. "I just meant those scriptures that you hear about all the time, like, 'Joy comes in the morning' *Psalm 30:1:5, or 'faith without works is dead' *James 2:26. He has a knack for expounding on those."

Natalie smiled in appreciation and chimed in to help him out. "Yea, we know what you meant. And he does. That's one of the things I love about your pastor. He makes the scriptures come alive, and you see them in a way you never saw them before."

Kate's smile widened, successfully flashing all 32 chicklet teeth. "Exactly! And he's not afraid to *go there*, you know? Like he doesn't shy away from uncomfortable topics." Golden strands fell across her face as she leaned over the table.

"Right. Remember when he did the speech on politics during the election?" Devon offered. "I swear I thought half the congregation was gone up and leave. But he stayed true to his stance and didn't let man determine what he would preach."

Natalie's stomach dipped a little. "Um. What was his stance exactly?"

"Y'all know what chu' want?" A small Asian woman traipsed to their table with an impatient look scarring her tiny face.

"Oh. I forgot to look at the menu." Natalie grabbed one from the rack in the middle and sped her eyes across it.

"We'll need a few," Devon suggested, but Natalie shook her head in protest. She didn't want to hold everyone up.

"No, it's cool. Y'all go ahead and I'll figure it out by the time it gets to me."

"It's ok, Nat." Devon slid the waitress an apologetic smile. "My girlfriend's never eaten here before, so can you just give us a sec?"

Natalie couldn't help beaming. *I'm Devon's girlfriend!*

The waitress tossed an annoyed nod before rushing off while Natalie browsed the list of sandwiches and drinks. She was ready by the time the woman revisited but was more concerned about Pastor Luis's political stance than the grilled cheese and tomato soup she had ordered.

"So. Back to what you were saying earlier, Devon. What exactly was the political issue you thought the congregation would leave on?" Natalie tried to minimize the nerves grating her tone. Her church back home had been very divided over politics and just thinking about going through something like that again taunted her with dread.

"Oh. Pastor Luis doesn't believe in using his pulpit to sway people with political views, and some folks were angry that he didn't want to share what his own were," Devon said, filling in the gaps. "I mean, he has his own stance, of course, but he doesn't think leaders should use their influence to manipulate others into falling in line with their beliefs."

Natalie expelled a relieved sigh. "Wow. That's rare. My last church was super politically vocal. It was the worst when election time came." She made a face.

"Oh yea. Mine too," Kate jumped in. "I went to a Catholic church for several years and it was the same deal. Even on the issue of race, it's been such a blessing to be in an environment that doesn't shun interracial relationships." She sandwiched Lamont's hand in hers over the table, and the couple's eyes locked into an intimate gaze.

"So. How *did* y'all meet exactly?" Seeing the rare opening, Natalie dove into the topic she'd been wondering about. *Kate just does not look like the type to be out here kicking it with a brotha,* she couldn't help thinking. She tried not to reveal her thoughts through her eyes.

"Lamont and I actually met at New Life," Kate volunteered along with a dreamy expression. "We worked on the same committee to serve the homeless at Christmas. We worked so well, they put us on another team to lead the youth in summer day camp." Lamont swiveled his bald head up and down in agreement before the waitress reappeared with their orders and he manhandled his steak and cheese sub.

Natalie snuck a peek at the couple while engaging her meal. Lamont was decked in a flannel and canvas sneakers, while Kate wore a chic light green sheath dress. *They just don't seem to fit,* she thought and had to admit to herself she had weird feelings about the girl dating a brother. There were so many issues within the Black community, and Black love was hard to come by. Black women needed Black men to honor and value them in every aspect of life, especially romantically. But ultimately, Natalie knew in her heart, love wasn't about color.

And I guess her dating a Black man inspired her to learn about his culture. I can't be mad at that. She figured this, since Kate was the lone Caucasian person still attending their Black writers' class. As Natalie munched on one of Devon's sweet potato fries, the conversation turned to his upcoming open mic.

Which reminds me, I need to follow up with Lisa about his interview and tidy up some things for Monique's orders for the event. But after Devon stole a bite of her grilled cheese, Natalie's thoughts reverted back to her initial musings.

But I mean, who am I to judge someone's relationship? Devon is almost 10 years older than me. With a half-smile, she watched her boyfriend use a napkin to erase the provolone dripping from the side of his mouth.

Your grandfather was 10 years older than me! The flashback of Grams making that statement to Ashley at the Sunday dinner popped into Natalie's brain. *Leave it to Grams to be speaking to me without even knowing she was speaking to me.*

Devon peered over at her. "You good?" he asked, concern denting his forehead. In newfound contentment, Natalie fell back into her seat while thinking about Grams's story of dating an older man; her own grandfather. A joyful smile oozed from her lips.

"Yep. I'm perfect."

The couple left lunch with their friends, and as Devon held open the door from the restaurant, his eyes bloomed with anticipation. "Come on. I want you to meet my mom." He spoke with excitement before sabotaging Natalie's hand and guiding her to the subway.

"Oh! O-k." Natalie was a mix of elated nerves and giddiness. *It's like a dream,* she thought as they smooshed between a slew of New Yorkers in the frantic busyness that marked the constant state of the city. She tried not to grin the whole ride, but the foggy reflection in the subway glass behind a redhead reading the New York Times betrayed her joy. Natalie had met Devon's other family members at the diner and figured when he was ready to introduce her to his mother, he would. *I guess he's ready!* She hid another goofy grin.

In what felt like no time, an older woman with shiny silver hair and a pleasant smile welcomed Natalie at the door with open arms. "So. *This* is Natalie."

So, this is home, she couldn't help thinking, then expelled a breath when bathed in the woman's slender arms. "Hi, Mrs. Woods."

The two women strolled into the middle of the living room like old friends, leaving Devon behind. The Woodses' had a beautiful brownstone with high-vaulted ceilings and a balcony right off the kitchen. Perfect for hosting family gatherings.

"And this is Bella!" When Devon picked up the little bundle of joy from her play area near the stairwell, she cooed with glee.

Natalie exclaimed, "It's nice to meet you, Bella." But Bella popped a finger into her mouth while in her uncle's arms and puckered her lips around it into a frown.

"Say 'Hi,' Bella," Devon prompted, but the child held no interest in complying. Instead, she whipped her head the other away and tossed it onto his shoulder, offering her back to Natalie.

"Oh now. Don't be that way, sweet Bella. Come meet Devon's new friend," Mrs. Woods encouraged Bella, pulling her from Devon's arms and turning her to once again, face Natalie.

"It's alright," Natalie said. An awkward smile crawled along her lips. "She probably just needs a minute to warm up to me."

Bella stared at Natalie with the same crooked frown, then shook her head and heaved it back onto her grandmother's shoulder. "No!" came her small defiant voice, now muffled by Mrs. Woods's blouse.

Devon suggested, while moving next to her, "I'm sorry, Nat. Let me take your coat." When he held out his arms, she obliged, eager for the distraction, and broke free from her double-breasted charcoal gray pea coat.

"Natalie, I love that scarf," Mrs. Woods commented in approval and Natalie caressed the burnt orange material draped around her neck.

"Thank you." She added in a softer tone, "It was my mom's."

"Well, she sure has good taste!"

A pang of hurt exploded in Natalie's heart like an unforeseen hurricane. "Yea. She did. She passed away earlier this year," she explained.

Mrs. Woods's face deflated into sorrow. "Oh dear. I'm sorry to hear that."

Devon came near and caressed her back as Natalie nodded. She never knew how to respond when people shared their condolences, but Mrs. Woods's genuine tone circled her heart, putting her at ease.

After Devon hung her coat along with his on the coat hanger by the stairs, he led Natalie to the long tan leather sectional stapled against the wall. A rectangular glass coffee table sat a couple of feet in front of it while a 75-inch TV straddled the opposite wall above a brick fireplace, facing the guests. *They're like modern day Cosby's,* Natalie thought while settling in next to Devon.

"Would you like tea, Natalie?" Mrs. Woods had tucked Bella back into her play area, and turned hospitable gray-brown eyes to her guests.

"I'll get it, Mama," Devon informed. He rushed to the kitchen before Natalie could even blink.

"Uncle Debon!" Bella took off after him, her long pigtails swinging freely behind. Devon smiled, his eyes cascading with love, and scooped her into his arms before the duo headed to the kitchen.

Natalie fell back into the plush cushions, making herself comfortable and admiring the decor. *They definitely have money,* she thought, then zeroed in on the painting above the couch. Several Black people dressed in their Sunday best were walking together in groups. "Funeral Procession," she mumbled.

"You know Black art, dear?" Mrs. Woods sat diagonal on the other side of the sectional, lovely in a violet silk blouse and gray dress pants with what appeared to be real pearls. Her crisp silver hair hung chipper and chopped in a blunt fashion at her shoulders.

She's the epitome of grace. Natalie was hugged by another wave of awe. "I know a little," she responded, then smoothed down her sandy-colored sweater dress. With slight hesitancy, she added, "My cousin Ashley is the real artist though." At the statement, another uncomfortable pang hit her heart, but she stifled it. *No need in thinking of her right now.*

"Ah. But Devon said you write. Correct?" Mrs. Woods lifted a razor thin brow while sitting as straight as a board. "That is art too, you know."

"Yep. She's amazing!" Devon reappeared with Bella on his hip, then reclaimed his seat near Natalie. The toddler busied herself by using his face as her playground. She extended her hands over his chin and laughed every time he pretended to bite her chubby fingers. They were like little sausages, and Natalie's heart melted at the sight.

Tearing her eyes away, she said to Mrs. Woods, "Devon literally has heard two school papers and a poem. And that's the only credibility I have at this point with my writing." She veered teasing eyes back to Devon.

Devon pitched a boyish grin and puffed out his chest. "Not true! I've been an avid reader of "Poetry of Passions" for the last two weeks now." His cream sweater tightened against his muscular frame with each movement, inducing an appreciative smile from Natalie.

"'Poetry of Passions'?" Mrs. Woods asked, perplexed.

"It's my blog," Natalie informed. "Mostly poems. But some short stories too." She added this last bit of information, hoping that it made her writing sound just a bit more vast.

Mrs. Woods offered a cool smile, saying, "Well. That's very nice, dear."

Disappointment sliced Natalie's heart, and her earlier insecurities about the age gap between her and Devon resurfaced. *Devon is a self-made man with his own business,* she ruminated, *and I'm up here writing poems on a blog.* She stretched down her sweater dress that didn't quite reach her chocolate knee-high boots. *Still, I* think *the dress is respectable. I just wish he would have told me beforehand we were coming over here.* Thankfully, the teapot whistle rescued her from her insecure wonderings.

Mrs. Woods called to her son, "Devon, would you get that, dear?" but he was already in action with Bella at his heels.

Natalie's eyes overflowed with adoration as his niece waddled behind in her pink OshKosh B'Gosh jumper. Devon had told Natalie that Bella's dad was MIA. *It's so nice she has her uncle as a good father figure.* Natalie thought of Malcolm, and that made her smile even more.

"I understand you're a student?" Mrs. Woods's tone was polite with only a hint of the protective mother-mode she was in.

While fingering her scarf, Natalie remembered having that experience once herself. "Yes, ma'am."

With the poise of a ballet dancer, the older woman crossed her legs at the ankles while leaning in just a bit. "Well, what are your plans for the future? I mean, *after* graduation of course."

Caught off guard, Natalie shifted at an awkward angle. "Oh. Umm. Uhh... I'm hoping to get a job writing." She paused and rubbed her thighs painted with black tights. They had flower designs cruising down her thighs and before this very moment, she had thought they were a great fashion statement. Now they just made her feel... *young.* "I'm just not sure in what capacity. But I honestly feel a call to the nations," she finished.

"Here we go, ladies!" Devon appeared with a porcelain tray crowded with complimentary mugs, various tea bags, and a small stout teapot.

Natalie marveled. *Is that* china?

"Thank you, dear." Mrs. Woods lifted her mug along with an earl gray tea bag while Devon hid Bella back inside her play area.

After she was settled, he handed Natalie a mug and eased down beside her. "What'd I miss?" he asked.

"Oh," Natalie froze, her eyes racing over the tea options. *Maybe I was trippin' thinking there could be something with us,* she wondered, choosing a bag of mint tea. Placing the mug and the little saucer on her lap to let it steep, her heart brittled with both disappointment and confusion.

Mrs. Woods's dainty tone floated an answer. "Natalie was just telling me her plans for the future." The woman crossed her legs again while massaging her mug on a saucer.

I don't think I'll ever be able to hold my tea like that, Natalie mused.

"Oh?" Devon slid closer to Natalie and stroked her arm. "Well, Ma, Natalie has plenty of time to figure all that out."

"Mmhmm." Mrs. Woods's shrug was light. "Of course. I just wanted to know if she had any *insight. That's* all."

Little Bella waddled over to the adults then, somehow squeezing her pudgy body between the coffee table near Natalie and Devon's feet.

Devon straightened, assuming she was coming to him, but she kept right on moving, ultimately stopping near Natalie. Surprised, Natalie gazed down as the little girl held up one plump hand and tugged a strand of her long, thick, wavy hair, fashioned into a twist out.

"Oh. Well!" Mrs. Woods proclaimed with gleaming eyes. "Look who's come around." Devon smiled and rested an arm on the back of the couch.

Bella extended both hands and said, "Up!" demanding to be held by Natalie. Grinning, Natalie complied, burying the child into her lap. It dawned on her in that moment that Bella was a great picture for the way God often moved in her life. She played with Bella for a bit before redirecting her attention to Mrs. Woods.

"Mrs. Woods, I've found it's best to wait on *God* to provide my next steps in life." Natalie paused, bending her head down at Bella, while pretending to steal her nose. "Sometimes it feels like it takes a while for Him to come around. But I know from experience, He's always right on time." She glanced at Devon, and the two hid themselves in an affectionate gaze.

Mrs. Woods pumped her sleek gray head up and down, both startled and impressed by the clarity of the young woman's words. "Well. I can't argue with that." She had had her own experiences of waiting on the Lord, and they had taught her well. While taking a long sip of her earl gray tea, Mrs. Woods's eyes stayed locked on the couple. "And please. Do call me Grace," she suggested before indulging in another lengthy sip.

"Oh! Ok... *Grace*." Natalie laughed to herself while bouncing Bella on her lap. The little girl bubbled with sounds of joy, her earlier shyness completely forgotten. Natalie smoothed down her pigtails, and Devon rubbed Bella's back as the toddler grinned from ear to ear at all the attention.

"No. I can't argue with that at all," Grace mumbled. She was still watching Natalie and Devon, but now, a mysterious smile was polished on her exquisite mahogany face.

CHAPTER 23

PAINT IT OUT

(ASHLEY)

In her opinion, Ashley's recovery was slithering at a snail's pace. She had physical therapy twice a week, but her pain meds were still needed daily. Not for the first time, she complained to Denise on the phone, "I'm just sick of not doing my usual," and sucked in a wad of air between her teeth in frustration. *It's Saturday night, and I'm freaking homebound.*

Denise spouted her ritual response on the other end. "Girl. You know what the doctor said. You don't need to be out and about unnecessarily."

Ashley lay sprawled on her back with a pillow beneath for support while talking on speakerphone. Snippets of people's lives from her newsfeed glazed the screen as her eyes glossed over in boredom. *Hmmm. Tam broke up with old boy, I see.* She hadn't seen any new pictures of Tamara and her new boo in weeks, so she figured as much. *I guess we in the same boat,* she mused with despair while thinking of her breakup with Jason. Ashley hadn't heard from him since he bailed on their museum date and harbored mixed feelings about it. On the one hand, she was pissed that he tossed her aside like that. On the other, she couldn't stop thinking about Darren.

As if she were monitoring Ashley's thoughts, Denise asked, "What's up with you and Jason?"

"Ugh. I haven't heard from that boy since he canceled our date for the damn museum."

Her friend's tone was soaked in disbelief. "Dang. He didn't even come see you at the hospital?"

"Naw."

"Well. I guess you should be glad he gone then if the brotha didn't care enough to come see you at the freakin' hospital."

Ashley gritted her teeth. "I mean. I ain't really tell him I was in there, so he didn't really know," she admitted. "But umm, Darren's ass came to see me." It was the first time Ashley had shared this information with anyone. She had been wrestling with it and still sorting through how she felt about it.

"Whaaaattt!" Denise was shocked. "He came to see you, and you just now saying something?"

"Cuz, I don't know what to do with it. I mean, he kissed me and brought me flowers, and I'm like, what the hell?" Another sigh jutted out before Ashley flipped onto her side. A sharp pain socked her back, reminding her to take it easy. "And we've talked, but not about the damn kiss," she informed, caressing her lower spine. "And like I said, I just don't know what to do with it."

"He kissed you? Dag. That's crazy."

"Yea. But it was on the damn cheek. I mean, *maybe* if he kissed me on the lips, *then* I would know where we stood. But naw. He tryna hit me with those player moves." She deepened her voice to sound like a man's and tossed her eyes upward. "Girl, you know I'm always here for you. No matter what happens between us, I'm here."

Denise released a hearty laugh. "I don't know if it was like that, Ash." After a pause, she added, "But really, I'm not that surprised."

Ashley's brows reached for the ceiling. "What chu' mean?"

"Cuz. Darren has always had a super soft spot for you. Why you think he distanced himself so much after the breakup? I think he still has feelings."

Ashley sucked her teeth in annoyance. "I don't *even* know. *All* I know is that I need to get some shit straightened out within myself before I even think about Darren. Or Jason. Or anybody, for that matter. If Darren and I were to ever have a chance, things would need to be different." Chewing in thought at the inside of her cheek, she pressed her eyelids closed. "*I* would need to be different."

"Wow. I guess your counseling is paying off, huh?" Ashley tried not to be offended that Denise sounded so surprised. "On *that* note. Have you talked to Natalie?"

"Naw. Not really." Ashley resumed her perusal on Instagram, but not seeing anything else of interest, she typed Darren's handle in the search field. *Just cuz we was talking about him,* she told herself. *Not cuz I'm thirsty to see what he doin'.* Darren had updated his page with a reel of him and his kid brother Eric playing basketball. They showed off for the person shooting the video with different plays and moves.

"You know it wasn't nothin' between her and Darren," Denise said. "Right? I mean, she's with Devon."

"Yea. I know." Ashley switched to a different page. She was tired of pining after Darren.

"Then why did you do it?"

"Do what?"

"Why did you put her on blast in front of Devon? With that cutting situation. I know I sent you her journal page, but I didn't think you would put her out there in front of Devon like that."

Ashley was silent. "I don't know, D. It's like, sometimes I get so angry that all I can see is red." Easing over onto her stomach, she slid her cheek onto one arm. "That's how I felt when I found out she was with Darren that night. And his whole damn family. I think I just wanted to hurt her as much as I felt like she hurt me."

"Yea. But 'chu do owe her an apology." Denise slid in. "That stuff that happened when y'all was kids. Y'all was *kids*! I did a lot of stupid shit when I was a kid. And foreal foreal, if I had known *that's* what your beef was about, I would a never shot you that intel."

Ashley had heard the same message from her counselor about them being just kids and kids doing stupid stuff. In addition to physical therapy, she had begun her mental and emotional treatment with Regina Caldwell. Talking to Regina was like reading a good book. There was peace every time she was in her presence, and Ashley couldn't get enough. She actually looked forward to their twice-a-week meetings.

"Yea. I'm starting to realize that," she responded, rubbing the scar on her head and thinking about how long she had harbored animosity towards her cousin for getting that scar. Her mind recalled her conversation with Regina in their last counseling session.

"I just don't know if I'm ready to let it go," Ashley told Regina while perched on the soft cushioned purple loveseat. Regina had good taste, decorating her office in shades of creme, grays, and pops of purple. The woman was a kindred spirit and dressed like she was on the runway. That day, she rocked a leopard-print top beneath a black Gucci blazer, fitted black pants, and midnight black Balenciaga high-heeled boots. One side of her hair was shaved as thick braids cascaded like waterfalls over the other.

"Does letting it go mean letting her back in?" Ashley continued voicing her concerns. "How can I trust her when she clearly betrayed me?"

Regina asked, "But did she really betray you?" She peered at her client with a thoughtful frown. "It sounds like she wasn't a part of the assault."

In a flash, Ashley slapped her arms over her chest. "She's the one who invited me to hang with those girls. You can't tell me she didn't know what they was planning!"

"Maybe she did. Maybe she didn't. But you won't know until you ask. And honestly, what would it have benefited your cousin to have you assaulted?"

Ashley was silent. After a moment, she replied in an uneasy tone, "To fit in with them. I guess."

"But you said she already fit in. That doesn't make sense." When Ashley didn't say anything, Regina continued. "Ashley, forgiveness is more for you than the other person. Think of how long you've carried this grudge against your cousin. And how that's affected your mental and emotional well-being." Her counselor watched her from the chair, a black pen poised to her purple lips.

Ashley was stubborn. "I'm fine." Tilting her head to peer out the window, she declared, "I ain't tweakin' on Natalie."

The older woman prodded, "You're fine? OK. Then what brought you into my office?"

Ashley's light eyes dipped as she caressed the edges of the knitted yellow scarf from Grams thrown over her black sweater from Express. "The panic attacks," she finally answered.

"Right. The panic attacks. What you've described is that when you're extremely upset, you suffer from these attacks. That means the anxiety and fear you have as a result of trauma is manifesting physically in your body. That last panic attack caused a severe incident where you were rushed to the hospital. Ashley, if you don't deal with this trauma now, what will it cause the next time?"

"All I'm sayin'," Denise's voice piped into her speaker, bringing Ashley back to the present, "is that your cousin was *devastated* when you were out cold at Devon's *and* when you were in the hospital. If you could have seen the look in her eyes." Her voice shivered with passion, and she stopped speaking to gain control over her quivering tone. "And that was *after* you straight up *dogged* her in front of her man! Natalie loves you. She loves you like *I* love you." Denise paused again. "Shoot, maybe even more, cuz I don't know if I could have dealt with *that* shit you pulled." When Ashley didn't respond, Denise went on. "She loves you like a sister."

Ashley shifted onto her side, wrestling with her inner being. She knew Denise was telling the truth, and it wasn't just because Denise always did. It was because she had felt that same message stirring in her heart since the accident. *Especially after she looked out for me with Darren.* But when it came down to it, Ashley was just too afraid to let the girl back in.

"I hear you, sis. But look, I gotta go. My dad and I are supposed to do a movie tonight. And it's been *forever* since that's happened. Plus, it's my only highlight for the weekend since I'm jailbait and all." Ashley tried to make her tone light while checking the time on her cell.

"OK, love. I'll check on you later."

"Thanks. And tell B 'wuz up'. Since y'all still goin' strong." Her voice was teasing, but she was genuinely happy for her people. *It's nice to see them settling down.* Ashley for sure had mixed feelings about them initially, but her accident had given her a different perspective. *If anybody can find happiness and love, I'm all for it. Hashtag Black Love, foreal.*

"Bet," Denise answered before hanging up.

Ashley lay there for a moment with her head buried in her pillow. It was 7:55 PM and almost time for her movie date with her father, but she couldn't get Regina's words out of her head. What would happen next time if she didn't deal with her trauma now?

Paint it out, she sensed in her heart, and a wispy sigh escaped her mouth at the thought. Painting and drawing had always been therapeutic for Ashley growing up, but she stopped doing that kind of creating a long time ago. *Probably the last intimate piece I did like that was that mural in the alley Darren hipped me to. And I only did that because he convinced me to.*

Paint for me.

The message resonated again. It was so strong, and she couldn't shake it. *Paint for* who? she wondered. "Mama?" Her body tensed as she eased from her bed and straddled the middle of the room, her back to the door. Not seeing a thing, she swiped her long, pointed Versace umbrella from her closet corner. It was the only weapon she could think of in her room. Ashley had never believed in ghosts, but just in case, she wanted to be ready.

"Ashley?"

Pain stabbed her neck when she whipped around to see her dad looming in the doorway. "Ow!" She grabbed and started rubbing.

Malcolm looked at her with a strange expression and a bowl of popcorn. "You OK?"

"Uh. Yea. You just scared me. That's all."

"Mmmm. OK. Well. You ready?" He held up the popcorn. "It's movie time."

Feeling silly, she answered, "Sure," and threw the umbrella back into her closet before trailing him down the stairs. *Ghosts,* she thought while laughing to herself. But that desire to paint was so heavy, and Ashley couldn't ignore this pressing feeling that there was something she had to release. That same energy accompanied her through the movie they watched: "Father of the Bride," one of her dad's favorites.

"Honey, you seem distant." Her father studied her in the dimness of the den.

"Yea. Just thinking..." The bowl of half-eaten popcorn stared at Ashley as she rocked her outstretched legs on the couch. Her dad was rooted on the other end in a pair of sweats she had bought him for Christmas. With his money, of course.

"About what?"

"You believe in ghosts, Dad?" she ventured, running a hand over the smooth leather cushion.

"Ghosts, huh?" Malcolm tickled his chin with his hand in thought. "Nah. I can't say that I do. Your mom was the more mystic one out of us."

"Funny you should say that." She stole a glance to view his reaction. "I think *she's* the one tryna tell me something," she confided.

Malcolm's eyes shined with compassion. "Oh? Well... then see what it is."

Ashley fiddled with her joggers. She only wore them around the house because they had a hole in the left pants leg, but they were so comfortable she couldn't bring herself to get rid of them. After a moment, she admitted her fear out loud. "What if I don't wanna know what it is?"

Her dad took a second to respond. "Well, if your mom is the same woman in the afterlife that she was in *this* life, then her message for you could only come from a heart of love."

"Wow. Thanks, Daddy!" Ashley was touched by her father's words. And not just his words, but also his willingness to talk about her mom. She mustered all her courage. "Can I ask you something?" One of Ashley's counselor's tips was to be more honest with her father. Instead of stuffing down her emotions, Regina said to try to talk to him so that her anger didn't build up until she lashed out like she did at their Sunday dinner.

"What's the deal with you and Samantha? I mean, you never even mentioned her to me until the day you brought her to meet the whole family."

Malcolm kicked out a weighty breath. "After our conversation that morning, I thought you were cool with meeting her. I had no idea you would flip like that. Or take it so hard."

Raw emotion drew Ashley upright in her seat. "I mean, you barely said two words about her, and then you bring her to meet the whole damn, I mean, freaking family? I would have thought you would have introduced her to *me* first." Hurt sparkled in her tawny-hued eyes, and her father grew quiet again.

"I honestly didn't look at it like that." His own eyes were just as pained. "I guess I was excited, and I thought I had the green light." Stretching a hand to caress her chin, he added, "I'm sorry, baby. I didn't intend to hurt you. I just got caught up in my feelings. I haven't felt this way since your mom and I mishandled the situation."

A burst of emotions exploded in Ashley's heart. "And how come we don't talk about her? Mom, I mean." The question rushed out from years of not having ever said it out loud, and her words tumbled forward like a toddler taking their first steps.

Malcolm rocked in his seat a little. "But we *do*." He looked at her perplexed. "We just did."

"No. No, we don't. I'm lucky if I get a few sentences out of you about her, like tonight, and then it's a closed topic until the next time you decide to give me two more sentences." Ashley spoke fast, afraid she would lose her boldness.

Malcolm looked surprised. "Wow. I didn't know you felt that way." His head collapsed onto his chest as he huffed a sigh bogged down by years of unsaid words.

"Yea. I do," she continued. "And there are no pictures. The only pictures I have are the ones Mom gave me. But you don't have *any* up. In the whole house. Not one." Ashley exhaled in freedom from everything she had wanted to say for so long, feeling lighter but still grieved. Tossing the bowl back and forth in her lap, the little kernels spun and twirled as her eyes fixated on their performance.

"I-I didn't realize," Malcolm whispered. Remorse slouched her father's shoulders, and when he finally did look at her, his eyes were soaked with tears. "I guess it just hurt too much," he croaked.

Ashley dropped the bowl on the coffee table in one fell swoop and scooted closer. "I know. It hurt me too. But it hurt me more *not* being able to talk about her. *Not* being able to keep her memory alive," she admitted. Her sad light eyes pierced his.

Malcolm cupped a tender hand on her face, his voice cracking as he spoke. "Ashley, you mean the world to me. Losing your mother so suddenly was devastating, and I can't fathom ever losing you after that.

When you were laying in that hospital bed..." He stopped and shuddered. "Well, it was a wake-up call." Motioning to her, he said, "I'll do better. I promise."

Ashley fell into the long-awaited embrace when her father opened his arms. Though it was a conversation she wished they'd had a while ago, her heart was still in need of it. *Better late than never*, she thought while coddled in her father's arms. *Better late than never.*

<hr>

Sunday morning, Ashley awoke as light as a feather. Her talk with her dad had given her peace, and her mind was clearer. Instead of her typical run, she went for a walk since she was still recovering. Bundled up in a CCNY sweatshirt, boots, and jean jacket complete with scarf and gloves, she browsed the familiar neighborhood. Even though she had lived there for several years, everything somehow seemed illuminated.

Ms. Jesse sat on her porch, rocking in her porch swing, which appeared as yellow as the sun. Old Mr. Roberts walked his golden retriever on the opposite side of the sidewalk, his dog's mane shining like a pot of gold. The trees were almost bare, but the ones that stubbornly held onto leaves radiated in hues of red, orange, and yellow, resembling flames of fire. It was like Ashley was seeing in 3D!

Paint it out. The message did laps in her heart, sharper than Michael Phelps, the Olympic swimmer. It was so loud she stopped her walk and peered behind with her hands tied to the inside of her jacket. But there was no one.

In absolute fear, Ashley whispered, "Momma?" but only the wind responded. Still, the words "paint it out" held her heart in their palm as she speed-walked to her car in the garage. She was the only one home. Natalie was at church, and her dad was at the office. Before she could question herself, before she could allow reason to override what was occurring in her being, Ashley clicked the key fob in her jacket pocket, hopped in her truck, and dashed out the driveway, nearly forgetting to shut the garage.

What is happening? The maddening thought plagued her as she turned down a road she hadn't driven in so long. She was *compelled*, even almost *desperate*, to get to where she was going.

"Paint it out," reverberated as she scurried onto the side street of Pete's Paint and Supplies just when Pete arrived.

With curious eyes, he squinted through his bifocals. "Ashley?" He was waiting at the storefront's door, his head cocked in her direction. Even from a distance, Pete seemed the same as he had when she would come years ago; short, bald, and sweet as pie.

"Hi, Mr. Pete!" She waved with animation, getting out of her truck after parking.

"Ashley. It's the strangest thing," Pete said in wonder. He rubbed his bald head and scratched the prickly gray hairs on each side. "We aren't even open on Sundays." His gaze was uncanny as he stared at her with a key postured near the keyhole.

"Really?" she asked. *I didn't even think about it being Sunday.* Ashley just knew she had to get there. Pete proceeded to open the door to the shop, and they hustled inside, seeking safety from the cool air. The smell of paint fumes engulfed her, engaging in a long-awaited dance with the tiny hairs in her nostrils. Ashley inhaled relief and exhaled pure joy. *I forgot how much I missed this smell!* Her eyes began drinking in the pallets and paints that crowded the small interior.

"But I had this urge to get here this morning and open the shop," Pete finished while bending over the windows and opening the three large blinds in the front of the store.

"Well, I'm glad you did!" And Ashley meant it. In unabashed eagerness, she dove into the supplies and picked out colors, canvases, and brushes, stuffing them all in the only cart Pete had stashed in front of the intimate space. Thirty minutes later, she drove the rickety thing up to the register where Pete totaled her purchases. His small, beady eyes sparkled behind his glasses. He seemed just as giddy as Ashley felt.

"Ashley, I've missed you frequenting my shop. It's always been such a pleasure."

Ashley's heart simmered at the statement. "Aww! Thanks, Mr. Pete. I used to love coming here with my mom as a kid. Great memories."

"I loved your mom. Seeing you is a reminder of her beauty and talent."

Again, she was touched. *The man is pulling on my heartstrings.* "Thank you. That means a lot."

"Sure thing," Pete said, handing her the receipt. "And Ashley?"

Clutching the bags, she placed them with care into her cart. "Yes, Mr. Pete?"

"Paint it out."

In utter shock, Ashley gasped. Did Pete even know what he was saying? "I intend to," she replied, marveling. Thanking the kind old man, Ashley whisked her bags to the car, then tucked them into the front seat before driving back home in record time. After parking in the garage, she lugged the items upstairs all in one trip. She was that determined. When Ashley got to her room, she set up the canvas, pulled out her paints, unleashed her brushes, whipped out her pallets, and went to work. Her hands were an electricity of creativity. She drew, brushed, and stroked. For hours she went, only stopping to use the bathroom and drink from her bottle of Smartwater.

"Paint it out," clung to Ashley's heart the whole time. With every stroke, "Paint it out" resounded. And so she did. It was late when she finished. Locked up in her room with the door closed while Alexa played 6Lack, she knew she was a sight, but she couldn't care less. Cheek-stained with various paint colors, baggy sweatshirt loose over a pair of black leggings, hair smothered with the scarf she woke up in; Ashley had been so driven, she forgot to take it off.

She teetered back to look at the completed work and studied the painting. A woman was running in the midst of water, nearly drowning, gaping behind in fear. The waves surrounded her, almost overtaking her. But there was a man. He walked on top of the water, full of peace and emanating love. So. Much. Love. With bloody hands, He reached out to her.

Ashley's eyes poured over the painting like a starving man eating a piece of bread; hungrily. She examined the man on the water, with tan skin and hair of wool, then stood in awe. All this time, she had been afraid, but there was no reason to be. She realized there was no reason to run because instead of fear, there was only love. *And I never saw it until now.*

"Jesus," she whispered, peering with intent at the man walking on water. And Ashley knew, at that moment, that it wasn't her mother who had been delivering that message, "Paint it out." It was God.

CHAPTER 24

OPEN MIC

(NATALIE)

It was Natalie's break time at Devon's, and she was in the middle of working on her poem for open mic night. The words sprung from her very depths right on time. "Better late than never," she mumbled while scribbling in her journal. Devon's open mic was tonight.

"Natalie, I want you to meet someone!" At the sound of Devon's voice, she yanked her head up from her desk, a ballpoint pen still in hand.

Wow. She's stunning. A honey-hued woman with thick, curly hair flowing well past her shoulders was planted just so against the doorway. She beamed at Natalie, and a deep dimple flashed in the cavern of her left cheek.

"Hi, Natalie. I'm Lisa Doris. Devon's told me so much about you." Perky and petite, Lisa hopped a few steps into the office and extended a gracious hand.

"Oh. Hi!" Natalie hopped to her feet, dropping her pen and adjusting her knee-length tweed pencil skirt. She raved, "It's a pleasure. You must be here for the interview?" Natalie checked her brown leather Coach watch her uncle had recently gotten for her and added, "I didn't even realize it was 1 o'clock."

"Yea. We're going to the conference room. You *did* get it ready for us, didn't you, Nat?" Particularly dapper in a blue tweed jacket over a white crew-neck sweater and khaki pants, Devon ambled within inches inside the doorway.

"Sure did," Natalie assured with a smile. "There's some water set out, and the printout of the keynotes you requested is waiting on your chair."

"Great." Devon lifted his chin in a take-charge kind of way. "Let's go, Lis."

"Ok," she replied but turned back to Natalie. "Natalie, given the information Devon has shared with me about you and your career goals, I would *love* to speak with you after the interview." Lisa looked hopeful yet regal, sporting a beige Kate Spade purse and a dark blue trench overlaid with a fluffy fuchsia scarf.

"Oh?" Natalie swept her eyes to Devon, who was grinning at her, then slid them back to Lisa. "Ok-ay." She was surprised and a little confused. *What could Lisa Doris, a journalist, want with me?*

"Awesome. *Jazz* Magazine has a great internship program. I think you might find it beneficial in helping guide you into your next steps with writing," Lisa elaborated. "Especially if you choose a profession in journalism."

Natalie was elated. "Wow! I didn't know that." Her eyes were ready to bust from their sockets as she shook her head in agreement. "Yes, that would be great."

"I'll come get you when we're done." Lisa's wave was promising before she tailed Devon out the door, and Natalie caught his eye before he left. He threw her an excited wink.

Alone in her office, she fell back into her chair, fluttering both eyelids to the ceiling. "Wow. An *internship!*" Natalie celebrated with one good swivel and entered into a short praise break.

Anything for you, Beloved, came the familiar voice as her heart cried out in song. *Anything for you.*

The show was about to start, and Natalie was nervous. It was her first open mic at Devon's. Just when she was looking for him, he appeared behind her.

"You need anything?" he asked in a caring tone.

"Shouldn't I be asking *you* that? This is *your* big event." She scanned the crowd. *I've never seen Devon's this packed before.*

"Yea, well, I have good people helping, so I'm a little more free than I've been in the past," Devon advised, his eyes watching several of his servers on the move.

"Yo. Can I get some service?" yelled a young brother with braids from the coffee bar.

Natalie teased Devon with a grin. "You were saying?"

"Actually, um, let me help my 'good people'," he answered with a sheepish chuckle.

She patted his hand in understanding, "Baby, do what chu' gotta do," then shifted her attention back to the front. People were loitering at the door and seated at every table. The servers, many of them now her friends, dashed around the cafe, taking orders.

"It's insane in here!" Denise announced, hurrying by. She emptied a tray in her hand and set the empty glasses on a shelf leading to the kitchen.

Natalie's twists stroked the air as she cocked her head in response. "Yea?" she asked, "But isn't it always like this on open mic night?"

"Yep. At least for the last couple of years that I've worked here," Denise agreed. When she started making drinks at the bar, she almost slammed into Alice, who popped up with her own tray to empty. "My bad, sis," Denise mumbled, stumbling out of the way.

Alice waved her off. "You already know what it is." She slid her mugs onto the back shelf and waited for Denise to finish her drinks. "Nat, how was your lunch with Lisa?"

Natalie smiled. "Amazing. I'm really grateful Devon connected me with her. I think she's going to be a great mentor in my career," she confided.

Alice gave her a thumbs up. "Nice. Oh. I have good news too. The publishing company accepted my manuscript!" Her eyes were aglow behind her rims as a broad smile swallowed her petite face.

Natalie's jaw dropped. "Alice, that's *great* news. I'm so happy for you!"

"Thanks. It's been a long time comin'." Once Denise rushed past them to serve her customers, Alice started making drinks. "I'll give you the details later," she promised before leaving.

Wow. Alice's good news made Natalie think about her own future in writing. *I wonder if I could get published one day?*

"Alright, alright, alright! Y'all know what time it is!" Chuck stood at the front with the mic, hyping up the crowd. "How y'all doin' tonight?" He gazed out as the spotlight pierced him, and the audience was rowdy in their response.

"Yea!"

"We see you, Chuck!"

"Let's go!"

Chuck laughed. "Ok. Ok. Welcome to our monthly open mic at Devon's." He raised a hand, and the group cheered, "Woohoo!"

The energy from the atmosphere enthralled Natalie as her eyes inhaled the slew of chocolate faces seated and standing. *Look what Devon has done,* she thought with appreciation. A memory surfaced from earlier today when she felt neglected in his office. She had stopped in, thinking they could connect, but Devon was too preoccupied. *I can't be mad at him at all. The brother is on fire.*

But within minutes, Natalie's beautiful browns lost a bit of their shine. Seated near the front, on the same side of her, was Ashley. Pain made a grand entrance into Natalie's heart, and she struggled to ignore its presence. She and her cousin hadn't spoken since the last time they were at Devon's and Ashley had fainted. Somehow, they had become pros at the game of avoiding each other in the house. Natalie was giving Ashley space to heal from her fall. At least, that's what she had been telling herself. But she had to be honest that since Ashley's outburst, she had struggled with her emotions. It had been such a difficult season with her mom passing and then Ashley's coldness. She felt so lonely while missing her friends, and then the added financial stressors had felt so overwhelming at times. Natalie wondered that she had even made it through all the tests and trials.

As she lay in bed the night before, journaling, a scripture she had memorized crept into her psyche.

1 Peter 1:6- *...though now for a little while you may have had to suffer grief in all kinds of trials. These have come so that the proven genuineness of your faith—of greater worth than gold, which perishes even though refined by fire—may result in praise, glory and honor when Jesus Christ is revealed.*

That passage had given her peace, and she understood that though her circumstances were difficult, they had purpose. Her faith was even greater as a result of withstanding the hardships she had experienced in this season.

Is that Uncle Malcolm? Natalie peered more closely at the man at Ashley's table. *I didn't even know he liked poetry,* she wondered to herself.

"The rules are the same," Chuck continued. "One. No negative feedback. We are always appreciative of local artists and talents. Two. Snap, don't clap. And three. Buy some coffee and sandwiches!" The crowd laughed, and Chuck announced the first open mic volunteer. A middle-aged woman with thick, short twists popped up in front. Natalie took the opportunity to read notes on her phone, but a male voice disturbed her concentration.

"Hey there." She glanced up at Darren before pulling him into a quick hug. Natalie had mentioned the open mic last week, but he never said he was coming.

"You made it," she whispered back, but then, her eyes grew.

"Hey, girl!" Jaida peeked out from behind Darren with Trisha in tow.

"Oh my God!" Natalie squealed, and all three girls fell into each other's arms. "How are you here? What is going on?" Natalie whipped her head back and forth between her friends.

Jaida grinned. "Darren here sent us the flyer." She nodded her head towards him, and Darren smiled at Natalie.

"I cannot believe this!" Natalie was undone. "I can't believe y'all came all the way up here. But how did you even contact them?" Her voice dripped with shock while gaping at Darren.

"Ever heard of Instagram?" Darren's playful tone goaded her.

"Girl, we not gone distract you. Just wanted you to know we was here," Jaida piped.

"Yea, we'll talk to you later!" Trisha added.

Before following her friends, Darren bent down towards her. "Um, Nat, Ashley helped me get the girls' info too. Just thought I should mention that."

Ashley? Natalie was thrown for a loop and searched for her cousin as Darren disappeared into the crowd, but Chuck's voice broke into her search.

"Give it up for Brenda, y'all. Great poem!" Chuck said, and the crowd snapped. "Next up is James."

Natalie decided to focus on the show to keep her mind in a good space. The first half of the open mic ended after about an hour, and she was truly blessed. *There's so much talent in this city!* When the lights came on, she greeted Lisa after spotting her walking towards the coffee bar. "You made it."

"Yes, ma'am. Natalie, meet my husband, Michael." Lisa gestured to a distinguished-looking brown skin brother behind her.

"Nice to meet you," Natalie offered while Michael smiled in greeting. He was debonair with light brown eyes, the perfect complement for her new mentor.

"Bruh, you tryna get wit' my girl?" Devon saddled up behind her and joked with Michael, then embraced Natalie.

"Yo, man. I got my own." Michael tackled Lisa's waist, pulling her closer. "Plus, I ain't tryna make you look bad in yo own spot." Lisa giggled and pecked him on the cheek, the love flowing in effortless ease between them.

Natalie gave a cheerful sigh. *I hope Devon and I will be just as happy.*

"Ugh! Is this spot just for couples?" Denise made a clacking sound when tossing her tray on the bar counter. "Cuz I gotta get my boo if that's the case." Using one hand to shield her eyes, she pretended to search for BJ in the mob of people. "B, where you at?" she fake-yelled, making everyone laugh.

"Babe, you have to meet my friends," Natalie gushed to Devon and shifted her eyes in their direction. Both Trisha and Jaida were pushing through the crowd to get to her.

"At last. We meet Devon, the entrepreneur!" Jaida quipped, holding out her hand.

"Yea. We've heard so much about you!" Trisha giggled, and Natalie shook her head with a huge smile plastered.

"Y'all are ridiculous." She looked at Devon, who seemed to be taking their goofiness well. He was gracious as the quartet dialogued briefly about hanging out after the open mic. Jaida said she and Trisha were driving back that night but could stay for about an hour afterward.

People were milling about, stretching, talking, and using the break for a coffee run. Natalie snuck a glance near the front in the corner, but Ashley wasn't there anymore. Instead, she found her chatting with Darren and BJ on the other side. *That's good they're talking*, she thought regarding her and Darren.

A Caucasian face emerged into Natalie's view as it zipped through the door of Devon's, gold hair shimmering among a forest of brown.

"Kate," Natalie called, and the young woman veered towards her with Lamont tailing behind. Her friend's face brightened as she locked eyes with Natalie.

"Hey, girl," Kate embraced her while Lamont jerked his head in greeting.

Natalie had come to learn he was the large, silent type. "So glad you guys could make it," she said.

"Oh, you know we couldn't miss it. Besides, Devon's open mics are legendary at New Life," Kate spouted. "We're all so proud of how he's built his business."

"Well, hopefully you can get a seat. It's packed."

After a short chat, the two wandered off to try and find a seat in the crowd. Kate held onto Lamont, letting everybody know he was her man.

Wow. That girl for sure puts herself out there. Natalie truly valued Kate's willingness to experience being the minority in various sectors. At Devon's, Kate was a singular marshmallow floating in a steaming cup of hot chocolate. She didn't know too many white people that conscious of their own privilege who took steps to immerse themselves in uncomfortable cultural environments. Natalie had learned a lot from her interactions with Kate.

Devon's heavenly touch brought her out of her musings. Sidling up behind her, he caressed her back and handed her a small mug of herbal tea. "For your nerves," he whispered. He was so thoughtful.

"Thanks, babe. Did you see Kate and Lamont?" But the lights dimmed before he could respond, and people were heading back to their seats

"Alright, alright, alriiiiiight!" Chuck blared in his best rendition of Kevin Hart. "I hope ya got what ya needed during the break, cuz we bout to get back to it."

Natalie blew out the nerves through her breath. Her friends had dispersed, some going to their tables, others sliding more to the side to lean against the wall. She peeked at her phone again, reviewing her notes as Devon massaged her shoulders.

"Next up, we have one of our own. This young woman has been a great asset to the Devon family, and I'm pleased to say she got my man Devon *all* the way together with his office!" People laughed while those who knew her applauded. "Please, y'all. Give a good welcome for Natalie Greene."

Devon whispered, "Get 'em, Nat," right before she took her first step to the front. With each step, she inhaled and exhaled. It had been a while since Natalie shared her poetry outside of her blog.

"Thank you so much for the warm welcome, everyone!" she said into the mic, then glanced at Devon, who grinned from ear to ear. "When I first moved to Jersey, I didn't know *what* I would find. I just knew that I needed a fresh start." Natalie gripped the mic in one hand and swallowed the lump in her throat. "But what awaited me was more than just a new school, a new home, or even a new job." She fiddled with her phone. "What I found was *community*. And *love*. And *family*." Natalie smiled at Devon. Then her eyes found Darren, Monique, and Alice. She even saw her uncle standing in the back with pride embedded in his face. "The piece I want to share is something I wrote after experiencing one of the greatest losses of my life. I hope to use the remainder of *this* life to honor *her* and the many who came before me. So. Here goes..."

Natalie cleared her throat, viewed the notes section on her phone, and started reciting.

"I am my ancestors' wildest dream.
I'm the writer for those who couldn't read.
The voice for those who couldn't speak.
I dance for justice and fight for peace.
I am free.

But only due to their bravery.
The men and women who went before.
Who paved a road of liberty.
Laced with sacrifice and suffering.

Families tattered and torn by a system of oppression
Brutal beatings armed with lynchings, filled with aggression
False lessons.
To prove they were lesser than their oppressors.

But we fought back you see.
And lifted arms under its weight until the system was dismantled.
We used our Hope and Faith as weapons.
And sliced through the enemy's camp of fear,
Set out to keep us under.
Instead, we went down under,
Ground.
And met Fear face to face.
We looked him dead in his eyes
And found, *he* was really the one afraid.

I am my ancestors' wildest dream
I dance the dance that David did,
With feet of a King.
And lift my head up high like Esther
Exuding the exquisite stature of a Queen
I march and shout like Martin and Harriet, Malcolm and Sojourner,
Frederick and them.
Their blood races through my veins at a considerable rate,
To fight in the war I was born to face.

The eyes of our hearts now having been open,
It was never about our skin but our purpose!
It was never about our race but our image!
And Whose we were created in.
They passed the torch to *us* to win!
We run not for ourselves, but like they did,
For our next of kin!

For houses built and businesses owned.
For laws that protect and injustices atoned.
We are our ancestors' wildest dream,
And they now find their rest, their joy, their love in the manifestation of
such a miraculous thing."

When Natalie finished, the silence was astounding. *Did they like it?* she wondered, chewing with fear on her lower lip. Then, the clapping started. And it didn't stop. Apparently, the rule about snapping was completely forgotten. People even stood to their feet!

"Say that, girl!" somebody shouted.

"That's my niece!" That was clearly Uncle Malcolm.

Natalie's face broke into a wide smile. *Whew. I did it!* Chuck met her on stage with a warm hug, and folks stopped her as she made her way to Devon.

"Excellent poem," one woman encouraged, planting a hand on her arm.

"Thank you so much," Natalie replied to the kind stranger.

Lisa stood from her stool and hugged her. "Natalie, that was beautiful."

Natalie's heart flooded with gratitude. "Thank you, Lisa."

"I knew you were a good writer. I could feel it," she added, and Natalie's face heated at the woman's praise.

"Wow. That really means a lot!"

"No doubt. Contact my secretary next week like we discussed so we can schedule your interview for our internship program."

"Yes, of course." Natalie was elated when Jaida and Trisha met her with bear hugs.

"We're so proud of you!" They showered her with compliments. "It's been so long since we heard you share anything. Your mom would be proud," Jaida whispered, and Natalie's eyes moistened. She gave her friend another squeeze.

I hope you are, Momma.

"Girl, I didn't know you had bars," Denise chirped when Natalie reached the mahogany countertop, and Natalie laughed.

She kidded back, "You know I spit sometimes,"

"Natalie." A hand rubbed her arm just then, and she turned to see a glistening-eyed Ashley. "That was beautiful." Her cousin's voice broke.

Was Ashley *moved*? A rush of emotions gripped Natalie, but she didn't want to scare her away. "Thank you," she said simply, risking a small smile. When Ashley turned back into the crowd and slipped out of Devon's as if she had never even been there, Natalie wondered to herself, *Had she come just for me?* She had only told Devon and Darren she was performing tonight.

Finally, she made it into Devon's arms. The next person was sharing at the mic, so he pressed his lips to the tips of her ear and murmured, "Remember when I said sometimes it's like heaven on earth at open mic?"

Natalie remembered. It was during her interview with him months ago. So much had happened since then. She nodded, "Yea," as her back curved into his crevice. She rested her chin on his arm covering her chest, and in response, he smothered the top of her two-strand twists with his lips.

"Well, that was it. *You* are it." Spinning her around, Devon brushed her chin with his fingertips. The speaker at the mic faded into the background, and all she saw was him. "Natalie, *you* are heaven on earth." Devon kissed her then. In front of everyone and everything. She was his, and that was all that mattered.

Natalie sighed with pleasure. After such a long road, she was home.

CHAPTER 25

WHEN LOVE WINS
(ASHLEY)

Winter settled in like a child in her momma's lap, and just like that, the fleeting fall season was over. Although Ashley was disappointed (the fall fashions were everything), she was learning that new seasons held new promises. These days, she spent her time differently than she had in previous seasons.

Her physical therapy was nearing its end, and she was almost ready to run again. She was still doing her therapy sessions with Regina. Ashley had learned so much about her own emotional and mental health, or lack thereof. She was also painting more. But, even more importantly, she was learning a lot about God and what He wanted to do in her life.

"Thank you for the invite." Natalie sat in front of Ashley at the little bakery around the corner from their house, Bill's Bakes.

Ashley had asked her to meet her there, thinking it was a calm and cozy environment, perfect for the occasion. She slipped on a quiet smile in response. "Thanks for coming. You want something?" Ashley pointed to the section where delicious handmade desserts were encased behind glass, but Natalie shook her head.

"I'm good," her cousin replied. "I actually just ate." She patted her stomach, hidden underneath an army green and black plaid shirt, then draped her large navy North Face Down on top of her chair. Malcolm had gotten the coat for her for the winter when she ripped a hole in her old one. He was spoiling her and supporting her in ways she was still getting accustomed to.

"I love their German chocolate cake," Ashley declared. "I mean, at that time of the month, it is *everything*." Her tongue splashed over her lips as she crossed her cream Prada combat boots. Natalie chuckled at her cousin's humor, a tad more relaxed.

"I know we could have talked at home, but I figured this little spot would be a nice space. I come here sometimes to read. Or study. Or whatever..." Ashley ran her hand over her cup of coffee as her voice drifted. "The coffee isn't as good here as it is at Devon's, but they kinda make up for it with the desserts."

At the mention of Devon, a warm smile tugged at Natalie. "Yea? I'll have to try something next time." She glanced around the small bakery that only held a few tables, but there was a fireplace someone lit with a microfiber sofa stationed in front of it. A classic by John Legend murmured in the background.

"I know I told you, but I wanted to say again how beautiful I thought your poem was at the open mic," Ashley said. This time, there was a slight tremble to her tone. "I know the message was what our moms would have wanted. For us to share their legacies with the world."

"Thanks. I appreciate that. Writing has always been a great way to express my heart." Natalie hesitated, then asked, "Did you know I was performing that night?" Her eyes tinted with curiosity as she studied Ashley.

A guilty smile played along Ashley's lips as she tucked her long, flowing hair behind an ear. "Yea," she admitted. "Darren told me. And then I mentioned it to dad."

"I knew someone had to have. Darren also said you helped with getting my friends there?"

"Yea. I kinda overheard a conversation you had with your counselor where you talked about missing them." Ashley lowered uncertain eyes while fidgeting in her seat. "I hope that was ok."

"Well," Natalie paused. "I guess something good came out of you eavesdropping." She folded her hands on the quaint, round table with a blank look and waited.

Ashley prayed. *God. Please help me through this.* That calming sensation she had been experiencing since she started asking God for help emerged. It was that peace she now realized she had been looking for all along. Who knew it was in Him?

"Natalie, I-I want to start by apologizing to you for how I've treated you since you've come to stay with us," Ashley began with a deep sigh. Natalie lifted both brows but remained silent. "I mean, I really didn't even *think* about the fact that you were grieving your mom and needed our support more during this time than you ever would have." Ashley cleared her throat, her stomach doing a million and one flip-flops. She had never been this vulnerable before, and it had taken her so many steps to get here. Just that morning, she stood in her room, reciting the points she wanted to make over and over. She even scribbled a few things on her hand, but the ink was now jumbled from sweat.

Peering at Ashley, Natalie rubbed all ten shaky fingers over her thighs and paused before speaking. "Ashley, I appreciate you sayin' that. And you're right; I did need you guys. I needed *you.*"

Guilt swarmed Ashley, but she didn't want to run from the feeling by deflecting blame like she had done so many times. As she discovered in her counseling sessions, she had wasted enough time doing that, so she pressed on.

"I, for one, know the experience of losing a loved one. Losing a mother," Ashley clarified, tearing up the napkin she'd used earlier for her muffin into little pieces onto her lap. The tiny shreds now lay like polka dots of dandruff on her skinny jeans. "And I know that, because of that experience, I should have been more sympathetic to your situation." She dropped the pieces of napkin to brush a few bangs out of her face. Tamra had cut her hair to give her bangs since she wanted to switch it up for the winter season.

"Especially since I loved Aunt Melissa too," Ashley added while cleaning up the mess she had made with the napkin. She dumped all the particles on her plate with the muffin before trudging ahead. "I'm sorry." Having heaved out the words, she waited. Her heart was in her throat as she stole a fearful glance at Natalie. Although her cousin was still quiet, her face had turned inviting, her eyes now shimmering with affection.

She really cares for me. Encouraged, Ashley continued. "I also want to apologize for how I acted at Devon's before I fainted. What I did. What I said... I—I can't imagine how I would feel if somebody put me on blast like that. If I had some personal shit, I mean, stuff, happening, and they told somebody I cared for deeply about it..." A heavy weight pressed against her chest as she peered down, thinking of Darren. If someone had spilled her dirt in front of him, how would she feel?

Natalie's eyes were a well of sadness when she replied. "Thank you for saying that. I didn't want to bring the topic up until you were ready, so I hope you understand why I've kept my distance." Beneath the table, Natalie's leg rocked with emotion, her umber riding boots tapping in rhythm on the hardwood floor.

"I was so hurt that you shared that information in front of Devon. And then I was thinking, 'How did she even find out about the cutting?'" Natalie's forehead creased in confusion. "And you went through my things." She paused. "To get the..." another pause with a drop of her eyelids, "the razor. But Denise called and apologized when you were in the hospital and filled in the pieces. We had a long conversation. I'm still hurt, but I'm working on forgiving her." When Natalie looked at Ashley, the pain in her eyes was evident. "But the fact that you had the razor..." Her voice trailed as she studied the table. "I don't even know what to do with that."

Natalie's whole body seemed to sink into her chair as horror engulfed Ashley's heart.

Lord, what have I done? Ashley sighed. *Well, here goes the hard part.*

"I was in your room. Looking through your things... when I found it." The weight on her chest seemed to travel to her throat as she reached for her voice to explain. "When Denise sent me your journal, I put two and two together. I'm so sorry." Ashley shifted to the table as she examined a crumb from the abandoned muffin, then gulped her room-temperature coffee over the rock stuck in her throat. "I'm so very sorry, Natalie. I-I can only say that I felt so betrayed at the time that I didn't care about betraying *you*. I didn't care about anybody but myself," she added bitterly, but when looking back at her cousin, she could still see the pain. *The pain I caused.* Finally, Ashley's sins had caught up to her. *But I don't know if I can bear them!*

Cast your cares upon Me, Beloved. The loving voice of God resounded, easing her grief.

Natalie was a statue of thought while staring out the window. "I can't imagine what you went through back then, Ashley," she finally said. "And how I would have responded. I understand where you were emotionally as much as I can without having gone through it." She turned back to her cousin. "I know how hard it's been since I lost my mom. And I'm way older than you were when you lost yours." Natalie stopped and gnawed at her lip in heartbreak. "However, it-it *hurts.*" Her voice was torn as she shifted back to the window. When she looked at Ashley again, tears clung to her eyes.

Ashley grazed her hands over her face, her own eyes burning. "Yea. Of course," she said thickly. "And I know it takes time to forgive. I-I don't even deserve it." Twiddling her fingers on the mug, she searched for the right words, thinking of what she had learned in her previous counseling appointments. "That mindset I had was so engraved in me believing that *you* were the betrayer. Not me," she tried to explain. "It-it doesn't justify what I did. I just want to share why I did it."

"I'm sorry, Ash," Natalie said. "I never intended to hurt you."

Suddenly Grams's words came back to Ashley, piercing her with their truth. *The people who love you never intend to hurt you.* Natalie's eyes were so ballooned with sorrow that Ashley's heart swelled with regret. "I know that now." Exhaling a sharp breath, she plowed ahead. "I realize after talking to my counselor and doing a lot of self-reflection that you would never have allowed me to be in that position at camp if you would have known the outcome." She looked off into the distance and rested her chin in her hand while thinking back. It had taken many a counseling session for Ashley's view to finally be purged of the perceived betrayal that had tainted it for so many years.

"I think, because of the trauma," she started slowly, reciting the revelations she had learned, "first of losing my mom just a few months before camp, then the assault, my 14-year-old brain needed *somebody* to blame for all the pain." Ashley paused, struggling to make eye contact.

"And that person was you." She finally glanced at Natalie, and her cousin nodded in response.

"I see what you're sayin'." Natalie trotted her tongue along the inside of her cheek, more out of her varying emotions than anything. "But I did feel horrible that I led you into that craziness. I should have known those girls were a hot mess. I never could have fathomed how bad, though." A shudder ripped through Natalie as she gripped her hands on the table to the point that her knuckles protruded. She was livid at the thought of The Hyenas attacking Ashley. It took several talks with Devon and Celia to realize she wasn't to blame, although that was her first reaction.

"I know. I know," Ashley replied. "I just wish I would have confided in somebody and maybe had a different perspective. After it happened, I didn't tell anyone. Not even my dad. I carried it inside, letting the pain fester." She huffed a stark breath of remorse. "I didn't know how to get it out."

Ashley's eyes drifted to the window. It was snowing now. She kissed her mug with her lips and took a slow drink, allowing the lukewarm liquid to flow through her. "But now, I do," she continued, feeling strengthened by all the changes that had occurred internally. "Now I feel like I have some better tools to deal with what I experienced. And maybe, also, for what's to come." In a shy tone, Ashley revealed, "I've started painting again."

"Really?" Natalie's eyes lit with excitement.

"Yep. And it's been so healing. God has been speaking to me through my paintings." Her voice was stuffed with tender wonder.

"God? *Wow.* That's... *amazing.*" Natalie's eyes widened as she looked at her cousin with surprise wrapped in pride. "You sound like you've done a lot of soul-searching and self-reflection. I know from experience that kind of work isn't easy. I'm proud of you." Natalie found her cousin's hand on the table and squeezed it.

Ashley squeezed it right back while sitting in awed relief. *She's so good with me.* "I'm definitely on a journey of learning how to be a healthier person, but I don't know if I'll ever be as considerate as you. Even when I was lashing out at you, you still put me first. You covered for me with Darren. You talked me off the ledge when I freaked out at the Sunday dinner. You took that thrashing at Devon's. Over and over, you still just kept trying to—*love* me. I don't know if I can be *that* good of a Christian," Ashley admitted.

Natalie's eyes brightened even more, and in a voice soaked in pleasure, she asked, "So... you're a-a Believer?"

In response, Ashley offered another shy smile. "Kind of. I mean. I guess," she shrugged. "I just know God is showing me a lot, and I want to keep learning more." Ashley killed the rest of her coffee while thinking again about Regina and how much she had been teaching her in their one-on-one meetings. "My counselor is a Christian-I mean, a Believer. And we've been having these Bible studies."

Natalie plopped her chin in her hand, marveling. "Wow, Ash. I'm so happy for you! You seem to have peace now."

"Yea. It's nuts, right? I kept wanting peace, but I didn't know that's what I wanted. I thought I wanted a dope house with a fine husband and 2.5 kids. I mean, I do still kinda want that stuff." Ashley gave a sheepish laugh, and Natalie laughed with her. "But now I realize those things won't give me peace. Peace comes from here," she said while patting her heart.

Natalie's face exploded with joy. "Yes! You're so right. It doesn't matter what our circumstances are. We can have peace in the midst of the storm. Or, we can have the whole world and lose our own soul* (Matthew 16:26)."

Ashley reflected on her cousin's words. "That's deep. I realize what I want for myself. I want to have peace. I don't want to lose my soul." With determination, Ashley studied the falling snowflakes and rallied her courage. "Do you think you can ever forgive me?" Her voice was fragile as she searched her cousin's face.

A sweet smile touched Natalie's lips. "I do. In time. I love you too much not to."

Ashley could no longer contain herself. Eyes brimming with tears, she leapt to her feet and embraced her cousin. "Thank you, God," she whispered, cleaving to Natalie, her head hugging tight to the top of Natalie's curls. *How long have I needed this?*

Natalie responded with heartfelt elation. "Thank you, Lord!"

Ashley and Natalie talked for hours. It seemed like they were catching up for all the years they had missed.

"I meant to ask you. Where is your truck?" Natalie had noticed her cousin driving a rental the last week, but since they hadn't been speaking, she didn't want to ask about it.

Ashley tossed her head with a scowl. "Ugh! This dude I was messin' with keyed my freakin' car."

Natalie's eyes bulged. "What? Are you serious?"

"I mean, he denyin' it, but I know it was him. Or at least, one of his thots that he got to do it. We was kickin' it for a minute, and he got in his feels and fount out I had some other thing happening. I think his roommate saw me on a date at the movies, and it got back to him." Ashley rolled her eyes in annoyance, thinking of Jeremy and Case. "So anyways, I guess he had one of his females jack up my ride the next time I was over cuz we got into an argument. I come outside, and the freakin' door is all slashed up. Then on top of that, my ride is sitting on some damn bricks! Somebody slashed it and stole my freakin' 28s."

Natalie was in shock. "That's *crazy*." She shook her head in sympathy for her cousin.

"Puh. You don't even know the half. I was so pissed. BJ and Denise came to get me, and BJ starts swinging on ol' boy."

"What?" Natalie gasped. "That's why he had that black eye when I saw him meet Denise at Devon's last week?"

Ashley huffed while rolling her neck. "Mmhmm. My dude, Jeremy, is super big, so he lost that one. But bless BJ's heart for tryin'. He definitely a real one. So anyways, I called the cops right away on his ass as soon as we got back home, and they got him for some weed charges. I made sure my ass was off the scene, though, before I did it. He know where I live, so I can't have that gettin' back to me. So anyways, I shouldn't a been messin' with him foreal foreal." Ashley frowned, and Natalie couldn't help but chuckle.

"Ash, you are too much. You could have seriously been hurt. What kind of neighborhood was this?"

Ashley smiled. "I know, girl. But I'm done with these fools. I can't have no dude tweakin' on being a side piece when he knew he was doing his one-two as well. Besides, my ride can't afford to be gettin' jacked over some random."

"I mean, I didn't even know dudes did stuff like that. I thought that was a female thing."

Ashley was adamant while making a face. "Girl, these brothas get in they feels just as much as we do. They just try to hide it. So anyways, my truck is in the shop and should be finished next week. *And* I'm 'bout to have daddy buy me some 30s."

The bakery owner, Bill, interrupted Ashley's colorful tale to explain to the girls that he was locking up.

As they snatched up their things, Natalie asked, "Sir, can we get a piece of that German chocolate cake before we go?"

Bill, a round man with a long beard and a slight resemblance to Mr. Woods, responded, "No doubt, honey. I got 'chu."

Natalie turned to her cousin, "I figured we could split it tonight if you don't mind. I gotta see what all the fuss is about, but I'm not tryna gain all those calories." She grinned while throwing on her coat, scarf, and gloves.

Ashley laughed. "Ugh. You and me both. I gained like 10 pounds since I haven't been runnin'. I just wish I would have gained it in my ass." She looked at her cousin mischievously, and they both cracked up.

Ashley rocked her white Calvin Klein jacket accented in gold with the large furry hood as they walked to their vehicles. While starting up her Civic rental, she was in awe. Ashley had never thought she could forgive Natalie, but what she learned was that she, too, needed forgiveness. And also, just as her counselor had said, *she* was the one who would benefit the most from offering it.

While driving the little Honda, Ashley thought more about what God had done for her by sending His Son. *I've received so much forgiveness myself. How could I not give a gift so freely given to me?* Even though the snow was coming down in herds now, Ashley navigated the streets and skidded into her driveway after Natalie in no time.

Exactly, Daughter! God responded. *Exactly.*

It was almost Christmas, and Devon's was decorated to the T. White lights were strung on the walls and around the windows as garland hung on every doorway. Large, red stockings swayed along the coffee bar counter with the server's names written in glitter. Mistletoe and a bell straddled the entrance while various Christmas songs chimed over the speakers. Even a plate of Grams's famous Christmas cookies was laid out, courtesy of Natalie. Ashley made sure to grab one when she walked in. *No doubt Denise and Natalie did the bulk of the decorating*, she thought in admiration. The decor was cute and classic. *It has Natalie written all over it.*

It was quiet in the cafe, and Denise wasn't working, but Ashley had plans to meet up with her and BJ to see a Christmas play his brothers were in. She jiggled her foot back and forth under the table, anticipating Darren. He had been on her heart for the last couple of days, and after much deliberation, she followed God's prompting to reach out. Although they had talked a few times since he popped up at the hospital, they hadn't had *this* kind of talk. Ashley knew it was time.

Devon came over, a calming distraction to her nerves. "You want a refill, Ash?" he offered in his usual amicable tone.

"Aww, naw, I'm good. Thanks, though." Ashley smiled, grateful they were on good terms. He could have really taken her outburst a few months ago to heart. But Devon seemed like a really good guy, and she was happy her cousin was with him. As he turned to leave, Ashley noticed an email had come through on her phone from CCNY. Popping it open, her eyes roamed the message. *Professor Simone!* Abruptly, Ashley shifted in her seat and started to read:

Ashley, I hope the holiday season is treating you well. I wanted to let you know that your design for the extra credit project was the selected winner! I fell in love with your take on the male and female ensemble-challenge. I seriously believe you could be the next Misa Hylton, if you decide to go in that direction.

If you're interested, I would like you to accompany me on the trip to Paris this spring for the Paris Fashion Week event. Please do not share this news before our last week of class, as I want to

keep students focused on finals. Thank you again for your participation and I'll speak with you soon!

Sincerely,

Simone, MFA.

Her mouth agape in disbelief, Ashley fell back into her chair. *I won!* She marveled at the screen and couldn't stop herself from reading the email repeatedly. Tears stained her vision as she bowed her head in wonder.

Thank You, Lord. Even though moisture decorated her cheek, she made no attempts to remove it. Ashley would have run from her emotions in the past, but she was learning to be honest with herself. And with others.

"Ash. You ok?" Darren loomed over, a worried expression adorning his nut-brown eyes.

"Oh!" She hadn't even heard him approach. Sniffling, Ashley fished inside her black leather Giovanni bag for something to wipe her face. She came up empty and snatched a napkin from the dispenser. "Yea. Just got some good news. Um. That's all." Blotting her face, she pitched him a watery smile, but Darren's smile back was uncertain.

"Oh. Ok. Well, cool." He kept his hands jammed deep into his coat pockets and rocked back and forth, adding awkwardly, "Congrats then..."

Ashley sighed. *Guess it's time for me to continue practicing being honest.* "Thanks. Can you have a seat?" She gestured to the empty chair across from her. "The Christmas Song" played on the speaker, and Natalie Cole's voice serenaded them.

Darren removed his muddy-toned leather bomber jacket and cream wool scarf. He then sat, landing his hands on the table before folding them together.

Ashley looked at him. All the guys she had been with since simply didn't compare. She was finally ready to admit that Darren was the one she couldn't get over. *I'm still in love with him.*

Ashley prayed, *Lord, please help me to share my heart,* and was met with strength. Whatever Darren's response was, she was ready and knew that she would be ok. *Because I have You now,* Ashley realized, thinking of her new relationship with God. *And that's more than enough.*

Epilogue

Eyeing her reflection in the mirror, Ashley added the final touches. "Just a little more mascara," she muttered, gliding on the thick black liquid with unmatched skill.

"You look gorgeous, cousin. Now, let's go. We're late!" Natalie posed in Ashley's bedroom doorway, incredibly stunning in a long, black dress that dipped low in the front and split on the side. Her hair, straightened and dripping well past her shoulders, was layered and highlighted with brown undertones. Natalie hoped it would stay since it had been a while since she had gotten it straightened, but Ashley had convinced her she should do something different for the New Year. Natalie, Ashley, and Grams went to Thelma's Hair & Style that morning, and the four-and-a-half-hour process (for all of them combined) proved to be worth it.

"Girl, I'm comin'!" Ashley ogled her cousin, a pleased smile gripping her plump lips. "OK-ayyyy! You got the 'girls' out tonight, huh?" With an impish grin, she cocked her head to the side. "Mmmhmm. And you swear you ain't given that man none..."

A humorous laugh shook Natalie's physique, and she flipped her hair over her shoulder. "You are too much."

"You love it!" Ashley cackled, then looked back at the mirror, continuing with her mascara. "Did dad leave yet?"

"Yep. He went to pick up Sam for dinner a half hour ago."

"Cool. I'll call him later after midnight. I must have been in the shower when he left." She studied herself.

Natalie leaned on the entryway and stuck out an impatient hip while slapping a hand over it. "Girl, we got to *go*. You know we have reservations, and the mens is waitin'. Come *on*."

Sneaking one last look, Ashley smiled with satisfaction. Dressed in a hot-red number, she slipped on her Jimmy Choo strappy black heels, then confiscated her small leather Chanel bag. "Yea, yea," she announced, "I'm comin'," then trailed Natalie down the stairwell where Darren and Devon waited side-by-side. They were the perfect picture of a delicious box of chocolate.

As Natalie descended, Devon whistled and stared in appreciation. "Now don't be startin' nothin' you can't finish," he joked, holding out a hand to help her down the stairs.

She gazed at him with a gleam in her eye and tossed back, "Oh. Is that what's happenin'? Well, baby, you just wait, and you'll find out it was worth it." Running her fingers up and down Devon's black Calvin Klein double-breasted coat jacket, Natalie pulled him close.

Devon grinned, holding her tight. "Girl, I ain't playin' wit 'chu." Laughing, Natalie let him lead her to the foyer, then pivoted around to watch Darren's reaction to Ashley.

When Ashley sashayed down, Darren slapped one hand over his charcoal sweater smoothed underneath a black Versace jacket and dropped his jaw. "Lord, I done' seen the light!" he announced in a throwback Red Foxx voice while taking her in.

In typical Ashley fashion, she took her time sauntering down each step, the material from her dress, straight-stitched to every curve. Secured by a thick gold clip, her hair was slicked into a high ponytail that sped down her mid-bare back, the look inspired by Sam. Soft, curly baby hair resting on her edges in small swoops was an added touch. The black choker wrapped around her neck with one single diamond perched in the middle belonged to her mother. It was so tender to her father that he kept it in his office safe but knew this was the time to share it with her.

"You look just like her," he said, holding it to her neck earlier that day.

Ashley whispered, "Thanks, Daddy," as her eyes teared up.

"I'm just sayin'. They gone' have to *carry* me in a stretcher to the restaurant cuz I ain't gone' be able to walk!" Darren exclaimed, and Ashley giggled, gobbling up all his praise.

She clasped his hand before sailing into his arms. "Boy, stop playin'." Her voice indicated, however, that she wanted him to do the exact opposite. Shining adoration colored Ashley's gaze as she whiffed his Gucci Guilty Black cologne. Then, in uncharacteristic coyness, she offered up her cheek for a kiss. *Only Darren makes me feel this way.*

Devon broke the couple's shared moment, "Y'all. The limo is waitin'," and Ashley put some distance between them.

"Okaaayyy. Let's *go.*" The men helped their women into their coats, and the foursome braved the cold night air. The temperature was brutal, but Ashley was just glad the snow was to a minimum. She was being risky and only brought her flats for the dance floor.

The limo driver, a young light-skinned brother with zig-zag box braids, led them to a nice, upscale restaurant on the outskirts of New York City called Devonte's. Devon had made the reservations, saying he had been there once and the steak was excellent.

Ashley's loved ones laughed and chatted in excitement over their meals consisting of lobster tails, shrimp, lamb, and, of course, steak. She sighed, her heart happy, and let the bubbles from the champagne tingle down her throat. But she knew the real fun wouldn't begin until later that night. *We're going to The Barn!*

"Yo! I thought y'all was never gone' make it," Denise shouted to the crew when they ambled into the club sandwiched in by the late crowd. A short, sparkly black dress with spaghetti straps accentuated her slender form while BJ was propped next to her in a white Armani suit and a huge grin. He and Denise had secured their table earlier when they arrived, and everyone greeted each other with daps and hugs.

"Sis. Now, what *'chu* tryna do tonight?" Denise's hands kissed her hips as she shook her head in fondness at Natalie. "I know yo cousin *had* to have dressed 'chu," she said. "Is that a *leg* I see?"

"Naw, girl. She did it all by herself," Ashley informed, eyeing Natalie with pride.

Natalie tossed her straightened hair to the side. "Yea! I know a little somethin' somethin'."

"Oh, you do, huh? Well, come on. Let's show IG what 'chu know then." When Denise announced to the group that they would be taking a picture, the guys put everyone's jackets on the chairs, and the girls started touching up their makeup and tidying up their hair.

Taking in the moment, Ashley peered at everyone all dressed up, then watched Natalie smiling in Devon's arms. *Thank You, Lord, for bringing her back to me.*

All the girls huddled in front of the guys, and the group squeezed tight to get everyone in one shot. "Ok. Happy New Year on three!" Denise commanded, stretching her arm and holding her phone sideways to take the picture.

Natalie looked at her, confused. "But, it's not the New Year yet."

"Nat. We gone' be *gettin' it in* at the New Year. And ain't nobody tryna take a picture then!"

Ashley laughed. "Just take the pic, Denise." She leaned her bare back against Darren.

Little shivers ran down her neck from his breath as he stared at her with love in his eyes. "Happy New Year, Ash," he breathed into her ear.

"One, two, three!" Denise shouted, and everyone posed and smiled. After reviewing the picture, she made them take three more shots from different angles. The DJ began the evening by playing some old-school songs. Usher's "Yeah" vibrated through the atmosphere, and party-goers hurried to the dance floor.

Ashley grabbed Darren's hand, drew him to her, and wrapped her arms around his neck.

"Happy New Year, baby," she replied before giving him a long, heart-felt kiss.

The End.

Acknowledgments

When I started writing *When Love Wins*, it became clear to me that though the story was about two young women desperately needing each other, whose relationship had been disconnected, it was really about a mother and daughter with the same tenacious need and the same disconnect. I wrote this book first and foremost for them. The original "A" and "N" who battled for many years, but in the end, the faithfulness of God's love brought them into an eternal union that can never be broken. I wrote this book for us, Mom. Thank you for being my inspiration, in so many ways.

I want to thank every single person who sat through the reading of *When Love Wins*, or read every single word of my blog, or commented and re-posted every single social media post promoting my work. It truly is a village that raises a child, and this book is my child. I thank God for my village.

Thank you to my sister of 20 years, Jamia Lewis, who literally sat through the reading of one of the final drafts of WLW. All 110k words! I so miss our "story times." You are one of my most precious gifts, and I am so grateful to be on this journey with you. Though it certainly is LONG (smile).

Thank you to my sister, Sophia Webb, for your honest feedback and the countless hours of reading and discussing WLW. You too have been the lovely recipient of "story time." I truly value your artistic perceptions and natural creative gene. I so love how the unfolding of our friendship has been like a good novel (smile).

My dear sister Esperanza Gallon, aka "Hopey G." Thank you for your expertise in mental health issues. I value your feedback and insight into Natalie's cutting struggles. Thank you for being the trailblazer for me and so many. May God reward us with the desires of our hearts, SOON.

Thank you Gwen Valerius for "shooting it straight" with me. Man, that manuscript critique still hurts, but was so needed! If not for you, we would have had a very shallow Natalie and a much more boring storyline. WLW would not be what it is now without your input. You are gifted at what you do. Thank you for sharing your gift. And thank you to Permission To Write (PTW) for introducing us.

Thank you Dr. Tamika Nunley for carving out precious time to sit with me and share your NY life experience. As soon as I saw your post on Instagram, I knew you were the one to go to. You were Natalie and Lisa all day! Thank you for squeezing me in between your own driven career, family life and new baby on the way. I'll never be able to repay you, but will surely try.

Thank you June Phelps for your much-needed feedback. I know you hated giving me the ins and outs, but it was so needed. Without you, my story would not have been as accurate in depicting NY life and therefore would not have resonated as much with my readers. I'm forever grateful for your honesty and encouragement.

Thank you to my beta readers Piper Youtzy, Silk Allen & June Phelps. Each of you are phenomenal writers, and I'm so honored you took precious time out of your busy schedules to read WLW. Your feedback is much appreciated, and I'm grateful you each enjoyed it :-) A special shout out to Literary Cleveland for hosting hubs of opportunities for upcoming writers in Cleveland, Ohio, and for bringing us together.

Thank you to my focus group Tommie Stanfield, Sydney Herriott & Iyanna Williams. This focus group was a desire of my heart. As "youthful" as people perceive me as being, the truth is, I'm getting old (LOL) and needed your vital input on the culture of the day.

I thank the people who gave me insight into "New York life." There are many of you who received random text messages at midnight (courtesy of Ms. Sophia Webb) and responded to questions such as "What is the kind of slang that young people use these days?" Thank you for your prompt responses! I couldn't have completed this book without you.

Thank you to my writing mentor, Sandra Heard, and her hubby,

Bobby Heard, for their support and prayers. I know we haven't known each other long, but our connection is divine and therefore natural time is meaningless. You have been there in ways I have needed most, and I do not take that lightly. Thank you for your generous heart to sow into my life in magnificent ways.

Thank you to Akron Summit Scribes for being a needed support. That very first virtual meeting I sat in was confirmation that I was in the right place. A group of prophetic writers writing for God? Yes please! I am honored to be amidst His last-day soldiers writing with His pen for the kingdom.

A special thank you to my friends. I have so many, yet they have all played such a vital role in the woman I have become which has contributed to the stories I am able to tell. This particular story drew inspiration from my good friend Marlene Morris, who demonstrated the power of love in a way I have rarely seen. She is Natalie through and through. Thank you, Marlene, for being His vessel during such a hard season.

I want to thank the men and women who went before. The ones who broke the barriers for Black writers to curate platforms for storytelling. Growing up, I was highly impacted by Urban Fiction and I aim to re-create our culture through storytelling as influenced by some of the greats. Black culture has its own "swag" and only *we* can accurately demonstrate that in the earth. Thank you, Omar Tyree, Sister Souljah, Terry McMillan, Robert Townsend (long live The Five Heartbeats!) and so many more, for being the *first* (at least in my eyes). Your gift made room for me.

I want to thank *you* dear reader. Thank you for reading. For supporting. For encouraging me to keep writing. My heart is to write stories that reflect the real-life spiritual experiences I and others have had. God is real, regardless of our hardships and difficulties. Regardless of what the media tells us. Regardless of the philosophies of the day. But most importantly, as someone who has chosen to live the last 20 years of my life His way, I can attest that His way is best. It may not be easy. It may look crazy. But in the end, it is always for our good.

Lastly, I want to thank my Abba. How is it that I just wrote a whole novel? How is it that we started out with just a blog? How is it that You know the end from the beginning? If it wasn't for Your leading, none of this would have ever occurred. If it wasn't for Your seeing the bigger picture and giving it to me in bite-size doses, I would never be crowned with the title "Novelist." Thank You for having so much in store for us (Your kids). Thank You for being the Great Author, knowing the last chapter before the first one is ever written about each of our lives. Thank You for crafting my life into a "magnificent novel." I aspire to make You proud in all that I do. Use every gift You've stored inside of me. Pour them out for the world to see. Receive Your glory from Your creation. You are most deserving. I am only a vessel.